THE UNWANTED CORPSE

Lady Fan Mysteries
Book Eight

Elizabeth Bailey

SAPERE
BOOKS

THE UNWANTED CORPSE

Published by Sapere Books.

20 Windermere Drive, Leeds, England, LS17 7UZ,
United Kingdom

saperebooks.com

ISBN: 978-1-80055-567-9

CHAPTER ONE

January 1794

Rays from diminishing daylight threw shadows across the daybed in the afternoon of a bleak Tuesday in January. A fire shed both warmth and illumination upon its occupant, comfortably ensconced and pleasurably engaged. The only sounds in the parlour came from Master Luke Fanshawe, suckling at his mother's breast.

Ottilia's attention was so concentrated she barely registered the opening of the door. But her infant son's mouth left her nipple and he turned his head slightly even as her mother-in-law spoke.

"You will be tied down for months, you foolish female."

Ottilia looked up. "Hush, Sybilla! You are disturbing him."

But Luke, having apparently registered the interruption, returned to his labours, unperturbed. Ottilia could not help smiling down at the little face, familiar both of itself after these first few weeks and from Luke's unmistakeable resemblance to his father. In more ways than one.

"When it comes to food, you are just like your papa, my tiny dear."

Her son acknowledged her words with a glance, but was not to be deflected from the important business of the moment. Presently, however, the effort involved overcame his appetite and he dropped to sleep.

Ottilia adjusted the bodice of her round gown with her free hand, as she had learned to do, lifting the fabric to re-cover her breast, and shifted her burden to make herself more comfortable before at last giving her attention to the Dowager Marchioness of Polbrook.

Sybilla had arrived earlier in the day, travelling to Hampshire in company with her dour maid once the Christmas festivities were done for the express purpose of making acquaintance with her new grandson. Or so she said. Ottilia suspected it formed a convenient excuse to remove from the Dower House with its too close proximity to Polbrook. Relations between Sybilla and her elder son, along with his French wife and children, were still strained. Her mother-in-law was proving to be more tetchy than usual and Ottilia supposed this to be a likely cause.

She kept her voice muted. "He is asleep."

"So I perceive." A gimlet stare did not abate. "I stand by my words, however."

Sybilla had seated herself in a chair by the fire in the small second-floor parlour that served for Ottilia's private sitting-room, opposite to her own favourite perch on her daybed which provided an excellent substitute for the nursing chair.

"What words?"

Sybilla raised her delicate brows. "Did you not hear me? Why could you not employ a wet nurse? You will scarcely be able to leave the house, nursing the boy yourself in this fashion."

Ottilia gave a tiny sigh, half of exasperation and part regret. "I cannot, alas, nurse him wholly myself. Susannah shares the duty with me."

"Who is Susannah, for heaven's sake?"

"The wet nurse."

"You have one?"

"Living in the house, yes. She and her baby moved in shortly after Luke was born."

Sybilla cast her eyes heavenwards. "One might depend upon you, Ottilia, to find an irregular way of doing things. Living in the house?"

Ottilia had to laugh. "Well, I could hardly spend my time going to and fro to her cottage."

"But why nurse the child at all?"

"Because I wished to, of course. Only I cannot produce enough milk to satisfy Master Greedy Fanshawe." She glanced down with fondness upon her son as she spoke, lifting him a little so she might plant a kiss upon his smooth brow. "Patrick has always advocated the mother feeding her own baby. He heartily disapproves of the practice of putting out babies to a wet nurse."

Sybilla let out a snort. "I might have guessed that doctor brother of yours was at the back of it."

"So you might. But it is not all poor Patrick's fault. It would not suit me to see little of my son for months on end. You know how I have waited for this day, Sybilla. Do you think I could endure to be parted from him?"

Her mother-in-law grunted. "I still say you are making a rod for your own back. You will not be able to take off in your impulsive fashion on one of these abominable adventures of yours."

"Well, what a good thing that will be. I am quite done with them, I assure you."

"Ha! I wish I may see it."

Ottilia surveyed her for a moment in silence. When Sybilla's gaze shifted towards the fire in an abrupt fashion, she ventured a throw. "Is there a particular reason you have chosen to visit at this time, Sybilla?"

The black eyes shot back to meet hers, their lids narrowed. "Why do you ask?"

"You are more than ordinarily tetchy, my dear mama-in-law."

Sybilla gave a short laugh, glanced away and then back again. "Must you be so acute? If you will have it, that wretch of a Mellis woman has decided to leave me."

"Teresa? Great heavens, why?"

An explosive sound escaped Sybilla. "That sister of hers, of course. Teresa went to her for Christmas and it seems the benighted female has grown so confused in her mind she can scarcely remember the time of day, let alone which day."

"Oh, poor woman!"

"Yes, that is all very well, and I suppose one must have pity, but if it means I must lose my companion, I find it difficult to be sympathetic."

This Ottilia could appreciate, typical though it was. "Am I to understand Teresa feels duty bound to devote herself to caring for her sister? She is a widow, is she not?"

"A very troublesome one too. Teresa is forever rushing off to succour her, but this is the outside of enough."

Ottilia made haste to soothe. "Well, but you will find another companion, Sybilla. Perhaps even someone a little more able to enter into your interests and sentiments." The suggestion did not appear to be finding favour. In haste, she added, "A woman with a little more to offer on the intellectual side would be a bonus, do you not think?"

Sybilla snorted. "If one can find any such. I only had one companion of the ilk and she can think of nothing better to do than rush about the country solving murders."

Ottilia let out a burst of laughter, hastily suppressed as she glanced guiltily down at her baby son, who seemed fortunately undisturbed. She lowered her voice. "I believe he would sleep through a thunderstorm." She smiled across at her mother-in-law. "And indeed, there is the rebuttal to your taunts. What need have I of such adventures now I have Luke to amuse me? Pretty too. She is so taken with him, she has overcome her shyness of me. Indeed, she was intrigued by the notion of his growing in my belly and could not resist coming close to me." She gave a low gurgle. "If I had a guinea for every speculation Pretty made as to whether she were to have a brother or sister, I should be a rich woman."

Too late Ottilia realised her mistake as Sybilla seized on this. Miss Pertesia Fanshawe, renamed by agreement from her original family name of Brockhurst, had recently been informally adopted by Francis and Ottilia. "Brother now, is it? You hold by that scheme then? Despite having a child of your own?"

Bearing in mind Sybilla's present dissatisfaction, Ottilia curbed her instant irritation and chose deflection. "Try asking that of Francis. He is quite besotted, you know."

The door opened even as she spoke and Lord Francis Fanshawe came in, the little girl in question held casually within one arm as she rested on his hip. He was clad in the country-wear he chose for comfort at home, a sporting frock coat of cloth over a plain waistcoat, buckskin breeches and boots. Ottilia greeted him with acclaim and a measure of relief. "Fan, my dearest, you are wonderfully *à propos*."

Before he could respond, Pretty set up a screech, wriggling to be free.

"Set me down, Papa! I want to see Luke eating Auntilla."

If she was not to be *Mama* to the child, it was balm at least to be *Auntilla*, culled by the little girl from the lips of Ottilia's two rambunctious nephews.

"You are too late, Pretty," she said as Francis bent to release the child, who ran at once to the daybed. Ottilia put a finger to her lips. "Quietly now. Luke is asleep."

Pretty began whispering a protest. "Ooh, did he eat already?"

"Yes, and with gusto as usual."

Pretty giggled. "He's so greee-dy." She bent to the infant, planting delicate kisses on his face, what time Ottilia looked up to find her spouse leaning down to listen to some murmured remark from his mother. She hoped Sybilla would not put him out of temper. Her arrival had not pleased Francis, his dissatisfaction finding expression the moment Sybilla had gone to her chamber to rest and recover from the journey.

"What in the world brings Mama here now? Cutting up our peace just when we are settling."

Ottilia had not been overly pleased herself, for the exigencies of her confinement followed by Christmas — made much of for Pretty's entertainment — had tired her more than somewhat. She was fond of her mother-in-law, but her irascibility could be trying. It behoved her to soothe her spouse however.

"Don't let her fret you, Fan. I dare say she will find much to complain of —"

"Yes, and I can guess where she will begin."

"— but it's my belief she is lonely."

Francis had produced a frown. "Lonely? With all her acquaintance round about, not to mention the Polbrook crew?"

"You know well she is rubbed by close proximity to Randal," Ottilia pursued. "From the tone of her letters, I think she is starved of intellectual stimulation."

"So she comes here to exercise her wit at my expense. I thank her."

It took time and patience to reconcile her spouse to the invasion, but Ottilia succeeded at last in extracting a promise that he would at least try not to let Sybilla's acerbic comments set him all on end.

"But if she starts on me, I warn you I shall leave the room and let you deal with her."

Ottilia was obliged to be content with this compromise, but for the present moment it did not appear Sybilla had as yet said anything untoward, despite her grievance, as Francis came across.

"Pretty, sweetheart, it's time you went back to Hepsie. She will be ready with your supper."

The child took the hand he held out, looking up from her diminutive height. "Is Luke coming too?"

Ottilia took this. "Indeed he is. Ring the bell, if you please, Fan."

"No need. Luke's nurse is waiting outside." He walked to the door, Pretty skipping beside him, and opened it to call out. "Doro!"

The erstwhile slave entered as he shifted out of the way. Ottilia could not resist looking towards Sybilla to see how she took this first sight of the Barbadian beauty. Dorote Gabon was slim-boned and graceful but her most startling feature was a pair of sky-blue eyes in a face as dark as midnight. She glided across and paused before the daybed.

"He is ready, milady?"

Ottilia took time to kiss her infant son before giving him up. "Yes, thank you, Doro. You may take him."

With reluctance, Ottilia allowed Doro to lift the infant out of her arms. Momentarily bereft, she fought down the urge to snatch him back. She could not, regretfully, take care of him herself. She had not the strength. Nor, sadly, in her privileged position in life, was it done. Sybilla would have a fit! The thought amused her, chasing melancholy away.

Doro carried her precious burden with practised ease, born, so Doro had told Ottilia, of helping to nurse infants in the slave compound at Flora Sugars.

"I have done it many times, milady. Pray let me take care of the babe. It is no trouble to me and you need not employ another for the task." When Ottilia demurred, saying she wished Doro to enjoy her freedom, "I am used to work, milady. I have been helping wherever I can, but I should like to have my own task, if it will please you."

Left with nothing to say, Ottilia had consented. Doro did not disappoint. Luke had taken to her with alacrity, and if there was a hint of envy in hearing Doro crooning to him, Ottilia did her best to banish it.

At the door Pretty paused, turning her face up towards Francis. "Story, Papa?"

"I shall come up when you are tucked in bed, never fear."

"Will you read me story?"

"Yes, you importunate infant! Off you go now. Doro is waiting."

Taking her cue, Doro set a hand to the child's shoulder and ushered her forth. Ottilia was not in the least surprised to see a pained look in the face of her mother-in-law. Sybilla's antipathy towards certain members of Pretty's real family had a long history. But the expected reproof did not come. As the door closed, Sybilla turned to Ottilia.

"You did an excellent thing there, my dear. That girl has a chance in life, thanks to you."

Francis, who had shifted across to the fireplace and was leaning an arm along the mantelshelf as was his wont, straightened abruptly. "You surprise me, Mama. I thought you disapproved of our taking Pretty into our home."

Sybilla flapped a hand. "I am talking of the maid, foolish boy. The less said about the other the better."

Ottilia made haste to intervene. "Dorote is very beautiful, do you not think, Sybilla? She caused quite a flutter in the servants' hall, so Mrs Bertram tells me."

"But did you not write that your steward fellow means to marry her?"

Francis snorted. "He won't secure her, though I've told him to stop shilly-shallying. The end will be that Tyler will snap her up from under Hemp's nose."

"No such thing, Fan. They have an understanding. Hemp is anxious not to force the issue, but you need not suppose he is backward in his attentions."

Sybilla exploded. "Heavens above! One would suppose you two were running a marriage mart here. What matters it who the girl marries?"

"Don't look at me, Mama. It is my wife who manages these things, not I." Francis grinned across at Ottilia. "She does not wish to lose Hemp's presence here and that is the matter in a nutshell."

"Well, I admit there is truth in that, but I agree with Hemp that Doro ought to enjoy her first taste of freedom of choice. Not that she will choose another. She is devoted to Hemp."

Ottilia was relieved when Francis dropped the subject for Sybilla had begun to look impatient. Instead he remarked upon the growing darkness. "Shall we repair to the withdrawing room until it is time to dress for dinner, or shall I send for candles here?"

About to reply, Ottilia hesitated, distracted by a familiar sound from outside that had been slowly impinging in the background of her mind. It now grew stronger, the clopping of hooves on gravel. Ottilia glanced to her spouse. "Is that on our drive?"

Francis shifted his head in a listening gesture as the clopping grew to a beat as if the rider had sped up. "Someone is in a hurry." He moved to the window and looked out, twisting towards the drive that led to the front of the house. "I can't see fully, but it sounds like a single horse."

"Is it an express, do you think?"

Francis came away, heading for the bell-pull. "We shall discover soon enough."

As he tugged on the bell, the hoofbeats abruptly halted. Ottilia expected to hear the distant ring of the front door. Instead, there came an odd thump. Francis raced back to the window and looked out just as the horse's hooves sounded again and fairly thundered as the rider galloped away.

"What in Hades —?"

"Some prankster, Francis, I'll be bound," said Sybilla, entering the lists. "I have had idiots riding up to the Dower house and ringing the bell for nothing before now."

Ottilia balked. "But he didn't ring the bell. Something is amiss."

There was a moment of strange hiatus, as if the world held its collective breath. Ottilia felt as if an eon passed. Then footsteps sounded, running up the stairs below.

"For pity's sake!" Francis headed for the door, wrenching it open and walking out into the galleried vestibule.

Ottilia was seized with the oddest impression of impending catastrophe. As she listened for more, she could hear Sybilla muttering but the words had no meaning.

Came her husband's voice, "What the devil was all that about, Rodmell? What did that rider want?"

The butler appeared at the top of the stairs, just within sight through the door, out of breath and uncharacteristically flustered. "I cannot say, my lord — is her ladyship within?"

Ottilia called out at once. "I am here, Rodmell."

The butler entered, his gaze fixed on Ottilia. She saw him shadowed, the deepening dusk lending him a sinister air in keeping with the mysterious happening. She hardly took in her spouse shifting into the doorway.

"Tell me, Rodmell."

The butler moved closer. "That rider, my lady, he … he dropped a man's body at the door."

Ottilia heard the exclamations emanating from both Sybilla and Francis, but she kept her gaze on the butler. "Dead?"

"Yes, my lady."

"Did you recognise him?"

Rodmell passed a hand across his balding pate. "I had no chance to see who it was, my lady. I went to the door when I heard the hoofbeats, but he was off before —"

"She means the body, man," Francis broke in with impatience. "Who is the dead fellow?"

"I cannot say I know him, my lord. I cannot remember to have seen him before." Rodmell turned back to Ottilia. "My lady, there is more."

"Yes?"

"He bears a label of sorts. It is addressed to 'Lady Fan'."

"Heavens above, what an impertinence!" Sybilla was up, shifting to join the coterie about the daybed where Ottilia still sat, her attention roving over the extraordinary occurrence.

"Whoever dropped it — or sent it — means me to find out what happened to the man." A gust of energy shook her and she rose with a briskness she had not felt for weeks. "Very well then. Let us go and see."

Her husband was at her side in an instant. "Are you well enough? Do you want me to look?"

"Don't be absurd, Francis. Of course she must see the body. You cannot tell its tale."

He ignored his mother's interjection. "Take my arm, Tillie."

She was glad enough to do so, but turned to the butler. "Fetch Tyler and Hemp, Rodmell, if you please. Also candles. Plenty of them. We will have to bring him inside, I dare say."

The butler hurried out, but her spouse held back a moment. "Capital. Just what we wanted. A corpse on the premises."

Ottilia let out an involuntary giggle. "The world is set on trying you today, my darling lord." As he led her forth she became aware of Sybilla on her heels and halted. "Sybilla, you need not see this, you know."

Her mother-in-law drew herself up. "I am coming. Do you suppose I mean to miss all the excitement?"

"It may yet prove to be but a storm in a teacup. We don't know the fellow has been murdered."

Another of Sybilla's snorts hit the air. "Of course he's been murdered. Why else would whoever did this bring him to your doorstep?"

"I am entirely of your opinion, Mama."

Ottilia glanced up at her spouse's face. "You need not sound so resigned, Fan. I can always repudiate the office."

"And pigs might fly."

"You take the words out of my mouth, my son. So much for no more adventures, Ottilia."

CHAPTER TWO

The body lay in an ungainly heap upon the flagged porch. Ottilia could see little in the fading light beyond the lumpy shadow made by the contour of its back and its legs, part folded.

"He must have been heaved off that horse to land in such a way," she remarked.

Francis had gone to the other side of the body, crouching to look more closely. "I should say the rider had him thrown across the saddlebow, head down. No hat and his hair is awry. His face is hidden so I can't tell who it might be."

"We must get him inside."

At this, Sybilla, who was standing in the doorway, predictably raised an objection. "Into the house? Surely the stables would be more appropriate."

"I dare say, but I cannot examine him in the stables. Nor do I suppose Williams and Ryde would welcome his presence in their domain."

Francis rose to his feet. "He's not precisely welcome in ours, for the matter of that. Ah, here come the bearers. Excellent."

Ottilia caught sight of her steward and the footman hovering behind Sybilla. "Pray let Hemp and Tyler through, Sybilla."

Her mother-in-law grunted, but shifted onto the porch, making way for the two men. "Where do you mean to put him?"

Ottilia likewise was moving out of the way. "In the little morning room for this present, if you would, Hemp. Set him on the sofa there."

Her husband took a hand. "You'd best take his shoulders, Hemp, and Tyler the legs. I'll help if you can't manage."

But Hemp was already taking his place at the head. "No need, milord. We will manage it between us."

Leaving her husband directing operations, Ottilia beckoned Sybilla to follow and went inside where she found Rodmell, armed with one candelabrum, and accompanied by the boots and one of the housemaids, similarly burdened with means of lighting Ottilia's intended examination.

"Ah, thank you, Rodmell. The little morning room, if you please." She opened the first door to the left of the hall herself and waited for the procession to enter, following close behind. "Set the candelabrum on that side table to give me the best light. Ida, put your candles on that chair and bring it nearer. Jonas may set his candelabrum on the mantel. We will bring it close if we need it. Ida, pile those cushions to one end. No, no, my dear, not that end. Under the light. Yes, good. Thank you, that will do very well."

The arrangements were completed just in time as noises betokening the arrival of the corpse sounded without. Ottilia directed everyone to move away from the sofa to give room and watched as the two bearers came in, Tyler walking backwards, his arms tucked about the body's knees, the trunk sagging between them. She made haste to intervene as they neared the sofa.

"His head where the light is, Hemp."

As the unknown unfortunate was lowered to the sofa, Ottilia's gaze became riveted upon his face. Handsome even in the pale waxiness of death, and shamefully young. "Why, he is just a boy!" She went to the sofa, vaguely aware of Sybilla coming to her side and Francis's voice, dismissing the servants with a word of thanks. Ottilia bent over the body, looking at once for any obvious signs as to why he might have died.

Sybilla spoke beside her. "That is no boy. He is a man grown. Young, I grant you, but I should be astonished if he does not prove to be of age."

"He may be so, but that makes it no better."

"I take it you don't know him?"

"Not to my remembrance. Fan may recognise him perhaps."

Sybilla called over to the master of the house. "Do you know this fellow, Francis?"

He appeared behind the sofa, leaning to look down at the man's face. "I can't say I do. He may well be visiting one of the neighbours. There are always strangers about at this time of year."

Ottilia touched her fingers to the pallid cheek. "Poor creature, whoever he is, to be cut off so soon."

Sybilla interjected. "For all you know, Ottilia, he may have been a vile reprobate, perfectly deserving of his fate."

Francis straightened. "Let us first discover what *was* his fate, Mama. Can you tell anything at all, Tillie?"

Ottilia sighed, trying to master the stirrings of compassion. "As yet I have scarcely begun. There is nothing obvious to the eye, beyond the blue of his hands which is to be expected." She picked one up and examined the fingernails, so pale as to be almost white. She released the hand and it fell heavily, as limp as the body itself, evidenced by its sag while it was carried in. "The only thing I may say with confidence is that I believe rigor has passed. Also he is somewhat malodorous."

Sybilla had fingers shielding her nostrils. "That one could scarcely fail to notice."

"I am afraid it is inevitable, Sybilla. But it confirms that he has been dead for many hours."

"How many do you think?"

"Hard to say, Fan. But it is likely he died yesterday, at some time last evening perhaps. I think we will be obliged to remove some of his clothing."

"Remove his clothing? Heavens, child, what would you be at?"

"Only enough to see what may be seen, Sybilla, so pray don't fret. I must discover how the blood has pooled and whether there is any wound."

Francis was on the move. "I thought of that. I kept Hemp and Tyler back. How much do you want removed?"

Ottilia glanced along the body and made a discovery. "He must have been at one of these Twelfth Night parties. His coat and breeches are certainly evening wear, and that floral waistcoat is silk, if I am not mistaken."

"You are right as usual, my love." Her spouse had moved to the feet. "Shoes, not boots. And no coat against the cold."

Sybilla snorted. "He will hardly have felt the cold in his condition."

"True, Sybilla, but it gives us a starting point, do you not think?" Ottilia received only a grunt in reply and looked across at Francis. "I think it will be sufficient to remove everything but his shirt, but tug that out and leave his breeches merely unbuttoned."

"Shoes?"

"Yes, those too, Fan. We will replace it all when I have done. Oh, and leave the label on the coat in place, if you please."

Ottilia shifted out of the way again, allowing the two servants to take her place. Sybilla, with whose company Ottilia could well have dispensed, chose to take occupation of a chair near the fire, clearly determined to see the business through. Once Francis had apparently satisfied himself that the servants knew what to do, Ottilia claimed his attention again. "We had better send for Doctor Lister at once."

"Don't you want to wait until you've done."

"I shall be finished by the time he gets here."

Francis's look as he eyed her was dubious. "You trust him to see all right?"

Ottilia shrugged. "He saw me through Luke's birth. I think he will manage. It is his business to call in the coroner, and he may arrange for the disposal of the body."

"What if it is murder?"

"We shall cross that bridge if we come to it, Fan."

His eyebrow quirked. "Motherhood has not changed you one bit, my dear one."

She laughed. "Should it?"

His glance swept across to Sybilla and he lowered his voice, turning to meet her gaze. "I am persuaded Mama thinks it ought. But I know you too well, Tillie. You'll be deep into this in a heartbeat."

A gurgle escaped. "Well, I must at least find out what wretch it was who addressed the body to me."

"Don't tell me, my lady Fan. You'll be beating at all our neighbour's doors."

"I have to start somewhere, don't I?"

They were interrupted. "Milady? Is this sufficient for your needs?"

A rush of eagerness went through Ottilia as she turned to see how Hemp had carried out her instructions exactly. "Excellent, thank you. Will you wait to dress him again when I am finished?"

"Whatever you need, milady."

She smiled at Hemp and moved forward, reflecting ruefully that her mother-in-law was right. Her adventures were not at an end.

In the background of her mind, she heard Francis at the door, speaking to Rodmell. "Tell Ryde to go for the doctor. He may take my curricle and bring Doctor Lister back with him if he can. If not, he will be the faster than he would be on horseback."

In which case she had best waste no more time, Ottilia decided. A familiar flurry of anticipation grew within her as she began, her first care being to sink her fingers into the man's light hair, feeling the head for indentations or lacerations. There were none. The face had the waxy, translucent look of death, although a slightly greenish tinge was beginning to show — another sign that rigor was past and decomposition begun. The lips were pale, undamaged beyond a tiny trickle of dried blood at one corner of the mouth. Lifting the eyelids showed nothing beyond the milky cloudiness to be expected of a body many hours after death.

Ottilia shifted her focus, pushing the shirt open at the top so she might examine the throat and neck. "Fan, lift his head for me, if you please."

He had returned to his post behind the sofa again and was watching what she did. He went at once to comply. "Shall I turn it?"

Ottilia dropped to a crouch. "I need to see behind." In a moment, she rose. "Nothing at all. No bruising either to tell us where the blood sank."

"Isn't that a little odd?"

"Very." But she was already pulling at the shirt. Francis laid down the head and moved to assist. As the naked torso became visible, Ottilia let out an exclamation. "Well, that explains it!"

"Explains what?" came from just behind her.

Turning, Ottilia found her mother-in-law had re-joined the coterie about the sofa, which included, she now saw, both Hemp and Tyler, attentive where they stood at the feet end of the corpse.

A bubble of mirth attacked Ottilia. "Dear me, I feel like one of these anatomical tutors at the hospital." The two servants shifted back but she beckoned them forward again. "Come, I am jesting merely. I have no objection to you watching."

"Will you explain yourself, Ottilia? What did you mean just then?"

Ottilia turned back to the corpse. "Look there, Sybilla, at his lower back. See how dark it is. That is the blood pooling after death." She bent to the body and took hold of the fall and band to the breeches, casting a look up at the dowager as she did so. "Pardon me, Sybilla, but I have to see." Without more ado, she pulled both away so that the breeches fell open, exposing the upper part of the man's groin, but more importantly the side of his hip.

"Good heavens! Is that bruising on the fellow's posterior?"

"Just so, Sybilla. We may deduce that he was seated when he died. I don't doubt the dark colour will show along the underside of his thighs too." She signalled to her steward. "Unroll his stockings, Hemp. Ah, there it is. Pooling around the ankles and feet."

"As expected, I surmise?"

"Indeed, Fan. If you will raise his sleeves, I dare say we may see the same under his forearms." He did so and Ottilia saw with satisfaction that she had gauged the matter correctly. "He died in a seated posture."

There was silence for a moment or two, her auditors apparently engaged in taking this in, staring as one at the indicative signs. Ottilia dropped to her haunches with the object of looking more closely around the visible skin for any sign of a wound.

Francis was the first to break out. "How is that possible? I mean, wouldn't he move at the moment of death? If he was choking or in pain…"

"Just what I was thinking, Francis. A man does not remain still in the throes of death." Sybilla's words washed vaguely over Ottilia as she continued her task. "I recall my father, when he had his apoplexy, thrashing about in a wild manner."

"My grandfather? Did he so?"

"It was excessively frightening, I can tell you."

"But we don't know this young man died of an apoplexy, Mama. Have you found anything else, Tillie?"

Ottilia glanced up. "There seems to be no wound that I can find. The post-mortem may reveal more." But she spoke absently, her attention concentrated on a faint discoloration on the left side of the chest. "Someone bring me the other candelabrum, if you please. Ah, thank you, Tyler. Hold it close. I need to see this more clear."

The added light revealed a bluish tinge in a small area precisely on the point above the heart. Ottilia kept her gaze fixed upon it, her mind working, only peripherally aware of the ongoing discussion between her spouse and Sybilla. One word kept repeating, both in their voices and in her head. *Heart …* *heart…*

She spoke aloud her thought without realising it. "If it proves to be so, I have only heard of it once. That boy was but a child though. Could it be possible in a man grown?"

Her spouse's voice impinged upon her consciousness. "Of what are you talking, Tillie? Have you fathomed it out?"

With reluctance, she shifted her gaze from the bruise, faint but telling, and rose to her feet. Tyler moved away, removing the added light as she stepped back from the body and passed her gaze about the eager watchers.

"There is a slight contusion just above the heart."

"Aha! A heart attack. Did I not say so, Francis?"

"Hush, Mama. Let her tell it."

"Thank you, Fan. I can by no means be certain. Such a thing is rare, so much so that I recall only one case in Patrick's purview."

"But what is it?"

"I am coming to it, Sybilla." Ottilia drew a breath. "A blow to the heart, not necessarily a heavy one, has been known to cause instantaneous cardiac arrest."

"Lord above! I have never heard of such a thing."

"As I said, Fan, it is very rare. I doubt I should have heard of it myself had not Patrick been obliged to delve into the matter when a young boy died, quite inexplicably. There was, as here, this slight contusion over the heart. Patrick conferred with several surgeons of note and discovered the existence of this odd phenomenon. It is thought that some arrhythmic disturbance in the heart must be responsible, but no one truly knows why it should result in a death so immediate and unexpected."

For a moment no one spoke, but at length Hemp ventured in. "Milady, I think I may have seen this in Barbados."

"Indeed? What happened there?"

"Some boys were engaged in a rough game. One of them dropped where he stood, quite suddenly. No one could understand why he died like that. There had been blows exchanged, but none deliberate. It was purely accidental and Master Matt concluded the child had some unknown disease. But by what you say here…"

"Then we are not dealing with murder," said Francis, his tone not entirely free of relief, Ottilia noted. "This fellow's death was an accident."

Ottilia shook her head. "With regret, I fear I must disagree."

Sybilla's proverbial snort came. "You would, of course."

"Ma'am, enough! Why, Tillie?"

Ottilia drew a breath, feeling perfectly reluctant to proceed. "Someone dealt this man a deliberate blow. If it was not meant to kill, it was certainly intended to harm. We may discount murder in favour of manslaughter perhaps. But someone is responsible for this young man's death."

Doctor Lister arrived just when the company had changed and reassembled a little before the dinner hour, for this once in the front withdrawing room in preference to the usual parlour which happened to be situated on the opposite side of the hall to the morning room. Knowing the physician's views, Ottilia left it to her spouse to conduct the man to see the body. The doctor was inclined to be sceptical of Ottilia's knowledge of medical lore and did not take kindly to any suggestion of hers in relation to diagnostics.

"Which is why," she told her mother-in-law, "I rarely call him in."

"Doctors!" Sybilla wafted a hand in that habitual dismissive way she had. "Don't tell me. A race of leeches. Pellew is forever prescribing me cordials I don't want and charging me a fortune into the bargain. Never believe anything a doctor tells you, that is my motto."

Ottilia could not help laughing. "If I were to abide by that, Sybilla, I should never have solved any of the problems with which I have been confronted."

Sybilla let out a scornful breath. "Oh, your brother! A paragon, of course."

"Well, he is. Patrick is truly an exceptional physician, even if I say so. Because — before you ask — he never takes anything at face value and he is forever increasing his store of knowledge. I fear he has left me far behind by this time."

"Well for you. High time you left off these adventures of yours and settled to comfortable domesticity."

The twinkle in Sybilla's eye belied the words and Ottilia gave her a comical grimace. "It becomes a trifle difficult, do you not think, if people are going to drop corpses at my very door?"

At that, the dowager let out a crack of laughter, swiftly turning it into a cough. Ottilia was not deceived. She was perfectly aware her mother-in-law took pride in her achievements, although nothing would induce her to confess as much to Ottilia direct. The onset of this new adventure might well be opportune, she reflected, in supplying a diversion for Sybilla's mind.

"Have you any notion who might have brought that unfortunate young man?"

"Sent, I think, Sybilla. I should be astonished to learn that whoever it was rode here himself."

Sybilla digested this. "A servant then?"

"A trusted servant too. A groom in all likelihood."

"Why a groom particularly?"

"Gentlemen — and ladies too, we must not assume the sender was a man — tend to develop close associations with a groom. I know Francis would trust Ryde with his life. It is a pity no one caught a sight of the fellow on horseback. One of the servants might have recognised him. We are a small community in this locality."

"Then it should not prove difficult to enquire among your neighbours. Whom do you have here?"

"A handful of families only." Ottilia did not add that these were of a class with whom it was appropriate to her station to associate. It grieved Ottilia to be obliged to exclude those considered lesser beings from her social circle, although she had made it her business to get to know the tradesmen and those with authority in the parish. A pity she was unacquainted with the working individuals of the various households she visited, but Mrs Bertram and Rodmell likely knew those serving local families.

Sybilla persisted. "Did you not say this fellow must have been at a Twelfth Night entertainment? Who hosted that?"

"I have no notion. Everyone knows I have been confined and could accept no invitations for this present. Besides, Francis and I rarely do the rounds of these incessant wretched gatherings that go on after the Christmas festivities. The same faces, the same gossip day after day. It is tedious beyond words."

Ottilia received a somewhat narrow look from her mother-in-law, who nodded in a decisive fashion after a moment. "I see what it is. You are plagued with awkward questions about all these murders and you cannot be teased with answering them time after time."

Ottilia burst out laughing. "You wretch, Sybilla! How came you to guess that?"

A grim smile curved the elder lady's mouth. "I know you too well, my good girl. You don't relish the notoriety."

"No, I don't. I hate it, if you wish to know the truth. Particularly as it irks Francis beyond measure to hear these idiots bleating about how exciting it must be when in truth it is beyond taxing and often dangerous. It never occurs to any of them that every murder is accompanied by grief and suffering for those left behind, like my poor little Pretty, or who must come to terms with the hideous truth that one of their number is a killer."

An explosive snort came from Sybilla. "Then they are about to learn a sharp lesson, I don't doubt."

Ottilia shifted with discomfort. "If indeed it proves out that this young man was deliberately slain."

Sybilla's delicate brows drew together. "If this strange circumstance you spoke of is in fact how he died, how would any individual know that a blow would kill the fellow?"

"Just so. But that does not mean there was no intent to be rid of the man. Perhaps to incapacitate him?"

The door opened to admit her spouse before anything more could be said.

"Lister will send his fellows to fetch the body in the morning. I have locked the room meanwhile."

Ottilia frowned. "What of the coroner? Will he come before or after the body is taken?"

"As the man did not die *in situ*, Lister thinks it does not matter, thank the Lord! We will see the back of it early tomorrow, though we are stuck with the corpse for tonight."

"Had Doctor Lister any notion to put forward?"

"His examination was but cursory." A faint smile crossed Francis's lips. "He has not your assiduity, my dear one. He claimed he could tell very little until he had the body on his examination table."

"But what little, Fan?"

A shrug came. "Nothing indeed. I mean, he said there was nothing to be seen. Which is pretty much what you said until you were able to see the fellow's naked skin. A waste of time for him to bother with that tonight, he said."

Ottilia thumped a fist on her knee. "How very frustrating. Did he not even make any observation about that dratted Lady Fan label?"

Francis grinned. "I'm not going to repeat that one."

"Impertinence!" Sybilla cried.

"Do you mean Lister or me, Mama?"

"That leech, of course. I will wager he won't find what Ottilia found."

Ottilia broke in. "But will he report back to me? Or to you at least?"

"He didn't say so, but I more or less commanded him to do so. I thought it politic to take a high hand. Since my wife has been involved in this rude fashion, I said, it was only right he should relate his findings back to me."

"Tactfully put, Fan, thank you."

"Well, I didn't want him delaying merely because his pride is hurt that you know more about his profession than he does."

"Oh, I do not claim that. He is competent enough, I grant, even if he holds the stuffiest notions."

Ottilia was treated to a quirked eyebrow. "Don't tell me, my lady Fan. You are decidedly put out."

"Well I, for one, don't blame her," declared Sybilla. "There is nothing more galling than for a stupid man to be lording it over us women merely because of his masculinity. Let him stew. It will not be he who solves this puzzle, be sure."

CHAPTER THREE

Mrs Honeybourne was a plump woman in her middle years, of a garrulous disposition and an avid interest in the doings of her neighbours. Ottilia chose her with deliberation as her first port of call upon the following morning. Leaving a disgruntled husband to entertain his mother, she walked into Knights Inham with her steward for escort.

"Not that I suppose Hemp can glean anything of much value from Mrs Honeybourne's servants, but you, my dearest, must remain to oversee the disposal of our unfortunate victim."

Francis emitted a groan. "I might have known I would be saddled with all the unpleasant tasks."

Ottilia eyed him in some amusement. "Well, unless you truly wish to spend a half hour or so listening to village gossip?"

"Be quiet, you wretch!" A gleam appeared in his eye. "But should you not take Mama?"

"To divert her?" Ottilia had confided the reason for Sybilla's present ill mood to her spouse during their nightly cherished moments of privacy, in hopes it would reconcile him somewhat to his mother's presence. But she had no intention of saddling herself with Sybilla's company at this first interview. "She will overawe the poor woman and I shall get nothing out of her, as you well know, you fiendish creature." Mischief burgeoned. "Besides, I am very sure Sybilla will relish a chance for a rare tête-à-tête with her favourite son."

Francis threw out a pointing finger. "Go! Never darken my door again!"

Instead, mirth bubbling over, Ottilia came close, setting a hand to his chest in the intimate gesture she was apt to use, and leaned in for a kiss. Her spouse returned the embrace, but gave notice that retribution would follow in due course. Ottilia left the house in a mood of deep content edged with decidedly heightened expectation.

She had not missed the thrill of the chase during the long months of her pregnancy, her mind concentrated upon the far more important issue of maintaining the health of her unborn infant, the ghost of the past disaster sitting on her shoulder. She obeyed without question every dictum laid down by her doctor brother, having taken advantage of his coming to fetch his two sons home. Patrick advised a regime of quiet, with healthful walks, good food and, above all, rest. It thus proved easy enough to follow the dictates of Doctor Lister and the somewhat autocratic commands — as she took care to inform him — of her darling lord.

"I will be good, Fan, I promise you. I am as anxious as you are for success. You may cosset me as much as you like."

In the event, Ottilia was saved from overmuch pampering by the demands upon "Papa" of little Pertesia, who rapidly became the focus of Francis's attentions whenever they might be diverted from his wife.

With the birth of a perfectly healthy baby boy, the household underwent a series of changes which occupied Ottilia for some time, along with learning the surprisingly demanding skill of nursing the infant Luke. She had not thought she could manage anything more. Yet the advent of this random body upon her doorstep had brought back all the old enthusiasm for the kind of puzzle that must tax her ingenuity to the utmost. Ottilia did not go so far as to thank the unknown messenger in her mind, but she was conscious of feeling more alive as she took her steward's arm, dependent upon his strength if hers should fail.

Mrs Honeybourne was a widow, and her modest establishment sat on the edge of the village of Knights Inham, the closest to Flitteris Manor, and the walk did not occupy many minutes, although Ottilia was well wrapped up in her woollen cloak against a sharp wind. The remnants of the first snows which ended as the New Year broke were still evident, with icy patches in the ruts of the road and under the hedgerows. Booted, Ottilia took care to walk where Hemp led as he sought a safe passage through.

The creak of the gate as it opened must have been heard, for as Ottilia walked up the path she caught sight of a head capped in a lacy mob bobbing about in the downstairs parlour window. Arrived before the door, it opened just as Hemp reached for the knocker. He stepped back as the matron herself, clearly flustered, appeared in the aperture.

"My lady Francis! Gracious me, is it indeed you? I declare, I could scarce believe my eyes! Come in, come in, do."

She bustled ahead, what time Ottilia signed to Hemp to leave her, knowing he would seek entrance at the back and no doubt receive a welcome from the Honeybourne cook. She then entered the square hall, undid her cloak and found her hostess popping back again from where she had been standing at the parlour door, at once urging action upon the maid who had evidently heard the sounds of an arrival.

"Take her ladyship's cloak, Sarey. What are you doing just standing there? And bring tea at once." She turned back to Ottilia, who was handing her cloak to the equally flustered maid. "You'll take tea, my lady, I'll be bound."

Ottilia demurred. "Coffee, if it is not too much trouble, ma'am."

Quite aside from the fact she preferred it, Ottilia knew it would be easier to serve coffee, not to mention less expensive.

Not that Mrs Honeybourne was purse-pinched, but tea was always a precious commodity for the less well-to-do.

Mrs Honeybourne chuckled, making her mob cap flutter. "Oh dear, if I had not forgot you like it better. Coffee, Sarey! And don't dawdle. Now, do pray come into the parlour, my lady." She began to usher Ottilia towards the door, but halted again, calling after the departing maid. "Sarey! Biscuits too. Or the seed cake Cook made yesterday. You'll take a slice, my lady, I hope. I venture to say it is very good."

Fearing that her mission would never get under way, Ottilia accepted and added a rider. "Yet I do need to sit down, if I may, Mrs Honeybourne. I am not yet fully recovered, you must know."

"Gracious me, how thoughtless! I quite forgot. Come in, my dear Lady Francis. Here, take this chair by the fire." She bustled to a comfortable-looking armchair, well cushioned, which Ottilia guessed was her own customary resting place. "There now, sit you down, do, my lady. I would not suggest we go up to the saloon, which I ought in conscience do, for it is sadly cold at this season. These big rooms are so hard to heat, my lady, and this parlour is particularly cosy."

Taking the indicated seat, Ottilia agreed to it and wondered how quickly she might be permitted to arrive at the business of her visit. As it chanced, her hostess offered the opportunity in short order, although not without first enquiring after the health of the infant Luke and Ottilia's own.

"I am very well on the whole, ma'am, I thank you, if a trifle tired still."

"No wonder, my lady. I recall my own confinements were perfectly exhausting, but I am happy to say both my daughters were healthy babies. Such a blessing, for I feared I might lose the second." She then threw a hand to her mouth. "Oh! I do beg your pardon, my lady. I did not mean to remind you —"

Ottilia broke in hurriedly. "Pray don't trouble your head about it, ma'am. I have Luke now and he more than makes up for that loss. There is our little girl too, as you know, so we are becoming quite a family at Flitteris."

Mrs Honeybourne became wreathed in smiles. "Indeed, indeed, and everyone is so very happy for you both. Lavinia Thorpe was saying only the other night how charming it is that you and Lord Francis have taken her in."

Ottilia seized her chance. "About the other night, Mrs Honeybourne. The party that took place. It is on that account I have come."

Mrs Honeybourne looked a good deal taken aback. "The party the other night? Gracious me, my lady, whatever do you mean? Were you and his lordship hoping to attend? I cannot think Mrs Thorpe would not have sent an invitation."

"Ah, so the event took place at Thorpe Grange?" Ignoring the rest as irrelevant, Ottilia went for the pertinent point. "I take it this was a Twelfth Night party? Monday was the sixth, was it not?"

Mrs Honeybourne's bewilderment was evident. "Yes, of course. But I don't understand, my lady. I believed you and Lord Francis —"

Ottilia waved this away. "That is not to the purpose, ma'am. Rest assured neither of us were ready or able to attend. But the party may well be of significance."

"How so? I cannot think what your ladyship may mean."

It was perhaps fortunate, Ottilia decided, that the maid chose this moment to enter with a tray of refreshments. While Mrs Honeybourne directed the girl with conflicting instructions about where to set it down and how to serve it, changing her mind once or twice, Ottilia took stock. If she continued in this evasive fashion, the widow would inevitably question and wonder throughout. If she could not be kept on track, a short, sharp shock might be salutary. There was, Ottilia decided, little future in attempting to conceal what had happened. Indeed, it might rather be advantageous to inform Mrs Honeybourne, who would undoubtedly carry the news to others, both saving Ottilia from tedious explanations and priming the local gentry for questioning. That it might also give time for the guilty party to think up ways of blinding her to the truth could not be avoided. Once the news was out, that was inevitable in any event.

As soon as Mrs Honeybourne settled again and the door was at last closed behind the unfortunate maid, Ottilia set down the cup from which she was sipping. "Mrs Honeybourne."

The portentous tone appeared to have its effect, for the widow gave her a startled look. "Yes, my lady?"

Ottilia smiled. "Don't look dismayed, ma'am. The fact is I need your help."

"Oh! I see. At least, I don't know how I may be of service to your ladyship, but —"

"Tell me, if you please, who was at the Twelfth Night party," said Ottilia, breaking in with haste. "I have a particular reason for asking which I will relate to you in a moment."

The plump features brightened, presumably at this hint of gossip. "Well, I cannot guess what it might be."

"Don't try. Who was there, ma'am?"

Thus urged, Mrs Honeybourne began counting off upon her fingers. "Well, nearly everyone, I believe. The Reverend Newton and his ward. Lord Vexford and his daughter Richenda. The Thorpes, of course, including Mr Thorpe's brother Jarvis, who is down for the festivities. Indeed, all the young men were there. Well, with Richenda Vexford in the vicinity, what can one expect? They are all after her, you must know, my lady."

Ottilia's senses prickled. This became interesting. She was aware that the local beauty, a brunette with the added charm of a fat dowry, was much sought after. "Which young men specifically, ma'am?"

Looking now a trifle surprised, Mrs Honeybourne eyed her visitor with avidity as she spoke. "Young Jarvis, as I said. My own nephew, of course."

"Oh, is Mr Botterell here again?"

Aubrey Botterell was generally thought to have an eye to his aunt's property, she having no son to whom to bequeath it. Both her daughters being settled, there was every reason to suppose he stood a chance, especially as Mrs Honeybourne doted upon him.

"Yes, the dear boy came down after Christmas, which delighted me, as you may imagine, for dear Maria and her husband were able to spend only the one night with me."

Ottilia brought her ruthlessly back. "But the party, ma'am. Jarvis, Aubrey. Which of them more?"

"Oh now, let me see. That godson of Lady Stoke Rochford's. She did not attend naturally, but her young companion came with Claydon." Mrs Honeybourne wrinkled her nose. "Such airs he gives himself, speaking in that condescending way, looking down his long nose as if he is one of the fashionable set, which I know for a fact Botolf Claydon most certainly is not."

Disregarding these animadversions, Ottilia demanded a description. "I have never met him. What does he look like?"

"Young Claydon? He is nothing great, I assure you. Too thin, if you ask me. His legs are quite spindly."

Then he was unlikely to prove to be the dead man, hopefully no longer cluttering up the morning room at Flitteris. Ottilia had no knowledge of any other young men in the vicinity. "Is that all of them?"

"Gracious me, no! There was that excessively good-looking young fellow who has set them all at each other's throats."

Ah, this was more promising. "What fellow is this, Mrs Honeybourne?"

"An upstart fortune-hunter, if ever there was one, coming among us to set all the young men at odds over that wretched Richenda." Mrs Honeybourne's feathers appeared to be seriously ruffled. "Marmaduke, he calls himself. I'd Marmaduke him, if I could! Poor Aubrey has been quite cut out, I declare."

Ottilia was mentally buzzing. "Marmaduke who? Does he have a second name?"

"Of course he has a second name," snapped Mrs Honeybourne, her annoyance overcoming the obsequiousness she thought proper to Ottilia's presence. "Gibbon. Marmaduke Gibbon. As if he was not bad enough, he must needs introduce a friend of his as well. Lavinia Thorpe felt obliged to welcome this Percy Pedwardine, even though Mr Gibbon did not think of asking her permission before he brought him along."

A *fait accompli*. One could scarcely blame Mrs Thorpe for acquiescing. But another possibility? This needed sifting. "What does this Percy look like? Is he equally good-looking?"

Mrs Honeybourne shifted with discomfort. "I dare say some might think so, but to my mind, he is cast quite into the shade by his fair friend. Fair of face and fair of figure. Not to mention a fair head. If you ask me, my lady, it is perfectly unfair for one young man to be so extremely well endowed. He has put all our young men's noses out of joint."

No longer, if Ottilia did not miss her guess. But the intelligence that the unfortunate left at her door had made enemies among his rivals for the hand of Richenda Vexford had raised a plethora of suspects at the outset.

It took a little time for Mrs Honeybourne to come to the end of her catalogue of dissatisfaction. Ottilia let her run on, making sympathetic noises and storing up the titbits of information that might prove useful as she sipped her coffee and nibbled at a slice of the promised seed cake. At length the widow ran down and Ottilia seized her chance to set the cat among the pigeons.

"Well, I fully understand, Mrs Honeybourne, but I fear you, and all these young gentlemen, may be in for a rude shock."

The startled look came back, laced with question. "Whatever can you mean, my lady?"

"I am sorry to ruin your morning, ma'am, but you must know that last night a dead body was brought to my door and left there. From what you have told me, I believe the body may prove to be none other than this Marmaduke Gibbon."

CHAPTER FOUR

Francis was conscious of inordinate relief, once the undertakers sent by Doctor Lister had boxed up the dead man and taken the coffin off on a cart. There was no avoiding the inevitable investigation. One could scarcely blame his darling wife for pursuing the matter, yet it galled him to be dragged into another of these affairs just as life was settling into a pleasant domestic routine.

Beyond the confines of Flitteris and the surrounding estate there was little to engage his interest, apart from keeping up with reports of the Coalition's engagements with the French. Even these had been desultory of late. Although the execution of Queen Marie Antoinette in October had been the subject on everyone's lips, little had occurred militarily since except for the Navy's evacuation of Toulon in December. Royalists and occupying soldiers alike were rescued from French forces under the control of a young fellow by the name of Buonaparte. Reports of his growing reputation had reached Francis via his friend Lieutenant Colonel George Tretower, commanding a battalion on the South Coast.

Although he kept up with such items of news, Francis could not but admit his fullest attention was concentrated upon the domestic affairs of Flitteris, such as the increased need for coal in this unusually hard winter and his wife's health, always a concern. Odd to discover at this late date that family life suited him. To be forced into gadding about after the identity of the dead man's killer did not sit well with him at all.

"I must be growing old." He entered the withdrawing room as he spoke, not fully realising he had said it aloud until his mother responded, her tone tart.

"Poppycock! You are no more than four and thirty, ridiculous boy! When you reach my years you may talk of growing old."

Curbing his irritation, Francis closed the door and walked across to the fireplace where Sybilla was occupying Tillie's customary chair. He was not obliged to take up the point as his mother spoke again.

"Well? I see those men have taken the body away. What now?"

Was she watching from the window? Francis leaned his elbow on the mantelpiece. "That must depend upon what Tillie finds out from Mrs Honeybourne."

"One of these gossipy women, Ottilia told me."

"A toad-eater too."

"Heaven help your poor wife! Nothing is more tedious than to have a fawning idiot paying one fulsome compliments."

"Tillie can handle her, don't fret." He did not say, as he would have liked to point out, that his dear mama was apt to become haughty when lesser beings failed to acknowledge her superiority of rank. No doubt it was unconscious in her to expect what she professed to despise. Francis had besides no desire to set up her back. She was twitty enough as it was.

The sound of approaching hooves came as a distraction, if less than welcome. "Who the deuce is that now?"

"The coroner perhaps, come to question you," surmised Sybilla as Francis crossed to the window that overlooked the sweep of the drive.

He set one knee upon the window seat and looked out. "A curricle. I can't see who is driving. He has someone with him and a groom up behind." The vehicle drew out of his line of vision as it came towards the front entrance. Feeling assailed, Francis left the window and returned to his post at the mantel.

"You look disgruntled, Francis. What ails you?"

"Need you ask, Mama? In these discommoding circumstances?"

His mother's brows rose. "You may find it discommoding. Ottilia is in alt."

"Hardly. She has to pursue it, I see that."

Sybilla snorted. "But you don't desire that she should. I did not think to hear you decry what gives your wife so much pleasure. Did you expect her to be content to settle to minding the baby and running your household? If so, you married the wrong woman, my dear boy."

Nettled, Francis retaliated with some heat. "I expect nothing of the kind! I know my wife's predilection for murderous adventures, I thank you, ma'am. Only just at this moment —" He clipped off the words, closing his lips upon the burgeoning dissatisfaction.

But his mother proved relentless. "Just at this moment, when she has at last given you an heir, you would cherish a period of peace, is that it? Well, I regret to be obliged to inform you, my son, that life does not operate to order."

"I know that."

"Then cease being boorish like your wretched brother and give Ottilia your unconditional support."

Incensed, he let fly. "Do you suppose I would do anything other? Tillie knows well I will do whatever she needs of me. But allow me a moment of irritation. It is not as if you are yourself a paragon of patience, Mama!"

A crack of laughter escaped Sybilla. "Far from it. Ottilia's antics irk me beyond bearing, but I defy anyone to decry her talents. She is what she is and I, for one, greatly admire her for it. She will always go her own way and that is rare in my sex. You are a very fortunate man, Francis."

A wave of emotion gripped him, a curious mixture of despair and elation, making speech impossible for a moment. He adored his darling wife, yes he did. Yet the advent of children had added a difficult dimension. Previously he had trembled for his own loss when Tillie was endangered. How much worse now, when she would leave those innocents motherless?

As if she read his thought, his mother spoke again, unwontedly tender. "Don't torture yourself, my FanFan. Ordinary life is just as uncertain. There are no guarantees."

He could not speak, but he met the sympathy in her eyes and gave a nod of recognition. He could not decide whether or not it was opportune that the door opened at this moment to admit his butler, who made a wholly unexpected announcement.

"Mr Maplewood, my lord."

Startled, Francis watched the entrance of the young man last seen in Tunbridge Wells whose oddities had attracted the interest of his niece, Lizzy Fiske. He strode forward as Maplewood entered the room. "You must be the last person I expected to see here."

The gentleman gave a careless bow. "My lord Francis."

Typical of the fellow. Called himself an artist and dressed the part. Although, Francis admitted, one could not fault the clothes in which he had travelled if one discounted the roughly knotted neck-cloth and the two undone buttons of a brightly-striped waistcoat beneath a double-breasted cloth frock coat with wide lapels and large mother-of-pearl buttons. Maplewood had been very much to the fore in the affair at the fashionable watering place which had resulted in Pretty

Brockhurst entering into the protection of the Fanshawe household.

Maplewood turned his eyes upon Sybilla and seemed a trifle taken aback. He executed another bow. "Ma'am, your servant."

"What in the world brings you to these parts, Mr Maplewood?" she demanded without preamble.

The young man, known for his insouciant manner, produced a smile. "My mother, ma'am, sent me to enquire after Pretty." He turned back to Francis. "She heard how my uncle was disposed to turn Pertesia over to your care, sir. She wishes to know how the child is faring and sent me to, as it were, spy out the lie of the land."

This last was said with a faint air of mockery that reawakened Francis's earlier irritation. Reminiscent as it was of certain remarks the fellow had made at Tunbridge Wells when his involvement with the victims of that debacle showed how his light, teasing manner — addressed for the most part to Lizzy — hid a depth of attachment to his unfortunate cousin, father to the orphaned Pretty.

"Be that as it may, I must tell you, Maplewood, that you arrive at an awkward moment."

The young man eyed him with an air of puzzlement. "How so, my lord? Is Pretty not upon the premises?"

"Of course she is upon the premises. Where else would she be if my son has taken her in charge?"

Francis gestured his mother to patience. "Give me leave, ma'am. The fact is, my young friend, we have just become involved in another unexplained death."

Instead of showing either alarm or interest, Maplewood's mouth twisted in a wry grin. "I apprehend it is very much a habit with Lady Francis to involve herself in these things. I gather there was a similar happening last year in Bristol?"

Francis exploded. "My niece has been busy, I take it. Do you know everything, sir?"

The grin vanished. "As much as Lady Elizabeth is disposed to tell me. She is not always forthcoming."

Which, if his suit had not prospered, was scarcely a surprise. It was no secret in the family that the lady Elizabeth Fiske, eldest daughter to Francis's sister Harriet, cherished hopes of a union with this young fellow, which had, by all accounts, been thwarted by the not unexpected opposition of her parents. But the intimation that the pair were carrying on a correspondence was disturbing. Did Harriet know? He glanced at his mother and found her tight-lipped, her black gaze fixed upon the visitor in a look of rigid disapproval. Francis hastened to change the subject before Sybilla could express her patent outrage. "Allow me to conduct you to the nursery at once, Maplewood. You may see Pretty for yourself."

Excusing himself to the dowager, Francis left the room, Maplewood at his heels. Relieved of his mother's presence, he ventured to satisfy his urgent need of discovery as soon as they had mounted the stairs to the upper floors. "Tell me at once, Maplewood. Is this correspondence of yours with my niece clandestine? Or does my brother-in-law know of it?"

The young man halted in the galleried passageway that ran around the space open to the hall below. "Is that an accusation, sir?"

"A question. I am not yet accusing you of anything."

It seemed to Francis that the fellow's ruffled feathers smoothed a trifle. "To tell you the truth, my lord, I don't know. Eliza writes to me every so often. As a friend." This last very much emphasised. "There is no exchange of ardour, if that is what you fear."

Francis became explicit. "The only thing I fear, sir, is whether my sister and her husband are subject to my niece's deception. I am not interested in the content of your correspondence. Though if you know of our sojourn in Bristol, I dare say I may guess at it." He began to walk on towards the stair to the nursery floor and Maplewood followed, surprising him with a change of subject.

"What is this new venture that has transpired, if I may ask?"

Francis told him in a few terse words.

The young man whistled. "Someone was determined to involve your wife, sir."

"With a vengeance." They were approaching the nursery door, Pretty's childish treble audible behind it. "Here we are. From the sound of things, my infant son is not asleep or Pretty would not be permitted to talk so loud."

"I had heard that your wife had given birth, sir. May I offer you my felicitations?"

"You may, and thank you. It is a great happiness to us both." Francis opened the door as he spoke and entered the nursery.

The large room had undergone a second transformation since the birth of Luke. Tillie had avoided making change until the child was born, fearful of tempting fate, but now the nursing chair and infant's cradle had been brought into prominence on the side given over to Luke's needs. Pretty's accommodation remained largely as it had been, with the addition of an extra toy cupboard and a larger space for play. Her small table with suitably sized chairs had been moved closer to the wall, along with the bookcase, leaving the carpeted area free to allow even for a grown man to engage in a tumble and tussle on the floor with an adoptive daughter shrieking in delight.

The little girl, all over golden curls without her cap, who was engaged in earnest discussion with her nurse Hepsie, broke off upon the opening of the door. She no sooner saw Francis than she set up a shriek, running to greet him. "Papa! Papa! I made a dance with my dolls. Hepsie did the song and we danced and danced."

Francis scooped her up as she related this history and planted a kiss on her cheek. "You may show me your dancing dolls presently. But first, you have a visitor. Here is Mr Maplewood come to see you."

He hesitated as the big blue gaze turned upon the fellow now watching this byplay with an odd expression in his eyes which Francis found hard to interpret. How to explain Maplewood without referring to events of which Pretty remained ignorant?

He was forestalled. "Vivian, please. Hello, Pretty. It is a long time since I saw you. We are cousins, you know. Of a sort."

Unsure whether he approved of this manner of describing their relationship, Francis intervened. "You might not remember him, sweetheart, but he remembers you."

Pretty disconcerted him, turning her gaze back. "Is he your cousin too, Papa?"

"Just a friend." It felt a lame compromise, but it was far too soon to be burdening the child with her tragic history of the death of both her parents. If she wished to know it later — much later — Francis had prepared himself to tell it. But not now. He set the child down. "Let's see this dance of yours then."

Nothing loath, the little girl scampered back to her nurse and picked up two of her dolls. Hepsie began to sing a simple rhyming song and Pretty skipped about, turning this way and that with the dolls held high and twisting to her motions.

With the child occupied, Maplewood spoke again, but quietly. "I see you have adopted my cousin's identity."

"The boot, my friend, was on the other leg." Francis had not meant to speak harshly. The fellow did not know, after all. He mended his tone. "The fact is that Pretty adopted me. I suspect she had lost the proper image of her father's face and took me for a substitute." He glanced at Maplewood and found the man frowning. "You don't like it, I dare say, but let me tell you she is the happier for having at least one parent."

The other's brows relaxed again. "I have no objection at all. I am glad for Pretty." After a pause, he added, his tone a trifle gruff, "I suspect Dan would also be glad. It is certainly a deal better than the future my uncle Leo had planned for her."

Viscount Wem's plan for his despised granddaughter had not been formed, other than to be rid of her unwelcome presence in his family. This had made it easier than it might have been for Francis to arrange for a transfer of responsibility to himself. Yet Maplewood's reticent response annoyed him. Was that all he could say of it? Or was that unreasonable? One must remember that the man had lost a dear friend in Daniel Brockhurst as well as a cousin. Francis schooled his voice to a friendly note. "She is a delightful addition to our family, sir, of that I can assure you with confidence. We have grown very fond of the child."

"Even to renaming her, I gather."

Did that rankle? "It was politic. I don't want Pretty to question her identity other than as a Fanshawe. That can only lead to distress, if she retains memories of that unfortunate contretemps."

"Contretemps?"

Francis faced him. "What would you have me call it? If I make lighter of it than it was, you ought to understand. It is your own method of dealing with unpleasant matters, is it not?"

A rueful look overspread Maplewood's features. "I am justly rebuked. I ask your pardon, sir."

"Granted. But pray take care how you speak to Pretty while you are here."

That wry grin returned. "You don't mean to evict me at once then?"

Despite himself, Francis laughed. "Even should I wish to, my wife would not countenance it. Pray make yourself at home. I will give order for a room to be prepared."

"Mrs Honeybourne was very much shocked, and extremely voluble," said Ottilia, settling onto the sofa.

Her husband threw a glance to heaven. "I'll warrant she was. She always is."

"Just so, Fan. I am very glad I pumped her about this party beforehand or I should have found it impossible to keep her to the point."

"What said she? Anything of use?"

About to launch into a recital of her visit, Ottilia was forestalled by her mother-in-law. "One moment, before you go into all that. Francis, have you told her?"

A faint sense of unease flitted into Ottilia's bosom at the portentous note. What now? Her spouse looked a trifle put out.

"I have not yet had a chance."

"Told me what, Fan?"

But it was Sybilla who cut in ahead of him. "Guess who has arrived here?"

"For pity's sake, Mama, how the deuce do you expect her to guess?" He turned his gaze upon Ottilia. "Maplewood is here."

Astonished, Ottilia could only stare for a moment. "Lizzy's Mr Maplewood?"

"The very same. Says his mother sent him to check on Pretty. I took him up to meet her and sent him off with Mrs Bertram to be housed wherever she deems suitable."

Sybilla gave Ottilia no opportunity to comment. "You are allowing him to stay?"

"I could hardly turn the fellow out. He's come from Kent."

"It will lead to trouble, Francis, mark my words. I can scent it already."

Ottilia made herself heard. "If he has come to visit Pretty, of course he must stay."

"I knew you would say so, my love."

"Only think what Lizzy would have to say to us if we did not receive him hospitably." A snort from the dowager made Ottilia add in haste, "But did you warn him we are all in an uproar here?"

"Yes, and he seemed to find the matter amusing, damn his eyes!"

"There is no necessity to use such language, boy!"

Again, Ottilia intervened as her spouse showed signs of imminent explosion. "It may be best if we discuss what next to do directly, before Mr Maplewood chooses to re-join us."

Francis hailed this with obvious relief. "An excellent notion. Tell us what you learned."

Ottilia's mind flashed instantly back to Mrs Honeybourne's disclosures. "Enough to guess at that unfortunate young man's identity, for one thing."

"You don't say so!"

"Well? Well? Who is he?"

"Marmaduke Gibbon. Or at least he is the likeliest candidate."

Both mother and son looked blank. Then Francis shrugged. "Never heard of the fellow."

"Nor more had I. He was here in pursuit of Richenda Vexford, it seems, and has put all the noses of our local young gentlemen out of joint."

"Aha! You think one of them may have taken steps to remove the threat?"

"Very possibly. Which supplies us with at least three suspects at the outset."

To Ottilia's secret amusement, Sybilla rubbed her hands together in a show of glee. "Then it begins."

"So we have the victim. Was he killed at a Twelfth Night party as you thought, Tillie?"

"At Thorpe Grange in Tangley, yes." Glad to have averted a battle of words between mother and son, Ottilia launched into a recital of all she had already discovered, not without several questions directed at her from her mother-in-law which she was not equipped to answer. But one name that caught Sybilla's attention afforded an inkling of possibility.

"Did you mention Lady Stoke Rochford?"

"I did, but she was not present at the party."

Sybilla snorted. "I should think not indeed. I thought she was long deceased. She must be in her dotage by now."

Ottilia jumped on this. "Do you know her, Sybilla?"

"In my youth I did. She was an acquaintance of my mother's, which gives you an indication of the years she must have in her dish. She was a good deal younger than Mama, but still."

"It is providential that you know her."

"How so?"

Francis took this. "She's a recluse, Mama. No one has seen her, to my knowledge, since Judith was alive."

The mention of her spouse's first wife, who had died in a carriage accident within a few years of their marriage, could not but give Ottilia a slight pang. Not on his account, but on her own. Her first husband, a soldier, had been killed in the American wars within a few months of their union. She could not regret her happiness with Francis, but a tiny corner of her heart still ached for Jack. The brief moment passed as her mother-in-law took up the point.

"It hardly seems Lady Stoke Rochford could add anything of value to your needs, Ottilia."

"Ah, but she has a young godson who is one of the rivals for Richenda's favours. Botolf Claydon. It is possible his godmother may supply some clue to his character. I may say that Mrs Honeybourne finds him supercilious and sarcastic, but I dare say that is merely prejudice on behalf of her nephew."

Francis rapped his fingers upon the mantel. "To the point, if you please. Mama may visit Lady Stoke Rochford, but don't you think we ought rather to begin with Thorpe?"

Ottilia gave him an amused smile. "You are reading my mind again, my dearest. I was going to suggest you make the first foray."

He did not look to be delighted at the prospect. "Leaving you to do what, if you please?"

"I shall visit Reverend Newton. If Marmaduke Gibbon is our man, then Virginia Grindlow is bound to know all about such a handsome prospect."

"Seth Newton's ward? Setting her cap at him, you think?"

"Would not any young woman? Mind you, according to Mrs Honeybourne our Marmaduke was a fortune-hunter and Virginia could not benefit from any such."

"Then why bother with the girl?" asked the dowager.

"Because, Sybilla, although matrimony might not be her object, I cannot suppose any young woman would not seek the attentions of such a handsome fellow. Especially if he was after Richenda. She is the beauty of the district, you must know."

The discussion was brought to a close by the entrance into the room of Mr Maplewood, obliging Ottilia to take up her mantle of hostess. She was also able to enquire after all the Brockhursts, a matter of interest since they were Pretty's legitimate family.

Sybilla, declaring that if the conversation was to turn upon the Dowager Viscountess Wem, who was her arch enemy, then she had done, chose to retire to prepare to take a walk in the grounds. "Pellew insists I must walk daily, silly man. Venner loathes it, but if I must suffer, so may she also." With which she departed to bully her dour maid into accompanying her on her constitutional in the Flitteris grounds.

Ottilia gave the visitor a smile, patting the sofa beside her. "Pray sit by me, Mr Maplewood. How did you find Pretty?"

"She seems to be admirably suited, ma'am," said the young man, taking his seat beside her. "I confess I found it odd to hear her address his lordship as Papa, but as I told your husband, I believe Daniel would be both relieved and happy to know his daughter was in such good hands."

"I am glad to hear you say so. She is an enchanting child. Amusing too." Ottilia laughed. "I think she has taken Luke for a live doll produced for her entertainment."

She was glad to see Mr Maplewood's rather solemn expression break into a smile. It recalled to her mind the teasing way he had adopted with Lizzy which had tantalised and intrigued her into forming an attachment. Yet was he similarly smitten in truth? He had not come up to scratch when he had the chance. A man in earnest would not be put off by the disapproval of parents. Or he ought not. Ottilia was inclined to wonder if Mr Maplewood was a little too weak a fellow for Lizzy's buoyancy.

But the matter was not pressing at this moment when she had more important fish to fry. Yet might she test him out? Could he prove useful in her current need?

He was addressing some remark to Francis about the prospect from the window of his allotted bedchamber. Ottilia waited for the inane exchange to come to a natural end and dived in.

"Mr Maplewood."

He turned back to her with the smile that had charmed her niece. "Vivian, please, ma'am. You must know I abhor formality. Lady Elizabeth was wont to complain of it often enough."

Ottilia had to laugh. "She might complain, but she liked it, of which I am sure you are quite aware."

A wry look came. "Shrewd of you, ma'am."

"Come, let us drop all pretence, sir. Or Vivian, if you prefer."

A sharp interjection came from Francis, who had dropped into one of the fireside chairs. "Ottilia! What are you about?"

She threw him a reassuring glance. "Nothing alarming, Fan. I am merely admitting Vivian into the family circle, as it were." She put up a finger as the young man beside her frowned. "Do not take me up wrongly, sir. I mean our little family circle here. You are Pretty's cousin. We are her surrogate parents. That applies, whether or not your interest in Lizzy comes to anything."

"You are very frank, Lady Francis."

"I have that reputation." Mischief burgeoned. "If you mean to make a habit of visiting Pretty you may as well accustom yourself."

Vivian grinned at that. "If candour is to be the order of the day, allow me to say that this strikes a dismaying resemblance to my Eliza."

He spoke, Ottilia was certain, without realising his use of the possessive for he looked wholly unconscious. Nevertheless, she shifted ground. "Well, since you are here, Vivian, may I invite your participation in this fresh investigation of mine?"

"I? That is more in Eliza's province than mine, Lady Francis. What in the world can I do?"

Francis took this, rising and coming to the sofa. "You can befriend the various young men who are potentially responsible for Marmaduke Gibbon's demise." He nodded to Ottilia. "Well thought of, my love."

It did not appear that Vivian Maplewood was similarly approving. Indeed he looked quite horrified and Ottilia had to bite back on a bubble of merriment. "I am of course at your service, ma'am," he said, in a tone which did not bear out his words.

Ottilia seized upon the spirit of acquiescence. "Excellent. According to Mrs Honeybourne, these gentry are apt to frequent the Plough in the village. You may begin there perhaps."

Vivian brightened. "Now that is a task I may embrace with enthusiasm."

Ottilia laughed. "Just so. Let me bring you up to date with our findings so far."

CHAPTER FIVE

The Reverend Seth Newton was out visiting one of his parishioners when Ottilia arrived at Foscot vicarage on Thursday morning. She had vetoed pursuing any further enquiries for four and twenty-hours in the hope Mrs Honeybourne's tongue would have done its work first. Besides, she had no intention of neglecting her baby son and his feed must come first. Having performed that duty, she set out for Foscot village in the phaeton with Hemp driving. Finding the vicar absent turned out to be a blessing, for his ward, who received her, was readily brought to engage in the necessary discussion.

Virginia Grindlow was pale, her tell-tale eyes a trifle puffy, reddened at the edges of the lids.

Ottilia wasted no time. "You have heard the news, I take it?"

The young woman's features crumpled for a moment and then she stiffened her spine and dashed at her eyes. "My guardian will not have me grieve, my lady."

"That seems a little harsh." Ottilia had taken a proffered seat on the sofa in a comfortable little parlour, well warmed by a good fire in the hearth. "You have sustained a severe shock."

Miss Grindlow caught a breath. "Oh, it is so horrid. To think of him at that party, so gay and full of vitality. And now…" She faded out, setting a hand to her face and turning away a little.

Ottilia observed her while she waited for Virginia to recover sufficiently to talk again. She was a pretty enough young woman, with soft sandy-coloured hair caught up in a top-knot, a straight nose in a rather narrow face and, her best feature, a pair of striking green eyes. Her figure was a trifle angular and she had not the grace of movement that characterised the beauty of the district. Nevertheless, it was evident at once to Ottilia that she had cherished a tendre for this Marmaduke.

In a moment, she visibly shook off her melancholy. "I beg your pardon, ma'am."

"Don't, my dear. I quite understand." This elicited nothing more than a fleeting smile. Ottilia took the bull by the horns. "I am not here on a courtesy visit, you must know, Miss Grindlow."

Virginia met Ottilia's gaze with a bold look. "No. You wish to ask me about the Twelfth Night party, do you not?"

"Mrs Honeybourne?"

A reluctant smile came. "She told me you posed all manner of questions. I will tell you whatever I can, ma'am." Her brows drew together. "Although I dare not believe that argument was serious."

Ottilia pounced on this. "Which argument?"

Virginia looked conscious, throwing a hand to her mouth. "I did not mean to say that."

"Yet you told me you are happy to answer any questions I may have."

Virginia looked down at her fingers, now twisting together in her lap. "I had not meant to cast blame on anyone."

"As yet there is no reason to suppose there is blame to be assigned," Ottilia said on a soothing note. "Until the results of the post-mortem are known, we will not know whether Marmaduke — if it is indeed he — died a natural death."

An eager look was cast at her. "It may not be him after all? But Mrs Honeybourne said —"

"Oh, I think there can be little doubt of his identity, my poor girl, even though we do not yet have anyone who may say so for certain. None of our young gentlemen in these parts can lay claim to being either blond or so excessively handsome."

"He *is* beautiful, is he not?" Virginia drew a sharp breath, her eyes clouding. "I cannot say it now, can I?"

"It is never easy to accept that one you knew well has gone." Better to bypass the death and pump Virginia for memories. "Tell me of this argument, if you will. How did it arise?"

Virginia let out a noisy breath, redolent of frustration. "Richenda, of course. It was all her doing, setting them off one against the other in that spiteful way." An alarmed look crossed her face as she glanced at Ottilia. "Oh! Now I sound like the veriest cat. I did not mean to decry Richenda. We have always been on good terms. Or we were."

She bit her lip and Ottilia cut in at once. "Before the advent of Marmaduke Gibbon, I take it?"

Virginia let out another overcharged breath. "Yes! I tried not to be jealous, but how could I help it? She has them all at her feet. Aubrey, Jarvis. Even Botolf Claydon, though he pretends otherwise."

Ottilia grew impatient. "But the argument, my dear. You said Richenda caused it? How, pray?"

Virginia looked down at her hands and, in a fastidious gesture, straightened her fingers which had curled into claws. "Perhaps she was not so much to blame. We were all intrigued by that fellow Mr Gibbon brought with him."

"Ah, yes. Who was he?"

"Pedwardine, his name is. Percy, Marmaduke called him. He made a point of presenting Mr Pedwardine to everyone. I dare say it would not have happened if Marmaduke had not singled out Richenda. 'And here,' he said, 'is the lady whom we both know and admire.' Just as if Henrietta and I were of no account!"

Ottilia began to wonder if it had not rather been Virginia herself who set the quarrel in motion. "You felt slighted, I dare say?"

"For a moment only. It seems Mr Pedwardine is acquainted with Richenda."

"And admires her?"

"To my mind, he did not appear to be particularly interested in her, only —" Virginia hesitated, fidgeting with her petticoats, her colour rising.

"Only?"

The prompt had its effect. "It entered my mind that Marmaduke meant for his friend to divert Richenda's attention from himself. Especially after the way he behaved towards me, using that caressing tone, hinting at it that my sentiments were…" She faded out, looking even more conscious.

But Virginia could not be allowed to wriggle out of this one. "Reciprocated? When was this, Miss Grindlow?"

"At our dinner last Friday. Marmaduke drew me into the conservatory. He paid me all manner of compliments, saying my complexion was like the pink flowers there and — and plying my fan for me and…" All at once she burst out, her eyes filling. "But it was all false! I see that now. He did it to make Richenda jealous. She was in the conservatory too, with Aubrey Botterell. I thought nothing of it at the time, but at Thorpe Grange, when Aubrey began upon him, I should have realised it then."

"Why, what happened with Aubrey? Was this the beginning of the argument?"

Virginia nodded with vehemence. "It must have been, although they were not loud to begin with. The gentlemen had come upstairs from the dining-room and had just entered the drawing room when it began. Aubrey grew angry and began shouting that enough was enough and Mr Gibbon should take himself and his friend off. The other gentlemen went to intervene and Mrs Thorpe ushered us females away to the Yellow Saloon next door. Not that any of us could settle for we could hear them all and it went on for several minutes."

Why had the widow not mentioned this? "Where was Mrs Honeybourne at this moment?"

"Mrs Honeybourne? She was there. Or, no. She did go to the ladies' retiring room. It might have been then."

"You heard nothing of what was said?"

"In the drawing room? No, for Mrs Thorpe encouraged Etta to go to the pianoforte and play for us."

"Etta?"

"Henrietta Skelmersdale. She is Lady Stoke Rochford's companion, you must know. Botolf Claydon brought her." A touch of defiance entered Virginia's voice. "A very good thing too. She does not have many opportunities for pleasure, poor Etta. So lively as she is too. We are friends."

A friendship that excluded Richenda? But Ottilia did not ask. Disappointing that Virginia had heard no more of the quarrel. "What happened afterwards? Did the gentlemen come into the saloon?"

"All except Marmaduke and his friend. Oh, and Botolf. They may have come back later, but my guardian insisted we must leave. He said it was growing late and he had to be in church upon the following morning, but it's my belief he just wanted me out of there. He doesn't approve of Marmaduke."

It crossed Ottilia's mind that the Reverend Seth Newton was likely not the only guardian to hold this view, if the young man was indeed a fortune-hunter.

Armed with the information gleaned by his wife at Foscot

vicarage, Francis drove to Tangley to tackle the Thorpes in a more hopeful frame of mind. He was received in the library by the man of the house, who professed to have no previous knowledge of the death. Francis took this with scepticism.

"The news has not reached you, sir? I confess I am surprised."

Martin Thorpe, occupying the space to one side of the mantel in his spacious den lined with shelves of books, pursed his lips and looked down his long nose through the spectacles perched thereon. "I never pay heed to gossip, my lord."

Tall and thin, wearing a tye-wig worn over a high brow and with a tendency to fold his hands together, he reminded Francis of a praying mantis. But he was not going to be permitted to hop his way out of this one.

"You have heard rumours then?" Francis prompted.

"Some nonsense about a delivered corpse. Who would do such a thing?"

"Precisely what I am here to find out, sir."

Thorpe's head came up. "You mean to tell me it is true?"

"Perfectly. Much, I may say, to my chagrin. A horseman dropped the body on our doorstep at Flitteris."

"Singular."

"Oh, I think not, Thorpe." Francis rocked back on his heels where he stood on an ornate rug set in the space before the hearth, and folded his arms. "Somebody, sir, saw fit to involve my wife. It is well known around these parts that she goes by the sobriquet of Lady Fan and has been successful in uncovering the perpetrator in several instances of murder."

Thorpe's expression grew bland and he released one hand to wave it in an arc. "All this, my lord, is common knowledge. Yet I fail to understand why you come to me."

Francis gave a somewhat grim smile. "That is easily explained. The fellow in question was in evening dress and arrived on Tuesday evening, a day after your Twelfth Night party."

"Good heavens!" Was Thorpe's surprise feigned? His expression turned to dismay. "You cannot suppose it was I who sent this corpse? My dear Lord Francis, I can assure you that all persons who attended my party departed quite safe and well."

Did they indeed? The insistence seemed a little too pat. Had Thorpe prepared for this interview? Francis changed tack. "What I need from you, Thorpe, is the tale of what occurred that evening during an argument between two of the gentlemen. To wit, one Marmaduke Gibbon and Aubrey Botterell."

"Oh, that." Thorpe hesitated. Was he deciding whether to be open? Francis watched him shift from his stance at the mantel and cross to a window, staring out for a moment at the frosted lawns. Shortly, Thorpe turned and gestured to one of the chairs with leather to the seat and back, which were set either side of the bay, close enough to catch the heat from the fire. "Will you sit, my lord? I can ring for wine."

He moved towards the bell-pull as he spoke, but Francis waved the offer away. "Nothing for me, I thank you." But he took the indicated chair and watched his host fold himself into the other, setting his elbows on the arms and steepling his fingers. Thorpe looked over them at his guest. "That young man was becoming a confounded nuisance."

"Gibbon?" Francis hit hard. "So someone got rid of him?"

The fingers dropped, alarm crossing Thorpe's narrow features. "Is that what you suppose?"

Francis backtracked. "It is by no means certain. There will be a post-mortem."

Either the alarm increased or Thorpe was busy thinking up excuses for he raised long fingers to his face, caressing his chin in a manner that spoke of agitation. Francis let him stew for a moment before applying a goad. "The quarrel, Thorpe?"

The hand dropped, but Thorpe set both on the arms of the chair where his fingers drummed briefly and then became still. He looked across, poking his head forward. "Very well, I will tell you." Francis gave a nod and waited for him to continue. A sigh came. "I had not thought it serious. Young Aubrey was jealous of Gibbon monopolising the girls. I regret to say he lost his temper, throwing all manner of nonsensical accusations at the fellow."

"What sort of accusations?"

"Oh, that his motives were mercenary, that he was a peacocking upstart, that sort of thing. Wild talk, but quite enough to justify Gibbon calling him out, if he had a mind so to do."

"He didn't?"

Thorpe adjusted his spectacles. "On the contrary. He merely laughed, taking the line that all is fair in love and war. Then Aubrey began upon the friend Gibbon brought with him, I forget his name."

Francis supplied it. "Percy Pedwardine."

A startled look came Francis's way. "You are remarkably well informed, my lord."

Francis ignored this. "Did they come to blows?"

"Gibbon and Aubrey? Not to my knowledge. But there was a scuffle. My brother Jarvis was one of the men who intervened."

"You did not?"

"I was more intent upon getting my wife to remove the ladies from the vicinity. By the time I re-entered the drawing room, where all this was taking place, Jarvis had hold of Aubrey and both Botolf and that other fellow were hustling Gibbon away."

"Where did they go with him?"

"Downstairs, I believe. They commandeered the breakfast parlour. Meanwhile, Jarvis took Aubrey outside to cool off."

"What happened to Botolf Claydon?"

Thorpe frowned. "I don't recall. He may have re-joined the ladies. I was preoccupied with Vexford, who had become heated."

Francis jumped on this. "Because of his daughter? Do I take it he disapproved of Gibbon's suit?"

Thorpe sniffed in a manner distinctly contemptuous. "Vexford disapproves of all Richenda's suitors. He is after a title."

A stray thought occurred. "I'm surprised she did not secure one last year when she came out."

Thorpe gave vent to a noise very like a snort. "With her father peering over her shoulder in that fierce way he has and frightening all comers away? Lavinia will have it the girl enjoys more freedom here than she did in Town. It appears, however, that this Marmaduke met her there." A note of dissatisfaction entered in. "He seems wondrous great with her. None of our young men have received such encouragement as she gave this interloper." He then appeared to recollect himself, putting a finger to his spectacles and resettling them upon his nose. "However, that is neither here nor there."

In fact it was very much to the point, but Francis refrained from saying so. He essayed a throw. "If I may be a trifle indelicate, sir, do I take it your brother Jarvis has an interest there?"

Thorpe's mouth tightened and he looked away briefly. Then he brought his head up. "My wife would like to see him marry well. I have taken it upon myself to warn him against the disadvantage of saddling himself with Vexford for a father-in-law, but what would you? He will take his chance, I suppose."

Now that Marmaduke Gibbon was no longer an obstacle. It was tempting, but Francis let it go. "I wonder if I might have a word with Jarvis perhaps?"

"He is out."

It was said rather too quickly. Once again, Francis was inclined to doubt his host's veracity. He pressed the pertinent point. "You are certain Gibbon left with the rest?"

The other's brows drew together. "Why should I not be? I certainly bade all my guests farewell."

"Including Gibbon?"

The persistence did not rattle Thorpe. "I believe so. It was all rather a flurry, you must know. Lavinia was principally involved. Seeing everyone's carriages were called for, that sort of thing."

A pity Mrs Thorpe had made no appearance. Francis began to feel he might have done better with the wife. Was there anything more to be got out of the man? "Is there any other little thing you recall?"

"Such as?"

Francis shrugged. "To do with the scuffle perhaps? What precisely occurred?"

"As I said, I was not present at that time. Jarvis might know more. The fellow you need, I dare say, is Botterell. He began it."

There did not seem to be much profit in pursuing matters with Thorpe, but just as Francis rose to make his farewells, the door opened and a flustered Mrs Thorpe entered the library.

"Gracious goodness, my lord, I do apologise, I do indeed!" As plump as her husband was lean, she bustled across and looked up into Francis's face out of rounded features which were nevertheless pretty. "I would have come at once had I known, my lord. So rude not to receive you properly." She turned on her spouse, indignant. "Why did you not send for me, Mr Thorpe?" Giving him no time to respond, she tucked a hand in Francis's arm and drew him towards the door. "Do pray come into my front parlour, my lord. It is a good deal warmer. I cannot think why Martin did not think to offer you refreshment, but we will remedy that upon the instant." Releasing him, she called to a footman standing to one side of the front door. "John, tell Mrs Strumpshaw we need wine and cakes. Immediately."

Accepting the inevitable, Francis made no attempt to break in upon the woman's monologue, but followed where she led, talking all the time, and presently found himself installed in a chair by the fireside in what he guessed was Mrs Thorpe's personal parlour, judging by its distinctly feminine air. The curtains and chair coverings were of chintz, cushions abounded and a closed sewing box stood close beside the comfortable armed chair opposite to the one into which his hostess had urged him.

Mr Thorpe, Francis noted, had trailed in their wake and now hovered in the doorway. Wondering whether he might make himself scarce? The matter was settled by his garrulous spouse.

"Do sit down, Martin. I cannot think why you are standing about in that foolish fashion." She settled on the chair opposite Francis and continued without pause, "I dare say I may guess what you have come about, Lord Francis. Such a dreadful business. Terrible news. So young, so handsome. A tragedy, is it not?"

Francis broke in at last as she took breath. "You believe the dead man to be Marmaduke Gibbon then, ma'am?"

"Well, of course. Mrs Honeybourne said as much. And if, as I understand Lady Francis intimated, the poor young man is fair-headed, then most certainly it is he. There are no other blond men in this part of the world. Certainly not in our circle. Indeed, I am sure that is what made him so very attractive to all our young ladies." She gave a sigh and a chuckle. "I do recall becoming quite enamoured of a fair fellow in my youth. That was before I married you, my dear."

This was said with a compensatory glance at the silent Thorpe, who had taken a seat a little removed from the fire. Francis could scarcely blame him for wishing to escape. He was beginning to wonder if he would ever be permitted to utter a word. Fortunately, the footman appeared in the doorway at this moment, burdened with a tray. Francis seized his chance while Mrs Thorpe stopped talking momentarily to observe who entered.

"There is one thing you may be able to help me with, Mrs Thorpe."

She signed to her husband to do the honours with the wine and turned with an eager look towards the guest. "Yes, my lord? You are enquiring on behalf of Lady Francis?"

"I am, and I would be glad if you can tell me what time Marmaduke Gibbon and his friend left the house."

Mrs Thorpe's brows drew together. "I am not entirely sure. Reverend Newton and his ward left almost immediately after the contretemps. That must have been — oh, around nine o'clock perhaps? Lord Vexford took Richenda a little later. But the rest of them went off in a bang after we had drunk tea. Goodness, such a hurry and bustle as there was, I don't believe I remarked the time."

"They all left then? You are sure of that?" He cast a glance up at Thorpe as he spoke, for the fellow was hovering over him, holding a full glass.

"I said so, did I not?" It came out in a snap and he thrust the vessel towards Francis.

Francis took it. "Corroboration is always helpful, sir."

"My dear Mr Thorpe, what in the world would you be at? If his lordship wishes to ask me as well as you, I have no objection." The chubby features smiled as the wife met Francis's eyes. "Of course they all left. Even Jarvis went off with Botolf Claydon. I heard him come in after we were tucked in bed. Did you not, my dear?"

Thorpe gave his wife a sour look. "I don't remember. I dare say I was sound asleep."

So Jarvis was abroad that night, as also Botolf Claydon. A thought occurred. "Did not Claydon escort Miss Skelmersdale home?"

Mrs Thorpe threw up a hand. "Did I not say? Henrietta went with the reverend. She and Virginia Grindlow are quite bosom bows." She gave another chuckle. "A little gossip, I expect, talking over the happenings of the evening, and likely reviling poor Richenda too. Yes, Seth Newton kindly said they would take Henrietta, Penton Mewsey being, as you must well know, sir, only a little way beyond Foscot."

"About those happenings, Mrs Thorpe," Francis broke in. "I understand from your husband that there was a quarrel between Botterell and Gibbon."

Mrs Thorpe threw up her hands. "Yes, so silly. Young men will do these things. Most reprehensible, but what would you?

When girls will flirt it is bound to set their suitors at each other's throats. You may be sure I questioned Jarvis closely. He said it was no great matter. A little pushing and shoving, sheer horseplay."

Horseplay that may well have resulted in death, if Francis's darling wife had it right, and she usually did. "It would be useful if I could hear Jarvis Thorpe's account from his own lips."

"I told you, my lord," came in an irritated tone from Thorpe, "my brother is not in the house."

Francis looked from him to his wife and her smile turned on at once. "It is very true, alas, my lord. He said at breakfast that he meant to meet with one of his friends, I forget which. Oh, and that he might call on Richenda. We do not expect him until the dinner hour."

Francis tossed off his wine and rose to take his leave. There seemed nothing more to be gained here for the present. But a niggling dissatisfaction persisted. Neither Thorpe could positively state that Marmaduke Gibbon had left the house.

CHAPTER SIX

Ottilia had just settled her infant son, replete from his feed, when a knock at her parlour door was followed by her maid's head peeping into the room. Ottilia put a finger to her lips, gesturing towards Luke and beckoned Joanie into the room. Everyone in the household knew it was her habit to nourish the baby after partaking of the customary snack, set in place around midday to stave off her hungry lord's complaints of starvation, and in general none disturbed her until she rang. It must be important. She kept her voice to a murmur. "What is it, Joanie?"

Her maid responded at a like level. "Mr Rodmell did not wish to trouble you, my lady, but the lady insisted."

"What lady?"

Joanie leaned in, becoming confiding. "She's in a bit of a tizzy, Mr Rodmell thinks. It's that Miss Vexford, my lady."

"Richenda!" Ottilia's mind jumped to the problem of the dead man. How fortunate the young woman chose to seek her out. "I will see her. Ask Doro to come for Luke, if you please."

"Doro's waiting in the gallery, my lady. I'll fetch her in."

While Joanie slipped out for the Barbadian nurse, Ottilia reflected on the convenience of Richenda Vexford arriving just at this moment. Sybilla had opted to take a nap while Francis went off to tackle the Thorpes. Vivian Maplewood had gone out, armed with his sketching pad, to which Ottilia had raised an objection.

"You are going sketching, sir? Do you not mean to find those young men for me?"

Vivian had waved the pad. "A ruse merely, ma'am. I shall pursue my task, never fear."

With which she had been obliged to be content. While she fed Luke, the puzzle faded from her mind, enchanted as she was still with the miracle of her infant boy's existence. But when she had kissed him farewell and allowed Doro to take him away, her attention veered readily, increased by the demeanour of her visitor as Joanie ushered Richenda into the parlour.

In contrast to Virginia Grindlow's angular form, Richenda Vexford was a buxom creature, endowed with a generous bosom enhanced by a narrow waist. A quantity of dark curls fell down her back and framed a face charming by any standards with a neat nose, pouting cherry lips and a pair of pansy brown eyes, just now shadowed with distress. Her voice was husky with it as she burst out at once.

"Madam! Lady Francis! I pray you, help me!"

Ottilia rose, holding out her hand. "My poor child, you are discomposed indeed."

Richenda came forward, seized the proffered hand and gripped it. "I am utterly cast down, my senses wholly disordered. Forgive me, but I had to come!"

Ottilia covered the hand, trying not to wince. "I am very glad you did. Come, sit by me and we will talk."

She made to draw Richenda back towards her sofa, but Richenda released herself, hanging back. "You must know why I have come. You are so clever. Lady Fan, they call you, do they not? Oh, if ever you deserved that sobriquet, pray, pray do so now!" She threw her hands over her face and the words came muffled. "Marmaduke! My love! My heart! I shall never recover. Never!"

Ottilia struggled for patience. Was this genuine? She could not avoid the suspicion these histrionics were turned on especially for her benefit. Or was Richenda habitually this dramatic? "Come, my child, this will get us nowhere. Strive for a little control, if you please."

The hands dropped. Were her eyes wet or merely reddened? At least she sounded contrite. "Yes. I beg your pardon. I am overwrought." The brown gaze became soulful. "You did not know him, did you?"

"I did not."

"I wish you had, for then you would understand." Richenda's hands curled tight and there was anguish in her tone. "We loved one another. We would have married but for my father. We were betrothed."

Ottilia studied her, unconvinced. "Secretly, I take it?"

A wild gesture. "Yes! What would you, when my papa remained so stubborn? He has no regard for me. He wishes me to make a *good* match. As if Marmaduke was the veriest nobody."

Ottilia tried for a calming note. "It is a habit of fathers to wish their daughters to marry well. Especially where there is a substantial dowry."

"So mercenary." Richenda flung away, taking up a pose by the mantel and setting one hand thereon. "It is all of a piece. My happiness is of no account. He wishes to sell me to some horrid old peer, to be miserable for the rest of my days."

It was noticeable that her father's iniquity possessed more power over Richenda's mind than the death of her lover. Indeed, Ottilia was struck by the tone of her language, which suggested she had already accustomed herself to the fact of Marmaduke's death. Yet his corpse had not been identified.

"Richenda — if I may?"

Richenda batted a hand in the air. "Oh, call me what you wish to, Lady Fan, I care not." Turning, she held out pleading hands. "I ask only that you do your utmost to find out who did this thing? Who would harm him? Why? What had he done that someone should take his life?"

Ottilia applied a damper. "It is by no means certain that anyone did so. I wish you will sit down, child. I am going to do so, for I cannot stand for long." She retook her seat on the daybed as she spoke, gesturing to a chair set close enough to be cosy. "Sit, Richenda!"

The visitor flung up her hands. "Behold me then!" Moving to the chair, she threw herself into it, but at once sat up, leaning towards Ottilia, her brows drawing together. "Are you saying he was not slain by another?"

"I am saying we don't yet know. There was no outward sign of injury." Ottilia withheld her surmise of a blow to the heart.

A long sigh escaped Richenda. "Nothing to show how he died. No wound. No blood."

The oddity of these utterances grated. These were not questions, but statements rather. Moreover, where had all the despair and grief gone? It returned in a bang as Richenda raised her eyes to Ottilia's again, a plea in her voice now.

"Will you find it out? Can you? I cannot bear it that he is gone if I do not know."

Ottilia seized opportunity. "I will do what I can to relieve your mind, but you must help me in your turn."

"How? What can I do? I am bereft, of no use to a living soul!"

Tempted to give a sharp retort, Ottilia instead threw in a question. "You can tell me, as a start, what happened between you and Marmaduke to cause a tussle to spring up among all the young gentlemen at the Twelfth Night party."

Consternation covered Richenda's face, followed by a frown and puzzlement. "Between Marmaduke and I?"

Ottilia chose not to spare her. "He was flirting with Virginia. Was it to make you jealous? Had you quarrelled?"

Richenda looked away, fiddling with the petticoats of her round gown of green kerseymere, worn with a fichu over the low bosom that did little to conceal her charms. Ottilia waited. At length, Richenda's gaze came back, an earnest look within it.

"I had best make a clean breast of it, I suppose."

"It would be of use."

Richenda drew in a breath. "We did quarrel. Not that night. We had made up by then. But Virginia must have tattled."

"What makes you think so?"

"Aubrey would not have said what he did if she had not."

"To Marmaduke? What did he say?"

Richenda shifted her shoulders. "Oh, that Marmaduke ought to be content with one conquest. Merely because Marmaduke introduced his friend to Virginia and Henrietta."

"This Percy?"

Richenda's lip curled. "Percy! Why had he to come amongst us, making it his mission to drag Marmaduke away?"

"From you? He wanted to part you?"

"No, no, not that. But I knew he would find pursuits for Marmaduke to engage in, just as he had in London."

Ottilia became dry. "Gentlemanly pursuits such that Marmaduke would not be dancing attendance upon you." Richenda's lovely features grew pink. Ottilia was glad to see she was capable of blushing. "Is that why you quarrelled?"

An instant change. The beauty's eyes flashed. "Not that. Not only that."

"What then?"

A toss of the head. "He thought he knew better than I, but I know Papa. Consent? A foolish dream. There is only one way to best Cosmo Vexford."

These cryptic assertions set up a train of thought in Ottilia's head, a growing suspicion that the professed attachment to Marmaduke Gibbon was in truth a tool, perhaps even fabricated, for use as a skirmish in Richenda's war with her father. Such griefs as she displayed appeared spurious, unlike that shown by Virginia Grindlow. This belief was fostered by a sudden disturbance in the galleried hallway outside and an irate voice calling the young woman's name.

"Richenda! *Richenda*! Where the devil is the girl?"

"Oh, no! Papa!" Richenda leapt from her chair and raced to the window, as if she sought to exit by that way. Balked, she turned there, standing at bay, her gaze fixed upon the door as her name continued to ring out around the galleried vestibule.

"Richenda! Where are you, wretched female?"

"Oh, don't let him come in! He will punish me dreadfully!"

Ottilia thought she heard her butler in a confused medley of voices as she looked back to Richenda. "Don't be afraid! There is nothing he can do to you in this house."

Even as she spoke, the door burst open and the red-faced, contorted features of Lord Vexford confronted her. Ottilia had met him upon few occasions and found him brusque but civil. He was a man of less than average height, which he made up for with a loud voice and proudful manner. He was sporting a toupee with a high front and wings that did nothing to complement his stature, and his features, though they resembled those of his daughter, were set in harsher lines, the brown eyes fierce as they looked across at Richenda, wholly ignoring the rightful inhabitant of the parlour.

"So! I find you, do I? Disobedient, wilful child! Come here at once!"

Belatedly, from behind Lord Vexford came Ottilia's butler, out of breath and looking outraged. "My lady, I could not stop him!"

He attempted to slide in front of Vexford as he spoke but was thrust off. "Out of my way, fool!"

Concern for the elderly servant loosened Ottilia's tongue. "Let be, Rodmell. You may go. I will deal with this." Turning on Vexford, she began, "As for you, sir —" She got no further.

"Richenda, do you hear me? Don't make me fetch you, wretched girl! This nonsense must cease forthwith! You will smart for this, I promise you."

Ottilia, beginning to recognise that Richenda's tendency to the dramatic was inherited, could not let this pass. Disregarding the fellow's rudeness to herself, she rose and put herself directly in his eyeline so that he might not ignore her. "Lord Vexford!"

He blinked and reared his head back. Evidently he had been unaware of her presence. "Lady Francis."

Ottilia chose a deliberate note of cool reserve. "A polite greeting might have been more appropriate, sir, than this violent entrance. How dare you assault my servant?"

His mouth worked, his gaze resentful. "I came for my daughter."

Was no apology to be forthcoming? "So I gather. I imagine the whole house is by now aware of it."

Again, he appeared to struggle with himself. "No wish to intrude. I'll take my daughter and leave."

"Not if you mean to approach the poor girl in this deplorable spirit," Ottilia returned on a tart note. "Have you no compassion at all?"

"Pah! She'll get no pity from me, mooning over that damned wastrel! No loss to the world. If he's dead, I'm glad of it." Speaking across Ottilia, he addressed his daughter, his voice rising again. "Come here, I said! I'm taking you home. You can do your grieving in your room, but you'll be standing for days, my girl, when I've finished with you."

Once more Ottilia intervened. "This bullying, sir, is the outside of enough. I am minded to keep the child here if you are intent upon a petty vengeance. What has she done, after all?"

"That, madam, is none of your affair. You have no rights in the matter. She is my daughter and she will come home with me. How dare you interfere?"

Ottilia's temper betrayed her. "How dare you, sir, address me in such a fashion? If my husband were here, he would deal you short shrift, let me tell you."

"He had better try! Richenda, are you coming or do I have to drag you forth?"

Before Ottilia could protest further, a welcome interruption came in the icy voice of her mother-in-law. "What in heaven's name is the meaning of all this commotion?" Sybilla strode into the room, black eyes snapping as she moved to a point where she could confront Vexford. With a surge of admiration, Ottilia saw how the intruder remained silent before her, such was the command of her presence. "You are the author of it, are you? I take leave to tell you, whoever you may be, that your manners are atrocious. By what authority do you barge your way into my daughter-in-law's private sanctum? By what right do you stand there and attempt to browbeat her? Take yourself off, sir!"

Though he took a pace back before this onslaught, Lord Vexford did not immediately obey. "I leave with my daughter or not at all."

At this, Richenda re-entered the lists. "I won't go with you! You don't care that my heart is broken! Oh, Marmaduke, Marmaduke!"

But the dowager had marched to the still open door. "Rodmell? Fetch Hemp and the footman too. Then throw this —" with a contemptuous gesture in the direction of the invader — "this *gentleman* out of the house."

As Rodmell hurried out in obedience to Sybilla's command, Ottilia's sense of the ridiculous was beginning to get the better of her and she found it hard to resist the urge to laugh. Vexford would undoubtedly take it for an insult if she did. Would he yield? She glanced back to find Richenda had moved a little way into the room, her brown gaze alight with excitement rather than the alleged despair. Was she enjoying this? Perhaps she thought to see her father bested for once. If so, she was disappointed.

With a sudden spring, Vexford leapt past Ottilia, seized Richenda's arm and tugged her, with some violence as she resisted, screeching the while, towards the door.

Ottilia could not think how to stop the assault, but with a vague intent of intervening, she moved towards the pair, only to be brought up short by Sybilla, who grasped her arm.

"Leave be, Ottilia. There is nothing you can do."

"But he means to beat the poor girl."

"I dare say it will not be for the first time. She will survive it."

The interchange was not heard by the combatants and Ottilia followed as they exited the room, both making the maximum amount of noise. She stood at the balustrade, watching the pair descend the stairs to the first floor, Richenda now tearful as she struggled still, reviling her father with every breath.

"Beast! Brute! I hate you! I will hate you forever!"

"Hate me if you will, but you'll obey me, girl, or take the consequences."

Ottilia lost sight of them as they made their way to the main staircase, although she could still hear their voices. Down in the chequered hall were waiting Hemp, Mrs Bertram and a collection of other servants hovering at the edges. Rodmell hurried behind the departing pair towards the front door which Tyler was holding open. Vexford dragged his daughter through and the door closed behind them. Ottilia remained at her post, listening to the echoing row which persisted right up until the horses' hooves could be heard carrying the unwelcome visitors away.

"Well!" Sybilla was at her side. "A vulgar exhibition, if ever I saw one. I dare say it has not occurred to that foolish man that the tale will be all over the countryside before the night is out."

Which was all too true, rendering null and void the vague hope burgeoning in Ottilia's mind that Francis would not hear of it.

CHAPTER SEVEN

No sooner had Vivian Maplewood entered the taproom of the Plough than he spied a coterie of three young men seated in earnest and low-voiced conversation at a table by a latticed casement window set at the front of the room. Vivian was pleased to note an empty table a little way from where they all sat. They were by no means the inn's only clients. An elderly pair were engaged in a desultory game of dominoes at a table near the fire and a man who looked like a well-to-do farmer from his countrified frock coat and leather breeches stood at the counter.

The place was clean, its atmosphere cheerful with brasses on the walls, a plethora of wall-sconces throwing light on the ancient timbered beams and a well-dressed fellow manning the casks at the counter.

Vivian approached this individual, taking surreptitious stock of the fellows he assumed to be his quarries. Two of them had their backs to him. Both looked to be of slim build, one with narrow shoulders, the other a trifle more robust as far as one could tell. Neither wore wigs which indicated an adherence to current fashion among young men who tended to the loose look of the French style, if not as shaggy as his own. But the one facing Vivian wore his brown hair tied behind, flowing back from a high brow. There was a lean cast to his countenance and his nose was rather long. His stance, even seated, showed him to be taller than either of his companions, in particular as he straightened upon catching sight of his appraiser. Vivian looked away just as the tapster addressed him.

"What can I get you, sir?"

Vivian slipped fingers into his money pocket and brought out a couple of coins. "A tankard of your best ale, if you will."

The tapster smiled appreciation as he upended a tankard and began to fill it at one of the casks. "Ah, we've a good brew, sir. I venture to think it'll please you."

Vivian set his sketchpad down upon the counter and lifted the tankard to his lips, quaffing a mouthful. It was of average quality but he chose to praise.

"Excellent. What's the figure?"

The tapster named his price and Vivian set the appropriate coinage down, returning the rest to his pocket. Picking up his sketchpad again, he looked about as if he sought a place to sit and then made as if he spied the free table beside the young men. Making for it, he was aware that he became the focus of the gazes of all three as they fell silent. He set down both sketchpad and tankard, nodded casually in their direction and took his seat, gazing out the window as he took a pull from his drink as if he inspected the prospect outside where a small green was surrounded by the buildings that made up the centre of the village of Knights Inham.

The three young gentlemen resumed their conversation, but in lowered tones and huddling towards each other, elbows on the table so that he could not inspect the second two men. Vivian strained to hear what was said but could make out snatches only.

"... another stranger..."

"Not seen him since..."

"... so this Lady Fan told my aunt."

Ah, they were discussing the murder. Or rather, the death. Had not his hostess insisted there was as yet no real reason to suspect foul play?

He let the conversation run on for a while, but could descry no opportunity to interrupt. Recalling Eliza's forthright methods, he decided, with some reluctance, that he would have to make his own time to intervene. He was dubious as to being able to discover anything at all, but he had given his word and must follow it through.

Accordingly, he turned his chair, making a deliberate noise about it, and addressed them all impartially. "I beg your pardon, but are you residents around these parts?"

The three turned towards him and Vivian was able to take in the looks of the other two as the tall one he had first noted spoke. "I am, sir, more or less. I was born and raised at Tangley, nearby, but for the most part I live in the capital these days." He gestured to his companions opposite. "Botterell here and Claydon are frequent visitors."

"Ah, then you are well placed to advise me." Vivian nodded at the two indicated. The fellow Botterell was a chubby-cheeked young fellow, just now wearing a discontented pout though he returned the nod. The other man gave Vivian back look for look, making a thorough examination of it as he regarded Vivian with a faintly supercilious air. "What advice do you require, sir?"

Vivian was ready for that, having prepared his story in advance. He set a hand on his sketchpad. "Prospects. Or, to be more specific, trees."

Claydon's eyebrows rose. "Trees?"

Botterell gave a somewhat high-pitched laugh that caused the florid style of his frilled neck-cloth to flutter. "Are you a forester, sir?"

"An artist. Or I aspire to be so. I am engaged in a study of trees. To be more precise, bark."

Claydon, who evidently considered himself a wit, let out a ululating howl like a dog. The other two burst into laughter, hastily muffling it with hands over their mouths as Vivian showed no disposition to share their amusement. He caught the eye of the mocker.

"I like the patterns that appear in bark as it ages and cracks. I dare say you have observed as much." From the expressions of all it was clear they were as far from observing anything so aesthetic as they might be to fly to the moon. Vivian permitted himself a smile. "Where may I find aging bark?"

The three exchanged glances. The man who had first answered took it at length. "I imagine there must be trees enough in Chute Forest."

"Ah. Is that far?"

"A few miles only. Take the road to Tangley and you will find it to the west. A short drive. Unless you are on foot?"

"Oh, no, I have my curricle at Flitteris."

Vivian observed with satisfaction how this announcement produced an immediate change in all three gentlemen.

Botterell showed consternation. Vivian's informant, who was dressed with propriety in a sober blue coat, his neck-cloth neatly tied, stared at him rather hard. With suspicion? It was left to the artist in mockery to take it up.

"You are staying with the Fanshawes then."

"I am."

The man looked to the others, each of whom half shrugged. He turned back. "I must suppose you know what's been happening here?"

"You mean the body dropped on the doorstep? Yes, I have been informed. I was not here then. I arrived upon the following day."

Botterell chimed in. "Are you well acquainted with this Lady Fan?"

"Not well, but I was present when she solved a murder." Vivian did not add that it involved members of his family. He judged it time to introduce himself and stood up. "I am Maplewood. Vivian Maplewood."

All three men came to their feet. Claydon, whose attire of long-tailed cloth coat over buckskins and top boots looked rather more suited to the metropolis, was the first to hold out his hand in a more friendly spirit than he had shown hitherto. "Botolf Claydon."

Then Aubrey Botterell introduced himself, and finally, Jarvis Thorpe. He it was who resumed the questions as they all sat down, Vivian drawing his chair nearer at his invitation and shifting his tankard to their table.

"So you have actually witnessed Lady Francis in action?"

Vivian did not much care to recall the events of that episode in Tunbridge Wells. His grief was no longer raw, but it had revived upon sight of Pretty and the reminder did not sit well with him. It was ever his practice to eschew such deep emotion, a habit that had earned him the reprimands of Lady Elizabeth Fiske. The memory of those too intimate exchanges between them was another area from which he preferred to slide away. He turned his attention back upon his task, feeling relieved that it had proved thus easy to infiltrate the den of Lady Francis's chief suspects. Not that he had any notion how to worm information out of them. He did not answer the question directly.

"I take it Lady Francis's prowess in this direction is known hereabouts?"

Botterell spoke with some eagerness. "She is famous for it."

"Or notorious, some might say," said Claydon. "Hardly what one expects from a female of her rank and position."

Aware that Eliza would have at once taken up the cudgels in her aunt's defence, Vivian let this pass. "You may have reason to be glad of it, I gather."

Jarvis Thorpe took this, with a frowning glance at his friends. "How so? None of us are in any way involved."

"Are you not?" Vivian looked around their faces with an air of innocence. "I quite thought you had all been at this party the other night. That is when the fellow died, is it not?"

This was productive of a flurry of protest.

"Nothing of the kind!"

"He was very much alive when I last saw him."

"Don't you think we would have said something if he had died in my brother's house?" This last from Jarvis Thorpe was said with some degree of heat.

Vivian threw his hands palm up. "Hey, hey! I am making no accusations. I was not suggesting this Marmaduke died there, but he did die that night. So Lady Francis says. She seems to know these things."

"How the devil does she know?" Thus Botterell, his puffy cheeks somewhat flushed.

Claydon produced a mocking laugh. "She's no physician, one presumes."

"She is not, but her brother is. She was used to live in his house before her marriage, as I understand it, and learned medical lore from him." Vivian shrugged at their faces of patent disbelief. "Don't blame me, my dear sirs. I am merely the purveyor of information. But I can say, with some authority, that her diagnoses in all cases where I — er — was witness, were accurate. Corroborated by the doctor too." He very nearly grinned at their changing expressions, from disbelief to decided dismay. He took pleasure in applying a hot coal. "She was uncannily accurate too in finding out the culprit. According to — er — one who knows her well, Lady Fan has never yet failed."

Well, if he did not manage to extract any valuable information, he had succeeded in reducing Botterell and Thorpe at least to gibbering apprehension.

"She won't find anything for which I am to blame. I had nothing to do with it."

"Which of us did? We were mere bystanders."

Claydon opted to contradict. "You can't claim that, Aubrey. There's no denying Gibbon's arrival put the cat among the pigeons. If Lady Fan is as good as Maplewood says, she'll know that already."

Botterell pouted. "I wish she had not chosen to tell my aunt Honeybourne. Fond as I am of her, I can't deny she's a blabbermouth."

From his knowledge of Lady Francis, it occurred to Vivian that she had likely chosen with deliberation. Eliza stigmatized her as being perfectly unscrupulous where it would serve her needs. No need to say so, but he seized on the cue. "You heard about the event from your aunt then, Botterell?"

Claydon let out a laugh tinged with the mockery that appeared to be habitual. "As did we all. None of us had reason to suppose Gibbon dead."

"So you have explained. I wonder, did any of you see him leave the premises?"

Jarvis Thorpe's brows drew together. "My brother's house, you mean? Not I. I came away with Claydon ahead of the rest. I have no notion what happened to Gibbon and his friend."

Claydon took this up, his tone precise. "I was obliged to assist that fellow to remove Gibbon to another room, matters having become a trifle heated." He glanced as he spoke towards Botterell, whose cheeks flew colour as he gave his friend an unloving glance. "No need to blush, old fellow. If this Lady Fan has not already discovered the facts about your contretemps, I shall be astonished."

Vivian took his glance and gave a wry smile. "Undoubtedly. She has a knack." He paused a moment, but Botterell was clearly sulking, Thorpe's lips were tight and Claydon looked inordinately satisfied with himself. Dislike of the man rose up, but Vivian kept his countenance bland. "Contretemps?"

"A mere nothing." Jarvis Thorpe spoke with impatience. "That fellow put up Aubrey's back, that is all."

At that, Botterell reared up. "All our backs! I spoke up, but you need neither of you pretend you were not just as disgusted with that fellow. Not content with monopolising Richenda, he must needs start upon Virginia too. The wonder is he did not draw in your Etta into the bargain." His heated gaze turned on Claydon.

"She's not my Etta, I thank you. She's my godmother's companion. Not that Gibbon meant anything serious with either she or the Grindlow chit. If you did not take his measure, Aubrey, I did."

"Do you think I don't know? He was after Richenda's fortune, of course."

Jarvis Thorpe cut in, low-toned. "Be quiet, you fool!" He cast a significant glance towards Vivian who instantly held up a hand.

"Don't fear me! I am simply an idle passer-by."

Jarvis Thorpe produced a look emulative of Claydon's brand of disdain. "You have the ear of Lady Francis."

"True enough. It does not therefore follow that I shall use that advantage."

A scoffing sound came from Claydon. "Do you take us for a set of flats? She set you on, I'll wager!"

Now how was he to do? Vivian eyed each face in turn, noting the accusation and apprehension appearing in the other two. He opted for compromise. "As it chances, Lady Francis did make a request of me. She wished me to discover the whereabouts of Gibbon's friend. I forget his name now."

"Pedwardine," supplied Jarvis Thorpe. "He was staying at the same inn as Gibbon, in Wyke village."

"To be near his inamorata." The mockery was back in Claydon's voice. "Vexford's estate is near there."

Vivian tried to look suitably gratified. "Ah, excellent. Is Wyke far from here?"

"A matter of a mile or two merely."

"Thank you. Which inn?"

"There is only the Fox. You can't mistake."

Botterell spoke up, his tone grumbling. "You'd think Pedwardine would have come looking for his friend by this. But no sign of the fellow."

Jarvis Thorpe took this. "I wondered that. Unless he's left the area."

The sinister note was marked. Vivian chose to bat it out into the open. "You are suggesting this fellow may be complicit in Gibbon's death?"

A shrug came. "As well him as any of us."

"Yes, and he likely left with Gibbon that night." Thus Botterell, eager now.

"Did you see them leave together?"

"I was escorting my aunt. I had too much to do to persuade her to leave off talking and come away to be noticing who went with whom."

A spurious excuse, and no actual answer. Vivian let it go. He changed tack. "Was Gibbon injured in the — er — contretemps?"

That he had taken all three aback was patent. There was a pause before Botterell, defensive in both tone and manner, took it up. "I never hurt a hair of his head!"

Claydon intervened. "Come, Aubrey, the fellow lost his breath." He gave Vivian a direct look. "It was scarcely a brawl, merely shoving and words. No use denying it, however. Something made the man catch his breath. He staggered back and I caught him. Jarvis held Aubrey off, didn't you?"

"He had no need to hold me off, I tell you! I didn't touch the fellow!"

Claydon ignored this. "Pedwardine and I took care of Gibbon. He had a hand to his chest and grew red in the face. Once he was sitting down, he got his breath back. When he was somewhat recovered I left them and went in search of Aubrey, but Jarvis had taken him outside."

"I didn't need taking outside! Officious, that's what it was. I was perfectly in my right mind."

Jarvis Thorpe set a hand to Botterell's shoulder. "You'd lost your temper, my friend, and there were ladies present."

"I never hit him!"

"You struck a light blow. I saw it."

"Light! There, you see. I didn't hurt him. What, are you saying I killed the fellow? Jarvis! I thought you were my friend!"

The sneering Claydon cut in. "Friend or no, there's no sense in concealing what happened. I knew you must have struck him. Enough to knock his breath out for him at least."

"I never meant that! I don't even remember doing it."

"No, because you were too hot-headed to know what you were doing, you fool!" Thus Jarvis Thorpe.

Vivian was certain his presence was forgotten. The altercation had attracted the attention of the other patrons and the tapster. He deemed it time to call a halt. "Gentlemen, we are in a public place."

All three swung upon him, stared, and then cast glances across the taproom. Jarvis Thorpe cursed under his breath and Botterell flushed all over again, dropping his head and seizing his tankard wherein he buried his face. Claydon, perhaps predictably, gave a nonchalant laugh which did not quite come off. He was the first to recover, shooting Vivian one of his contemptuous looks.

"You can't run fast enough with this to the famous Lady Fan, I'll be bound."

Vivian chose to turn it off. "In fact, I was thinking rather of making my way to Wyke."

Ottilia became abstracted during dinner, her mind roving the ramifications of the pooled reports. The intelligence that Marmaduke Gibbon had indeed received a light blow was offset by the lack of certainty about the place where he died. A niggle of an idea lurked but as yet it would not come to fruition, no matter how much she poked at it.

She had but one ear on the discussion going forward at the table. Her spouse, between chewing mouthfuls of his favourite beef from his laden plate, was comparing what he had learned at Thorpe Grange with Vivian's tale culled from the three young men. Fortunately Francis's indignation with Vexford had cooled. Much to Ottilia's chagrin, her spouse had been regaled with the tale by Sybilla with the result that she had been obliged to waste time soothing him instead of changing her dress, making the hosts late to the parlour where the other two members of the party had foregathered. Francis had desisted at last upon being assured Ottilia had taken no sort of hurt having been rescued by his mother in short order.

She was relieved to see his attention taken up instead by making comparison with Vivian's account. The stories matched in several particulars, but the salient point, upon which so much rested, remained elusive.

"We still have no firm witness to state that Gibbon actually left the premises. To my mind, Thorpe was evasive."

"Evasive how?" demanded Sybilla.

"He was not inclined to tell me anything at first. When he did, he made out that the bulk of the guests left all at once and in the muddle he did not notice Gibbon."

Vivian raised an objection. "That won't fadge. If his guest had been somewhat incapacitated, a conscientious host would ensure he was fit to leave, would he not?"

"If he is a conscientious host."

The dowager re-entered the lists. "What matters it? The fellow who must know is this friend of his, Percy whatever it is."

"True, my lady, but unfortunately I failed to find Pedwardine at the inn in Wyke where he was allegedly staying."

"He was out?"

"No, my lady, he had left the morning after the Twelfth Night party."

"Significant, don't you think, Tillie?"

Before Ottilia could rouse herself to answer, Sybilla banged the table. "Aha! Absconded, did he?"

Vivian gave a short laugh. "One might think so, my lady, if he had no intention of coming back."

This caught Ottilia's attention and she eyed Vivian. "He means to return?"

"Tomorrow apparently. He did not take his luggage."

"Which would indicate that he does not yet know of his friend's demise, don't you think, my love?"

Again, her mother-in-law forestalled her, giving forth one of her scoffing snorts. "Obviously."

"Not necessarily, Sybilla."

Ottilia came under the questioning gaze of Vivian. "Why so, ma'am?"

"It might be a ruse."

"What, you mean he did the deed and then went off so that he would not come under suspicion?"

"Just so, Fan. Though I think it unlikely."

"Why?"

"Because, my dear Vivian, as far as we know, he had no quarrel with his friend. Richenda complained only of his insistence on dragging Marmaduke off on male pursuits that must necessarily exclude her. That does not sound as if they had fallen out."

Her spouse pointed his empty fork at her. "It sounds as if he was doing his utmost to keep Gibbon away from the girl."

"Why should he so?" Thus Sybilla.

"That we will learn only from the man himself," said Francis. Then Ottilia was treated to a raised eyebrow. "Why, pray, are you staring at me in that odd fashion, wife of mine?"

She shook herself free of a roving thought and laughed. "I was merely thinking."

He eyed her bodingly. "Have you come to some conclusion and don't mean to tell us?"

"Certainly not. I have no conclusions."

The dowager blew out a disbelieving breath and Francis glanced at her, giving a decisive nod. "Precisely, Mama. Share, Tillie!"

She set down her utensils and spread her hands. "But I have nothing, I promise you. Only questions."

"Let's have them then."

Sighing, she capitulated. "Very well, if you insist." Noting young Vivian's glance going from one to the other, she let out an involuntary giggle. "You will have to excuse us, Vivian. We stand upon no ceremony in this house."

Francis rapped the table. "Yes, yes, we speak as we find. Cut line, woman!"

"Don't bully her, Francis!"

"I'm not. I am merely —"

Ottilia cut in strongly. "Richenda is the focus. Nothing can be examined unless it is looked at in the light of her intentions, her scheming."

"Scheming? What in the world do you mean, Ottilia?"

"Oh, come, Sybilla, you must have taken her measure, even from the little you saw of her. She is a play actress. I do not believe for one moment that she cared the snap of her fingers for Marmaduke, despite her protestations."

Both gentlemen looked puzzled and her mother-in-law was clearly taken aback.

"How so? I thought you said she told you they were betrothed."

"She did and I am inclined to doubt that too. Indeed, if I am not mistaken, it was not Marmaduke who set the cat among the pigeons with all these young gentlemen, but Richenda herself."

After a moment of silence while her auditors seemed to be digesting this, Ottilia was a trifle surprised to find that Vivian raised an objection.

"I don't understand how you can deduce this with no statement to support it."

Ottilia smiled. "Well, there is one. Virginia Grindlow gave me to understand that Richenda plays the flirtatious game of setting one against another among her suitors. Virginia retracted it at once, stigmatizing herself a cat, but I am inclined to trust her judgement. A straightforward girl she is too, whereas Richenda, if one did not read through her histrionics, would be an enigma."

Francis signed to Rodmell, discreetly waiting in the background, to see to the remove, before turning to Vivian. "She doesn't need proofs, my friend. That is her forte. You cannot hope to match my wife's jumping mind. I gave up trying years ago."

Ottilia felt her cheeks grow warm. "Nonsense, Fan! I wish you won't say such things. I assure you, Vivian, he outguesses me more than half of the time."

"Not nearly half, but I have been lucky enough on occasion, to beat you to the post." Her spouse raised his glass to her with a teasing grin and put it to his lips to drink.

Sybilla groaned. "Pay no heed to either of them, I charge you, Maplewood. This rivalry is as feigned as that girl's vaunted grief."

Ottilia pounced on this. "So you do believe she is faking."

Her mother-in-law gave a wry smile. "I believe you know what you're talking about. After all this time, I've learned to trust to your notions, however outlandish."

"I will remind you of that, ma'am, the next time you pooh-pooh what I say."

She was rewarded with one of Sybilla's rare cracks of laughter. "Impertinent chit!"

Ottilia laughed but was called to order by her spouse as the dishes of fruit, nuts and tartlets were set upon the table, together with the cheeseboard.

"Enough of this frivolity. What are we to do next, light of my life?"

Ottilia reached for the cheddar that had become her favourite ever since she craved it during her pregnancy. "I have been thinking about that." She sliced a generous piece and set it on her plate. "Your task, Vivian, is to track down Pedwardine tomorrow. Pray don't come back without him."

Vivian, evidently succumbing to the prevailing mood, made a smart salute. "As you command, my lady Fan."

Francis gave a shout of laughter. "You will do very well in this family, Maplewood."

Ottilia frowned him down as Vivian's cheeks darkened and he took refuge in his wine glass. She hastened to shift the focus. "Tartlets, Sybilla? Or will you take fruit?"

"Neither, I thank you. Venner will bring me up hot milk when I retire. But you were saying, Ottilia? Have you a task for me perchance?"

"I have, but not until Francis has tackled Vexford."

Her spouse's genial expression turned to horror. "You're saddling me with that appalling curmudgeon?"

Ottilia could not forbear a giggle. "You will charm him, Fan, as I could not."

"Charm him? I am more like to plant him a flush hit to the jaw!"

"No, no, pray don't. You will only make matters worse and we need his testimony."

"Then perhaps you had better tackle him after all."

"To what end, Fan? He won't talk to me. He disapproves of women of my ilk. Besides, he thinks I am in his daughter's camp."

"Which you patently are not."

"But he does not know that. I tried to protect her from him, and that is all he will remember."

Her spouse grunted, but Ottilia resolved to make it up to him when they were alone. As it chanced, Francis proved to have his attention on something other.

"I believe I may have been wrong about Maplewood, my dear one," he said, as Ottilia completed her nightly routine and set aside the hairbrush.

She came across and slipped into the bed beside him. "That is quite an admission, my dearest dear. Why?"

She blew out the candle and pulled the curtains to. Francis drew her down and cuddled her close. "I think he might suit Lizzy after all. He has the common sense she lacks."

Ottilia snuggled into him. "He will provide the leaven? But he is not a solemn young man."

"Not at all. I believe he may be strong enough to control her quirks."

"Like you, you mean?"

"Wretch!" His kiss was accepted with fervour. "Nothing will serve to control yours. I abandoned that hope long since."

She giggled. "Which I appreciate deeply, my darling lord. You have been tried too high of late. Allow me to do what I may in mitigation."

CHAPTER EIGHT

Buoyed by his wife's affectionate overtures, Friday saw Francis setting out for Wyke in a more contented frame of mind than he had experienced since his mother's descent upon their peace. The distance being too short to provide sufficient exercise for the curricle's team, he chose instead to go on horseback, leaving his groom to turn the rest of his stable out to roam the paddocks. Vexford, a hunting man, would have no objection to the aroma of horseflesh. When he arrived at Wyke Hall, however, he was received instead by Richenda Vexford's duenna, a pallid woman of middle years whom he recalled vaguely from past gatherings.

"Lord Francis! Oh, dear. You have come for his lordship, Thomas said."

A footman had shown him into an austere apartment on the ground floor, saying he would inform Lord Vexford. Francis kicked his heels for several moments, unimpressed by the sparse furnishings. A small dresser to one side, a wooden settle and a collection of chairs which looked to be decidedly uncomfortable demonstrated scant evidence of Vexford's vaunted wealth. Either it had been exaggerated or he was parsimonious to a fault.

The entrance of the dowdy female who had lent Richenda countenance since her mother's death was an unwelcome surprise. Francis felt obliged to apologise for his attire.

"I have come to speak to Lord Vexford, yes, and did not anticipate meeting the females of the household. I must beg your pardon if I reek of the stables, for I rode here, Miss —

er…" Memory failed him, but the duenna thankfully came to his rescue.

"Poynton." She blinked up at him from under round spectacles. "I could not expect you to recall it, my lord."

Francis was conscious of a tug of conscience, mixed with sympathy. It could not be a comfortable existence at the beck of such a man as Cosmo Vexford. "I take it Lord Vexford is out?"

Miss Poynton tutted. "It seems so, my lord. I had not known he intended it, but it is not his custom to keep me informed of his movements."

This was said not in any spirit of resentment, but in a matter-of-fact fashion that suggested the duenna was inured to being disregarded. Irritated by the thought of a wasted journey, Francis was about to enquire if the master of the house was expected back soon, uselessly he supposed, when Miss Poynton surprised him.

"It is vexing for you, my lord, since I take it you have come about that young man's demise?"

She had not moved, still peering up at him in her deferential way. He abandoned his first impulse to admit it and take his leave.

"Do you know anything of it, Miss Poynton? Have you any knowledge of what went on that night?"

A faint crease appeared between her brows. "I was not in attendance at the party, my lord."

Francis eyed her in a considering way. Was this evasion? Or did she truly know nothing. "That does not answer my question, ma'am."

Her lips widened in a tiny smile. "No, it does not."

He had to laugh. "Would you object to it if we sat down, ma'am. I feel sure you have something to offer on this subject."

For a moment she said nothing, her gaze limpid under the spectacles. Then she gave a decisive nod and moved to the only sofa, a plain piece of furniture with a bare claim to upholstery in its linen-covered seat, which was at least placed to catch the heat from a meagre fire, though even that was at too much of a distance to be effective at supplying any useful degree of warmth. He noted that Miss Poynton's round woollen gown and large paisley shawl were appropriate to the chilly atmosphere as, with a gesture, she invited him to join her.

"I will be glad of any little detail, ma'am, that may shed light upon the happenings of that night," he said, as he took his seat in a sideways stance that enabled him to face her.

"I cannot add anything to what you may know of the events at the party, although I have gathered the gist from what Richenda and my cousin Cosmo have said."

Francis did not beat about the bush. "Is it true that Richenda had contracted a secret engagement to Marmaduke Gibbon?"

Under the spectacles, her eyes widened. "Is that what she told Lady Francis, my lord? I am aware she went to Flitteris yesterday, but her account of what happened there was somewhat garbled."

"She was, as I understand it, voluble upon the subject. Also upon the matter of her father's having forbidden the banns."

Miss Poynton gave a resigned little shrug. "Banns were never in question, my lord. She may have been trying to persuade the boy to an elopement."

Francis balked. "*She* was persuading *him*?"

"Oh, yes. Mr Gibbon would not have broached such a course. For one thing, I doubt he could afford to carry a female all the way to Scotland and back. For another, Cosmo warned him, when he proffered his suit in London, that he would cut Richenda off if she ran away to marry."

"I wonder then at his pursuing her to her home environment."

Miss Poynton gave another of those quick little smiles. "I doubt he would have come without being sent for."

"You mean Richenda sent for him?" Once again Tillie was in the right of it. A scheming baggage, if ever there was one. "Yet what could she hope to gain by it? If Vexford —"

"My lord, you can have no notion of the situation that prevails in this house." She made a placatory gesture. "Forgive my interrupting you, but you may as well know at the outset that the only thing Richenda cares for is besting her father."

Francis with difficulty refrained from saying he could scarcely blame the girl with a father of Vexford's ilk. "I take it he is a strict parent?"

"A harsh one, sir. Richenda is confined to her room at this moment."

"Because she went to see my wife?"

"Because she disobeyed Cosmo's orders. He told her to keep out of the business and instructed her to refuse to answer any questions she might be asked. That, of course, was guaranteed to send her off hotfoot to interfere."

It sounded plausible, but Francis felt curiously dissatisfied. "Are you suggesting she cannot throw any light upon this business of Gibbon's death?"

Hesitation? Miss Poynton looked away towards the fire for a moment. Then turned back. "Are you cold, my lord? I can get a servant to build up the fire."

Prevarication, definitely. "Miss Poynton, I asked you a question."

She let another of those smiles loose. "I find it hard to answer that one, my lord."

"Try." Again, she hesitated. Francis pushed. "You know something, don't you? Something you suppose may be relevant."

Her fingers were resting in her lap, but they shifted, fiddling one with another as she looked down at them. Francis waited, not unhopeful. He had learned from his wife that one got further by leaving a silence than by pressing for a response. It proved out.

Miss Poynton looked up, sounding rueful. "I meant to tell you at the outset, but it struck me I was being disloyal. To both."

Now he might apply a spur. "If it turns out that Marmaduke Gibbon was in fact murdered, ma'am, such scruples will cease to be of importance. Pray don't withhold what may be of use to my wife in discovering why someone brought this matter to our very door."

A sigh escaped her. "Yes, that was very wrong."

"Or very right. Whoever did it meant the death to be investigated. Which would indicate that person at least supposed there might have been foul play."

Miss Poynton seemed to make up her mind. She turned more fully towards Francis. "I was in bed when Cosmo brought Richenda home, but I was not asleep. I heard them arguing, but that was nothing untoward. It happens all the time. At length the house went quiet and I assumed Richenda had gone to bed."

"Vexford too?"

"Not he. He retired to his library for a nightcap. He invariably does so when he comes in from an evening engagement."

Miss Poynton appeared to be labouring under suppressed agitation, the remnants of earlier calm now seeming forced. Francis judged it politic to prod for more. "And then?"

She nodded several times. "There is an *and then*. I was dropping off when an odd sound jerked me alert. A door closing, but an outer door." Her eyes almost pleaded with him through the glass of her spectacles. "You see, I know Richenda too well. She can be a naughty piece. I got up out of my bed and went to the window. It is a casement and I keep it a little open for air. I saw the light at once. She was making for the summer house."

"It was Richenda? You are sure of that?"

She waved her hands. "It could be no other. She had a lantern. I knew she was up to her tricks."

"What did you do?"

"What should I do, my lord?"

"Follow her. Inform Vexford. Anything, I should suppose, to stop her."

"Stop her from what? I knew she had no real intention of making off to Gretna, though she threatened it. As for telling Cosmo... I did in the end. I tried to ignore it and returned to my bed, but I knew it would not do."

"You think she meant to meet Gibbon?"

"I cannot think what else would take her out to the summer house at that hour."

The scent grew stronger and Francis's blood was up for the hunt. "You said you went to Vexford?"

Miss Poynton shuddered. "I knew how it would be. He roared and raged, swearing he would horsewhip the Gibbon boy and thrash Richenda into the bargain."

"What, you told him you suspected she was meeting Gibbon?"

"I had no need to do so. The moment I said Richenda was out in the grounds and making for the summer house, Cosmo assumed as much. He tore off then and there."

"He went out?"

"I presume so. I went back to bed. I could not endure to hear it all." That smile again. "You will think me a coward and I fear I am, but I hid under the covers."

Francis let this pass. "You did not look out of the window again?"

"I did before I went to Cosmo, but Richenda was out of sight. I thought I saw a faint light in the summer house, but I cannot be sure. I have no notion what happened afterwards."

"You heard no altercation?"

She shivered. "Nothing. If there was one it was too remote to reach my ears. By morning, Cosmo was back to his usual self and Richenda was defiant and close mouthed. She would tell me nothing."

Yet, for all Miss Poynton knew, Marmaduke Gibbon might have been in that summer house that very morning, cold and dead in a chair.

Ottilia had spent an agreeable hour with Pretty and her infant son, for once awake and alert to his adoptive sister's efforts to amuse him as he lay in his mother's lap.

"Rattle, Luke, listen! It's your rattle." And to Ottilia, "He likes me to sing better." Upon which utterance, without further prompting, her childish treble piped up in a song of her own invention.

"Lukey Luke, Lukey Luke, you can puke, Pukey Lukey Luke."

Ottilia had to laugh, but she thought it proper to object. "Fie, Pretty! Will you encourage him?"

Pretty left off singing to proffer an explanation. "He can't help it, Doro says, and Hepsie says I was a pukey too when I was small."

"I believe all babies are, yes."

"Pukey Luke, Lukey Puke. See, he likes it." An assertion borne out by Luke's smiling gurgle.

Several nursery rhymes later, recited largely at random and incorrectly by the little girl, Ottilia was interrupted by Doro, come to remove both children to the nursery.

"Mrs Bertram wishes to see you, milady. Pray let me take Master Luke and Miss Pretty away now."

With reluctance, Ottilia bade her son goodbye with a kiss. She was watching him settling in Doro's arms, the usual pang of regret in her bosom, when Pretty, still curled up at her side, astonished and gratified her by reaching up her arms. A hug? Was she to be so honoured?

She complied with the invitation, catching the child lightly to her for fear of seeming so eager that she suffered another rejection. But Pretty clung tightly and Ottilia could not but return the pressure.

"Be good, Auntilla," came the childish treble in her ear, turning the threatening prickle at her eyes to laughter.

Releasing the child, she said, "I will if you will."

Pretty dissolved into giggles, slipped down from the daybed and ran off in obedience to Doro's beckoning finger. Ottilia watched the trio leave the room, a burgeoning of joy in her heart. But the immediate entrance of her housekeeper, accompanied by a stout woman in bombazine and a fellow in the garb of an outdoor servant, seized her attention.

"Begging your pardon, my lady, but I thought it proper to bring Mrs Strumpshaw and Yelland here directly to you."

Ottilia took in the anxious features of the visitors. "This is quite the deputation, Mrs Bertram. Very well, please close the door." She waited while her housekeeper complied and, folding her arms, stood sentry before it. Ottilia turned to the two newcomers. "Now, how can I help?"

The woman designated Mrs Strumpshaw dropped an awkward curtsey. "If you'll excuse the intrusion, my lady, I'm Mr Thorpe's housekeeper and this here is groom to the poor young gentleman."

The fellow Yelland touched his forelock. "Mr Gibbon's my master, my lady. I've been that worried."

Surprised, Ottilia eyed him. "You did not know of his unfortunate end? It has been known in the area for some three days now."

The man's ruddy cheeks darkened further. "Aye, my lady, but I never knew where he'd been, nor where he were took. Last I seen he were alive and well."

Ottilia seized on this. "When did you last see him?"

"Twelfth Night, my lady, when I drove him to the party."

"Did you not fetch him afterwards?"

The groom, who had his hat in his hands, began to turn it round and round in clear agitation. "Master Gibbon said as Mr Pedwardine would bring him back to the Fox. I never thought nothing of it when he didn't call for me next day, see. He'd have slept in likely is all. And if he were wishful to go and see Miss Vexford, I knew as he'd walk. Only when I never seen him the day after, I fretted a bit, my lady."

"I imagine you might well." Ottilia was thinking fast. "I take it you returned to Thorpe Grange in hopes of discovering what had become of him?"

"Not then, my lady. The rumours reached me by way of the tapster first. I didn't rightly believe it were master as had died. I thought he might've gone off with Mr Pedwardine to see that mill."

"Ah, that is why Mr Pedwardine was absent too, is it?"

"That's right, my lady. Only this morning, when Mr Pedwardine come back, master weren't with him."

"At which point you hastened to the Thorpes?"

"That's it, my lady. And Mrs Strumpshaw here told me … told me…"

Ottilia cut in quickly as the fellow looked ready to burst into sobs. "Yes, I see. Thank you." With deliberation, she turned to the Thorpe housekeeper. "I have a question or two for you, Mrs Strumpshaw, if you will be so good."

Puzzlement and a touch of apprehension entered the woman's face. "Me, my lady? I don't know as I can tell your ladyship anything to the purpose."

"That remains to be seen." Ottilia smiled, throwing a glance to her own housekeeper. "Mrs Bertram did right to bring you to me."

The apprehension deepened, quickening Ottilia's senses. Was there something here after all? She opted for a soft approach. "The thing is, Mrs Strumpshaw, we have not yet been able to establish whether or no Mr Gibbon left the Thorpe household after he was taken ill."

A frown came. "Ill, my lady? He wasn't taken ill, not to my knowledge."

"Breathless? Perhaps from a light blow?" Consternation was to be read in the woman's face. Ottilia raised the stakes. "As I understand it, there was an altercation. You will not, I hope, tell me that this was unknown to the domestic staff?" No response, but a furtive glance towards Mrs Bertram. As if she wished to escape? "Mr Pedwardine and Mr Claydon, I think it was, were obliged to take Mr Gibbon downstairs to recover. The breakfast parlour, I believe."

She waited, half an eye on the burgeoning dismay in the groom's face as Mrs Strumpshaw appeared to debate within herself.

Mrs Bertram moved to her side and patted her shoulder. "Come, Betty. It's no manner of use keeping anything from her ladyship. She'll find it out in any event."

Mrs Strumpshaw met the other's gaze and let out a sigh. Capitulation? She must remember to thank Mrs Bertram.

Mrs Strumpshaw's tone was subdued. "It's as you say, my lady, though I didn't see it."

"What did you see?" Ottilia felt sure there was something.

Mrs Strumpshaw flicked a troubled look towards the groom. "I took in a glass of water as Mr Claydon requested."

"Mr Claydon did?"

"He caught — he saw me coming through the hall. He said Mr Gibbon was in the breakfast parlour and needed water. I didn't know he'd been taken bad, my lady, not then."

Ottilia had not missed the slip. Listening at the door, was she? No doubt the noise of the quarrel had penetrated to the domestic quarters. "But you saw as much when you went into the breakfast parlour?"

"Not as such, my lady. Mr Pedwardine met me at the door and he took the glass. I only caught a glimpse."

Not for want of trying perhaps. "What did you see?"

The words came easier now she had begun. "He was leaning back in a chair. Looked a trifle pale in the face."

"What more? Think back, if you please. Try to recall that glimpse."

Mrs Strumpshaw frowned. "He had a hand to his chest. He didn't look to be breathing free. Sort of gasping."

"You heard that?"

Mrs Strumpshaw looked surprised. "Now you say, my lady, I think I did."

At this point, the groom stuck his oar in. "Why didn't nobody fetch a doctor to him? If he were labouring like."

Ottilia's ears pricked up. "Had such a thing happened before, Yelland?"

The groom shook his head. "Not as such, my lady, not from a blow. But master did labour now and then. His breath, I mean."

"Asthma?"

"I don't know what that may be, my lady."

"An airways disorder. Finding it hard to breathe sometimes and wheezing."

"Might be. He seen the doctor one time after. But it weren't nothing bad. It weren't like to kill him. I don't understand how he upped and died, my lady."

"The post-mortem will determine that."

The fellow registered horror. "You mean they'll cut him up?"

"I'm afraid it is standard practice when a person dies of an unknown cause. Especially a gentleman of Mr Gibbon's youth. He will be returned to his normal state afterwards, never fear." She bethought her of her first supposition. "How old was he, Yelland?"

"Three and twenty, my lady. All his life before him too."

Except that if he had indeed suffered from a weak chest, his life was unlikely to have been prolonged. Which in no way excused his being sent to his maker before his natural time. Yet still the salient point remained unanswered. Ottilia turned back to Mrs Strumpshaw.

"Were you present when the guests were taking their leave?"

"John was, my lady, the footman."

"You did not, perhaps, help the ladies with their cloaks, or...?" Ottilia left the word hanging, not unhopeful that Mrs Strumpshaw had indeed been about at the pertinent moment.

"I did pop into the cloakroom to see that the maids were doing their duty, my lady."

"So you saw who left the house, I assume."

"Not all." Anxiety again? "The mistress will have me wait in the hall in case any needed anything. I was kept busy sending for the carriages."

"Mr Pedwardine's carriage?"

Mrs Strumpshaw looked upset. "Really, my lady, I don't remember. I've thought and thought for it seemed to me he must've gone with the rest."

"Mr Gibbon?"

Mrs Strumpshaw nodded. "All I know is there was nobody in that breakfast parlour when I looked in to be sure the candles were doused. There was only one left burning near the door."

Then either Marmaduke had walked out or he had been moved. There remained only one more point to raise. "Did your master and mistress go straight to bed?"

"The mistress did. I left John to see to the master's candle."

So it was possible that Martin Thorpe knew more of the business than he had seen fit to tell Francis. On the other hand, it appeared the friend Pedwardine was back in Wyke. Which meant that Vivian Maplewood might have better intelligence about Marmaduke's movements. Assuming he had been capable of moving.

Having furnished the groom Yelland with Doctor Lister's direction, and sent Mrs Strumpshaw on her way with a word of thanks, Ottilia left her parlour with the intention of awaiting her mother-in-law in the front withdrawing room. Sybilla had sent her maid down with a message to say that she meant to rise late and would breakfast in bed at her leisure. By this time, she would likely be up and about and Ottilia was keen to discourage a tendency to use her parlour, meant for a private retreat, as a morning room. She could not blame Mrs Bertram for seeking her there, but it was too much to be disturbed by the dowager's acerbic tongue. Besides, it was the one apartment where she and Francis could get away from the visitors. Or it ought to be.

She had just settled into her usual chair by the cheerful fire when she heard the opening of the door. Expecting to see Sybilla, she turned her head just as a youthful face peeped into the room, mischief written all over it.

"Lizzy!" Ottilia rose with alacrity as Lady Elizabeth Fiske tripped into the room, her grey eyes brimful of laughter. "Where in the world did you spring from?"

"A surprise, dearest Aunt! I hope you are pleased."

CHAPTER NINE

Lizzy threw her arms out and Ottilia received her in a strong embrace, laughing as she released her and held her at a little distance. "Dreadful child! I am delighted to see you, though I should much have preferred to be notified. But how? I did not hear a carriage."

"Oh, I came post and hired a gig from Winchester. I drove round to the back and left it with Ryde."

Lizzy spoke in an airy fashion that filled Ottilia at once with foreboding. "Pray don't tell me you have come alone."

Lizzy seized her hands and squeezed them. "You don't look a penny the worse for having given me a new cousin, Aunt. Of course I did not come alone. I have Nancy with me."

Ottilia squeezed the hands in response, but remained dissatisfied. "Does Harriet know you have come here?"

Her niece, a petite creature with a piquant countenance and a marked tendency to engage in unconventional conduct, released Ottilia's fingers and threw her hands in the air in a wild gesture. "For what do you take me? I told her I must make the acquaintance of my baby cousin before I was overtaken by the Season. She quite understood."

Worse and worse. "What you mean is you nagged her day and night, and when she would not yield, you applied to your father for permission."

Lizzy went into a fit of the giggles. "You are far too knowing, dearest Lady Fan. To be truthful, Papa was not happy at the prospect, but I managed to bring him around."

"I don't doubt it. But did he permit you to travel post alone?"

"Oh, no. Papa sent Charles along as well as my maid and hired an outrider too. So ridiculous, but he insisted. I was so eager to escape I would have agreed to anything."

"I take it you stayed at an inn last night?"

"Yes, the Wykeham Arms in Winchester. I did not wish to incommode you, arriving late at night. I was well protected, for Nancy slept on a truckle bed in my room and my footman remained in the corridor all night, poor Charles. I've asked Rodmell to let him sleep somewhere as soon as he's had a good meal."

Ottilia was a little cheered to hear that she was accompanied by a footman as well as her maid, but Lizzy's arrival just when Vivian Maplewood was in residence could not but set up the gravest suspicions in her mind. The thought of her spouse's reaction made her stomach swoop with dismay. Lizzy, however, appeared wholly unconscious.

"What do you think of the new fashion, Aunt? Is it not delightful?" She twirled and her lemon-coloured petticoats floated about her in rippling folds. "See how the muslin behaves?"

Taking notice of her niece's attire for the first time, Ottilia realised she was clad in one of the new-fangled gowns of soft fabric, made high to the waist and emphasising the bosom, although Lizzy wore a short spencer over all, buttoned to the throat. "I have seen it in Heidelhoff's Gallery of Fashion but not in the flesh, as it were, until now. Are you wearing no stays?"

"Oh, yes, but they are very short. What do you think?"

"It looks to be comfortable, I must say, although it is strange to see a waist so high under the bodice."

"You will adjust to it in no time, dear Lady Fan. But enough of fashion, come!" Lizzy drew Ottilia to a sofa, threw herself down beside her and tugged on her hand. "Sit, Aunt, do, and tell me all!"

"All what?"

"About little Luke and how you fared. Is he well? What of Pretty? Is she madly jealous?"

"On the contrary, she is delighted with Luke and spends her time entertaining him. But I had much rather talk about you just for the moment, Lizzy." Ottilia gave her niece a straight look. "Why are you really here?"

A touch of tell-tale colour rose in Lizzy's cheeks, but she laughed it off. "But I have told you, Aunt. I must meet my new cousin. Besides, I am tired to death of being chivvied from pillar to post and told to consider this or that eligible male. Mama thinks she has secured a match for Candia and so she is determined to procure one for me this year."

It was news to Ottilia that Francis's other niece had formed an attachment. She had shown no disposition to like any man since she had lost the Frenchman she was convinced was the love of her life.

"Is Candia betrothed?"

"Gracious, no. She is still hankering for Pierre. But Sebastian Davidge is *épris*, Mama says, and Candia seems not to be objecting."

"Who is this Sebastian? Is he titled?"

"He is Lord Askern's son and will inherit the earldom. Grandmama is his sister Louisa's godmother."

"Ah. Is the match of Sybilla's contriving?"

"Yes, it is. Which is another reason I had to get away. Mama talks of consulting her on my behalf. The last thing I need is Grandmama interfering."

Ottilia could not forbear a laugh, albeit in a sympathetic spirit. "My poor child, you are quite out of luck. Your grandmother is here."

Scarcely were the words out of her mouth than the door opened to admit Sybilla, who came in speaking. "Ottilia, I am going out for my —" She broke off, her black gaze falling upon her granddaughter. "Elizabeth!" The construction she put upon this unexpected appearance was not at all what Ottilia had anticipated. "Good heavens, child, what is amiss? Don't say someone is ill? Met with an accident? Your father? Not my Harriet, pray don't say my Harriet is injured!"

Ottilia rose, but Lizzy was before her, jumping up and throwing herself into her grandmother's arms. "No, no, Grandmama! No one is ill or dead, I promise you. Be easy, pray!"

Sybilla's voice came muffled. "Thank heavens! What a fright you put me into, child!" She extricated herself from Lizzy's embrace and regarded her, brows drawing together. "Then if you have not come on that account, why are you here?"

To Ottilia's immediate consternation, her face changed, her brow growing thunderous. Ottilia hastened to intervene. "The very point we were discussing when you came in, Sybilla. Lizzy has come to make acquaintance with Luke, of course."

But it was no use. The black eyes began that dangerous snap that signalled trouble. "Don't tell me! You are here for an assignation with that Maplewood fellow."

To Ottilia's secret admiration, Lizzy managed to feign astonishment. "Vivian is not here, is he? Gracious, how fortuitous! I had no notion." She turned on Ottilia. "Why did you not tell me at once, Aunt?"

"I had no chance, my child, but —"

"Do not allow the baggage to bamboozle you, Ottilia. As for you, Miss, you need not think to pull the wool over these old eyes. I am far too fly to be taken in. Disgraceful!"

"Sybilla —"

"No, don't make excuses for her. Your conduct is shocking, Elizabeth. I make no doubt you have taken in your poor parents into the bargain."

Lizzy looked a trifle shame-faced, but she rallied, coming back strongly. "They sent me on my way, Grandmama, so you need not suppose they don't know I have come to Flitteris."

"I'll wager they don't know you meant to meet Maplewood here, however. Even your father would not countenance such a thing."

Ottilia cut in fast. "Well, there is nothing to be done about it now, Sybilla. We can scarcely send her away again."

The dowager ignored this. "Only wait until your uncle is home, girl. He will have something to say to you, I'll be bound."

Only too likely, but Ottilia again tried to avert her mother-in-law's thunder. "Shall we sit? Has Mrs Bertram found you a room, Lizzy?"

"It is of no use to behave as though nothing untoward has occurred, Ottilia. This child is in want of both conduct and honesty. How dared you embroil your aunt and uncle in your tricks?"

"But I didn't," pleaded Lizzy, sinking back down onto the sofa. "Truly, Grandmama."

"I don't believe you. Are you telling me you did not know Maplewood was to visit."

Lizzy had the grace to blush. "I knew he had the intention of coming to see Pretty, but I did not know when he proposed to make his visit."

Ottilia sat down beside her and took her hand, speaking in a matter-of-fact way. "Not precisely, I expect."

A mischievous look was cast at her and Lizzy squeezed Ottilia's hand. But she resumed a solemn expression as her gaze returned to her grandmother's face where she continued to lour over Lizzy like a gloomy cloud.

"Dear Grandmama, pray don't be out of reason cross. You know how I dote upon Aunt Ottilia, and I did so want to see little Luke."

There was no softening in Sybilla's expression but she grunted and straightened her back. "Well, I suppose there is little to be done about it now. If I had my way you would be confined to your chamber."

"Now, Sybilla, you know that would not answer. Lizzy would escape in a heartbeat."

"Yes, I should."

"Besides," Ottilia pursued, ignoring the interjection, "we cannot be troubling our heads too much at this present. We have enough on our hands as it is with this unexplained death."

Lizzy's gaze turned back on her, a sparkle in her eye. "A murder? Oh, are you back to Lady Fan?" She released her hand and clapped in a gleeful way. "I could not have timed it better. May I help?"

Ottilia could only be glad Sybilla had been persuaded to take her constitutional and Lizzy had gone up to wash off the stains of travel when Francis returned, accompanied by both Vivian Maplewood and a stranger.

"I met them both in the hall, my love. This is the missing Pedwardine."

Ottilia's gaze appraised the young gentleman who had clearly been brought back from Wyke by Vivian. He was well looking with dark hair and a pleasing countenance just now solemn and a trifle pale. He was dressed for travel in buckskins and frock coat and must have been intercepted before he could change. He in no way rivalled the beauty of his deceased friend, but his eyes were marked with the distress of recent loss. Ottilia greeted his arrival with warmth.

"You found him then, Vivian. This is excellent. How do you do, Mr Pedwardine? I am very pleased to see you. Allow me to offer you my condolences."

Mr Pedwardine did not approach her, but acknowledged her words with a bow. "Maplewood here suggests you may be able to furnish me with more detail than he was able to give concerning my friend's death."

"Alas not much." She noted the use of the dread word did not appear to dismay him, although his reaction looked to be genuine. "On the contrary, I am hoping you may be able to enlighten me instead."

Vivian spoke up, lightly touching the fellow's shoulder. "I warned you she would have questions, sir."

Mr Pedwardine barely spared him a glance. "You did, yet I am at a loss to know how I may assist you, ma'am. I was not present."

"Precisely the point," her spouse cut in before Ottilia could answer. "Present or no, you are likely the last person to have seen Gibbon alive."

The young man winced. "How so?"

Ottilia took this. "We have been unable to discover for certain that Marmaduke left Thorpe Grange. Can you confirm that he did?"

"I cannot, ma'am."

"You did not leave together?"

"Indeed not. Duke said he had an assignation."

"Ha!" The exclamation came from Francis. "At Wyke Hall?"

Ottilia's mind jumped. Is that what he had discovered there? Had Vexford told him so?

Mr Pedwardine seemed reluctant to answer. "It may have been. He did not say."

"But you assumed it, I must suppose?"

"As I say, sir, I do not know. Duke had earlier made a play for the other female. One who lives at a vicarage? I forget her name."

Ottilia supplied it. "Virginia Grindlow. That, however, is far less likely. Virginia is convinced your friend merely flirted with her to make Richenda jealous."

A flicker of distaste crossed Mr Pedwardine's lips. "That is in Duke's mode, I fear."

"He was determined then, to make a play for Richenda?"

The young man hesitated. To Ottilia's surprise, Vivian applied a spur, impatience in his tone. "Oh, come, Pedwardine. Every man in the area knows the fellow came here for no other purpose."

Ottilia received an odd look from her spouse, who gave a tiny shake of the head. He knew something other? But did not wish her to ask in company. She gave him a quick, reassuring smile and turned back to Mr Pedwardine.

"Pray be open with me, sir. I cannot unravel this matter without your assistance. Did you think Marmaduke meant to visit Richenda?"

He gave a sigh. "Yes, ma'am, I did."

Her mind on possibilities, Ottilia pursued it. "Did you in fact drive him to Wyke Hall, sir?"

At that he looked startled. "Why would I, ma'am? He had his phaeton."

"Ah, but he had it not, sir."

"He did. He led the way to that party and I followed in my curricle."

"Why did you not travel together?"

"Because I wished to leave betimes as I had an early start in the morning."

"To go to this boxing match."

He blinked, and Ottilia found both her husband's and Vivian's eyes upon her.

"How in Hades do you know that, Tillie?"

She gave a gurgle. "I had it from Marmaduke's groom who came here this morning." She turned back to the newcomer. "He also told me that your friend instructed him to drive the phaeton back to the inn at Wyke because he had the intention of returning in your company, Mr Pedwardine."

He merely stared. Francis took it up instead. "But this is mad! If he meant to go to Wyke Hall, how did he propose to get there? Walk from Tangley in the middle of the night? It's all of five miles."

"Then perhaps it is safe to assume that Wyke Hall was not his objective," suggested Vivian.

"Where else, for pity's sake? What, had the fellow a harem in this place? He had scarcely been in residence five minutes!"

"Wait, Fan! Let us not be hasty. We have not yet established who of the company was still at Thorpe Grange when Mr Pedwardine left." She looked a question.

"Really, I scarce know. I am little acquainted with any of them. Nor do I suppose Duke would have begged a ride from any of those fellows, if that is what you suggest, ma'am. They were all jealous of his success."

"That we know too well." Vivian glanced at Ottilia. "But I am not convinced of that fellow Claydon. I don't believe he is a serious contender."

"For Richenda's hand? Why not?"

"He regards his fellows with mockery, contempt even. He might give Gibbon a ride, if only to spite his so-called friends."

"You paint a charming portrait, Maplewood."

"Indeed, Fan. But it raises a possibility. Do we know when Botolf Claydon left the party? Specifically, was it before or after you, Mr Pedwardine?"

He looked regretful. "I cannot say. He was the fellow who helped me take Duke to a room where he might recover, but he left us there and went in search of a servant to bring water. I don't recall seeing him again."

"Then he may be a possibility. Where precisely did you leave Marmaduke, sir?"

The young man's brows drew together. "What do you mean, ma'am?"

"Exactly what I say. You were with him in the room. When you took your leave of him, was he still there?"

"No, we parted at the door. He wished to go in search of — " He hesitated, clearing his throat and glancing rather at one and the other of the two gentlemen than Ottilia. She applied a prompt.

"In search of whom or what, sir?"

Mr Pedwardine seemed reluctant to voice his thought, again looking to the men.

Francis rolled his eyes. "Spit it out, man! You need not mind your tongue before my wife, if that is the difficulty. She is not missish."

Ottilia emitted a gurgle. "No, indeed. What is the matter, Mr Pedwardine? Pray don't be embarrassed. Do you mean to imply that Marmaduke wished to relieve himself?"

His startled gaze caused Francis to let out a snorting laugh. "I did warn you, Pedwardine. Was that it?"

A glance at Vivian found him looking wryly amused and Ottilia took pity on the victim. "Pardon my candour, sir. You must know that I have been obliged to witness a great deal that is considered unsuited to a lady's delicate sensibilities. We will make better headway if you bear that in mind."

The young man let out a breath, looking rueful. "I will do my best, ma'am. You have gauged the matter correctly. I helped Duke to his feet. He was a trifle unsteady at first, but he managed to walk unaided."

"I could wish you knew if this assignation was with Richenda or Virginia."

He gave a half-shrug and Ottilia read discomfort in his features. "I assumed the former. But as I said, he showed more interest in the vicarage girl."

"Who is all but penniless," put in Francis on a sceptical note.

Was it wrath in Mr Pedwardine's face now? "Why must everyone assume Duke was fortune hunting?" His voice shook. "He is heir to a good estate in Oxfordshire."

This was new. "Is it so indeed? He was then well provided for?"

"Not precisely. He lives on an allowance at present and it may be many years before he inherits. It is not a rich patrimony, but adequate for any man."

With pity and in passing, Ottilia noted his use of the present tense, but her mind was concentrated upon this fresh information. It would seem Mr Pedwardine thought poorly of the notion Marmaduke Gibbon might seek a fortune, but an allowance and a long-term prospect of a better future could have been irksome. Why not help himself to nearer and more substantial means with an advantageous marriage? She kept this thought to herself.

"Let us return to the moment you parted from him, if you please."

"There is no more to tell. I told him I was for my bed and left him. I found our hostess in the saloon, made my farewells and departed."

"You don't know who was still there at that point?"

"The younger girls were no longer there, but I cannot say if they were in the house. There was a matron with Mrs Thorpe."

"Mrs Honeybourne?"

"It may be. I can't recall the names."

"What of the gentlemen?"

"I heard voices in the drawing room, so I must suppose they were still there. Some of them at least."

"No one left when you did?"

"No, although there appeared to be a general exodus in train as carriages were being brought up. The fellow who began all the commotion and one of his friends — Mr Thorpe's brother, I think he was — were walking in the grounds when I drove out."

Which made both Jarvis Thorpe and Aubrey Botterell unlikely candidates for disposing of Marmaduke, assuming the original blow was not responsible for his demise. Her husband voiced the thought in her mind.

"The question is then, where did Gibbon end up?"

A spasm crossed the young man's face. "You think he died there? At Thorpe Grange?"

Ottilia was about to answer when she caught sight of her spouse's face. He was looking a trifle grim. What in the world had he found out from Vexford? Thinking she must seek a private moment to discover it, she gave a belated response to Pedwardine.

"That, sir, is yet to be determined. The only thing I can tell you with certainty is that Marmaduke died in a sitting posture." A blank stare was his only response. She softened her tone. "You are shocked. These things are quite easy to fathom with a little understanding of medical lore, which I have from my doctor brother."

"If I am shocked, ma'am, it is only at the thought of Duke succumbing in such a fashion to whatever illness it was that killed him. I see now why you wished to discover where he went."

Ottilia refrained from speaking of the notion of manslaughter or murder, which had evidently not entered the man's head. "I understand from his groom Yelland that he suffered from a chest condition akin to asthma. Was he often taken short of breath?"

"Rarely. I recall only one instance, after we had done some hard riding. It took several moments for Duke to recover, but I thought nothing of it at the time. He had been subject to breathlessness as a boy, but he grew out of it. He never spoke of having a permanent condition."

"Understandably," put in Francis. "A man does not care to have his friends think him disabled in any way."

Mr Pedwardine looked upset. "I cannot imagine why he should die so suddenly. Dear God, I suppose I must inform his family."

Vivian spoke up at that. "You had best write. I can't think Lady Fan will wish you to leave the area until she has this matter sifted out."

Ottilia smiled. "Why, thank you, Vivian. You are very right." She looked at the visitor. "Yet I don't believe we need keep you any longer, Mr Pedwardine. For the moment, I thank you for your help."

He took his dismissal in good part, bowing. "I am glad someone is taking the matter to heart. You may count upon me, ma'am, at need."

Yet he left the room with alacrity and Ottilia wondered if grief was overtaking him. She turned at once to Francis. "You are big with news from Vexford, Fan, are you not?"

He grinned. "Obvious, was it? Not Vexford. He was not there. But Richenda's chaperon met me instead and was most forthcoming."

"Well, what news?"

His eyebrow went up. "Oho! I have the advantage of you for once."

"Don't tease, Fan. Tell me!"

"There is every reason to suppose —"

But what was to be supposed remained undisclosed, for the door opened at this moment and Lizzy entered the room, causing Francis to break off. Dismay overtook Ottilia. She had momentarily forgotten the imminence of disaster. She'd hoped to break the news gently, but it was too late.

Francis shot one look towards Vivian Maplewood, who looked quite as astonished, not to mention discomforted, and exploded. "What the devil is the meaning of this?"

CHAPTER TEN

In the privacy of his study whither he had commanded the fellow's presence, Francis confronted Vivian Maplewood, his words coming clipped as he kept his temper in check. "Now, sir, perhaps you would care to explain your presence here with more truth than you have hitherto seen fit to impart."

Rather to his surprise, Vivian came back in a manner equally biting. "Your assumptions, my lord, are as insulting as your words."

Francis eyed him, suspicion veering. "Are you going to claim you did not know Lizzy meant to meet you here?"

Vivian's jaw tightened. "The only thing I claim, sir, is the right to be heard without prior judgement."

Francis hesitated. Had his abominable niece engineered this without the fellow's knowledge? The devil! Of course she had. Typical of the child. Now what was he to do? Apology stuck in his throat. After all, Lizzy must have known by Vivian's agency that he intended coming here. He compromised.

"You have not taken my niece's measure, my friend. What possessed you to tell her of your visit?" He flung up a hand. "Pray don't try to make me believe you did not do so, for you've already confessed to engaging in a clandestine correspondence."

Vivian bridled. "I did not say it was clandestine."

"Clearly it is so or my brother-in-law would have warned me of the danger. Gil is too well acquainted with his daughter not to guess what she would do the moment she knew of your intention to visit Pretty. I presume you did not seek Dalesford's permission before writing to his daughter?"

"I did not suppose it needful. Nor did I gain the impression that Eliza's —" He broke off, compressed his lips for a moment, and then began again. "That Lady Elizabeth's parents were of such strict disposition as to oversee her correspondence."

"Any father would do so when the correspondence in question is with an unwanted suitor." Francis then wished he had held his tongue for Vivian winced as if he had been hit in the face. He backtracked. "I did not mean quite that."

"You did not mean to say it? Why not? It is the truth. You will allow that I have withheld any further overtures."

Francis snorted. "One can hardly regard a correspondence as withholding."

"We are friends, sir, that is all."

Francis threw up his eyes. "For pity's sake! Are you saying you don't wish to marry the girl? If that is so, you do the child harm by leading her on to suppose you do."

Vivian's cheek darkened. "You are making assumptions again, my lord."

"With good reason. I thought you a man of honour, Maplewood. I grant you Lizzy is a handful and her conduct in coming here in hopes of encountering you is disgraceful, but —"

"One moment, sir. If I have not encouraged Eliza to expect an offer from me, I will admit that my attitude is to blame for her taking such a step. She knows I care little for convention. If she supposed anything, it would be that her antics would amuse me."

"Well, they don't amuse me! What the deuce am I to say to my sister and her husband, I should like to know."

Vivian's mouth quirked, as if he was now amused. "Must you tell them?"

"Lord above, man, you must see that I can't condone this nonsense!"

Vivian drew himself up. "Then I had best leave at once."

"Oh, no, you don't! You'll stay and face the music, my friend. What, would you leave Lizzy to take the brunt of everyone's displeasure? You've met my mother, I take it."

A laugh, hastily choked, escaped Vivian. "Eliza can handle her far better than I, my lord. So she would tell you."

Francis waved this away. "That is nothing to the purpose. Tell me this. Are you or are you not desirous of marrying Lizzy?" There was no immediate response, and Francis balked. "Come, you commit yourself to nothing with me. I'm not the girl's father. But if I don't know your wishes — I am not asking for your intentions, take note — I can't know how to act. Nor how to advise my wife, who has Lizzy's ear and will best be able to steer her."

Vivian still made no answer. Instead, he shifted to the window and looked out over the prospect that encompassed some part of the lawned terraces beyond the drive, the fountain and wooded areas to the side. Francis waited, curbing the rise of impatience. At last the fellow turned.

"The truth is, my lord, I have not allowed myself to care for her as strongly as I might. When I visited at Dalesford, some months after that business at Tunbridge Wells, I hoped, in renewing our acquaintance, that we would — that things between us would resolve. But it was made abundantly plain to me that an earl's daughter was above my touch." His lips twisted. "It is not in my nature to sue for approval. I made a decision then to…"

"To let Lizzy go? Is that what you would say? But she would not permit it, is that it?"

A light laugh came. "Eliza is nothing if not determined. I admire her independent spirit, her persistence in going her own way regardless of what others might think. She is an original."

"Like you perhaps?" Despite himself, Francis was warming to the wretched man all over again.

Vivian shrugged. "I won't conform to the dictates of Society. If that makes me an original, then perhaps. But I do not have Eliza's zest for life. I go my own way because I don't care to be coerced. Eliza does so because she is carried by her enthusiasms."

Francis could not forbear a grin. "I was wrong. You do have her measure. Yet you have not answered me."

"Because I cannot. It is not a future I could predict with any confidence. But I do care for her a great deal."

He did not mention love. Francis began to think the only way the fellow would enter the married state would be if Lizzy forced him into it willy-nilly. Which did not augur well for his controlling her quirks. On the other hand, it simplified his own role.

On the thought, a knock at the door produced Lizzy herself, peeping into the study. "Uncle Francis, may I come in?" She sounded contrite for once, and there was a trifle of apprehension in her features as she slid into the room and closed the door.

Francis raised an eyebrow. "You appear to be in, with or without my permission."

She cast a glance towards Vivian, who retreated back to the window, removing his gaze from hers. Lizzy turned to Francis. "I came because I cannot have you berate Vivian when it is all my fault."

"So much I had deduced, I thank you."

The piquant features were turned up to him as she came closer, the grey eyes pleading. "Yes, but you dragged him away because you meant to ring a peal over him, and I cannot bear that."

"Eliza —"

Lizzy flapped a hand in Vivian's direction but did not look at him. "Pray don't interrupt, Vivian. I must say it all. You see, sir, I did know Vivian was coming here for he mentioned it in his last letter. I guessed at the approximate date because he spoke of not troubling you until the household had likely settled after Luke was born."

"Then you schemed to come here at the same time." The wrath Francis had earlier felt was seeping back. "I'll wager you did not mention this to Harriet or Gil, did you? Nor did it occur to you, I dare say, that you would put your aunt and myself into an awkward position thereby."

Lizzy threw a hand to her mouth and her eyes grew moist. "No, I swear it never did occur to me. Oh, Uncle Francis, forgive me, pray. I had not thought."

With difficulty Francis refrained from pouring his fury over her head. "You never do think! That's the trouble. You jump in head first, just as you did over that wretched female in London, not to mention —" He clipped the words off short, turning to Vivian. "You'd best retire, my friend. I need to speak to my niece alone."

"As you wish, sir." Without once looking at Lizzy, Vivian circled around where she stood, she turning as he did so and watching him walk out.

"Lizzy!"

She turned back, her eyes brimming. "I have embarrassed him, haven't I? He doesn't want me here!"

The misery in her voice went straight to Francis's heart. Without thought, he gathered Lizzy to him and let her sob into his shoulder for the space of several moments. When she quietened, he shifted her away and gave her his handkerchief. Then he pushed her into a chair and turned the one at his desk around for himself.

"Thank you, sir. I'm sorry, truly."

The husky note was marked and Francis gave her a wry smile. "You are filling me with foreboding for the future when Pretty is grown."

Her features broke into a smile. "Aunt Ottilia wrote that you have taken to Pretty as if she was your daughter."

The warm glow that his relationship with the orphan always engendered entered his chest. "To all intents and purposes she is my daughter. She adopted me for her father and that was that."

"What if Aunt Ottilia gives you a girl next time?"

"Then I will have two daughters. But we are not concerned now with my daughters, actual or potential, but with my niece. What possessed you, Lizzy?"

She sniffed into his damp handkerchief, looking woebegone again. "I love him, Uncle Francis. I cannot think of marrying anyone else."

Francis's heart cracked for her. Should he give warning of Vivian's words? For the life of him, he could not bring himself to distress her further. "Well, if you are determined, you should tell your father. Gil only wants your happiness."

Her gaze became fixed upon him. "But does Vivian?"

The direct question was altogether disconcerting. He prevaricated. "I gather he has received no encouragement."

"From me he has! I could not have been more explicit without positively turning the tables and offering for him."

Francis was very nearly lured into saying that perhaps she should. He bit his tongue on the words. Lizzy was eminently capable of doing exactly that. Fortunately, she resumed speaking before he was obliged to say anything.

"After all, why should it be the gentleman who takes all the risk? If I were a queen, I would have to ask him to marry me."

"Well, as you are not a queen —"

"But it is the principle of the thing, Uncle Francis! A woman is never allowed to make the choice. It is unfair, both on us and on men too. It ought to be equal, and Vivian would be the first to say that a female might justifiably have such rights."

Alarmed, Francis pointed a finger. "Don't you go asking him, for pity's sake! Vivian may have adopted this eccentric stance, but his upbringing is steeped in convention. You would shock him to the core."

She giggled, fast returning, it would seem, to her usual cheerful mien. "I wish I might shock him. Vivian is so cool as a rule, I want to shake him sometimes."

Francis judged it time to call a halt. "Enough, my child. Maplewood offered to leave, but I told him he must remain to face the music. Your grandmother will not let this lie, believe me. However, I am going to write to Gil immediately."

"Oh, no!"

"Oh, yes, my girl. You can't expect your aunt and me to house the pair of you without your father's knowledge, and I won't do it."

Lizzy sighed in an elaborate way. "You must write, I see that." She leaned forward to seize his hand. "But not to Mama, pray!"

"I've no intention of writing to my sister, I thank you. But make up your mind to it because your father will undoubtedly tell Harriet."

She released his fingers. "Yes, but he won't go into hysterics."

Francis subdued a laugh and rose. "All I can say is I'm glad you are not my daughter."

"So am I. I much prefer you for my uncle." She then stood up and flung her arms about him. "I do love you and Lady Fan. You are neither of you at all stuffy."

"I should think not. Now, Lizzy, don't go plaguing Maplewood's life out, I charge you."

She stared up at him, serious all at once. "Did he say something? Does he not like me enough?"

What in the world was he to say to that? "I have no notion. I will say that he defended you."

Her smile was radiant. "Did he indeed? Dearest Vivian!"

"Lizzy!"

"Oh, don't fret, sir." She patted his cheek, quite as if she were the elder. "I will be circumspect. Besides, Aunt Ottilia has need of me. I am to go with Grandmama to visit Lady Stoke Rochford."

"What you mean is that Mama intends to keep you under her eye."

A giggle escaped. "That, yes. But I am to pump the companion, you must know. She was at the Twelfth Night party."

An uneasy atmosphere reigned at the dinner table. What with Sybilla glowering at Vivian, her target close-mouthed with his attention on his plate and Lizzy unusually subdued, Ottilia began to partake of her spouse's complaint of being under a veritable siege. She had managed to escape to her parlour for the purpose of doing her duty by her infant son, where first her mother-in-law invaded to voice her animadversions upon the conduct of her granddaughter and her supposed swain.

"A flighty piece she has been from birth, but this is the outside of enough. Harriet will be mortified. Not that she may avoid part of the blame. She ought to have nipped the child's mischief in the bud at the outset, but no. She spared the rod at Dalesford's behest, if you please. As for that Maplewood fellow —"

Ottilia let the tirade wash over her, pretending concentration on Luke's needs, although her baby boy was eminently capable of drinking his fill of her milk without the slightest prompt. As soon as he dropped asleep Ottilia was able to shush his grandmother, to whom Luke had paid no attention whatsoever, on the score of not disturbing his rest. Balked, Sybilla at length took herself off with the stated intention of writing to her daughter before changing her dress for dinner.

No sooner had she departed than Francis appeared, big with an account of his interviews with the guilty parties. Ottilia listened without comment, but was moved to utter a warning note. "You had best speak to Sybilla at once, my dearest. She is writing to Harriet and you ought to tell her that Vivian knew nothing of Lizzy's intention."

Her husband threw up his eyes. "For pity's sake, why must she interfere? I am about to write to Gil and we don't need my sister going into a panic which she will do, as sure as check."

Which thought so wrought upon him that he left her there and then. Ottilia breathed a sigh of relief and called out for Luke's nurse, who was sure to be waiting outside.

"Doro!"

The maid came in with alacrity, ready to take her charge in hand again. For once, Ottilia did not linger over her farewell to her son, her mind roving the mounting complications. Not least the fact that this fresh fracas had prevented Francis from relaying what he had found out at Wyke Hall. She was almost dressed by the time he joined her in their bedchamber and time was short.

"I had best hurry, I suppose." Francis began to strip off his coat, heading for the dressing room where his valet awaited him. "Not that I am looking forward to dining with this crew."

Ottilia ignored the rider. "What did you tell Dalesford?"

Her words caught him at the door, where he paused and turned. "The truth, of course. I dare say he will be the next to descend upon us." With which bitter remark, he vanished into the adjoining room.

Ottilia sighed with frustration and allowed her maid to set a Paisley shawl across her shoulders, complementing the blue of her chemise gown, favoured since Luke's birth for comfort with her still fuller figure. "Thank you, Joanie. I will do now."

In the downstairs parlour where the family foregathered before entering the adjacent dining-room, she found Lizzy already in possession and looking woebegone. Ottilia tried for a light note. "Ah, there you are, my dear child. You have set the cat among the pigeons indeed this time."

Lizzy was seated in the sofa, clad in a flowing muslin gown of pale jonquil with the new high waist reaching just under the bosom. She straightened her shoulders, her chin coming up. "I don't care for that, Aunt."

Ottilia softened her tone. "But you care for Vivian and you are afraid he does not return your regard, is that it?" Francis had been specific on this point.

She had expected tears, but they did not come. Lizzy was defiant rather.

"There are other fish in the sea besides Vivian Maplewood. Be sure I will be casting my line this Season."

Ottilia paid this scant heed. "It is possible he is being chivalrous."

A disbelieving stare came. "Vivian? Chivalrous? You don't know him, Aunt Ottilia, if that is what you think."

"I didn't say I did think it. I am merely cautioning you not to place too great a reliance upon appearances. They are very often — indeed one might say almost always — deceptive."

The notion did not appear to find favour with her niece. She began to look mulish. "I hate shams. He is far too cryptic. He should say what he means."

"As you do."

"Yes! No. No, of course I don't want him to be like me. He is who he is. Only I am discovering I don't much like who he is."

This was said with an air of such blatant rebellion that Ottilia had no hesitation in wholly disregarding it. She could not resist an amused laugh. "All in a minute, I dare say."

Lizzy flashed her an indignant look but was prevented from replying by the entrance into the room of the man himself, who held the door for the dowager. Sybilla accorded this courtesy a dignified humph and stalked into the parlour, casting an unloving glance at her granddaughter. Ottilia gave an inward sigh. A trying evening looked to be in store.

Mere manners precluded any sort of confrontation at the dinner table, especially while the servants were in the room. But the atmosphere of stilted conversation drove Ottilia almost to screaming point. Once the soup tureen was removed and dishes including a ragout of lamb, cutlets and her husband's favourite beef were set upon the table, together with sides of pickled beans and mushrooms along with an omelette, she opted to break the tension.

"Francis!"

He looked down the table from his seat at the head, surprise in his face. She rarely called him by his full name but she needed to command everyone's attention. All eyes had turned to her, much to her satisfaction. Ottilia smiled.

"The death, Fan. We are missing your information."

She watched him glance around the table and was amused to see that the other three diners were now looking to him instead of herself.

"Wyke Hall?" she prompted. "You said you spoke to Richenda's duenna there."

"Ah, yes. Did I not tell you?"

"You have scarcely had an opportunity." Sybilla chiming in, with a flash of her black eyes towards Vivian, seated to her left, and thence to Lizzy across the table. "Let us have it then."

Much to Ottilia's relief, her spouse launched into his recital with gusto clearly born also of relief. Within a moment, the events of the last hours faded from her mind as she took in the salient points.

"That is why you flashed me a warning look when I asked Mr Pedwardine if he thought Marmaduke died at Thorpe Grange. You thought it as likely he died at Wyke Hall."

"In the summer house, yes."

Before Ottilia could answer, Lizzy spoke up, her interest clearly aroused. "But if he was there, Uncle Francis, why should both Richenda and her father return to the house? If he was dead there, I mean."

Ottilia took a hand. "He might not yet have arrived."

"He must have been expected," Vivian objected, "if this Richenda went out with a lantern. Why else would she go there?"

Only Sybilla appeared not to relish Vivian's intrusion into the discussion, for she cast him an unloving look. Lizzy, on the other hand, gave a decisive nod.

"Vivian is right. An assignation must have been made."

Francis pierced another piece of meat as he spoke. "That's the one thing we do know. Marmaduke told Pedwardine he had an assignation."

Ottilia listened to the ensuing discussion with only half an ear, her attention on the problem of just where Marmaduke went when he parted from his friend in the parlour. At length she became aware of silence and discovered everyone was once again looking at her while they resumed eating. Ottilia sent an enquiring glance towards her husband.

His eyebrow lifted. "You were off in your thoughts, my love."

Ottilia set down her fork and shifted her plate away a little. "I was concentrating on what we don't know."

"Well?"

"Yes, pray don't keep us in the dark, Aunt. We are pledged to help, after all."

Ottilia saw denial in the dowager's eye and hastened to comply. "The question most exercising my mind is where Marmaduke actually died."

"At Thorpe Grange, you mean? But he would have been found."

"If, Fan, we assume Martin Thorpe was speaking the truth. Perhaps he was found and summarily disposed of."

Francis made a face. "What, and then sent here the following night? It seems hardly credible."

"Yes, Uncle Francis, and where would you put a dead body for all that time?"

"Good point, Lizzy."

Lizzy, reviving from her erstwhile dejection, became eager. "Isn't it more likely that he went to this Richenda's summer house, later than expected, and succumbed there to his injury."

Ottilia demolished this at once. "How did he get there? He sent his groom away and he refused a ride with his friend."

"I agree, Tillie. He could not have walked it. At least he might, but why? It doesn't make sense."

"That is the difficulty, Fan. None of it makes much sense. For a start, we don't yet know if my supposition of what killed him is correct."

"If you ask me, Lister won't find it even if it is."

"True, Fan, but even if I am right, Marmaduke could not have lived long enough to walk to Wyke Hall, or even to drive there, supposing some other man gave him a ride."

Vivian set down his glass with a thump. "Botolf Claydon! He is unaccounted for."

Ottilia threw him a smile. "Well done, Vivian. Just so." She put up a finger. "But if he did — and lied to you into the bargain — he might have had a corpse on his hands before he reached the place."

Lizzy jumped in her seat. "Then he must be the one who sent the body to you!"

"We don't know that, Lizzy."

"True, Fan. Nor can we be sure that the person who sent the body to me is the same person who found Marmaduke dead."

The dowager threw up her hands. "Oh, this becomes beyond ridiculous! Do you know anything at all?"

"Yes, Sybilla. We know that a quarrel took place, that Marmaduke was still alive when Mr Pedwardine parted from him —"

"If he is telling the truth," cut in Vivian on a sour note.

"— and we know," Ottilia pursued, "that an assignation was made, presumably with Richenda." She turned her gaze upon Lizzy. "What you may discover, if you will, is whether that was known. Also what time Botolf Claydon returned to Lady Stoke Rochford's house, and whether Marmaduke had indeed shown any serious intentions towards Virginia Grindlow."

Francis raised an objection. "Didn't she say he was merely leading her on?"

"Yes, she did. But if the facts will not fit together then someone is lying. The question is who. We need to eliminate as many options as we can."

CHAPTER ELEVEN

Lady Stoke Rochford proved to be a diminutive old lady with an oddly loud voice, attributable, as her companion informed Lizzy in a mutter, to her profound deafness.

"The poor thing can barely hear and one has to speak up. Perhaps you will explain to Lady Polbrook, ma'am?"

Lizzy had to look up to Miss Henrietta Skelmersdale, who was a tall female, with a generous figure and a large smile to match. Lizzy, watching her grandmother attempting to explain her identity to their hostess, who looked positively drowned in her large, winged armchair stationed by the fire, could not but be amused by the contrast the robust dowager made against the frail figure of Lady Stoke Rochford.

"I gather she is a recluse?"

"Oh, yes, very much so. I have been with her near five years and might count her visitors on one hand. She cannot go out, poor lady, unless I take her into the garden in a wheeled chair on a fine day. Lately, even that…"

Miss Skelmersdale faded out and Lizzy spied a distressed look in the other girl's face. Girl? No, a woman, for she must have been a good few years older than Lizzy's twenty. Recollecting that she had been asked to inform her grandmother of the other lady's deafness, she was about to move to join them when it became obvious that Sybilla had divined the problem for herself as she raised her voice to a strident note.

"You may not remember me, my dear Robina, but I remember you. You were the queen of society, a reigning belle, when I was a girl. Every debutante for years sought to emulate your style."

This had been heard for a chuckle emanated from the elder woman. "Foolish gels. I told them. Find your own style, I said. Don't hanker for my life. None of my children survived and I buried my husband. Who wants that?"

A whisper came from Miss Skelmersdale. "If I have heard that once, I have heard it a hundred times. She says it every time she remembers she was once young, though that has become rarer these days. She is failing, I fear."

Lizzy knew not how to respond, but seeing her grandmother take a seat close enough to converse with the old dame, she looked up at the companion.

"May we sit somewhere a little out of range? I would like to ask you something, if I may, Miss Skelmersdale."

The other's eyes grew merry as she looked down. "Ah, you are Lady Fan's deputy, I take it?"

Lizzy laughed. "I am indeed. Do you object?"

"Not in the least. It's the most immensely exciting thing to have happened around these parts since I have been in residence." Her brows drew together. "I am sorry for the poor fellow, of course, but I hardly knew him. Ridiculous to pretend grief for someone quite unknown, it seems to me."

Lizzy warmed to her. "I heartily agree. Nor am I surprised you are finding it exciting. I have seen my aunt in action twice before and she is astonishingly good at finding things out."

"Even though she sends you?"

"Oh, I have done so before on her behalf," said Lizzy on an airy note, consigning to oblivion the unauthorised activities she had undertaken in the affair of the woman Lady Fan had found in the road covered in blood. "Besides, she is not in a fit condition yet to be gadding about talking to witnesses."

"Ah, her recent confinement."

"In the production of my baby cousin, yes indeed. A very fine little fellow he is too."

As they talked, Lizzy had been following Miss Skelmersdale across the room and joined her in a square alcove before the windows in the substantial drawing room into which they had been shown on arrival. Two sofas occupied the spaces either side of the centre of the room, a round table set behind one of them, overloaded with knick-knacks. Lizzy spotted an open box of chessmen beside a chequered board, skeins of wool atop a tambour embroidery frame and several leather-bound books piled higgledy-piggledy. A baize-topped card table was situated near the inner wall and several comfortable armchairs were placed in a haphazard fashion about the room, one opposite to Lady Stoke Rochford's winged chair. Into this the dowager had settled.

With a gesture, Miss Skelmersdale invited Lizzy to the window seat, taking her own place to one side so that they were more or less facing for ease of conversation. The companion folded her hands in her lap and produced her wide smile.

"How may I help, Lady Elizabeth?"

Lizzy flung up a hand. "Lizzy, please. I do hate ceremony, don't you? And I shall call you Henrietta, if you don't object."

Miss Skelmersdale surprised her. "I do, most emphatically, for I can't bear the name. My friends call me Etta."

Lizzy seized the cue. "Who are your friends? Richenda Vexford?"

A merry laugh rang out. "Gracious me, no! Perhaps I should have said friend, for here I have only the one. Ginny and I found we had a deal in common at the outset, and even kept up a correspondence when she was away at school."

"In Bath? Who is Ginny?"

"Virginia Grindlow. She lives with her guardian, the Reverend Newton. I expect you have heard of him?"

"Hardly. I have only been here a day upon this occasion. But my aunt did mention Virginia Grindlow." Lizzy hesitated. Should she be blunt? Etta seemed willing enough to answer questions, but would she be cautious when it came to her friend?

The other woman evidently divined the reason for her hesitation. "You need not be afraid to ask. I don't know anything secret in any event, so I have nothing to withhold."

Lizzy made up her mind. "Excellent. Do you know anything about an assignation this Marmaduke had with someone?"

"Richenda? Or are you supposing he meant to meet Ginny?"

"That is just it. We don't know." Better at this point not to say that it appeared Richenda had expected to meet someone in the summer house. "I was hoping you might have an idea."

Etta pursed her lips, looking away from Lizzy towards the card table. Prevaricating? Or was she merely trying to remember? In a moment, her gaze returned to Lizzy.

"I can't think it was Ginny for she and the reverend drove me home. She was not in any sort of suppressed excitement, which she would have been if Marmaduke meant to follow her to the vicarage. Nor do I think she would have appointed a meeting there for fear her guardian might find them out."

Lizzy was impressed. "An eminently practical way of looking at it, Etta. But Ginny did have a tendre for Marmaduke, didn't she?"

Etta rolled her eyes. "Utterly ridiculous, but yes. Bowled over by his handsome face, if you ask me. Ginny is much too intelligent for such an empty-headed fellow."

"Empty-headed?"

"That is how he struck me. Why, he could think of nothing but paying fulsome compliments to the females — not me, of course, but then men never do — and talking of sporting matters with the gentlemen. Indeed, he infuriated Richenda by saying he was off the next day to see a mill in some village or other."

"The one Mr Pedwardine went to!" Having been given all the relevant facts by Lady Fan, Lizzy was primed. "But he didn't go."

"No, because Richenda made such a fuss he was obliged to say he would forego it. His friend was severely disappointed. I believe they had quite an argument over it."

This was news to Lizzy. According to Ottilia's account, Mr Pedwardine claimed he had parted from his friend on the best of terms. "When? I mean, when did they have an argument? Before he had one with that Botterell man?"

" Aubrey? Oh, he was being absurd. Mrs Thorpe ushered us females out just when it was beginning to be interesting. I thought the two of them were bound to come to blows."

"Yes, but the other argument, with Mr Pedwardine. When did that take place?"

Etta raised her brows. "I didn't witness it. I heard it from Botolf."

"Then it might have been afterwards, might it not? Didn't Botolf Claydon help Mr Pedwardine to take Marmaduke to another room?"

"I believe he did but I really cannot say for sure. I told you, Mrs Thorpe must needs move us off to the parlour where, after she obliged me to take to the pianoforte for a while — just when these interesting happenings were in train, can you imagine? — we had nothing to do but take tea and wait to be taken home. In the event, Reverend Newton ushered Ginny and me off before the tray came in, so we witnessed nothing of the aftermath."

"How disappointing." Not just on account of having no information, for Lizzy could keenly appreciate the frustration of being excluded from the males at combat.

"It was. I asked Botolf about it afterwards, but he wouldn't tell me anything, the wretch."

"Except that there had been an argument between Marmaduke and Mr Pedwardine?"

Etta threw up her eyes. "Is that of importance? I really can't recall when he mentioned it."

Even more disappointing, but Lizzy did not say so. She turned her attention to another of her tasks. "What time did Botolf get home, do you know?"

Etta shrugged. "I can't tell you that either. I did hear his steps on the stairs, or so I thought. A door slammed too. Well, not absolutely slammed, but loud enough for me to hear it being shut. His chamber is at the other end of the hallway to mine, but who else could it have been?"

"What time was that?"

The wide smile came. "I wish I might tell you, but I don't know. I had been asleep. I dare say his entrance woke me for I have learned to be a light sleeper in case Robina needs me in the night."

"Then it is safe to say he returned in the early hours. What time were you abed?"

"Not until midnight. At least, I was in bed, but I like to read by the light of my candle. My vice, if you will." She laughed. "I have a little clock in my chamber that chimes the hour and if it goes to twelve, it reminds me to get my sleep."

"Gracious, doesn't it keep you awake chiming all night?"

"Not after twelve, for it's a mere tinkle."

"A pity it didn't chime when Botolf came home." Aware of dissatisfaction in her tone, Lizzy made haste to disclaim. "Pray don't think I am blaming you. I am most grateful for your help." Etta merely smiled. Mindful of her instructions, Lizzy returned to Virginia Grindlow. "Do you think Marmaduke was wholly for Richenda? Or had he any design upon your friend Ginny?"

"If he had, he concealed it well. Ginny thinks he used her to make Richenda jealous and I dare say she is right. Or perhaps he meant to show Richenda he was not at her beck and call. That would accord with the sort of fellow he was."

"What sort is that?"

"Oh, you know the type. Conceited enough to think any woman must be glad of his attentions, but unwilling to play the game as she would have him play it."

This remark served Lizzy an unwelcome reminder of the brief encounter she'd had with Vivian earlier in the morning. He would not play the game her way, would he? He might not be conceited, but he had been perfectly unkind when they met at breakfast before anyone else in the house had come down.

Having served himself from the covered dishes on the sideboard and taken his plate to the table, not, Lizzy noted, on her side, he disconcerted her with an attack direct.

"If you had told me you meant to come here, I should have postponed my visit."

"That's why I didn't tell you." It was out before Lizzy could control her tongue. She felt warmth rise in her cheeks at his pained look and her tone grew gruff. "Scold me if you wish, but it's an age since we met. I knew you wouldn't come to London."

He addressed himself to his bacon without answering and Lizzy's ire rose. She buttered a roll in silence, but the urge to hit out would not be suppressed. "Is that all you have to say to me?"

Vivian looked up, his fork poised. "What would you have me say, Eliza? The less we converse the easier this will be."

Goaded, Lizzy snapped back. "If you don't wish to be in my company, why don't you leave?"

"I was going to but your uncle insisted I remain. To *face the music*, he said."

"Oh, you are abominable!"

"I know it." To her increased fury, he gave an odd laugh. "It doesn't appear to have put you against me."

Lizzy's heart dropped. "Do you want me against you?"

"It's the popular opinion. You ought to abide by it."

"Well, I don't, so there."

An echo of his old mocking smile flitted across his face. "Just the sort of remark I would expect from the Eliza I remember."

A constriction in her throat made it difficult for Lizzy to speak with any sort of clarity. "At least you admit to remembering."

He gave her a straight look. "I've an excellent memory."

Words poured through her mind, things she could not bring herself to say. Then why didn't he remember the shared moments? The half promises made for a future together. Or had she completely misread him then? Either that, or he had changed his mind. Yet he kept up a correspondence with her. Desultory, but nevertheless persistent. The question came without intent. "Was it always only friendship then?"

Vivian's gaze dropped from hers and he dug a fork into bacon, rather more forcefully than he need, she thought. "That is what it has to be." There was a lengthy pause and then he looked up again, his tone flat and unemotional. "Until you marry. It would cease to be appropriate then."

The message was clear. The air squeezed out of Lizzy's bosom. A sort of numbness invaded her mind. In a hypnotic fashion she reached for the teapot and refilled her cup. The silence dragged.

All at once, Vivian laid down his utensils, pushed away his plate and, shoving back his chair, stood up. Lizzy watched him walk out of the room and the conviction he was lying to them both settled into her head.

Recalling it now, she marvelled that she was able to behave with normality. Except that it had become less about hope, she realised, and more about how to shake Vivian out of his misplaced notion of chivalry. Lady Fan had said it, had she not? He was bowing out to spare her. Well, that was not *appropriate*, Vivian Maplewood. Not by a mile.

"You look quite fierce, Lizzy. Is anything amiss?"

She came back to the present in a bang, catching Etta Skelmersdale gazing at her in a good deal of concern. Her face became heated and she at once disclaimed. "Nothing at all. I was just ... you made me think of something — someone — when you spoke of Marmaduke refusing to play Richenda's game. Men can be so stupid."

A merry laugh emanated from Etta. "Perceptive, my dear. They can and they are. Take Botolf. He imagines no one sees through his pose of aloofness and disinterest when nothing could be more obvious that he was positively green with envy to see Richenda under Marmaduke's spell."

It was plain to Ottilia that Doctor Lister would have preferred to discuss his findings without her presence. But her darling loyal husband had refused to budge from the withdrawing room into which the doctor was shown.

"Ah, Lister, excellent. I take it you are come with news?"

"Indeed, my lord." A formal bow was directed towards Ottilia. "My lady." With which he turned immediately back to the man of the house. "If I might take up a few moments of your time, my lord?"

"As many as you like. We are quite as leisure. And eager, moreover, to hear what you have to say."

Lister coughed. "I thought perhaps in private, my lord?"

Francis let out an explosive sound of derision. "My dear man, if anyone has need of your information, it is my wife. Say on!"

Ottilia concealed a smile at the flash of chagrin that crossed the man's face and adopted an expression of meek interest. Silence was likely the best policy, though she was agog. The more so since the acquisition of facts from various sources which belied her original notions.

Lister looked resigned. "Very well, my lord. Yet I must say at once that we discovered very little to indicate the cause of death."

Ottilia eyed him, a beat of excitement burgeoning. Just as one might have expected, if the new direction her thoughts had been taking was correct.

Her spouse was frowning. "What, nothing at all helpful?"

"I did not say that, my lord. We believe, my colleague and I, that from the pooling of the blood, the fellow must have been seated when he died." Ottilia caught a quick look of triumph thrown at her by her husband, but she kept her attention on the doctor. "Otherwise, the only indication we found was a faint contusion to the skin on the left side of the chest."

"Ha! My wife saw that at the outset. What did you make of it?"

Lister's countenance took on a pained expression. "Nothing very much, my lord. It was so slight as to be negligible and might have been caused by any collision, and at any time before death, perhaps days even."

Seeing Francis's sceptical look, Ottilia took a hand. "Indeed, sir, but perhaps hours rather than days, do you not think?"

"Possibly." He pursed his lips.

"A blue discoloration, I think it was."

"Hard to tell, my lady, with so faint a mark." He gave her an austere look as if daring her to contradict. Ottilia gave him a spurious smile and held her tongue. A look flicked at Francis was productive of instant reward.

"Well, and is that all, sir? I suppose you opened the poor fellow up?"

"Naturally, my lord." Said on a tight note of evident irritation. "As I said at the outset, the body revealed almost nothing to indicate trauma of any kind."

"Almost, you say?"

Another formal little bow. "Quite so. We found nothing until we ventured to cut into the heart itself."

An involuntary little sigh escaped Ottilia. This was what she had been waiting for. For the life of her she could not prevent the words from escaping. "Bleeding? Were there clots?"

"Lacerations." He was turning towards her, as if his professional interest was overcoming his prejudice. "They had bled but little, but damage there was. It was not extensive. Indeed, we almost missed it. Had we not cut on a transverse path, I doubt we would have seen it. But as the blood emptied, there it was."

"Upon the side closest to the chest?" Eager now, Ottilia made no attempt to conceal her understanding.

"Indeed."

"What was your conclusion, doctor?" She almost held her breath as his lips pursed again.

"My colleague would have it there had likely been blunt trauma. However, I myself believe the fellow must have had a defective heart."

Ottilia smiled, glad to be in a position to flatter the man. "You may well be right, sir. I gather, from both his groom and his friend, that there have been a couple of episodes of shortness of breath."

Lister looked gratified. "As one might expect."

"Just so." Ottilia gathered her forces. "However…" His face changed and she softened her tone. "At first, you know, I supposed he had died swiftly, after perhaps receiving a blow."

"But —"

"A light blow, Doctor Lister, enough to cause cardiac arrest. I am sure you must have heard of that rare phenomenon?"

If he had not, it was plain he was not going to reveal his ignorance. "Hm. Extremely rare."

Ottilia exchanged a brief glance with her spouse whose eyebrow flickered in the ironic fashion she knew well. "Yes, indeed, and after subsequent questioning, we have reason to wonder just when Mr Gibbon did die. According to two of our sources, he was alive for some little time after a quarrel took place when he might or might not have taken a blow to the chest."

Lister was clearly unmoved. "Pure supposition, my lady. In my report to the coroner, I have stated precisely what I have told you. There is no convincing evidence to support the idea of a blow, nor indeed to say the man had a defective heart, despite my personal opinion."

Francis spoke up, impatience in his tone. "Then what have you given as the cause of death?"

"Oh, cardiac arrest, my lord. That much we may be sure of. Anything further is mere speculation."

"You are saying my wife is wasting her time then?"

A faint shrug came together with supercilious smile. "That is her ladyship's prerogative. From a medical point of view, there is nothing further to investigate."

His patronising manner so incensed Ottilia she had difficulty in bidding him goodbye with politeness as he made to take his leave. "I must at least thank you for what you have been able to add, sir. It was enlightening."

He bowed. "I am happy to have been of service." A laugh came. "Should you stumble over any more corpses, pray do not hesitate to call upon me."

Ottilia waited until he had been ushered out and could hear his footsteps receding before letting out an infuriated expletive.

"I heard that," said her husband, coming back into the room in time. "Impertinent little man!"

Ottilia drew in a breath and let it out again. "It was his heavy-handed attempt at humour that proved my undoing."

"I am not surprised." He came over to where she sat in her customary chair by the fire and leaned an arm along the mantel. "What now, wife of mine? Does this make a difference?"

Ottilia shrugged. "Not a great deal, Fan."

"You hold by your notion of a blow, I take it?"

"How can I not? Lacerations in the heart? A faint contusion on the skin? The man is blind!"

He made no response to her frustrated comment. "But you now don't think it was this rare condition you spoke of?"

"No. I began to discard that as soon as Mr Pedwardine claimed he left Marmaduke alive and walking unaided."

"But you still say it was the blow that caused his death."

"Precipitated the condition that caused it. I am ready to accept it was accidental death. At least, that must stay until we know just when he died."

"And where, if we are to presume he was in no condition to live long enough to remove from Thorpe Grange."

Ottilia watched him drum his fingers on the mantel. "What is in your mind, Fan?"

The fingers stilled and he looked down at her. "This notion of Lister's that he had some sort of heart defect. What do you make of it?"

"It may well be so, but that does not preclude his having died because he was hit."

"Would it not explain the discrepancy of time though?"

Ottilia considered this. "Perhaps. I don't know enough of heart disease, or defects as Doctor Lister has it, to be able to make such a judgement."

"Well then, what now?"

The repetition rankled. "I wish I knew, Fan. If we are to talk of discrepancies, I am more concerned with those in the various accounts."

"You did say someone was lying."

"Just so. Which presupposes there is something to hide. We are left with two unanswered questions. Where did Marmaduke die and who sent his body to me?"

"Aren't you forgetting the when? When did he die?"

She flicked him a smile. "I am ahead of you, Fan."

His lips quirked. "How so, Madam Mischief?"

She let out a gurgle. "I conflate the when with the where. Once we know where, we should also know when."

CHAPTER TWELVE

Ottilia was becoming hopelessly muddled. She began to wish Francis had not ridden out with Vivian, but as his expressed intention was to make for the village inn, once they had shaken the fidgets out of the horses, in hopes of encountering one or other of the young gentlemen not yet individually questioned, she could not wholly regret his being absent.

Yet what with Lizzy's disorderly relation of all she had learned at Lady Stoke Rochford's, punctuated by her mother-in-law's commentary upon that lady's failing health, she was obliged to intervene. Laughingly, she called over from her stance on the sofa in the withdrawing room, "Pray stop, the pair of you! If you will both talk at once, I can make neither head nor tail of anything."

Sybilla, seated on one side of the fire, was the first to hit back. "That is because you have filled my granddaughter's head with nothing but this wretched nonsense."

"Pooh, Grandmama!" This from Lizzy, standing at bay near the fireplace. "It is you who will keep on about that poor old woman, when —"

"Enough, I beg of you!" Ottilia covered her ears. Both parties ceased talking, Sybilla casting glares upon Lizzy, who stood mumchance but with dancing eyes. Ottilia cautiously removed her hands and eyed each in turn.

"Now then, let me see if I have managed to grasp your findings, Lizzy." Ottilia held up a finger as the dowager opened her mouth. "One moment, Sybilla, if you please. We will talk together presently."

Sybilla humphed. "I might have known my opinions were of less account."

"Not in the least. But Lizzy was on a mission for me and I need her information." Ottilia waited a moment, but Sybilla had evidently opted for the sulks. Suppressing a smile, she turned to her niece, who tripped across and took a seat on the sofa beside her. "If I have understood you, Lizzy, this Etta does not think the assignation was with Virginia. She heard that Mr Pedwardine quarrelled with Marmaduke because Richenda did not wish him to go to this mill. Have I that right?"

"Yes, and Richenda made a big fuss and Etta thinks Marmaduke used Virginia to make Richenda jealous."

"That is her opinion? She does not know it for a fact?"

"Goodness, how should she? She barely knew Marmaduke. Enough to stigmatise him as empty-headed and interested only in sporting pursuits."

Ottilia breathed out. "So far, so good. Was there anything else?"

Lizzy looked triumphant. "Botolf!"

The dowager stared. "What in the world does that mean?"

"She means Botolf Claydon, Sybilla. He is Lady Stoke Rochford's godson. Another of the young men who hung about Richenda, don't you recall?"

"How should I remember a plethora of names?"

Ottilia chose to ignore this. "You were saying, Lizzy?"

"I wasn't. I did not get the chance."

"How dare you, Miss?"

Ottilia threw her gaze heavenwards and was relieved when her niece, sounding penitent all at once, leapt up and ran to Sybilla, dropping down beside her chair and seizing her hands.

"I beg your pardon, Grandmama. Forgive me, pray. I did not mean to be rude."

"You would do well to learn better manners, child." But the apology had softened Sybilla for she disengaged one hand and flapped it in that dismissive way she had. "Very well, very well, get on then."

Nothing loath, Lizzy sprang up and returned to stand before the sofa. "Etta heard Botolf come in. Very late."

Ottilia's mind leapt. "How late?"

"She could not be sure," said Lizzy on a regretful note, "but it was after midnight and she had been asleep."

Time enough then to have taken up Marmaduke Gibbon and set him down somewhere — at Richenda's for the summer house? — before seeking his own bed. But Lizzy's eyes were a-sparkle. "Is there more, my dear?"

"Well, if Etta is right, there is. She believes Botolf is indeed one of Richenda's suitors though he pretends to indifference."

"Interesting." In which case, it was unlikely he would drive Marmaduke to his assignation with the beauty.

Then there was this quarrel with Mr Pedwardine. He had confessed nothing of the sort. Indeed, he claimed they parted on good terms. "How did Etta know that Marmaduke and his friend quarrelled? Did she hear them?"

"Oh, did I not say? Botolf told her."

Which at once made the story suspect. From all Ottilia had heard of Botolf Claydon, he looked to be one of these men who took delight in stirring the coals. Was anything he said to be relied upon?

"Have you finished?"

Sybilla's grim tone captured Ottilia's attention, but before she could speak, Lizzy leapt in, flitting back to the fireplace and plonking down into the opposite chair. "Yes, I am quite done,

Grandmama. What was it you wished to say of Lady Stoke Rochford?"

The studied interest in her voice did not deceive Ottilia. Nor was Sybilla fooled. She gave a snort.

"You think you are the only one to have been busy, do you? Allow me to disabuse you."

Lizzy's merry laugh rang out. "Oh, Grandmama! You are not going to tell me that poor old creature had anything useful to impart?"

Sybilla eyed her with a sort of quiet triumph. "Merely because she is physically weak does not mean her faculties are gone. Nor is she ignorant by reason of being a recluse." Her black gaze turned on Ottilia. "She is perfectly acquainted with your antics, for one thing."

Ottilia had to laugh. "I dare say she is. If it is not Mrs Honeybourne who carries tales thence, no doubt this Etta is *au fait* with what goes on around these parts."

The dowager gave one of her rare cracks of laughter. "Well reasoned, my good girl. Yes, the Honey woman goes regularly. Robina relies upon her tongue for the latest *on dits*."

Lizzy was clearly astonished. "Gracious, Grandmama, did she tell you anything of use?"

"Whether it is of use remains to be seen. She is shrewd, I'll give her that." She looked again to Ottilia. "This fellow Botolf, for instance. He hopes to be made her heir but she will not tell him whether or no she has made him so."

"So you did know his name!"

Sybilla's mouth twisted. "I am not yet in my dotage, Elizabeth."

"Lady Stoke Rochford means to keep him on a string to ensure his good behaviour, is that it?"

"She did not say as much, but it is a fair inference, Ottilia. Robina is not pleased with this Richenda business. If you ask me, she is angling for the boy to marry the companion." Sybilla threw a wry glance at Ottilia and added, "An event not entirely without precedent."

Ottilia had to smile at this reference to her brief tenure as Sybilla's companion which had culminated in becoming betrothed to Francis, but before she could comment upon the supposition, Lizzy broke in. "I don't think that would fadge, Grandmama. Etta doesn't even like Botolf. At least —" She broke off, frowning.

"She sounds to be on good terms with him," supplied Ottilia. "Perhaps her interest is stronger than you suppose."

"Oh, no, it can't be. She was altogether disinterested."

Ottilia refrained from pointing out that this might argue an opposite view, especially if she believed Richenda to be her rival. "Sybilla, why does Lady Stoke Rochford not make provision for her companion herself?"

"She may well have done. She seemed inordinately concerned for the girl's future. Particularly as Robina believes she is not long for this world."

"It is to be hoped a malevolent spirit does not help her out of it." The words escaped before Ottilia could bite her tongue. The result was everything she would not wish.

"Good heavens, child! Does your mind run on nothing but murder?"

But Lizzy clapped her hands. "That is why she will not reveal the contents of her will to Botolf, depend upon it, Aunt!"

"Poppycock!"

"But it isn't, Grandmama. Only think! If he is evil enough to do away with his godmother for his expectations, why should he not as well be rid of a rival in Richenda's affections?"

"Don't talk such nonsense! You are letting your imagination run away with you. You too, Ottilia. You have no evidence to support any such supposition."

"Too true, alas." Ottilia waved a placatory hand. "I spoke a thought aloud."

"But —"

Ottilia frowned Lizzy down. "Your grandmother is right, my dear. Don't let us put the cart before the horse." She drew a breath. "Nevertheless, I should welcome an opportunity to have a little talk with young Claydon." She ignored her mother-in-law's explosive sound of protest. "Along with Jarvis Thorpe. Both of these gentlemen have some explaining to do, I fancy."

"Why Jarvis Thorpe, Aunt?"

Ottilia got up. "Because he is another whose movements after the party are unaccounted for. But no more. It is time for Luke's feed."

In fact she was early, but she needed the haven of her eyrie. Besides, an hour with the children would be just the thing to clear her mind of too many questions.

Before she could reach the door, it opened and Vivian Maplewood strode in, stopping short just before they collided. He made no apology, his gaze merely sweeping the room to take in the other two occupants by the fire. Then he addressed Ottilia, his tone sharp and urgent.

"We thought you would wish to know at once."

Ottilia's attention snapped in. "Know what, sir?"

"We met Lord Vexford riding like a madman. He is scouring the countryside. Richenda has vanished."

Ottilia's mind was leaping with conjecture. If Richenda was missing, who else might be unaccounted for? She wasted no time. "I take it my husband is assisting Lord Vexford?"

"He is, ma'am, and desired me to ride back to apprise you of the situation."

"Well, what is the situation, Vivian? When was Richenda last seen? How long has Lord Vexford been searching for her?"

He spread his hands, casting a glance at Lizzy who had risen and was hovering halfway between the fireplace and where Ottilia and the young man stood near the door. Unusually hesitant for her forthright niece. Had there been further disagreement between them? She brushed the thought aside as Vivian answered.

"I hardly know, ma'am. She dined yesterday, if I heard him aright, but has been confined to her chamber. His lordship was somewhat incoherent in his fury."

"Exacerbated by anxiety, no doubt. So she was seen last night. Are we to take it that she escaped from her confinement?"

"Presumably. I really have no notion." He gave a slight bow. "If you will forgive me, ma'am, I promised Lord Francis that I would return to join in the hunt."

He made for the door, but Ottilia moved swiftly to intercept him. "Stay!"

Then Lizzy was beside her. "Yes, stay, Vivian! Let me come with you!"

His gaze raked her person. "You are not dressed for riding."

"We may take your curricle. I only need to get my pelisse."

He hesitated, long enough for Ottilia to cut in. "No, Lizzy."

"But why not, Aunt? I can —"

"Wait!" Ottilia turned her gaze on Vivian. "Do not join the hunt, if you please. You would be better employed in seeking out the young gentlemen."

His brows snapped together. "You are thinking of an elopement?"

"At this present, I am thinking only of discovering whether one of those fellows is also missing. When you find them — if you do find any of them — pray request them to come to me here at once."

He looked dubious. "What if they refuse?"

"Remind them that I am trying to unravel what happened to Marmaduke and I need their assistance."

"But —"

A spur came from an unexpected quarter as Sybilla, who had risen moments before, swept up. "Don't shilly-shally, boy, but do as she asks! Ottilia knows her business."

"Thank you, Sybilla. Hurry, Vivian!"

"As you wish, ma'am." He gave a slight bow, cast a glance at Lizzy in which Ottilia read a trifle of apology or regret, and departed.

Lizzy's disappointment was patent. "What can I do, Lady Fan? You surely don't expect me to sit about twiddling my thumbs in all this excitement?"

"Excitement, you say?" Sybilla blew out an impatient breath. "If the girl has eloped, it is more serious than you know."

"Well, of course I know that, Grandmama. But I must do *something*."

Ottilia set a hand on her arm. "Come with me, my dear. I must feed Luke and I need you."

Lizzy brightened but the dowager intervened. "You need her while you are nursing? What in the world for?"

"To entertain Pretty, of course. I cannot think if she is to be chattering in my ear throughout, and I do need to think."

Sybilla eyed her. "You cannot have solved it."

"Hardly. But there are so many contradictions. I need to sort them all out in my mind. Especially if Vivian does indeed manage to find one or other of these interested parties. Which reminds me, I need Hemp."

This catalogue was productive of a dissatisfied grunt. "And I? You have no use for an old woman, eh?"

"On the contrary, Sybilla. I would be most obliged if, when you are rested enough, you will walk into the village and inform Mrs Honeybourne of what is going forward."

"Gossip? It is not in my style, girl. Besides, I do not know the woman."

"Just so. She will be overcome by your condescension and eager to tell everyone how you favoured her. I can think of no surer way of frightening the individual who is trying to pull the wool over my eyes than to set the whole community buzzing with conjecture."

"But what possible excuse have I for visiting this creature?"

Ottilia had no need to suggest a ruse for Lizzy chimed in. "I know, Grandmama! You will send Venner to knock on the door and ask that you be permitted to rest a moment as the walk has been too much for you."

"In all likelihood it will be the death of me," grumbled Sybilla.

"Oh, Aunt Ottilia, it won't do. I shall have to accompany her."

Sybilla drew herself up. "Nothing of the sort. Do you take me for a nincompoop? I am quite as capable of subterfuge as are you, I thank you." She thrust at Ottilia. "Go, child. I shall do my part, never fear."

Ottilia leaned in to kiss her cheek. "I have no fear that you won't, Sybilla. Thank you. I had best hurry or my son will be protesting his hunger. He is the perfect copy of his father."

When she and her niece were out of earshot of the withdrawing room, Ottilia took hold of Lizzy's arm as they made their way around the gallery towards the stairs to the second floor. "I wish you will be a little patient with your grandmother, my dear."

Lizzy let out an explosive breath. "She has no patience with me, Aunt Ottilia!"

"That is quite untrue, and you know it. But it happens," Ottilia added, holding up a finger to prevent any retort, "she is much exercised because Miss Mellis desires to leave her."

Lizzy came to an abrupt halt at the bottom of the stairs. "What, Teresa Mellis is retiring at last? I thought she never would!"

"She is forced to, it seems." With which, Ottilia furnished her niece with the unfortunate situation of Miss Mellis's sister. "Oblige me, therefore, if you please, by taking more care not to annoy Sybilla with ill-considered remarks."

"Oh, very well, if I must." Lizzy followed as Ottilia began to mount the stairs. "What will Grandmama do then? I hope to heaven she does not request me to live with her!"

Ottilia had to laugh. "Nothing of the sort. You would be at each other's throats in no time. She will find a new companion, of course. The necessity does not sit well with her, which is why —"

"Yes, yes, I perceive the difficulty, Aunt. You need not warn me all over again."

Ottilia repressed an inward sigh and held her peace. Once in her parlour she rang the bell. Tyler appeared at the same moment that Doro arrived, bearing the infant Luke and leading Pretty by the hand.

"Pretty, dearest, here is Lizzy come to have a talk with you." Pretty cast dubious eyes upon the visitor but Lizzy produced a merry smile and a bright greeting won the child over in an instant. Satisfied, Ottilia turned to the nurse. "Have I kept you waiting, Doro? Pardon me, pray."

"I had but just prepared upon coming down, milady. Will you sit?"

"In just a moment. Tyler, pray request Hemp to come to me here at once." The footman bowed and retreated. "Let me tell Hemp what I need of him and then I will feed Luke." Ottilia peered into the infant's face and met his eyes, the brown that had shown light in his first weeks now darkening to his papa's deep colour. "You are quiet enough, my little man. Is he not hungry?"

Doro chuckled. "He will eat, milady, never fear."

"I don't doubt it." A flitter of unease went through Ottilia. "But he usually looks so eager, seeking for my nipple. Are you sure he is not sickening for something?"

"Milady, he is the healthiest baby I have ever known. You will see. When he is in your arms, he will be looking for sustenance, you can be sure."

Ottilia would have argued further but that a knock at the door produced her steward, bringing the events of the day back to mind. She moved to greet him. "Ah, Hemp, thank you for being so quick. I need your help, if you please."

His deep voice came as he gave a small bow, casting, rather to Ottilia's amusement, a quick glance at his inamorata. "I am always at your service, milady."

Ottilia smiled at him, warmth catching in her breast. "I know it." If only he did not grow impatient for his Doro and wish to leave Flitteris at last.

"How may I serve you, milady?"

Ottilia pulled her thoughts back. "Mr Maplewood is herding a coterie of young gentlemen to this place. At least, I hope he may find them. When they come, which may well not be for an hour or so, pray keep them in the withdrawing room and do not permit any to leave before I am able to join them."

One of Hemp's rare smiles crept into his face. "It will be my pleasure, milady. Am I to know who they are?"

"An excellent thought." Ottilia counted them off on her fingers. "Messrs Claydon, Botterell, Thorpe — the younger one, Jarvis Thorpe, that is. Oh, and a Mr Pedwardine too, if the luck favours us. But he I have already spoken to, although it will be well to know if he —" She broke off, recalling the presence in the room of Pretty. The child's ears were sharp. Best to withhold all mention of Richenda.

Her plans laid, she was able at last to turn her attention to the business of replenishing Master Luke Fanshawe's stores of energy. True to Doro's prediction, no sooner was she seated and had taken the boy in her arms than he made immediate signs indicative of his wish to partake of his meal at the earliest possible moment.

Lord Vexford kept up a frantic pace which made it impossible for Francis to put the questions hovering in his mind. By the time the man slackened the rein both mounts were blowing and his temper was rising.

"If my horse suffers for this, Vexford, you will know my wrath," Francis announced, sidling the animal up close enough to be able to converse.

The other turned an irate glare upon him. "Did I ask for your assistance? Go, if you have no appetite for the hunt."

"What I have appetite for, sir, is to rid my wife of this pestilential business as speedily as possible." He held up his whip hand as Vexford opened his mouth to retort. "Pray don't presume to tell me my wife may ignore this death. Someone —

you, for all I know — dropped that boy's corpse on our doorstep with a note referring it to Lady Fan."

Vexford's ruddy countenance, already suffused from his hectic exertions, reddened the more. "You dare accuse me?"

"I might, but it happens I won't. I should doubt of your taking any such devious action. If you are anything, Vexford, you are direct."

The fellow harrumphed, holding in his horse to a walk with an iron hand. Not that the poor beast looked to be in any condition to hare off again. Vexford had ridden him hard.

Francis seized the chance to put his questions. "Why have you confined your search to the local area? Might your daughter have gone further afield?"

"Ha! Not on that mare of hers."

"You are sure she was riding?"

"Had the mare saddled and rode off without her groom, disobedient chit."

Then it seemed unlikely Richenda had taken off with one of her paramours, which was what Francis had supposed. "Was it to infuriate you? Is that why she went off?"

Vexford grunted. "Up to her tricks again. Should have kept her locked up."

Abandoning the immediate problem, Francis pursued the more pertinent point. No sense in beating about the bush with this fellow. "Can you tell me what took your daughter out to the summer house on your return from the Twelfth Night party?"

Vexford's gaze was shifting from one clump of trees to another, as if he thought to catch sight of the errant Richenda hiding behind, but at this his head whipped round. "How came you by that information?"

"From Miss Poynton. She saw Richenda from her window and came to inform you."

Vexford let out an explosive curse. "Useless female! If she'd any gumption, she'd have curbed the wench years ago, but no. I am obliged to intervene. I tell you, I'll be happy to get the girl off my hands."

"Then you would do better to stop driving away all her suitors," Francis said, exasperated.

"When she picks a suitable man, I shan't drive him away. The wench is bent upon thwarting me, but she'll dance to my tune if I die for it!"

It was plain the man was quite as obstinate as his offspring. Francis returned him to the point. "Did you think Richenda meant to meet Marmaduke Gibbon in the summer house?"

"How the devil do I know whom she meant to meet? Or if she meant to meet anyone?"

Francis suppressed a strong desire to flick the man's head with the thong of his whip. "Well, was there any sign of him, or some other if you must have it so, in the summer house?"

"Pah! If there had been, he'd have had the thrashing of his life!"

He had been armed with the means for dispensing his rough justice presumably. "You saw no one?"

"Have I not said so?"

"No, as it happens. So far you have answered no question directly." Which surprised Francis, though he refrained from saying so. "Is it not possible there was a fellow there, who hid upon seeing you approach?"

Vexford let out a short laugh. "If there was, he'd no chance to prosecute his design. I had the girl away from there in a trice."

And dealt her short shrift, no doubt, poor child. "Did you lock her in her room then?"

"No need. She'd not have dared venture forth again."

Was the fellow deluded? Or was he prevaricating? A girl as rebellious as this one could be counted upon to do precisely what she chose. If Lizzy could escape out of a window, which Francis knew from his brother-in-law she had done, for Richenda to sneak back to the summer house must be a bagatelle. Had Miss Poynton not seen her by chance, Vexford would have known nothing of her excursion in the first place. Or had it been he who went back there in time to discover Marmaduke dead? Or to discover him and take opportunity to dispose of him?

Francis changed tack. "Could your daughter have ridden to meet someone this morning, do you think?"

"Not if she knows what's good for her."

The man was impossible. Francis let fly. "Which, clearly, she does not. Has it not occurred to you this may be a ruse to cover a more determined escape?"

"To where? She has no refuge from me, sir."

That was well seen. "I am asking if she might have eloped."

"With whom? She don't want for sense, despite her determination to outwit me. She's known the boys in these parts for years. No danger there."

Was the man blind or merely a fool? At least his temper had cooled. "You don't mean to check for her in the houses round about?"

"What, to advertise her folly? She'll be back with her tail between her legs, if I don't find her first."

Francis gave it up. He tried one more throw. "Can you tell me anything of the argument that broke out between those young men?"

Vexford's snort was comprehensive. "D'you think I waste my time listening to the bleatings of whelps?"

"Apparently you became heated at the time." No answer being forthcoming, Francis applied a goad. "Moreover, since the quarrel appears to have concerned your daughter, if indeed she did not instigate it, I should have thought it might indeed interest you."

He was treated to an amazed stare. "What care I? If they've not sense enough to know I'd not consent to any of them marrying my daughter, let them quarrel to their heart's content. It is nothing to me."

"Yet you refuse to entertain the notion one of them might persuade Richenda to an elopement."

"Not she! Knows where her bread's buttered. It's all posturing and protest with my girl. She won't marry against her inclination and she don't incline to any yet. Least of all that dunce of a fellow with the pretty face."

"The dead man?"

"Aye, he. Only dragged him here to flout me. Declared her undying love. Pooh! Didn't believe a word of it, and she knows it."

Not so blind then. This tallied with what Miss Poynton had revealed. Yet Francis could not shake the notion there was more to this business with the summer house than Vexford was willing to state. He began to chafe to be gone from this fruitless quest.

"What do you mean to do now?"

"Ride home, what else?"

Admitting defeat? An idea occurred. "Did you think to check for your daughter in the village?"

Vexford kept his horse on the move but subjected Francis to a frowning stare. "What should she do there?"

Francis brought it out flat. "Keep an assignation?"

"Pah! She'd no chance to make any such. Been locked in her chamber for the better part of a week."

"Her chamber has a window, I presume."

"Of course it has a window. What the deuce are you getting at, man?"

With his own niece's antics in his mind, Francis could not keep in a derisive sound. "Use your imagination, Vexford! Richenda is plainly an enterprising girl. I can think of half a dozen ways she might find means to send or receive a message."

Vexford blew out an impatient breath. "The chit wouldn't dare. She knows my temper."

Which had not prevented her from disobeying her father's express commands. But Francis refrained from pointing this out. Apart from anything else, he could not unleash further punishment on the child. Bad enough she was like to fall under Vexford's gravest displeasure for merely riding out. On the other hand, he could not place any dependence on the man's conviction that his daughter had not gone to meet some cavalier. Which of them though, now that Marmaduke Gibbon was out of the picture?

CHAPTER THIRTEEN

The three young gentlemen assembled in the withdrawing room looked to be disconcerted, at the least. Perhaps, Ottilia thought with a gleam of amusement, at being held captive by the large frame of Hemp, standing like a gaoler between them and the door, his arms folded. She produced a smile.

"I must apologise for keeping you waiting, gentlemen." She had taken the opportunity to replenish her system with a light luncheon of rolls, her favourite Cheddar cheese and coffee, brought to her on a tray in her parlour. Lizzy had been likewise served, but with a more robust repast of beef and a selection of patties.

The tallest of the reluctant visitors, whom she recognised as Jarvis Thorpe, gave a small bow, but his tone was grudging. "Lady Francis. That fellow Maplewood said you wished to see me."

"Indeed I do. All of you."

Aubrey Botterell stepped forward, his round countenance bearing a pout that made him look like a discontented baby. "All but arrested us, that fellow. I can't think what you want with us. You must know everything already, ma'am."

Ottilia waved him away. "I only wish I did, Mr Botterell. Unfortunately, there are one or two gaps in my knowledge. I am in hopes the three of you might be able to fill them."

"Highly doubtful." This came from the last of the trio, a thin young man whom Ottilia appraised with interest.

"We shall see. You are Mr Claydon, I take it?" He had the grace to give a bow of acknowledgement. "How do you do?

Do pray take a seat, all of you." Ottilia waved them to chairs as she took a central position on the sofa.

None of the young men took up the offer, instead electing to assume stances at a discreet distance. Was it to signal a disinclination to remain for long? Ottilia glanced at Hemp, signalling with her eyes that he should retire to the side of the room.

All three turned to watch as he shifted his position. Claydon glanced towards the door. Ottilia gave a laugh.

"You wish to escape, Mr Claydon? Have no fear. I merely desire information. I will make no accusations today."

He flushed and pointedly settled his spindly frame in a chair by the wall opposite to Ottilia's seat. Botterell hovered a moment longer and then sat in one of the chairs by the fire. Only Jarvis Thorpe remained standing.

"Well now, if we are all settled, I must first ask if any of you have seen Richenda this day?"

Surprise flickered as she looked from one face to the others.

Thorpe spoke first. "Why? What is the wench up to now?"

"That is what we would all like to know. You have not seen her?"

"Not I."

Ottilia shifted her gaze. "You, Mr Botterell?"

He shrugged. "I've not seen her since the party. Word is she's been kept close by old Vexford."

"You had that from your aunt, I dare say."

Botterell reddened, letting out a self-conscious laugh. "Aunt Honeybourne does enjoy a trifle of tattle."

"I did see her, if you must know."

The statement, rough with aggression, came from Claydon. Ottilia wasted no time.

"Where and when? Was she on horseback?"

Claydon's brows drew together. "How the deuce do you know that? Yes, she was. At least, she had been, for she had the rein in hand. She was talking to a fellow outside the Fox in Wyke."

"What fellow? Did you know him?"

Claydon shrugged. "A servant. None I recognised."

"Did you speak to her?"

Claydon's mouth curved in a sneer. "Not I. I've no wish to embroil myself in that female's scheming toils."

This remark was productive of protests from the other two.

"Claydon, that's not fair."

"You'd scheme if you had Vexford for a father."

"Ha! You only say so, Botterell, because you want her for yourself. She's a little cat and I wish you joy of her."

Botterell was on his feet. "Unsay those words!"

Jarvis Thorpe seized his arm. "No, you don't, Aubrey! You've brawled enough and look what came of it last time."

Botterell turned on him. "Shut your mouth, you fool!" He gestured wildly towards Ottilia.

She called the gathering to order. "Gentlemen, if you please. No fighting in my drawing room, I thank you. Hemp!"

Hemp paced a couple of steps towards the two young men, who took one look and fell back, releasing hold of one another. Both turned resentful faces upon Ottilia but it was Claydon who spoke, an amused taunt in his voice.

"Thus we see why you installed a guard, Lady Fan. Very wise. Botterell's hot temper is to blame for this whole debacle, as I am sure you are already aware."

His victim turned on him, the snarl sitting oddly on his plump cheeks. "You'd blame me, would you? That fellow was alive when you — yes you, Claydon — took him off to that room downstairs. I'll wager she knows that too."

Ottilia clapped her hands in a manner calling for attention. "Enough! That will do. Be quiet, all of you!"

The authoritative tone, coupled with the menace of Hemp's solid form standing all too close, had its effect. All three subsided, Jarvis Thorpe at least looking shame-faced. He it was who proffered an apology. "I beg your pardon, my lady. This business has upset us all."

Ottilia became tart. "The more reason to co-operate in a bid to find out what precisely happened to Marmaduke Gibbon that night."

Thorpe stared for a moment, then nodded, glancing to his friend. "Come, Aubrey. Better to be rid of the business once and for all, eh? Sit down, man."

Botterell's belligerent pose did not abate, but he sat again at last, stiffly upright in the chair. A faint mocking laugh brought his head round to the third man and drew Ottilia's fire.

"Mr Claydon, I must request you to refrain from cheap jibes. Let us try to be civilised." She waited to see if he would venture upon a retort but he said nothing, though the sneering expression was not quite gone. Ottilia nodded at Hemp and he retired again, but this time remained closer to the door. She chose to tackle Claydon with the first of her queries.

"I understand you witnessed an argument between Marmaduke and his friend Percy Pedwardine."

Claydon's brows rose. "Well?"

"Concerning Marmaduke's decision not to accompany Mr Pedwardine to this mill?"

Claydon's face cleared. "Oh, that? A mere skirmish, I thought. That fellow took exception to Gibbon kowtowing to Richenda's demands — and who shall blame him?"

"Was this before or after the other argument?"

An apprehensive glance came from Botterell at this further mention of his contribution to the evening's troubles, but Ottilia kept her attention on Claydon.

"Oh, before. Afterwards, Pedwardine was too anxious for his friend's condition to be abusing him."

"What precisely was said, do you know?"

"I hardly paid heed, ma'am. Pedwardine was scowling but Gibbon could only laugh, holding that a lady's wishes were paramount. There was no more to it."

Except that Percy Pedwardine had not seen fit to mention the matter. If there was bad blood between the two, it rather changed the complexion of events. Well for him this little disagreement had taken place before the contretemps that resulted in his friend's death. But of more significance was the mystery surrounding Marmaduke's whereabouts. Ottilia cast a glance across the faces of her disgruntled visitors. "There is a discrepancy in the story I have managed to glean from various sources."

That brought a frown to two of the faces. Claydon's expression did not change. He merely stared at her, the supercilious smile again evident.

"It appears," Ottilia pursued, "that Marmaduke had an assignation, possibly with Richenda. He sent his groom home with his curricle and refused a ride with his friend Percy Pedwardine. Yet your brother, Mr Thorpe, is sure that he left the premises that night. I dare say you perceive my dilemma."

Jarvis Thorpe's frown had intensified. "I could not swear to his movements, ma'am. I left once Aubrey had escorted his aunt to her carriage."

"Where did you go, sir?"

"To — er — to the Plough in Knights Inham."

"Alone?"

He hesitated, threw a glance at Claydon, who gave nothing away. "I met Botolf there."

Ottilia pounced on this. "Then you did not leave your brother's house together?"

"No, ma'am. We left separately."

Ottilia turned to Claydon, who was smiling with obvious expectation. "Well, sir?"

"Well what, Lady Francis? You wish to know what time I left? Or whether I saw the dead man?"

Ottilia turned it back on him. "Was he dead?"

The smile vanished. A dull red crept into the lean cheek. "What are you suggesting?"

She did not let up. "Was he dead before you left, Mr Claydon?"

He looked decidedly taken aback. "How in the world should I know, ma'am? I did not see anything untoward after I helped that fellow Pedwardine to secrete the man into the breakfast parlour."

Ottilia gave a tiny smile. "Come, Mr Claydon, this is mere quibbling. Did you or did you not see Marmaduke Gibbon's corpse in the Thorpe house?"

"I saw Gibbon seated in a chair. He looked none too healthy, I'll give you that. Pallid. He might as well have been a corpse."

"Was he breathing?"

"He was when I set him down."

Ottilia's senses were prickling. The evasion rankled. She could not be sure if it was manifest of Claydon's character to be deliberately elusive, or if he was indeed hiding the truth. His supercilious tone indicated one of those individuals whose mission was to appear more clever than they really were. Yet was he indeed clever enough to avoid incriminating himself? Ottilia tried a throw.

"What I cannot understand, sir, is how a man who was, according to your description, next door to a corpse, could vanish from that house and disappear without trace until he reappeared dead on my doorstep."

Claydon spread his hands. "Beats me, ma'am. I wish I might help you, but I regret I know no more."

Tempted to let fly, Ottilia held her tongue. As her glance swept the other two, she became aware that Jarvis Thorpe had become a trifle rigid, his gaze fixed upon Claydon. There was more here than met the eye. How to probe? If she had Thorpe alone, she might break him. But not in the presence of his friend Claydon.

She looked to Botterell and found him more dejected than anything else. Clearly he knew nothing of whatever Thorpe and Claydon were party to. If her instinct did not deceive her. She changed tack.

"What about this business of an assignation? Had any of you knowledge of it?"

Jarvis Thorpe looked relieved at the change of subject, rushing into speech. "I'd not heard of it."

Both Claydon and Botterell shrugged. Ottilia persisted. "It seems there was one. With, one presumes, Richenda." No reaction. "Who lives at Wyke Hall."

"Yes, we know." Claydon's sneer was in both face and voice.

She ignored it. "I do wonder if Marmaduke did indeed leave the Thorpe house that night, aided perhaps by another, or others?" She flicked a glance from Claydon to Thorpe and back again. Neither countenance altered, not by a flicker. Both pairs of eyes remained trained upon her, apparently unmoved. Ottilia's suspicion deepened. She pressed on. "I am suggesting that he could not have removed from there unaided." Nothing. Weird blankness in either face. "A dead body is a dead weight.

It took both my footman and Hemp here to bring poor Marmaduke into the house and you see how strong he is. One man could not have managed it, do you not agree?"

Thorpe cleared his throat, looking away. "I imagine you are in the right of it, ma'am."

"But you have no personal knowledge of handling a corpse?"

His cheeks darkened, but he remained steadfast in denial. "None."

Ottilia rounded on Claydon. "You, sir? Are you similarly ignorant?"

Much as she anticipated, he held his nerve, emitting a jeering laugh. "My dear Lady Fan, I have not half the brawn of your fellow here. Even did I wish to, I could not possibly assist in such an endeavour."

Ottilia drove them harder. "If Marmaduke was already dead —"

"You can't know that!"

"I didn't hurt him enough to kill him!"

"Suppositions, Lady Francis, suppositions."

She waited for the interruptions to cease. "If he was already dead, I was saying, his body must have been moved since it ended up on our porch here. There are several possibilities." The faces of the two most likely concerned became wooden while Botterell merely frowned. "It may have been secreted into some ditch or outhouse for the duration. But since Marmaduke's clothes were relatively clean, that is unlikely. Besides, anyone might discover a corpse in the grounds of Thorpe Grange."

"Which they most certainly did not, Lady Francis."

"Just so, Mr Thorpe."

Claydon's gaze was almost inimical. "You said several possibilities."

"Well, I imagine there are other places where one might conceal a dead body, but I shall not trouble to enumerate them. The danger of discovery again. No, the only sure way to be rid of it would be to remove it from the Grange altogether, do you not think?"

She flicked a look towards Jarvis Thorpe as she spoke and noted, in passing, that Botterell was looking bewildered, his pudgy features frowning as he looked from one to the other of the speakers. Then he had certainly not been instrumental in disposing of Marmaduke's body. Her attention was claimed by Thorpe, who chose to become hostile.

"I take leave to tell you that I resent these accusations, my lady."

Ottilia let out a light laugh. "I have made none, sir. I am merely putting to you a hypothetical possibility."

"Well ... well, it sounded accusatory."

"Did it? In my experience, Mr Thorpe, those with nothing to hide do not in general take offence at suppositions. One is bound to look at all possibilities when trying to solve a puzzle of this nature. If you tell me that neither you, nor Mr Claydon, had anything to do with moving Marmaduke Gibbon's body from one place to another, I must accept your word — for the moment."

She waited, but no such word was forthcoming. Jarvis Thorpe closed his lips firmly together, his expression resentful. Claydon, by contrast, produced his condescending smile, brows raised in patent mockery.

Ottilia let out a sigh. "Shall I tell you what I know?"

At that, Thorpe took a violent thrust towards the door. "I am not staying to hear this!"

Ottilia signalled to Hemp, who stepped in front of the door, bringing Thorpe up short. He wheeled. "You can't keep me here!"

"Oh, I have no intention of keeping you. Not for long."

He lifted his chin in a gesture of defiance. "Say on then, if you must."

From behind him, Claydon rose and came to flank him, his gaze finding Ottilia's. "You are no doubt very clever, Lady Fan, but you mistake. Marmaduke Gibbon took no harm of either of us."

Ottilia preserved her calm. "While alive, perhaps not."

Botterell, leaping from his seat, came to join them. "He took no harm of me either!"

Hemp shifted and Ottilia was glad to see him move into position by her sofa, facing the trio. Not that she supposed any would offer her violence, but she knew Francis would fly up into the boughs if she had no protector at a moment like this. Her gaze raked across the youthful faces and she was seized by a raft of compassion.

"You poor young things, I am sorry for you. Through no fault of your own, you have been dragged into this affair, have you not? Just as I have. You should know that there is no question of murder as such."

Her auditors, all three, exhibited change at this. Relief was visible in Botterell's face, Jarvis Thorpe's defiance relaxed a little and even Claydon showed signs of interest tempering the spurious contempt he evidently thought proper to adopt.

"However…" She saw them brace again and almost laughed out. "Don't look so apprehensive, gentlemen. Let us be clear. Marmaduke died by cardiac arrest, whatever it was that caused it. That is not a slow death, though it may take some small time to manifest. Thus, he cannot have left your brother's house alive, Mr Thorpe."

No one spoke. The wall of silence would not be breeched. Ottilia gave it up.

"Well, you may go, all of you. Think on my words. You know where to find me."

Having watched the departure of the young men from a vantage point in the gallery above the hall, Lizzy lost no time in making her way to the withdrawing room. She peeped round the door and saw her aunt seated on the sofa, talking with Hemp.

"May I come in now, Aunt?" She had obeyed a strict injunction to remain aloof while Lady Fan questioned the visitors.

Ottilia waved her in. "Yes, come in, Lizzy. Has Pretty gone back to the nursery?"

"Hepsie came for her half an hour ago. She was mightily displeased that I allowed the child to share my beef."

Ottilia laughed. "Hepsie keeps her on a child's diet, but have no fear, you are not alone. Your uncle has been caught slipping bacon to Pretty when she hides under the table at breakfast while poor Hepsie runs around hunting for her. He has incurred the nurse's scoldings for it, I promise you."

"What, does Uncle Francis endure them?"

"Well, he does come the lord upon occasion, but not within Pretty's hearing. One cannot undermine her nurse's authority."

Lizzy grew impatient. "Well, Aunt? Was your meeting fruitful, while I have been twiddling my thumbs in your eyrie?"

"You could have read one of my books. There are several on top of the bureau." Ottilia's gaze went to the steward. "Thank you, Hemp. I may need you tomorrow, for I suspect I shall be obliged to venture forth if I am to glean anything useful."

"I am always at your service, milady."

Lizzy watched them exchange a smile before Hemp left the room. But her aunt spoke before she could put her eager questions.

"He says that, but I suspect he is beginning to chafe. I fear I will lose him sooner rather than later."

Lizzy plonked down beside her on the sofa. "Didn't you say he must needs marry this Doro girl before he leaves?"

"Not too soon, I hope. She is so good with Luke. I don't know how I should manage without her."

"Well, perhaps he won't go even if they do get married," Lizzy suggested, inwardly impatient of the steward's love life. Especially when her own was wanting. She gave Ottilia no chance to pursue the subject. "What did you discover, Aunt?"

A sigh came. "Nothing of great note. They were close-mouthed. But those two know something."

"Which two? Not that I will know whom you mean."

"Botolf Claydon and Jarvis Thorpe. If they were not involved in moving that corpse, they know a good deal more about it than they were willing to admit."

Lizzy balked. "But why do you think the corpse was moved?"

"I know it was."

"How, Lady Fan? How can you know?"

Ottilia laughed. "Purely by logic, my dear. Marmaduke had no carriage, nor did he seek a ride with another. He allegedly had an assignation, though that I am beginning to doubt, with apparently no means of getting to the rendezvous. Where in the world did he go then, if he was not at Thorpe Grange?"

"So someone took him elsewhere. Is that what you suppose?"

"What I suppose, my dear, is that someone, possibly more than one person, drove his corpse to Wyke Hall and deposited it in the summer house."

Lizzy gazed at her. "But why? Why move it?"

"Oh, merely to shove the problem off upon Vexford. I dare say there were reasons enough for the choice, but I have yet to discover them."

"Then Vexford sent it to you?"

"Gracious, no! That is not in Lord Vexford's style. If I am right, the culprit who involved me is Richenda."

Lizzy threw up her hands. "This goes beyond me, Aunt." She would have spoken further but that the door opened and Vivian Maplewood entered the room.

Lizzy's heart did a little flip and her tongue tied itself into knots. She caught his eye briefly, but he looked away from her at once, focusing on Ottilia.

"I'm afraid I failed to find Pedwardine, ma'am. I waited at the Fox where he lodges for some time, but he put in no appearance."

Lizzy heard her aunt's response only vaguely in the background of her mind, her attention taken up by Vivian's presence, her heartbeat awry.

"Is he still in the vicinity? He has not left the inn?"

"Not to the landlord's knowledge, ma'am." His lip quirked with a touch of amusement in a way Lizzy remembered with fondness from their early encounters. "I did have a small stroke of luck, however."

"How so?"

The grin appeared and Lizzy's heart squeezed in her chest. "Richenda was seen there this morning."

Ottilia gave a crow of delight. "Excellent! Botolf Claydon said he saw her there too. Did you learn anything of what she did there?"

Vivian gave the characteristic shrug, a mere shuffle at his shoulders. "Unfortunately not."

Ottilia fell silent, evidently ruminating and Lizzy was caught out staring at Vivian when he turned his head. She looked down in haste. A step sounded and she glanced up to see him retreating to the fireplace. Hurt rose up. Could he not even look her in the eye now?

She was distracted as Ottilia spoke. "I wonder if Mr Pedwardine's absence has anything to do with Richenda?"

Lizzy was moved to protest. "But she doesn't even like him! Didn't you say she objected to his taking Marmaduke away all the time?"

"She said so, yes. But I believe I have been told a number of falsehoods, and that may be one of them. Added to certain statements made by Mr Pedwardine himself." She struck her hands together. "This grows tediously complex. What is that dratted wench up to?"

Lizzy had no answer. Nor, at this present moment, did she care. The urge to force a confrontation with Vivian was strong, only how to do so with her aunt in the room? She had not much time. The letter her uncle had despatched to her papa would have reached its destination. Enough to bring Papa hotfoot to the scene, ready to drag her away. Before that happened, she must talk to Vivian. To know his true feelings, if there was indeed any hope. Or if she should instead despair of him forever.

The very thought sent pricking shards into her bosom and Lizzy at last felt kinship with her cousin Candia, who mooned still over her lost Frenchman. Until this moment, she had cherished scant belief in the reality of Candy's emotions. Yet if she was, like her cousin, obliged to cast all hope of marrying Vivian aside and allow herself to be betrothed to some eligible peer of the realm, she did not know how she could bear it. Not that Candia was as yet engaged, but if Mama had her way, she would be by the end of the Season.

"What do you say, Lizzy?"

She came to herself with a start, blinking into her aunt's face. Vaguely aware of a continuing discussion between Ottilia and Vivian in the background, Lizzy tried to capture what might have been said, and failed. "I'm sorry, Aunt, I was not attending. What do I say to what?"

A faint lift of the eyebrows gave question to her aunt's expression, but she spoke with her usual calm. "Vivian is suggesting it may profit us for you to make acquaintance with Richenda."

"Assuming she can be found," put in Vivian, his gaze at last meeting hers.

Ottilia waved this away. "Oh, I think she will reappear. I set no store by this notion of yours of an elopement, Vivian. Her duenna must know her best and she is adamant Richenda will not so prejudice her own future."

This pulled Lizzy's attention off her own matrimonial hopes and she cast a frowning look at Vivian. "Did you think she had gone off with this Mr Pedwardine then?"

For a wonder, he did not shift his gaze away. "It is a possibility, since he is also missing."

"And she was at the Fox in Wyke, true. But there might be any number of explanations for that." Ottilia turned back to Lizzy. "We know that neither Henrietta nor Virginia cry friends with Richenda. But you, my dear, have just the personality to engage her sympathies."

Lizzy was moved to protest. "You said she is a play-actress. That is not my style at all, Aunt."

"No, but you are both lively and shrewd and you do not hesitate to speak your mind. Richenda, I submit, would find the combination irresistible." Lizzy found herself in receipt of a meaning look as her aunt patted her hand. "Take heart, child." This in a lowered tone. Then, more loudly, "I must see Mrs Bertram before your grandmama returns from Mrs Honeybourne's and comes looking for me. The household is so augmented, my poor housekeeper is growing a trifle frantic."

Ottilia rose on the words, cast a smile towards Vivian and went to the door. Lizzy would swear Ottilia gave her a conspiratorial look before she left the room. Lizzy could not but suppose her aunt meant to give her the opportunity for a tête-à-tête with Vivian. Her heart was behaving in a recalcitrant fashion, but she determined to seize the moment. Before her grandmother put in an appearance and ruined her chance.

Lizzy sprang to her feet, forcing a smile as she looked at her quarry. "I have not been out at all today. Will you walk with me?" Vivian hesitated and she added on a light note, "Or are you wanting a luncheon?"

"I had bread and cheese at the Fox while I was waiting for Pedwardine to put in an appearance."

Lizzy gave him a bright smile. "Then there is no reason to wait. Come with me, Vivian, pray do."

CHAPTER FOURTEEN

Vivian should not have agreed. The situation was complicated enough without the added disadvantage of subjecting himself to Lady Elizabeth's forthright conversation. To do her justice, she had not yet said anything untoward, confining her remarks to the state of the fountain pool, overgrown with weeds around the edges, and the rare appearance of birdlife in this winter landscape.

But Vivian was aware, as he allowed his steps to be guided by her wanderings, that she was meandering away from the terraces, which were plainly overlooked from the house, and heading towards the wilder part of the Flitteris gardens where woodland was kept at bay from encroaching upon the ordered lawns.

"Oh, the snowdrops are out. How pretty!"

An excuse to hurry? She quickened her pace, moving with purpose to the edge of the lower terrace. His senses grew wary. Not that he disliked to be in her company. But letters could be controlled. In person, she was like to speak without restraint. He had tried to remain aloof, but her suggestion could not but appeal to his deeper desires, rigidly controlled.

When she stepped off the lawn into the wooded area, Vivian halted. "We should not go too far afield."

She turned then, regarding him from where she stood, outlined by the wild woodlands behind, appropriate to the rebellious streak Vivian both feared and admired. "Do you suppose I will kidnap you?"

He could not withhold the laughter. "I would not put it past you, Eliza."

The piquant features creased into a smile. "Perhaps I shall then. If that is the only way I may win."

His amusement died. "Lady Elizabeth —"

Her face changed. "Oh, no, Vivian! Never that. Pray don't call me that. If there can be nothing else, let me at least savour being your 'Eliza'."

He tamped down the rise of emotion. "I might know you would not be circumspect."

"So you might." She did not move from where she stood, but her voice took on a plea. "Vivian, my father may come here at any moment. Don't, pray, try to muzzle me. Let me speak freely, just this once."

"Just this once? When have you ever refrained from speaking your mind?"

She looked away and back again. "I can be discreet, you know. Only —"

He ought to ignore it, but instead found himself prompting, "Only?"

"Only this is not the time." Turning, she lifted her skirts a trifle and picked a way further into the woods.

Exasperation seized him as he followed perforce. "Why can't you behave like a normal female?"

"You wouldn't like me if I did," she threw over her shoulder.

It was true, but nevertheless irritating. Vivian chose deflection. "I've not had a chance to draw since I got here, and you are not helping."

She halted, turning on him. "How so? It's not I who sends you off on missions." She swept a hand in an arc to encompass the woods. "Here is a perfect spot. If you had your sketchbook, you could start now."

"Well, I don't have it. I only have you, driving me to distraction."

Her glare pierced him. "I can't think why I even like you, let alone lo—" She broke off and the flush overspreading her features told its own tale.

Vivian had no words. He watched her turn away, moving deeper into the wood. She leaned down and plucked a small white blossom from its stem close to the ground. Cradling it in her fingers, she stared at it for several moments.

The silence grew oppressive. Vivian toyed with the notion of walking away, but he could not bring himself to disappoint her, to be cruel.

All at once, she turned back and took several steps towards him, a look of determination in her face that filled him with immediate foreboding.

"Why won't you marry me, Vivian?"

Shock stopped his tongue. He could only shake his head, unable to think how to answer. Contrary to his expectation, she did not sue for one, only holding his gaze, a world of distress in her eyes.

He cleared his throat. "I didn't think you cared so much."

"Didn't you? Have I been reticent?"

A bitter laugh escaped him. "Anything but."

"Well then?"

He struggled for the right words. "Eliza…" Almost he wished she would speak again, but she said nothing, merely waiting for him to continue. He drew breath. "Marriage isn't as simple as you think it is."

"Why not, Vivian? Why can't it be simple?"

He shrugged. "Convention. Status. Money. They are all part of the contract."

Her features crumpled. "I thought all that didn't matter to you. Is it just a pose then, disregarding convention? The artistic soul is not real, is that it?"

He sighed. "Eliza, it's one thing to be careless of it for myself. It's quite another to drag someone else into sharing my views."

"Me, for instance?"

"Especially you. We inhabit different worlds. You might now deem the values and privileges of your upbringing well lost for love — if we must introduce the word —"

A smile trembled on her lips and he regretted having spoken thus. "At least you said it."

He moved swiftly, catching up to her and seizing one of her hands. "I said it, but I should not have done. Elizabeth, it won't work! Can't you see that? Give it a few years and you will yearn for the balls and parties, the fashionable life."

"How can you know that? Have you asked me?"

He ignored this, sweeping on. "I'm a countryman at heart. I can't bear all that pomp and ceremony, the futility of such a life. I can't give you that for I won't endure to live that way. All I want is to wander so that I may draw, until the day I am obliged to take up my place and run Maplewood, and may that day be far distant. My father is a man in excellent health and I don't anticipate being obliged to take his place for many a long year. Until then…"

He faded out, becoming aware that tears were trickling down her cheeks. She did not sob or sniff, but the wetness threw havoc into his breast.

"Don't weep, Eliza! I am not worth your tears."

She did sniff then, releasing her hand from his and dashing her fingers across her cheeks. "It is for me to judge your worth to me, Vivian. I'm not crying for you. I'm weeping because you are so selfish you won't even give me a choice. I would not have believed it of you. You are not the man I thought you were."

She picked her way past him without looking at him again. Vivian watched her as she reached the lawn and began a swift return up the terraces towards the house.

Her words lingered in his mind and heart, the latter abruptly and painfully bereft.

Hurting too much even to think, Lizzy hurried blindly up the terraces, retracing the steps she had made with such desperate hope so short a time ago. Instinct guided her feet, the one aim in her head to reach her aunt and succour. Ottilia would know how to help her.

As she breasted the final rise to the drive, a movement on its sweep touched the periphery of her vision. Lizzy halted and turned in that direction. A figure was coming down the gravelled approach to the house. Its condition impinged upon Lizzy's senses, driving her own concerns out of mind. A woman in riding dress, hatless, dark locks dishevelled, one hand holding up her petticoats as she all but staggered in a stumbling run.

"Heavens above," Lizzy murmured as she picked up her own skirts and took off to the rescue. She called out as she ran. "Wait there! I am coming to help you!"

The woman's uneven steps slowed and stopped. She stood swaying and Lizzy's brain ticked into gear as she noted the stained garments, the ripped neck-cloth and the streaks of dirt on the woman's face. As she reached her, Lizzy put out her hands to the woman's shoulders, grasping her strongly.

"Steady, now, steady. I have you safe."

A pair of large brown eyes, in a face lovely even under the pallor and dirt, focused on Lizzy. "Lady Fan?"

"I will take you to her presently. Come, lean on me." She went to the woman's side and slipped an arm about her, taking her weight. Her figure was both taller and more robust than Lizzy's, but it was plain from the gasping breaths that she had run some distance. "There. We will go slowly."

The woman consented to be led along and Lizzy ventured upon the urgent questions teeming in her brain. "How came you to this? What happened? Did you take a fall from your horse?"

A slanting glance came her way. "Who are you? I have not seen you before."

"I am Lizzy Fiske, Lady Fan's niece." If the woman had taken this in it was not apparent in the appraising look she gave. Then she was not wholly debilitated. A flip of memory threw question into Lizzy's head. Could it be? She wasted no time. "May I know your name?"

The woman drew an unsteady breath. "I am Richenda Vexford, and my father is going to kill me."

So this female was the cause of all the rumpus. Lizzy made haste to pour a damper over the exaggerated remark. "Of course your father will not kill you. He is out looking for you, however. My uncle went to help him in the search. Where in the world have you been?"

Richenda, despite her sad state, jerked a rebellious head. "I rode out for a breath of freedom. He has kept me locked up for days."

"Then you took a toss, is that it?"

Richenda grew haughty. "Nothing of the kind. My Raven would never throw me. It is all the fault of that horrid man."

"Which horrid man?"

"Percy Pedwardine and I wish very much I had never sued to him for help."

Her mind working, Lizzy drew Richenda towards the arched front door, becoming aware as she did so that Vivian was standing in the porch. All the upset of their encounter washed back, but his aspect was more of question than constraint.

"I have rung the bell. Is this the errant Richenda, by any chance?"

In spite of all, Lizzy was impressed with his immediate comprehension. "Yes, it is. She is asking for Lady Fan."

Richenda halted, staring at Vivian. "Who is this?"

He bowed. "I am Maplewood, ma'am. Your father is out searching for you."

"She knows. I already told her. And pray don't speak of it, for she is afraid of what he may do."

Richenda reared up. "I am not in the least afraid of Papa. Let him do his worst, I care not."

To Lizzy's relief, the door opened at this moment, revealing the footman in the aperture. "Tyler, thank goodness! Pray let us in, and explain Miss Vexford's sorry situation to her ladyship and ask her to come down to the morning room."

She ushered the fugitive to the small room to one side of the chequered hall, the footman darting ahead to open the door for them. Lizzy detained him before entering. "One more thing, Tyler. Would you have someone bring refreshments to this room?" She glanced at the wilting Richenda. "Tea, I think." Then she swept the woman in and deposited her on the sofa.

Richenda sank against its cushioned back in an attitude of exhaustion, closing her eyes.

Vivian spoke quietly behind Lizzy. "Shall I send a message to Vexford, do you think?"

Lizzy jumped. She had not noticed him follow them into the room. But she knew the answer to this. "No, don't. Wait until Aunt Ottilia has spoken to her. She will decide what is best to do."

"But the fellow will be frantic."

Richenda's eyes flew open. "Let him worry over me! It is no more than he deserves."

Regardless of their earlier confrontation, Lizzy was moved to exchange a glance with Vivian. It warmed her to see the same hint of amusement in his face that she felt. Had not Ottilia said this woman was a play-actress? And she was to befriend her, Lizzy recalled belatedly. How fortuitous she had chosen precisely that moment to appear.

Before she could take any action, Vivian addressed Richenda. "Miss Vexford, what were you doing at the Fox in Wyke?"

The lovely eyes appraised him in a predatory look that caused a stab in Lizzy's bosom. Did the wretched female now seek to add Vivian to her conquests? How dared she?

"I wanted to speak with Mr Pedwardine." Richenda's gaze grew stormy. "But I mistook his character. Oh, he made a pretence of sympathy, promised he would speak of Marmaduke, but he lied!"

"How so?"

Irritation rose up in Lizzy. Was Vivian determined to wrest this opportunity from her? But the response was nevertheless enlightening.

"He said I should not be riding alone and he would escort me. I waited for him to have a horse saddled and we rode out together. The more fool me to have trusted him."

Richenda stopped, throwing a hand to her head in a gesture of dismay or despair, Lizzy could not judge which. In a bid to recapture her position, she applied a prompt. "What happened? What did he do to you?"

Richenda's hand came down and her eyes flared. "He attacked me, the brute!"

"Attacked you?" Lizzy waved her hand in a gesture to encompass Richenda's dishevelled costume. "Do you mean he did all this?"

Richenda made no direct answer, returning to her plaint. "I thought he meant to talk to me of Marmaduke, to help me recover from my grief. I wanted to hear about him, you see. I needed to hear. But instead he ... he..."

She threw her hands over her face and Lizzy could not but feel sceptical. Extravagant gestures belonged rather to the theatre than to life. She glanced at Vivian and noted, to her secret satisfaction, an equally disbelieving glint and a raised eyebrow. Reticent to a fault, Vivian was never an admirer of emotional display. A characteristic no doubt engendered by his disgust at the violent theatricality of certain members of his family.

Before Lizzy could question Richenda further, the door opened to admit Tyler, armed with a tray, along with one of the maids bearing the tea-kettle.

"Oh, thank you, Tyler. Pray set it all down and I will do the honours." Lizzy noted how Richenda, apparently recovered, watched the servants lay out the accoutrements for tea. Lizzy was pleased to see several cups had been supplied. She could do with one herself. She stopped the footman as he crossed to the door. "Tyler, is my aunt coming down?"

He paused, looking back. "Her ladyship is a trifle occupied, but she said she would join you as soon as she could."

He left the room on the words and Lizzy moved to the table where the tea things had been set and sat down on the chair beside it. "We will soon have you feeling more the thing, Richenda. Do you take sugar and cream in your tea?"

A rather hysterical laugh came from Richenda. "Tea? Sugar and cream? After all I have been through, I cannot even think of it."

Forgetting their earlier exchange, Lizzy threw an exasperated glance at Vivian. He returned it with a smile and went to perch beside Richenda on the sofa.

"I suggest at least sugar will prove efficacious, Miss Vexford. Sweet tea is a known remedy for shock."

Richenda gave him a limpid look and Lizzy was moved to empty the boiling water from the tea kettle into the pot in such a rush that she almost spilled it over the edge.

"You are very kind," said Richenda, batting her lashes.

Lizzy upended a cup and dumped it into the saucer with unnecessary force. She picked up a spoon and stirred the tea in the pot, aware of a treacherous thought of slipping a trifle of poison into the delicately coloured liquid.

"Can you tell us more about how that hound of a Pedwardine upset you?"

Vivian's sympathetic tone, as much as the words, made Lizzy long to fling the contents of the sugar bowl in his direction. Was this ridiculous manner, so unlike his normal one, meant for mockery? Or had he, like so many others by all accounts, succumbed to the beauty's allure?

Richenda, rather to Lizzy's glee, supplied yet another evasive answer. "He was unkind and cruel. I could not endure it and I ran away from him."

Vivian's brows drew together. "Did he molest you, ma'am?"

Richenda blinked. "Molest? He attacked me!"

"Yes, but in what manner?" A trifle of impatience sounded in Vivian's voice and Lizzy's jealous qualms began to abate.

"In a cruel manner, berating me horridly. Was it my fault Marmaduke died? Did I lay a hand on him? No, I did not! Yet to hear Percy Pedwardine, you would suppose I had struck the blow."

Lizzy had just poured tea into a cup and was in the act of picking up a lump of sugar with the tongs, but her hand stilled and she looked across at Richenda. "What blow?"

Richenda's pose of outraged womanhood dropped out and she stared across at Lizzy. "There was a blow. Lady Fan said so. Someone dealt him a blow."

The action automatic, Lizzy dropped the lump of sugar into the cup. "True, but it is not proven that Marmaduke died from it."

Richenda's gaze grew round. "He didn't? I quite thought... Then, if it was not the blow, what was it?"

The change from despairing victim to matter-of-fact enquiry was marked. More than ever Lizzy was convinced Richenda's unsatisfactory account was suspect. Could one believe anything she said?

Vivian answered the query. "I understand it is not yet determined, but the doctor in the case stated that it was definitely cardiac arrest."

Lizzy rose and brought the cup and saucer across. "Here, drink this, Richenda. I have stirred it already."

Richenda took it, picked up the cup and sipped. A perfectly radiant smile came. "Thank you, that is much better."

After one sip? It was evident Richenda was recovering from whatever ordeal had actually occurred. Difficult to determine what that might have been. That she had been in enough distress to come running for Lady Fan was clear, but how much of that was to be laid at the door of Mr Pedwardine remained a question.

Returning to her chair, Lizzy upended another cup and looked at Vivian. "Do you want one?"

He declined, dropping his gaze to his folded hands laid across his thighs. Lizzy felt the returning constraint and her hand shook a little as she poured tea for herself. Feeling in need, she added a lump of sugar and stirred. The hot liquid put heart into her and she was just about to resume questioning Richenda when the door opened to admit Lady Fan at last.

Ottilia's gaze swept across the scene and focused on Richenda. She took in the disturbing state of her clothing, noting in passing that Vivian had risen on her entrance from a seat beside the beauty. Did this signal trouble between him and Lizzy? Filing that away for the moment, she crossed to the sofa.

"My dear child, what in the world has happened?"

Richenda threw out her hands as though she would clutch at Ottilia. "Lady Fan! I came to you. Will you help me?"

Ottilia was tempted to enter a caveat to say it depended on what was required of her. "If I can. But will you not first explain how it comes to be that you arrive here on foot, and in some distress. We knew you were out riding, you see."

Richenda flung back into the sofa, throwing a wild gesture towards Lizzy. "Ask her! I have told her all. I cannot repeat it."

As Ottilia turned to her niece, Lizzy spoke, in a good deal of indignation. "You have by no means told me all, Richenda." Her gaze, sparkling with wrath, shifted to Ottilia. "All she would say is that Mr Pedwardine escorted her —"

"Because he thought she should not be riding alone, quite rightly."

Vivian's interruption did nothing to improve matters. Lizzy became irate. "She asked me, Vivian!"

"I'm trying to help, that's all."

"Well, you need not. I am quite capable of telling it myself."

Ottilia threw up her hands. "Children, children, if you please!" Reflecting that the tête-à-tête she had fostered could not have gone well, she ignored Lizzy's glare and Vivian's tight-lipped smoulder and took a seat beside Richenda, whose eyes had gone from one to the other in a frowning glance. Was she jealous to have lost the centre of attention?

"Come, Richenda. It will be best if you tell me yourself, do you not think? You met Mr Pedwardine at the Fox, I take it?"

Richenda sat up and faced her. "I went there to find him. I wanted to hear about Marmaduke."

"What precisely did you want to hear?"

Richenda's dark gaze played over her face. "I don't know what you mean."

Ottilia strove for patience. "Did you want to hear about his death? About his last moments?"

Richenda looked away, veiling her gaze. "Not that."

"What then?"

A deep sigh came and Richenda spread her hands. "I wanted to hear about his life. I needed to hear, to talk of him, to keep his memory alive."

This was said in a tragic tone in which Ottilia placed scant belief. Were they back to that pretence? "Mr Pedwardine was willing?"

The gaze came back to her, soulful now. "He said he was. We rode together for a time and I asked him — oh, all manner of questions."

"Did he answer?"

"At first. But then he became surly and rude. He blamed me. He said if I had not been in question, Marmaduke would still be alive. But how can that be? I did not strike the blow, I told him. But he would not listen."

Ottilia weighed the words for truth and found them wanting. What had Richenda said to provoke Percy Pedwardine's ire? On the other hand, his reason for accompanying her did not accord with his alleged dislike of the wench. Ottilia probed for more. "How was it you came off your horse?"

"I did not come off. I dismounted. Raven was frightened by that horrid man shouting at me and she ran off. I chased after her, but I fell."

At this point, Lizzy intervened. "I thought you said you ran away from Mr Pedwardine."

"I did! Of course I ran away from him. He chased me."

"While you were chasing your horse?" Disbelief was rife in Lizzy's voice and Ottilia could not blame her.

"He was on horseback. I could not outrun him, could I?"

"So you fell as he was chasing you?"

"He shouted that he would go after Raven. So he should. It was his fault the poor beast ran away."

This time it was Vivian who put his oar in. "Then why did you not wait? Why come here?"

Richenda's gaze went from one to the other. "I needed Lady Fan." Her eyes found Ottilia's. "Only you can help me, I know that now."

"I fear that is true." Ottilia reached for one of Richenda's hands and held it tightly. "Is it not time you told me the truth, my dear?"

"I have told you all."

"Not quite all." Ottilia drew a determined breath and brought it out, albeit in a gentle tone. "It was you who sent Marmaduke to me, was it not?"

Richenda's cheeks drained of colour. Her voice was a hoarse whisper. "How did you guess?" Then she wrenched her fingers free and threw both hands over her face, breaking into sobs.

Genuine this time, Ottilia believed. She made no attempt to proffer comfort, but rose from the sofa.

"Vivian, will you send to Wyke Hall to let Lord Vexford know that his daughter is safe."

To her secret satisfaction, Vivian snapped smartly to attention. "I'll go myself. I'll take my curricle."

"Excellent." Ottilia watched him leave the room before turning to Lizzy, who had jumped up and taken her place beside Richenda, putting an arm about her. "Yes, well done, Lizzy. I think the best thing you can do is to take Richenda to your chamber and get her cleaned up. I dare say she is hungry too. A bowl of broth, perhaps. Mrs Bertram will arrange something. We will re-assemble in the withdrawing room when you are ready."

Lizzy did not move at once, speaking low despite Richenda's noisy weeping. "Don't you mean to get the rest of the tale?"

"Not just now, my dear. Let the girl recover first. Time enough to turn the thumbscrews when she is feeling more the thing."

CHAPTER FIFTEEN

Electing to accompany Lord Vexford to his home, just to be sure his errant daughter had not returned, Francis was both gratified and alarmed by the tale related by the fellow's groom.

"Miss Richenda's horse come in without her, my lord. I was just about to send a party out to look for her."

Vexford seemed less concerned than did Francis. "Ha! Raven found her way home, did she? Good for her."

The groom, looking up to where Vexford still sat his mount, touched his forelock. "Begging your pardon, my lord, but it weren't like that, not exactly."

"What the deuce d'you mean, man? The beast came in without his mistress, you said."

"Yes, my lord, but young Sam says as he saw her led up to the gates by a gentleman and turned loose there."

Vexford's features became suffused and Francis cut in before the man's temper could explode. "Did Sam see who it was?"

The groom gave another brief salute of recognition as he turned his attention to Francis. "If he seen him, my lord, he didn't nowise recognise him. 'Sides, he were mounted hisself and rode off smartish by Sam's account."

Vexford grunted, the promised outburst averted. "Trust you've seen to Raven's needs, Baines?"

"Yes, my lord. Rubbed down and watered. She were steaming and skittish, but she's quieted down now, munching at her oats, she is."

Had the wretched fellow no thought for his daughter? If she'd been in company with this man, where the devil was she now? Francis took up the point since Vexford appeared not to think of it. "Are you certain Miss Richenda has not come in unbeknownst, Baines?"

The groom's features became anxious. "Pretty sure, my lord. The whole house has been turned out, checking the grounds and all. Saxby ain't come back yet — Miss Richenda's personal groom he is — so he must be still out hunting for his mistress. He went off along of his lordship when we knew she'd gone off."

"When did this gentleman return the horse?"

"Not more'n fifteen minutes gone, my lord. I'd to see to miss's Raven first, but a call has gone out to gather the men for a search party."

Francis looked at his companion of the morning. "What do you wish, Vexford? I am content to ride out again, if you think it will answer. We might separate and take different directions perhaps."

But, to his consternation, Vexford threw his leg over the saddle and dismounted, handing the reins to the groom. "Take him. Serve him well." Then, to Francis, glinting up at him, "Go home, sir. The girl will find her way."

Francis became tart. "She won't if she's lying in the woods somewhere. If her horse came home without her —"

"Brought home, Lord Francis."

"All the more reason for concern, I should have thought. Especially when the fellow who deposited the horse here did not stay to explain himself. Does not that suggest to you a suspicious circumstance?"

Vexford snorted. "Suspicious? No, sir. It suggests my girl was up to her tricks. D'you think I'm going to waste my time on a fruitless hunt. She'll come home by and by, I tell you."

Francis was tired and irascible from hunger. He let fly. "This is callous beyond words! If my daughter was in such trouble, I should move heaven and earth to find her."

"Your daughter, Fanshawe — if you insist upon dubbing that brat of yours in such wise — is but an infant. You'll know better when she's grown and determined to flout you at every turn."

Seething, not least at the insulting terms in which the wretch spoke of Pretty, Francis turned instead to the groom, standing by in obvious awed and avid fascination. Had he never seen his master taken at fault before? "Send out your party, Baines. You may make a search in the immediate vicinity. I will try further afield."

"You'll do no such thing, Baines! How dare you, sir? I give the orders in my home, Fanshawe."

About to retort with some heat, Francis was distracted by the sound of a vehicle on the approach to Wyke Hall. He shifted in the saddle and turned to look. "This may be Richenda now. Perhaps she has been picked up by some passing carriage."

A glance showed him Vexford had taken note, for he moved out from beside Francis's mount, which was obscuring his view of the road beyond the drive, and raised a hand to shade his eyes. A curricle came into sight, but in a very short time, as it came down the drive and neared, Francis saw it contained only one man and a groom up behind. Disappointed, he was about to remark upon it when he recognised the driver. "Good grief, it's Maplewood!" Without more ado, he set spur to his horse and rode up to the curricle, which was slowing. "What's to do, my young friend?" A premonition struck, not altogether welcome. "Have you news of Richenda?"

Vivian brought the curricle to a halt. "Yes, sir, she's at Flitteris."

"Oh, for pity's sake!"

Vivian's gaze travelled on to where Vexford still stood, his expression unreadable. "My lord Vexford, I am sent by Lady Francis to advise you that your daughter is safe."

Instead of expressing relief or satisfaction, Vexford gave forth another of his explosive snorts. "What the devil is the wench doing there?"

Exasperated, Francis cut in. "Can you not even now be pleased to learn your daughter is secure? What ails you, man? Don't you care?"

At this, the man looked affronted. "Care? Of course I care! I've warned her not to hobnob with that Lady Fan of yours, and now look!"

Francis rode back to him, itching to use his whip on the man. "I've had enough of your insults, Vexford. Speak of my wife in such terms just once more, and you will answer to me at the business end of a pistol."

Before Vexford could answer, Francis found Vivian had driven up beside him, speaking in a lowered tone. "Have patience, my lord! Is he worth your ire?"

"Far from it." Controlling the savagery in his breast, Francis looked down at Vexford, who appeared to be indifferent to his threat. "We will return your daughter to you in due course, sir. Though if I were she, I should make all haste to marry and escape your despotic and miserable rule." He then turned to Vivian, ignoring the gobbling sounds coming from his quarry. "Go into the house and beg Miss Poynton to return with you. It is her business to take care of Richenda, since her parent is signally incapable of doing anything other than rail at the child."

Vexford found his tongue. "Get off my land, sir! I need no man's advice on how to handle my own flesh and blood."

"I will depart with the greatest of pleasure, sir." Francis gave an ironic bow, watching as Vivian drove on. He hoped Vexford would not interfere in the project to bring the duenna away, but he was far from sanguine.

"Well? Are you going?"

Francis returned his gaze to the ruddy features below him. "I'm going. But I warn you that if I find your hand behind this Marmaduke business, you will hear about it. Moreover, you will answer to a magistrate." With which parting shot, he wheeled his horse and set him to a canter, thinking hard thoughts of his erstwhile riding companion and conscious of a good deal of sympathy for the unfortunate Richenda.

"Are you sure you do not wish to eat something, Sybilla?"

The dowager, who had plonked down into Ottilia's customary chair, which she had appropriated for her own since her arrival, set a hand to her stomach and made a face. "After the plethora of cake and macaroons that Honey woman saw fit to stuff down my throat? No, I thank you. I am full to the brim. No tea either, if you are about to suggest that."

Ottilia laughed in a dutiful fashion, casting about in her head for some other way to be rid of her mother-in-law before Lizzy brought Richenda into the withdrawing room. "A glass of your favourite port then? I could send one up to your bedchamber if you wish to rest."

A beady eye was bent upon her. "What are you at, girl? What has occurred to have you fretting like a cat on a hot bakestone?"

Ottilia sighed. "Oh, very well. I might have guessed it would prove impossible to dislodge you."

"Ha! That is your game, is it? Well, make up your mind to it. I am going nowhere. What is afoot?"

Ottilia capitulated. "Richenda Vexford turned up here."

"The missing one?"

"Just so." She gave Sybilla a succinct account of the events that had unfolded at Flitteris while she was upon her errand to Mrs Honeybourne.

Sybilla grunted at the end and stared into the fire for a moment, before turning her black gaze back on Ottilia. "You really think she sent the corpse to you?"

"She as good as admitted as much." Ottilia became brisk. "But never mind that now. How did you fare with Mrs Honeybourne?"

Sybilla threw up her eyes. "Do not ask me to visit that female again, I charge you. A more scramble-headed creature I have yet to meet. My Harriet has a butterfly mind, but I would back my daughter against that Honey woman any day. Her mind is such a hodgepodge, I doubt she is able to hold two thoughts together without flitting off in some other direction."

Ottilia could not withstand a gurgle. "She is scatter-brained, I grant you. But said she anything of use?"

"How in the world could I tell? She flitted from this one to that in a heartbeat. I was scarce able to keep track of the names."

Becoming tart, Ottilia rapped her knuckles together. "Oh, come, Sybilla, that is poppycock, as you would say yourself. There is none shrewder than you. I am quite sure you made something out of her discourse, no matter how meandering it might be."

A somewhat sheepish smile appeared. "Well, I did, of course."

"I knew it. Let me have it, if you please."

Sybilla grew business-like. "The woman is terrified her nephew may be blamed. It seems this young Aubrey whatever his name is —"

"Aubrey Botterell."

"Yes, he. I will wager he is just such a chatterbox as his aunt for he seems to have blabbed the whole story to her, in some detail, of his argument with the dead man."

Ottilia's senses prickled. "Did you remark anything in particular?" She held up a finger as the dowager's features grew indignant. "I do not expect a verbatim report, Sybilla, so pray don't snap my nose off. I feel sure you will have noted any part of it that might be significant."

A bark of laughter escaped her mother-in-law. "I begin to think you know me rather better than I supposed."

"I have your measure, ma'am."

Sybilla wafted a hand. "Don't ma'am me, my child. Not in private at least."

"Well?"

Sybilla sat back in her chair, setting her fingers together in a steeple. "According to Honeybourne's account, if I unravelled it correctly, Aubrey did indeed take a swing at this Marmaduke. More than one, I suspect. She deprecates his temperament, which is readily inflamed."

Satisfaction entered Ottilia's breast. "Noticeably. I should rather call him excitable, but he is certainly capable of losing control."

"So Honeybourne said, with much embellishment and a tendency to shed tears over the boy. What is more, he is one of these young men who attend Mendoza's boxing academy."

"Mendoza?"

"One of these champion fighters. I have heard Randal speak of him. Francis will know, if you wish for more on the subject."

"I may well ask him. If Aubrey Botterell has knowledge of boxing, he might deliver a judicious blow and know just where to aim."

"You suppose he meant to injure that fellow?"

"I expect he at least wished to hurt Marmaduke. I acquit him of a desire to kill." Ottilia eyed her mother-in-law. "Was there anything else?"

Sybilla gave a sly smile. "You are too shrewd. It seems the two other young men acted differently. One that Honeybourne called Jarvis tried to defuse the situation, but Lady Stoke Rochford's godson egged on the aggressor."

So Botolf Claydon had been instrumental in adding fuel to the flames. It accorded with the impression Ottilia had gleaned of his character. But there was another in the case. "What of Mr Pedwardine? Where was he in all this?"

Sybilla spread her hands. "I cannot tell you. All the Honeybourne could say was that Aubrey did not blame him. More, he thought Marmaduke had brought him along on purpose to occupy the other girls so that he might have a clear field with Richenda."

"Unlikely, I think, but no doubt Aubrey might take that view. He did not say whether Pedwardine took Marmaduke's side or tried to intervene?"

"Not that I could tell. The burden of his complaint centred on Marmaduke's conquest, his perfidy, his flaunting his handsome face and all manner of just that sort of nonsense one might expect from a young man thwarted in love."

"Or ambition." Ottilia stared into space, her mind working. She spoke absently. "I am not persuaded that any one of these young men cherishes true affection for Richenda. I suspect she knows it too. Underneath her tendency to histrionics, she is remarkably acute. A pity she has such a dreadful father. She might have turned out quite otherwise under a different rule. It will take a kind and clever man with strength of character to effect any real change in her, I fear."

The door opened before Sybilla could answer, and Ottilia experienced a lift of spirits and a fillip at her heart as her own very kind, exceptionally clever and decidedly strong husband entered the room. Oddly moved to realise her good fortune all over again, she held out a hand to him. "My darling, welcome! I am so sorry you have had a fruitless chase."

He nodded a greeting to his mother as he crossed the room and took Ottilia's hand, but he did not sit. "Not altogether fruitless, but let that wait. I came in but to let you know I am home. I must rid myself of the stench of horse."

Sybilla spoke from her chair, addressing Ottilia. "Do you allow him to enter your withdrawing room in all his dirt?"

Ottilia rose, keeping hold of her spouse's hand. "It is his house. He may do as pleases." And to Francis. "I will come with you."

He had flicked his eyes heavenwards at his mother's remark but he pressed her hand and released it. "No, stay. Maplewood will be back at any moment with that girl's duenna."

"Sybilla will entertain her." Ottilia cast a mischievous glance at the dowager, adding, "Will you not, my dear mama-in-law?"

A snort was all the answer she received as Ottilia followed Francis from the room and halted outside, leaving the door ajar. She touched a hand to his chest, her heart aglow with affection. "You ought to eat something, my dearest dear. I am sure you are hungry."

"Ravenous. I told Rodmell to have bread and beef sent up."
He cocked an eyebrow. "Whence all this tenderness, my dear one?"

Ottilia smiled up into the brown eyes. "Only that I remembered how lucky I am, and how very much I love you." She reached up on tiptoe and kissed his lips.

He returned the kiss with interest and dropped another on her forehead for good measure. "I can't hug you, sweetheart. I reek of the stables. But hold to that thought for later."

Ottilia gurgled. "I look forward to it."

She shifted back a step, but Francis did not immediately leave her. His brows drew together. "I have a letter from Gil, by the by."

"Dalesford? In answer to yours about Lizzy and Maplewood, I surmise. What does he say?"

"I've not had a chance to read it properly, but the gist is as I supposed. He relies on me to stop any nonsense in the meantime, but we may expect him in short order."

A spurt of exasperation seized Ottilia. "As if we had not enough persons in the house! Did you tell him we are in the midst of this crisis?"

"What do you think? I could not have him descending upon us without knowledge of the business. The only comment I noted in my hurry was Gil's conviction that Lizzy would embroil herself in the matter without any loss of time."

"As of course she did. But Maplewood has been useful, I will say." Ottilia refrained from mentioning her earlier attempt to throw the pair together in hopes of their settling their differences, since it seemed to have gone awry.

The front door bell sounded and Francis became fidgety. "Hell and damnation, that is likely the boy now. Let us hope he managed to persuade Miss Poynton to accompany him." He began to move off. "I'd best make myself scarce."

Ottilia detained him. "Will you come down when you are done, Fan?"

"I must see Pretty, but yes. I promised her a story before bedtime tonight and Lord knows how I shall fit it in."

He went off towards the gallery above the stairs and vanished down the corridor towards their private apartments. Ottilia watched him out of sight and then looked over the banister as Rodmell opened the front door. A faded lady entered with Vivian Maplewood close behind. Ottilia's mind returned to the puzzle confronting her as she went back into the withdrawing room.

From a chair opposite the sofa, where she had seated herself in order to command a good view of both Richenda and her chaperon Ottilia surveyed the pair. Miss Poynton and her charge were seated side by side with Lizzy flanking the beauty. Vivian had made himself scarce after performing the introductions, but Sybilla remained in situ, her black gaze trained upon the visitors.

"I trust you are feeling more yourself, Richenda?"

In fact Richenda was unusually subdued, but she answered in a more normal manner than hitherto. "Yes, thank you, ma'am. Lizzy has been kind."

Her niece cast a speaking glance at Ottilia, from which she deduced that the half hour or so spent in Richenda's company had been somewhat trying. To her credit, Lizzy had managed to make Richenda look respectable again, for the splashes of mud and dirt had been removed from her habit and a fresh neck-cloth was visible beneath the jacket. Loaned by Lizzy in all likelihood. Richenda's hair was brushed and tidied though she had left it loose.

"I hope you have some food inside you, my dear."

"Oh, yes, thank you."

Miss Poynton here spoke up. "She has a good appetite as a rule, my lady, but riding often makes her queasy."

Richenda did not look at her duenna, although her hand was resting in the elder lady's. "I wasn't queasy. Not on the mare. Running so fast made me weak."

"Well, I am glad you feel more rested." Ottilia homed in on the pertinent matter. "Will you tell me what really happened after the Twelfth Night Party?"

Richenda hesitated, glancing at Miss Poynton, who gave her an encouraging smile. "Come, my dear, it is better to tell it all."

Richenda looked across to Ottilia. "You won't tell my father?"

"Not if he does not need to know."

The girl heaved a sigh. "Very well."

Ottilia waited but no further word was forthcoming. She applied a prompt. "I know you tried to go to the summer house that night." She noted the little shiver that shook Richenda. "Did you have an assignation?"

The answer came low-voiced. "Yes — but not with Marmaduke."

"With whom then?"

"Percy Pedwardine."

Ottilia blinked. This was unexpected. Both Lizzy and the duenna exclaimed.

"*What*? Then you lied!"

"Great heavens, Richenda, why could you not have said so?"

Ottilia cut in fast. "Leave the child be, if you please." Satisfied of their remaining silent, and grateful to Sybilla for saying nothing at all, Ottilia kept her gaze upon the blushing beauty. "Why did you make an assignation with Mr Pedwardine?"

Richenda shrugged. "Oh, to make Marmaduke jealous. To serve him out for flirting with Virginia."

Ottilia watched her face and felt dissatisfied. "No, my dear, that is far too simplistic. Moreover, it is not in your style. What was the real reason?"

Richenda's head came up, the brown eyes full of distress. "I had no desire for a rendezvous with him. I thought he would tell Marmaduke and that Marmaduke would come instead."

"But you could not get to the summer house, so you don't know which of them came, is that it?"

Richenda's gaze became luminous. "But I do! I went there in the morning as soon as I could escape without Papa seeing me. I hoped he would have left a note."

"Pedwardine?"

"Marmaduke. I was so sure he would come and I was right. I found him in there..." Her voice failed.

Lizzy's sparkling eyes were eager and Miss Poynton's shock was patent. Ottilia held up a finger and shook it a little to prevent either speaking. She waited.

At length, Richenda spoke again, her tone pathetic with the true distress that must have attacked her then. "Marmaduke was sitting in a chair. He was dead." She covered her face with her hands and the duenna put her arms about her and held her, hushing her in soothing whispers.

Lizzy was clearly bursting to say something, but her lips were obediently folded. Ottilia spared a glance for her mother-in-law and found her narrowed gaze trained upon the beauty. Sybilla trying to fathom whether Richenda spoke the truth? Ottilia was no longer in doubt. It had been as she supposed. Now it behoved her to discover how Marmaduke had arrived at his final destination.

"Richenda!"

She sat up in a bang, the look she cast at Ottilia fearful. "Yes?"

"When you saw Mr Pedwardine today, what did you truly want with him?"

Richenda began to revive. "I told you what occurred."

"Yes, but you did not go solely to ask him about Marmaduke's life, did you?"

Richenda had the grace to look shame-faced. "I wanted to find out what he had said to Marmaduke, but of course I could not ask him outright."

"Because you feared to tell him you found Marmaduke dead in the summer house?"

"I did not mean to tell anyone. I would not have if —"

"If I had not guessed at it. Yes, I understand that. What did you ask then?"

Richenda sighed. "I told him I came to apologise because Papa had prevented me from meeting him in the summer house."

"What said he?"

Richenda's lip curled. "That I would have found it empty in any event for he never intended to meet me. He was very rude."

Lizzy chimed in, evidently unable any longer to keep silent. "But he escorted you just the same."

"He did. I accepted of his escort because I hoped he might tell me how it was that Marmaduke came in his stead. But he didn't. Instead, he berated me. He said I had played fast and loose with Marmaduke's affections, trying to get up a flirtation with him. I was so provoked I told him I never did wish to see him and that I hoped he would have told Marmaduke. He said … he said…"

"He said, I surmise," put in Ottilia on a dry note, "that he would not distress his friend by informing him of the perfidy of his inamorata."

Miss Poynton's sharp intake of breath was echoed in Richenda's cry. "He did say so! He would not believe me when I told him I only said it so that he would tell Marmaduke and then Marmaduke would come to me. He said I was a shocking flirt and his friend was dead because of me. But it's not true, it's not true!"

Wishful thinking, but Ottilia refrained from saying so. There could be no doubt Richenda bore a large part of the blame, but it was clear she was not given to that sort of self-examination that would enable her to see it. However, that was beside the bridge. Percy Pedwardine had been less than truthful in his account to Ottilia and she wanted to know the reason why. She would not find it out from the beauty, that was plain. Instead, she moved on to the aftermath.

"So, let us shift our focus, my dear. After you found Marmaduke, what did you do?"

Richenda became agitated. "I did not know what to do. I did not dare go to Papa."

"You could have come to me, Richenda." There was hurt in the duenna's tone. "I would have helped you."

"What could you have done, Pinny?"

"Buried him? I don't know."

Ottilia intervened. "That would not have answered, Miss Poynton, as I am sure you must know."

Richenda sniffed. "I did think of asking the gardeners to do it, but they would not have complied and Papa would find out."

"So what did you do, Richenda? Marmaduke's body did not arrive at my house until the early evening."

Richenda studiously examined the fingers clenched in her lap. "I locked the door and left him there." Her gaze came up, pleading now. "I had to think and I could not while he … while he… I walked, I don't recall where. At last I thought of you, Lady Fan."

I am obliged. But Ottilia did not say it. "You did not lift a man's corpse onto the back of a horse by yourself."

Richenda shuddered. "I could not have touched him. I told Saxby."

Miss Poynton gave another gasp. "Your groom knew?"

"I had to tell someone. I knew Saxby would never betray me. He promised to do what was needful."

"Bring Marmaduke to me, you mean? Was it you who wrote the label to 'Lady Fan', Richenda?"

She gave a quick nod. "I gave it to Saxby. He did everything."

Alone? Or had he an accomplice, another groom conspirator? It would take a deal of effort to heave the dead man onto the back of a horse. Unless he could induce the animal to bend the knee sufficiently for the purpose?

"After we had dined, I found opportunity to go out to the stables. I found Saxby there and he assured me all was done."

"Did you check the summer house?"

"I had to know for sure."

"That is why you came to me upon the following day." With her Banbury tales and false assertions of affection for the dead man. Scant point in bringing all that up now. Ottilia got up and went towards the bell-pull. "I will call for my carriage to take you both home." She tugged on the bell and turned with a smile to Richenda. "Thank you for being frank. I hope it will not be long before we have this matter resolved."

"But you do, surely? If Marmaduke came to me —"

"We still don't know why he died when he did. Or where, come to that."

Richenda looked bewildered, but Ottilia did not mean to share the information she had so far garnered. There was no more the beauty could impart to assist. Her immediate quarry must be Percy Pedwardine.

CHAPTER SIXTEEN

To her acute disappointment, Ottilia did not again lay eyes on her husband until the company foregathered before dinner. When she went to her parlour to give Luke his last feed of the day, the nights being reserved to the wet nurse, Pretty made no appearance.

"Is she unwell, Doro?"

Doro set the babe in Ottilia's arms before she answered. "Milord has been with her in the nursery, milady. She will not come away when he is there."

A familiar pang smote Ottilia. There could be no doubt Francis was now wholly the child's papa. She kissed her son's smooth brow for consolation before adjusting her bodice to reveal her breast. A nagging question rose to her lips. "Doro..."

The nurse was en route to the door but she checked, turning. "Milady?"

Despising herself, Ottilia nevertheless voiced her concern. "Did his lordship take notice of his son perchance?"

The startling blue eyes in the dark features showed a trifle of bewilderment. "Milord asks after Master Luke always, milady."

"Asks after him." Hurt prickled Ottilia's bosom. "Does he look at him? Hold him?"

Doro swept across to her, dropping to her haunches, the mesmerising gaze full of understanding. "Gentlemen, milady, all men, take no account of babies. When Master Luke grows, when he can sit and look and show how the world excites him, then milord will see him more clear. It will be so, milady, you will see."

Ottilia managed a smile, but her voice was husky. "Thank you, Doro. You are a great comfort to me."

At this point Luke, notwithstanding his limited abilities, made known his desire that his mother should concentrate upon the task in hand. Ottilia was moved to laughter. "Very well, my little man, I am chastened. Here, you have my full attention." She watched him battle to take hold of her nipple and then basked in the glow of affection that never failed to materialise whenever he took nourishment from her breast. If only Francis could feel what she felt.

Doro, watching with her, smiled too. "It is pleasant to see him with you, milady. With Susannah he is not so contented."

Guilt seized Ottilia. "Not unhappy, I hope?"

"Happy enough, milady. But the bond is not so strong as it is with you." Doro touched the babe's cheek with one finger. "See how he rests quiet as he drinks? When he takes from Susannah he makes more noise and sucks faster."

"Is that bad?" Ottilia cursed her own ignorance. Her knowledge of medical lore far surpassed what she knew of the daily routine of babies.

"Susannah has to burp him before he sleeps, that is all." Doro's gaze came back to hers. "It is normal, milady. All babies have wind. I only wished you to know that Luke is aware which is his mother."

Ottilia could not speak. She hoped Doro might read the message of her eyes before she turned them back upon her infant son, love overflowing in her heart. For Luke, for Pretty too, and most of all, for Francis. She must not give in to petty jealousies.

"I am a very lucky woman."

Doro rose to her feet. "You deserve your happiness, milady. You give so much."

"Oh, stop, Doro. You will have me weeping like a fountain, and that will disturb poor Luke." Even now, the quiet of which Doro had spoken rippled as the baby shifted his limbs, the little arms wafting, tiny hands opening and closing as Luke's eyelids fluttered.

Ottilia crooned to him, bidding him to quiet until he settled again. She put a finger to her lips and gave Doro a smile. The nurse signalled that she would be outside and tiptoed away, leaving Ottilia to a precious few moments of peace before she must bend her mind once again to the troublesome business of Marmaduke's corpse.

When her spouse arrived in the parlour where the rest of the company were settled awaiting their exodus into the dining-room, he explained his absence in a few choice words.

"My daughter would not permit me to depart her bedchamber without reading *Puss in Boots* yet again."

Ottilia ignored Sybilla's raised brows and Vivian's odd look at this mark of possession of Pretty. "Ah, the favourite. How many times is it now, Fan?"

He threw up his eyes. "I've lost count. I know the wretched tale almost by heart."

"I dare say Pretty does too," Lizzy chimed in. "I was used to infuriate Papa by butting in with the words when he would read to me my favourite fairy tale."

"Not *Puss in Boots*, I trust?"

"No, indeed, Uncle. With me it was *The Sleeping Beauty*. I could not get enough of Prince Florimond and Princess Aurora."

Sybilla cut across these reminiscences. "Enough of this frivolity! We have a fairy tale of our own to unravel."

Ottilia's mind leapt readily to the present puzzle. "I only wish it were a fairy tale. Unfortunately, I fear it is rather more convoluted and sinister than I had supposed."

Only Vivian, less familiar with the vagaries of these affairs, took her up on this. "Sinister? What can you mean, ma'am? How sinister?"

About to answer, Ottilia was interrupted by the entrance of Rodmell from the dining parlour next door. "Dinner is served, milady."

"Thank the lord for that. I'm famished. Mama, will you take my arm?"

Francis led Sybilla from the room and Ottilia found Vivian offering his arm to her. "Thank you, Vivian, but do you take in Lizzy. I must have a word with my butler."

She had no real reason to speak to Rodmell, but Ottilia had not failed to note the underlying constraint between the pair and as yet had found no opportunity to question Lizzy as to what may have occurred. Nor to tell her of her father's letter.

This latter omission was rectified by her spouse as soon as the first course was in progress of being served. Francis placed several slices of beef on his plate from the salver proffered by Rodmell and then, rather to Ottilia's consternation, turned his gaze upon his niece, who was seated next to Sybilla.

"I've heard from your papa, Lizzy."

Ottilia caught a look of consternation on Vivian's face where he sat on the opposite side of the table.

Lizzy appeared unmoved. "I am surprised he took so long to answer you, sir."

"He is much occupied about the estates, he says."

One of Sybilla's snorts greeted this. "Poppycock! What he means is he and Harriet argued the matter for days before he put pen to paper. Estates forsooth!"

Ottilia was obliged to suppress a giggle as her spouse looked far from amused. "I dare say Harriet is much occupied too, preparing for the coming season."

"No, she isn't, Aunt Ottilia," stated Lizzy in a flat tone. "She is mothering Gregory who broke a limb."

"Good heavens, child, why did you say nothing before?"

"I only had the letter this morning, Grandmama. I'm afraid I forgot it in all the excitement about Richenda Vexford."

Francis pierced a forkful of beef. "Ah, that must explain what Gil meant by domestic crisis."

Lizzy lifted her chin, staring over her fork at Francis. "Does he mean to come, sir?"

"Not for several days, I gather." Ottilia watched her spouse turn a minatory eye upon Vivian. "I am deputed in the meanwhile to keep the pair of you from indulging in any foolishness."

Vivian's jaw visibly tightened. "None from me, my lord."

But Lizzy was not similarly compliant, a spark in her eye. "Is that what Papa said? Indulging in foolishness?"

"His very words."

"Well! I should like to know just what is his definition of foolishness. What, does he think we may elope?"

"Lizzy!" Ottilia's low-voiced reprimand had its effect. Her niece's cheeks grew fiery and she threw a quick glance across the table where Vivian was studiously regarding his plate as he ate. Ottilia was relieved Sybilla contented herself with one of her scorching looks and she tried to signal to her clearly irritated husband to let the matter lie.

But Lizzy, as ever impulsive, was not to be wholly silenced. "I'm sorry. I've embarrassed you all." Her tone implied anything but an apologetic heart and Ottilia reached across to clasp her arm for a moment. The warning went unheeded. "It's all very well for everyone to shush me, but you won't silence me forever."

To Ottilia's surprise, Vivian intervened, clinching the matter.

"Enough, Eliza. Leave it, if you please."

Ottilia was glad to note Sybilla casting, for a wonder, an approving look upon him from across the table.

Francis saved the moment, addressing her from his place opposite at the head of the table. "I have not had a chance, my love, to relay what I learned from Vexford."

Ottilia embraced the change of subject with relief. "Ah, yes. What said he, Fan?"

"He does not believe, any more than Miss Poynton, that Richenda had the least intention of marrying Marmaduke Gibbon. Nor anyone indeed. It is all posturing with her, he says, and done to thwart him."

"That is precisely the impression I received," Ottilia said with satisfaction.

"I don't mind telling you he infuriated me, wretched man. Much he cares about the girl! He gave up the chase, saying she would return with her tail between her legs, as he phrased it. He would not even come here when he learned she was safe at Flitteris. I'm sorry for the chit. Or I would be if she was not such a curst nuisance."

This provoked a general laugh before Ottilia in her turn, with Lizzy's eager assistance — making amends? — gave the gentlemen, who had not been present, Richenda's account of what had happened after the Twelfth Night party.

"One mystery solved then," Francis commented.

"And another raised." Sybilla sipped her wine and regarded Ottilia over the rim of her glass. "Did you not say this Pedwardine fellow holds a key?"

Ottilia sighed, setting down her fork and pushing her plate a little away. "I wish it might prove to be a key. All I know is that, if Richenda is to be believed —"

"She is, Aunt, I am convinced of it. Do you not think she was speaking the truth, Grandmama?"

"How can I possibly tell? But hush, child. You interrupted your aunt."

Ottilia allowed the brief apology and continued. "What I am saying is that Mr Pedwardine omitted, or indeed twisted, a number of facts within his story."

"Such as?"

"Such as, Fan, that he knew well Marmaduke had no assignation since the assignation was with himself. Whether or no he in fact went to the summer house at all. And, most importantly, what he told Marmaduke upon the occasion."

Vivian was tossing off the rest of the wine in his glass. He set it down, his eyes on Ottilia. "Have you a theory, ma'am?"

"Of course she has," came scoffingly from Sybilla. "She always has a theory."

"But does not always choose to impart it." Her husband cocked an eyebrow as he glinted at her. "Well, Tillie?"

Ottilia had to smile. "I dare say I have several, but what I am chiefly feeling is inordinate relief, after the fiasco of this day, that tomorrow is Sunday, thus preventing any further pursuit of this abominable affair."

"For a day at least, but it won't fadge, wretch of a female!" Francis wagged a finger in her direction. "You will not escape relating these theories of yours by turning the subject."

A general chorus of agreement made Ottilia laugh, but she sighed a little too. "The difficulty is that the thoughts teeming in my head have no real coherence or logic to them. I have only questions."

"Let's have them then."

"They keep changing, Fan." She held up a finger as he opened his mouth to protest. "There is one constant theme. I remain dissatisfied with Marmaduke's condition at the time Percy Pedwardine left him. Was he walking? Had he succumbed already? Was his alleged friend instrumental in hastening his end?"

CHAPTER SEVENTEEN

Ottilia had barely swallowed her breakfast upon the following Monday when Rodmell entered the withdrawing room to announce an unexpected visitor.

"Miss Grindlow, my lady."

Surprised and a trifle perturbed at what might bring the vicar's ward, Ottilia watched Virginia enter, on a quick step and with an anxious countenance. The quiet of the Sabbath had served to recoup Ottilia's energies, since she did not accompany the rest of the party to St Michael's in Knights Inham for the service, but her brain refused to dislodge the puzzle of the corpse. Was Virginia come to add another piece?

Virginia's gaze flitted across the room to find Ottilia in her customary chair. "Lady Francis! Forgive my intrusion, but I come on a mission of mercy."

Ottilia rose and came to meet her. "My dear Virginia, you are very welcome. But before you tell me what I may do for you, allow me to present my niece, Lady Elizabeth Fiske."

"Oh, it is not for me, ma'am, but — how do you do?" Virginia dropped a curtsey and Lizzy, who had also risen, followed suit.

Ottilia hid a sigh at the lost moment for a private cose. Sybilla had not yet come down and the gentlemen had ridden out, so that Ottilia was for once alone with Lizzy. She had meant to enquire into how matters stood between her and Vivian, but that must obviously wait. "What is amiss, Virginia?"

Virginia turned back to her, her manner distressed. "It is Lady Stoke Rochford. Etta sent to me early. She found the poor lady dead and she is perfectly distraught."

"Oh, my goodness! Poor Etta!"

Virginia's gaze returned to Lizzy. "You know Etta?"

"We met the other day. I dare say she is grieving but —" Lizzy looked to Ottilia as if for corroboration. "Etta did say she did not think Lady Stoke Rochford could live much longer."

"It is not that which upsets her." Virginia's eyes also went to Ottilia. "Etta is afraid her death may not have been natural."

Ottilia had taken one of Virginia's hands and she patted it, speaking in a soothing tone. "I dare say there is nothing for her to be concerned about, but we may readily set her mind at rest, I believe."

Virginia clasped the hand that held hers, eager now. "That is what Etta hoped. She begged me to come to you. 'Lady Fan,' she said, 'must be able to tell.' Etta asks that you accompany me to the house."

"For the purpose of examining the body? Has she sent for the doctor?"

"Yes, yes, but she had much rather trust in you. Etta thinks the doctor is bound to assume that Lady Stoke Rochford died of old age."

"Only too likely. Do you not think so, Aunt?"

"Hush, Lizzy." Ottilia waved her niece down and smiled at Virginia. "But you know, my dear, there is every reason to suppose that it is so. Why does she think it may not be?"

Ottilia saw eagerness in Lizzy's face and signalled her to silence. Virginia drew a visible breath. "With all this talk of murder and poor Marmaduke, Etta fears Botolf Claydon may have been tempted to hasten the end so that he may inherit the sooner."

Ottilia could put a damper on this on the instant. "Why, when the end could not in any event be far distant? No, no, my dear Virginia. From what I have seen of that young man, he is far too canny to take such a risk."

"But do you not think —?"

Ottilia held up a finger. "What I think is that your friend Etta's imagination is running away with her. But I will certainly accompany you and we may ascertain whether or no there are grounds for her suspicions."

"I will come too, Aunt." Lizzy changed her tone at a look, her eyes both apologetic and brimful of mischief. "If I may, dearest Lady Fan? I am acquainted with Etta and I may keep her from worrying while you are making your examination."

"Very well." Ottilia went across to tug on the bell-pull, then turned back to Virginia. "Go with Lizzy while she fetches her pelisse, my dear. I must do likewise and also leave word for my husband and inform my mother-in-law of my absence. I will order my carriage."

Virginia was about to follow Lizzy from the room but she checked. "You may come in mine, ma'am. There is no need to trouble your coachman."

But Ottilia had no intention of making herself reliant on another for her transportation. "Do you take Lizzy, then you need not wait for me. I may need to go elsewhere after I have seen poor Lady Stoke Rochford."

The elderly dame was lying in her bed in an attitude of sleep. A maid was sitting in the room, sniffling into a damp handkerchief. She was evidently happy to be relieved from her post by the competent companion.

"You may go now, Jenny. Thank you for staying." Henrietta Skelmersdale watched the maid leave and then turned to Ottilia. "I did not want anyone to lay poor Robina out until you had seen her."

"Very sensible." Ottilia moved to contemplate the corpse.

The usual aromas of death were there, but faint, presumably since a window had been kept open. Someone had disturbed the bedclothes, leaving the head and shoulders exposed and one hand lying on the outside of the coverlet. A nightgown had been disarranged at the neck and a frilled nightcap shifted so that a straggle of grey hair showed.

"She cannot have been found like this," Ottilia observed.

The companion, who was regarding the body with an expression of sadness, looked round. "That was me. Also Dimmer, who found her first. She came to me when she could not wake Robina."

"Dimmer?"

"Robina's maid. I'm afraid she is beside herself. I was obliged to send her to her chamber. The housekeeper is with her."

"What did you each attempt to wake her?" Ottilia was examining the observable signs as she talked, without yet touching the body. The waxy look of death was total, the skin already drawing tighter around the bones. The mouth was open, the eyes sunken and closed. There was no tell-tale redness or blue shadow to indicate other than a natural passing.

"Dimmer was in shock, but I think she tried to shake Robina for she spoke of seizing her shoulders when she would not respond to Dimmer's voice."

Ottilia bent over the dead woman and lifted each eyelid in turn, finding no abnormality. She slipped her fingers behind the head to feel for anomalies. There were none and she shifted the head to one side. It moved easily, which suggested rigor had already passed. "And you, Miss Skelmersdale? What did you do?"

"Oh, pray call me Etta, ma'am. I cannot be formal in these circumstances." A sigh came. "To be truthful, I saw at once she was dead, but I checked her pulse and felt for any warmth."

"I surmise there was none."

"She was quite cold."

Ottilia looked up in time to see a little shudder pass through Etta's frame. Etta was not as relaxed as she appeared. From Virginia's description, she had expected the distress under which the maid Dimmer apparently laboured, but the companion had been calm. Apart from a trifle of pallor and a rim of redness about her eyelids, she behaved with admirable composure and a deal of common sense, even rejecting Virginia's offer to show Ottilia to the bedchamber.

"This is a task peculiarly my own, my dear Ginny. Besides, I dare say Lady Francis has questions that only I will be able to answer."

Which indeed proved to be the case. Ottilia gave her a smile. "I am afraid I must examine the full torso. You may retire if you wish."

Etta straightened her shoulders with an air of determination. "I shall remain. There ought to be a witness, ought there not?"

"Just so. But that may as easily be some other if you prefer not to see this."

Etta lifted her chin. "It will not be the first time I have seen her in dishabille. I have attended her in sickness many times."

Ottilia gave a nod and wasted no more time. She drew the covers off the body. Lady Stoke Rochford's limbs were straight, one arm at her side. The other Ottilia shifted to match. Then she systematically checked the limbs and torso for possible fractures, and examined the fingers for any trace of blue. There was no blood on the nightgown, although the effluvia of death had stained the lower half. With an apologetic glance at Etta, who despite her brave words had the back of one hand against her mouth, Ottilia tugged the nightgown to raise it. A lift of satisfaction entered her breast. The blood had pooled at the body's back, just as one might expect. She made a cursory check for discolouration, cuts or abrasions and found nothing.

At length she replaced the nightgown as best she could and covered the body again, straightening up to address Etta. "You may rest easy, my dear. There is nothing here to suggest her ladyship died of anything other than natural causes."

Etta did not immediately look relieved. "No poison? No strangulation? A pillow was not held over her face?"

The anxious tone caused Ottilia to touch the woman's arm in a reassuring way. "Nothing of the kind."

"Then why did she die? Because she was old? There must be something!"

"A post-mortem would likely reveal merely that her heart failed, but I doubt a coroner will order one. Truly, my dear, there is nothing here to suggest foul play."

At last, a long sigh came. With it, Etta seemed to relax at last, her shoulders drooping. She swayed a little and Ottilia caught at her arms. "Steady now. Come, sit down. You are overwrought."

Etta allowed herself to be ushered to the chair vacated by the maid earlier and sank into it, leaning back and brushing her fingers across her brow. She gave a tiny laugh. "I think you may safely say I am overwrought, Lady Fan. I could not rid myself of a conviction that Botolf had done something to bring on this sudden death."

Ottilia made haste to soothe. "But it is not really sudden, is it? My niece Lizzy told me that you believed her end was not far distant. Is that not so?"

A vigorous nod came in answer. "She said it herself, poor Robina. I suppose I did not want to believe it."

"That she might die, or that Botolf might have slain her?"

The question, delivered on a tart note, drew a blush from Etta. "It was on account of his behaviour over Marmaduke. He has been so secretive, refusing to answer any questions. I think he believes I am in league with you to fasten the guilt upon him."

Ottilia refrained from stating that she was perfectly certain he had guilt in the matter, but not in disposing of Marmaduke's life. Or so she supposed. She might yet be wrong. But he had not, she was persuaded from her inspection, taken steps to remove his benefactor from this earth. But the opportunity to probe was not to be wasted.

"Had you any reason to think Botolf might be in need of funds that he would take such a drastic step?"

Etta shifted her shoulders. "Not that I am aware of, but he does not confide such things to me. His manner towards Robina is always caressing, which is an instance of his duplicity. If he truly cares for her beyond what benefit she may give him, I shall own myself astonished."

Ottilia repaired an omission. "Where is Botolf? Does he know Lady Stoke Rochford has left us?"

"Oh, yes. I went to his room on the instant, when I knew there was nothing to be done. He dressed and rode for the doctor."

"Did he come into this chamber before he left?"

"Yes. I brought him in." Etta hesitated, her glance flying to the bed and then shifting to her hands in her lap, her fingers plucking at her petticoats. "I wanted to see how he took it. I thought I might notice by his reaction…"

"Whether he had been instrumental in the death? What was his reaction?"

Etta's face of disgust was eloquent. "He said nothing. Merely looked for a while. I saw no hint of tears, no look of distress. Nothing at all. It was unnatural."

"Ah, I begin to see why you became alarmed."

Etta rose in her agitation. "Yes, yes, that is it exactly. How could he be entirely unmoved? He was so cold I quite thought he might come out with one of his obnoxious remarks that he makes when he intends to be witty. Not that anyone could think them amusing."

"No, indeed."

"You noticed it too?"

"One could hardly fail to." Ottilia felt obliged to soothe again, for it was patent there was a good deal of resentment here. "I suspect, you know, that it is a kind of shield. The fact he did not say anything untoward in the presence of Robina's body may perhaps be taken as a sign that he was indeed moved, but could not show it."

Etta remained unconvinced, a bitter note in her voice. "If he was moved at all, it was from the thought he might at last become master of this estate. That would be bound to give him pleasure."

Undoubtedly, but still he might have spared a moment of sorrow for his benefactor. But Ottilia did not say it, unwilling to add to Etta's store of rancour. She wondered if there was a trifle of apprehension in it, due to an uncertain future now that her employer had died. But that was a matter for later contemplation.

"We have finished here, I think, my dear. Let us go and await the doctor."

When they re-entered the large drawing room into which the visitors had originally been shown, Lizzy was found to be in animated discussion with Virginia Grindlow. Both parties broke off as Ottilia entered, Etta close behind.

Lizzy looked eager. "Did you find anything, Aunt?"

"Not at all. I am certain there is nothing about which to be concerned. Lady Stoke Rochford's death was undoubtedly a natural one."

A voice spoke from the doorway, rife with sarcasm. "No doubt you anticipated otherwise, ma'am." Ottilia turned in time to witness Botolf Claydon's ironic bow. "The inimitable Lady Fan, as I live and breathe. I do not know whether I should cry welcome or run for my life."

Etta turned on him before Ottilia could speak. "For goodness' sake, Botolf! Is this a moment to be exercising your wit? Moreover, it is not for you to welcome Lady Francis to this house."

Claydon strolled into the room. "I think you will find, my dear Etta, that it is indeed for me. I have sent for Aunt Robina's lawyer."

"Already? Could you not have waited? It's indecent!"

To Ottilia's consternation, Lizzy leapt into the fray. "And you may like to know, Mr Claydon, that my aunt was the only one of us who did not anticipate finding anything, so you need not sneer at her in that horrid way."

The mocking curl to Claydon's lip became pronounced and Ottilia thought it politic to call a halt. "Thank you, Lizzy, but there is no necessity to take up the cudgels in my defence."

"I know you can fight your own battles, Aunt, but —"

"Enough!" Satisfied Lizzy was silenced, Ottilia turned not to Claydon, but rather to Etta. "It is as well, my dear Etta, to bring in her ladyship's lawyer as soon as possible. He may help with the formalities and take a deal of trouble off your hands." She looked to the young man and found his expression both surprised and gratified. Ottilia smiled. "You wonder at my taking your part, sir?"

He did not immediately resume his habitual sneer. "I admit it is unexpected."

Ottilia turned the screw. "You may be a tiresome young man, Mr Claydon, with your affectations, but I do not think you are a fool."

A tinge of red crept into his cheek, but to his credit, he managed an echo of his habitual manner. "I am obliged to your ladyship."

Ottilia let this go. "Have you brought the doctor?"

"He is following in his gig." His glance went to Etta. "Do you want to show him up, or shall I?"

It was plain Etta had not looked for such consideration. She eyed him in a look of doubt, but the belligerence had lessened when she spoke. "I ought to do it, I believe. But if you are set on it…"

"No, I thank you." He put up a staying hand. "Once was more than enough." He cleared his throat. "I did not expect to be as much affected, I confess."

Ottilia cut in before Etta could voice her obvious indignation. "It is always a shock to see the life gone from one whom one knew well."

The clang of a bell somewhere in the region downstairs had Etta hurrying for the door. "That will be the doctor. Botolf, will you send for refreshments for these ladies, if you please?"

He crossed to a bell-pull and tugged upon it, but Ottilia demurred. "Nothing for me, I thank you. I have not long broken my fast."

Virginia was on her feet. "But I have not. Etta's note reached me before I could breakfast. I would be very glad of a roll, perhaps, and coffee."

The word stirred Ottilia's senses. "Well, if there is coffee, I will partake of it."

Lizzy laughed out. "She never refuses coffee, you must know. She is quite an addict."

Botolf Claydon, for a wonder, gave a genuine laugh. "We all have our failings."

The atmosphere lightened and Ottilia took a chair by the fire at his urging. Virginia settled back onto the sofa, at a little distance, which she and Lizzy had been occupying and Ottilia was unsurprised to see their heads together in short order. Lowering her voice, she addressed the hovering Claydon.

"Have you by any chance given thought to my words of the other day?"

His regard did not waver. "I cannot say I have, ma'am. Moreover, under present circumstances…" He spread his hands in a gesture as if to encompass his benefactor's passing.

Ottilia became tart. "Present circumstances notwithstanding, Mr Claydon, I have still a puzzle to solve."

He gave a small shrug. "I cannot help you."

Ottilia eyed him, noting the carefully neutral expression. Before she could pursue it, a servant entered. Claydon gave his direction to bring the requested refreshments to the drawing room. Ottilia waited for him to leave and then played her ace. "You have heard the outcome of Richenda's adventure, I don't doubt?"

"I told you I saw her."

"You did, and your observation was accurate. As far as it went."

His brows rose. "Meaning?"

"Meaning that she went there to find Mr Pedwardine."

This was plainly news to the man. He frowned. "For what purpose?"

"To find out what he said to Marmaduke at the Twelfth Night party." She was glad to see the bewilderment increase. "She had no assignation with Marmaduke, but with Pedwardine himself. But it was Marmaduke who arrived in the summer house."

Claydon tossed his head. "Did I not say he left in good order?"

"As it chances, I don't believe you did. You claimed to have last seen him in the breakfast parlour."

"Either way, it demonstrates that I had nothing to do with that business."

Ottilia struck. "Pardon me, but it demonstrates nothing of the kind. Marmaduke was dead."

"In the summer house? There you are then. Clearly he died there."

"Come, sir, we have discussed this before. How did he get there? Without a carriage. Nor could he walk the better part of four miles or so in his debilitated condition."

Another shrug, but the discomfort was beginning to show. "He must have persuaded someone to take him there."

"A convenient supposition. Whom do you suggest? Nobody who was at the party, yourself included, admits to having seen Marmaduke leave the house, let alone giving him a ride."

"One of the grooms perhaps?"

"Then either Jarvis or Martin Thorpe would have known of it."

The sneer was back, but it failed to convince. "I fear it must remain a mystery then, my dear Lady Fan." He snapped to attention. "If you will forgive me, with all this upset, I have matters to attend to. Etta will be back soon. Pray make yourselves at home." He left her on the words and vanished through the open door.

Ottilia was satisfied. He was severely rattled. It could not be long before he broke. The sight of a servant entering with the promised refreshments was welcome. A respite before Etta reappeared would give her time to think how to approach her next victim.

CHAPTER EIGHTEEN

"I have had the most famous notion, Aunt!"

Ottilia was holding the strap for support as the coach lurched a little over ruts in the driveway that led out of Lady Stoke Rochford's establishment. She spoke with a degree of irritation. "If it is that Botolf Claydon's first task must be to expend some of his inheritance to repair this avenue, I am before you, Lizzy."

"Not that, though I must say it is certainly in need of it."

"You may say so with confidence."

"Do but listen, Aunt!"

"Well, what?"

Lizzy's eyes were sparkling. "Etta is free now and here is Grandmama in need of a new companion. What could be more fortuitous?"

"Good heavens, child, I cannot suppose the poor girl is as yet thinking of taking up a new position. Her employer only died this morning."

"Well, I was not proposing to mention it at once, but it would kill two birds with one stone. And I *like* Etta."

"Which is as much as to say that you don't like poor Miss Mellis."

"How should I? She is years and years older than I and I am very sure she regards me with disapproval. I should not mind visiting Grandmama if Etta was in residence."

Ottilia could not help laughing. "I am not convinced Sybilla would thank you for organising her life for her, but by all means suggest it to her. For now, let us concentrate on bearding Percy Pedwardine."

Lizzy was instantly diverted. "Do you suppose you will find him?"

"Well, he is staying at the Fox, so one must assume he went back there after yesterday's adventure." Ottilia added, on an exasperated note as the carriage bumped uncomfortably, "I begin to wonder if there will be much inheritance to speak of after all for Claydon, if the state of this drive is anything to go by."

"Abominable, isn't it? Perhaps it was not expense, but merely that the poor old dame was past seeing to such things. New blood may take better care."

"Pray don't say what may cause me to regard that young man with any degree of approval."

Lizzy giggled. "I have never known you to take a man in such dislike, Aunt."

"I have not taken him in dislike. I am merely desirous of forcing him to tell me the truth. He is no worse than half a dozen youths determined to show off their mettle."

"At least Vivian does not behave in such a fashion."

Ottilia looked round at the piquant face. "On that matter, how are things between you two?"

"Oh, it is not worth discussing." Her niece did not meet her eyes, flicking in a nonchalant manner at invisible dust on her pelisse. "I dare say I would not care to marry him after all."

This was said in an airy fashion in which Ottilia placed no belief whatsoever. A coach was not the best place in which to pursue the matter, however. She turned the subject. "I noticed you and Virginia enjoyed a good gossip. Did you learn anything of use?"

Lizzy turned, eager now. "I was going to tell you. Virginia recalled a snatch of conversation."

"When? Upon the night of the party?"

"No, it was before, she said. At the parsonage when this Marmaduke made her think he was interested in her rather than Richenda."

The recollection popped into Ottilia's head. "In a conservatory, was it not?"

"I think so."

"What was said, Lizzy?"

"At the time, Virginia confessed her attention was distracted to think Marmaduke liked her, which is why she did not recall it when she spoke to you."

"Also because she was too distressed to think clearly, I don't doubt." Ottilia pressed for the pertinent information. "What has she remembered?"

"Let me recall it as precisely as I can." Lizzy thought for a moment. "Yes, I have it. Marmaduke mentioned his friend, who had not yet arrived, but was expected. He said, if I have it correctly, that Percy Pedwardine would serve to distract Richenda, allowing him to give his attention where it was more to his taste to give it."

Ottilia did not know whether to be glad of the point or infuriated with the perfidious Marmaduke. "Duplicity? As I understood it, Richenda was close enough to overhear."

"Well, Virginia says she made a point of flirting with Pedwardine the moment he was presented." Lizzy wriggled her closed fists in excitement. "Does it not seem to bear out Richenda's tale of making an assignation with Pedwardine rather than Marmaduke?"

"Just so. A devious wench. She used Pedwardine, even as it appears Marmaduke did."

"Will you accuse him?" Lizzy's voice squeaked a little. "Did he do away with Marmaduke, do you think?"

Ottilia tutted. "How many times am I to tell you not to jump to conclusions, Lizzy? All the evidence must be sifted."

"But everything points to him, Lady Fan!"

"Not everything. Besides, let us not lose sight of the fact that, as far as we know, Marmaduke was not murdered."

"But he was dealt a fatal blow. You said so, Aunt."

"Yes, by Aubrey Botterell — perhaps more than one according to his aunt — but it was by no means intended to kill. But it could have caused his death nonetheless."

Lizzy did not let it lie. "What if Pedwardine delivered another blow? A later one?"

"It is a possibility."

"There you are then."

Ottilia had to laugh. "No, indeed, Lizzy. There am I not! We have far too many imponderables to be certain of anything."

"Ah, but you are going to talk to Pedwardine. You may unravel it all in a heartbeat."

Ottilia emitted an exasperated sound. "I have a very good mind to instruct Williams to drive you back to Flitteris and return for me."

"No, don't." Lizzy seized her hand. "I promise I will be good. I won't say a word, if only you will let me be one of the party."

"I ought to gag you, impossible child."

Lizzy's irrepressible throaty laugh came. "You wouldn't. You are far too kind."

"Am I indeed? To be truthful, I think I will get further if I tackle Pedwardine alone. Assuming he is there to be tackled."

Lizzy did not cease to labour the point until the coach pulled into the yard of the Fox. Weary of the argument, Ottilia consented to allow her niece to accompany her, on her promise of keeping her tongue. "Not that I suppose you will be able to, because you never do. I hope Vivian Maplewood knows what he is letting himself in for."

This reminder had the salutary effect of silencing Lizzy and Ottilia was sorry for bringing the matter up. More than ever convinced that something had gone awry between them, she determined to plumb the problem to its depths in due course.

Meanwhile, upon enquiry of the landlady, who came bustling up as she entered the Fox inn's spacious hallway, she discovered her quarry was within.

"Would you kindly tell him I am here, Mrs Oake, and that I would be glad of a few words with him? May I commandeer one of your private parlours?"

The landlady was all too eager, though evidently agog. No doubt the news that Ottilia was engaged upon this investigation had travelled half across the county. Mrs Oake led the ladies to a neat parlour on the first floor and offered refreshment, which was politely declined. "If you would go to Mr Pedwardine directly, Mrs Oake?"

Thus adjured, the landlady curtsied herself out and closed the door.

The parlour was scantily furnished, but Ottilia took possession of a chair that was advantageously placed to glean warmth from the fire and bade Lizzy, who was fidgeting about the place, now at the window, now holding the back of a chair at the table, to be seated.

"Oh, very well." Lizzy drew out the chair and plonked into it. "What will you ask him, Aunt Ottilia?"

"That must depend upon his attitude."

"Well, if he is minded to be rude like that wretched Botolf creature, I shall know how to do."

Ottilia sighed. "Do, pray, remember your promise."

"I didn't exactly promise. I won't endure to hear you maligned."

"Very gratifying, Lizzy, but if you must speak, at least follow my lead."

Fortunately, the door opened even as Lizzy began upon a retort, and she stopped talking as Percy Pedwardine entered. He was frowning, his gaze going from Lizzy, whom he evidently saw first, and settling upon Ottilia.

"Lady Francis? You wished to see me?"

Ottilia beckoned him forward. "I did indeed. Do sit, Mr Pedwardine, or I shall be getting a crick in my neck."

He looked wary, his brows still drawn together, but he perched on a convenient chair at a little distance and closer to the door than the rest. "How may I serve you, ma'am?"

Ottilia eyed him with interest. He was not nearly as friendly in his manner as he had been upon the last occasion they had met. Had he reason to suppose she meant to be on the attack? She tried a neutral note.

"Richenda came to me yesterday, you must know, after your little adventure."

He drew back, snapping in a sharp breath. "We come to it. That wench wants both sense and manners."

Ottilia hit hard. "Yet by her account, sir, it was your manners which left something to be desired."

His lips folded tight, a spark in his eye. Ottilia waited, trusting to her admonitions that Lizzy would not break the rising tension. The ruse worked.

"What did she tell you?"

"Oh, no, Mr Pedwardine. Let me first have your account of what happened between you."

"Why should I say anything of it to you?"

She gave a faint smile. "Come, Mr Pedwardine. It is your friend's fate we are pursuing. Is it not in your interests to be open with me?"

He looked down, clasping his hands loosely together between his knees in an attitude of thought. Ottilia threw a warning glance at Lizzy, who caught it and gave a quick shake of the head as if to indicate her continued silence.

Pedwardine looked up, his air now seeming to show he was coerced. "If you must have it, Richenda came to me, not the other way about. It was her pursuit. I should not have attempted a meeting otherwise."

"Well? What transpired?"

His glance found Lizzy and he frowned. "Who is this?"

"My niece, Lady Elizabeth Fiske. She is perfectly discreet." A false assertion, but what would you?

His gaze returned to Ottilia. "Richenda wanted me to ride with her. She had questions about Duke."

"What questions, sir?"

His shoulders shifted. "Petty ones. Had he not died, would he have offered for her, that kind of thing."

Sceptical she might be, but Ottilia needed him malleable. "I see. Did she not ask about the night he died?"

She received a straight look. "Is that what she said?"

"I am asking you, Mr Pedwardine."

"Of course she did, ma'am. All manner of nonsensical queries which I could not answer. I told her just what I have told you, all I know in fact."

Evasive, to say the least. Ottilia ventured to increase the pressure. "She did not ask why Marmaduke did not keep his assignation?"

"She knew why. We all did."

"Enlighten me."

He sat up straighter. "Are you setting a trap for me, ma'am? My friend was dead. How would he keep an assignation?"

Clever. Unless he was innocent, or Richenda had once again lied. Ottilia changed tack. "What made you lose your temper with Richenda, Mr Pedwardine?"

A flash at his eyes gave notice this had hit home. Was he going to deny it? After a moment, he let out a taut breath. "You have that, have you?"

"I have one side of it."

He seemed to wilt a little. "I dare say she told it as it was. I don't mind confessing it, she infuriated me. I know well she had no real affection for Duke. I could not bear her protestations."

"She professed to love him?"

"She blamed me for his disaffection. For his death. Had I not interfered, she claimed, he would have come to her that night and been alive still. She refused to believe I had naught to do with his decision, if decision he made. I know not what occurred after I left him, as I told you. Richenda seems to think it was I who dissuaded him from the assignation, refused to drive him thence. In reality, it is she who caused his demise and so I told her."

"How so? How did she cause it?"

Pedwardine let out a guttural sound. "She commanded him here, to have him for her plaything, to flaunt him in the faces of her local suitors. She is a conniving Jezebel!"

"Harsh words, sir."

"Deserved, I assure you." His eyes flared. "What, have you been in her company and not taken her measure? And you by reputation so all-alive!"

A hasty motion and an intake of breath from her niece induced Ottilia to throw out a staying hand. "Yes, very rude,

Lizzy, but we must make allowances. Mr Pedwardine's patience has been sorely tried, and he is grieving. Is that not so, my dear sir?"

He closed his lips together, visibly tugging himself back under control. When he spoke, his tone was more moderate. "I beg your pardon. I have this day sustained a visit from Duke's uncle, come in response to my letter."

Ottilia had an instant premonition that she was also destined to sustain such a visit. "Does he know the circumstances?"

"I held nothing back. Duke is — was — Edmund Gibbon's heir. He was also Duke's guardian after his father died."

Reflecting that she might get a better notion of Marmaduke's character and physical condition from his uncle, Ottilia reconciled herself to the inevitable. "Where has Mr Gibbon gone now?"

"I directed him to the doctor. He is anxious to take possession of Duke's body and return him to his family."

"That is understandable. Does he propose staying in this inn meanwhile?"

Pedwardine's brows drew together. "You wish to speak with him?"

Ottilia gave a faint smile. "It was in my mind that he will wish to speak to me, assuming you informed him of the peculiar disposition of Marmaduke's body."

"On your doorstep? Yes, I told him that."

Ottilia slipped a thrust under his guard. "Did you also give an account of Marmaduke's last moments?"

She received a blank stare. "Did I not say I held nothing back?"

Mentally, Ottilia conceded defeat. If there was more to know, he was armed against careless exposure. But one point might be worth an attack. "Richenda told me that her assignation that night was not with Marmaduke, but with you."

Was there an instant of alarm in his eye? Quickly veiled, if so. The hesitation might be for a speedy hunt to extract himself. Or was he genuinely taken aback? At last, he relaxed back in the chair.

"The girl is raving. I can't abide the wench. Why in the world would I wish for a clandestine rendezvous with her, of all females?"

Lizzy chimed in at this point. "But you didn't wish for it. Richenda asked you to meet her in the summer house and you agreed."

He cast a brief glance at Lizzy, but addressed himself to Ottilia. "This is typical of her sort of trickery. I warned Duke to be wary. It's not as if he had not seen it for himself. I have lost count of the number of times she set up a meeting and then made no appearance."

"But her father —"

Lizzy got not further. Pedwardine turned a look of derision upon her. "Oh, yes, her father. He gave her every sort of excuse to blow hot and cold upon poor Duke. More fool he to believe it."

Ottilia cut in before Lizzy, clearly ready with another indignant objection, could pursue the argument. "You have met Lord Vexford in one of his more tetchy moods, I take it?"

Pedwardine shrugged. "He is a choleric old fellow, but the truth is Richenda runs rings around him. She could always escape him when she chose. But that is her forte, pitting one suitor against another, pretending to favour Duke and then dispensing her smiles to some other fellow. He was idiot enough to believe her wiles and more so to be drawn hither on a fool's errand. She never meant to have him, that I will swear to."

Since Ottilia had come to much the same conclusion, she found this difficult to refute. But she had been confident Richenda's account of yesterday had been genuine. Doubt crept in. If Percy Pedwardine's intent had been to fuzz the issue in her mind, he had certainly succeeded. She resolved to take her leave before her observations could be further undermined. She rose. "I thank you for your time, Mr Pedwardine. I may need you again. Pray inform Mr Edmund Gibbon that I will be happy to talk to him at his convenience."

Having returned from his ride with Vivian Maplewood and changed his clothes, Francis entered the front withdrawing room to find his mother entertaining a complete stranger. She hailed him on the instant from her seat by the fire.

"Ah, there are you, my dear boy. Come in, do, and give Mr Gibbon here your attention." She turned to the man who was standing in the middle of the room and looking somewhat bewildered. "This is my son, Lord Francis Fanshawe. You had better speak to him."

Francis found himself confronting a fleshy fellow in his middle years whose features bore the marks of good living, red veins criss-crossing his nose and cheeks, which did not quite conceal his faded good looks. He wore his own hair, silky smooth and tied back, the grey inlaid still with blond strands. The most remarkable thing about him was his clothes, black in every particular, including his neck-cloth. The name his mother had used flipped into his mind. Gibbon? His probable identity slipped into Francis's thoughts even as the gentleman spoke.

"Your pardon, my lord. I am come to confer with a certain Lady Fan, your wife as I understand it, concerning the demise of my poor nephew."

"Ah, you are Marmaduke's uncle then." Francis held out a hand. "My condolences, sir."

Gibbon took the hand in a limp hold and released it at once. "I thank you, my lord. It is a great sadness to me to lose the boy, although I am obliged to admit his taking off is not entirely unexpected."

Taken aback, Francis stared at him. "How so?"

His mother chimed in, her brows raised. "He must mean this heart business. Did not Ottilia find there was a history?"

Gibbon looked across at her, his brows drawing together. "Who found, my lady?"

"Ottilia, my daughter-in-law. She it is who bears the sobriquet of Lady Fan."

If Gibbon noticed the inflection of distaste he did not show it. His brow cleared. "I see, my lady. She heard of poor Marmaduke's condition? I wonder who could have told her."

Francis took this. "Your nephew's groom spoke of his having lost his breath once or twice."

"That Pedwardine fellow also said something of it, Francis, do you not recall?"

Gibbon looked pained. "He would know, yes. Friends from Eton days, you see. Percy spent many happy weeks with us at Whitney Park."

"Will you not be seated, sir?" Francis gestured to a chair, intending to take his own place on the sofa opposite.

Gibbon hesitated, hovering by the chair. "But Lady Fan? Your wife, my lord? I came but to request of her an account…"

"She is from home at this present, but I don't doubt she will return shortly." He gestured to the chair again and Gibbon at last sat, with evident reluctance. Francis crossed to the bell-pull. "You'll take a glass of something, I hope?"

The man looked surprised, but he gave a nod. "That would be welcome. It is an unpleasant duty to be undertaking."

"Indeed." The bell rung, Francis took his place on the sofa and eyed the man. "Would you elaborate on why your nephew's death was not unexpected?"

Gibbon spread his hands. "As I said, poor Marmaduke has been often at the mercy of these attacks."

Sybilla took the words out of Francis's mouth. "What kind of attacks?"

A pertinent point. He had not died of an attack as such.

The uncle shook his head in a melancholy fashion. "He was asthmatic. Coupled with a weak heart, which he inherited from my poor brother's wife, I regret to say. It has been a fear in my mind for years. I own I had begun to hope, for the attacks have been few since he grew to manhood. He seemed stronger."

Francis could not avoid feeling sorry for the man. "That is indeed a blow, sir." The word put him in mind of Tillie's suspicions and he toyed with mentioning them. Why distress Gibbon the more at this juncture? His mother, however, had apparently no such scruples.

"Do you think a blow to the chest could have killed your nephew, Mr Gibbon?"

His startled look drove in Francis's irritation. He intervened. "Nothing is fully determined, sir. There is a good deal of conjecture, but my wife is pursuing her enquiries in hopes of unravelling just what happened to your nephew."

But Gibbon fastened on the point, his gaze fixing on Francis. "A blow? Did someone deal him a blow?"

Before he could respond, the dowager was off again. "A scuffle among boys, it seems. A stupid dispute. One of them may have hit this Marmaduke, but not intending to do him harm."

"But a blow? He could never indulge in fisticuffs, you see. Far too dangerous for the boy. Any little thing might set him off struggling to breathe. One had to keep him from such indulgence, poor child. My brother was anxious all the while the boy was in school, but he survived, by a miracle." His face puckered. "Only to be brought down at the last in this horrible manner. I must beg you will not tell me he died of a blow for I do not think I could bear it."

Francis exchanged a glance with his mother, whose delicate brows were climbing. The visitor had set his hand to his forehead, shading his eyes. Francis seized the chance to give a fierce shake of the head in hopes his mother would refrain from further revelations. She cast up her eyes but indicated by a shrug that she understood. Relieved, Francis turned back to Gibbon just as Rodmell entered on the echo of his knock.

"Ah, in good time. Madeira, Rodmell. Or no —" with a glance at the sufferer — "brandy might better meet the case."

"Tyler is on the way with the necessary, my lord."

Francis blew out a breath. "Well anticipated."

Rodmell held the door wide as the footman entered, armed with a tray which he set down on the marquetry pier table by the wall. Francis rose.

"Leave it, Tyler. I will do the honours." He nodded dismissal to the butler as well and picked up the brandy decanter. Pouring a small measure into a glass, he brought it across to the afflicted mourner. "Here, Gibbon. Drink this. It will revive you."

The man looked up, and had recourse to a handkerchief he dragged from a pocket, blowing his nose and wiping the wet from his eyes. He took the glass, his voice husky. "Thankee, my lord. That is kindly done."

Francis left him to it, turning to Sybilla. "For you, ma'am?"

"I will take Madeira. Unless you have Port there?"

"Madeira or brandy only." He poured a measure from the wine decanter and took it across, giving time, he hoped, for Gibbon to recover.

Settled with a glass of Madeira for himself, he retook his seat and awaited the visitor's pleasure. With good fortune, Tillie would not be too long delayed at Lady Stoke Rochford's whither her note said she had gone.

At length, having disposed of most of his brandy, Gibbon spoke, the glass held loosely in his fingers. "I am at a loss in one instance, my lord."

"What is that, sir?"

"Why was my nephew's corpse treated in this despicable fashion? Who could be so callous as to drag poor Marmaduke's body across the back of a horse and drop it in a most disrespectful way? Upon your doorstep! Who would do such a thing? Why? What should it profit anyone to mistreat him so?"

The grief was burgeoning again and Francis hesitated over his reply. They knew now it had been Richenda who sent the corpse, but what profit in saying so? On the other hand, the fellow deserved an explanation. He prevaricated. "You are likely unaware, sir, that my wife has something of a reputation. She has dealt with several unexplained or unexpected deaths.

The person who sent Marmaduke to Lady Fan was desirous she should find out what had happened to him."

The man's features registered confusion. "But in such a fashion? Why not ask? Why treat him so shabbily?"

Why indeed? Francis tried for a light response. "The individual did not wish their identity known."

"But…"

Francis sighed. "Words fail you, sir? I am not surprised. I assure you, we were quite as dismayed." Not necessarily by the disrespect, but no need to mention that.

Gibbon seemed a degree less indignant. "Pray understand I do not attach blame to you or your lady wife, sir. Indeed, I am grateful you saw fit to bring a doctor to him, even if it was too late."

Far too late, but best not to say that either. Francis waited for what he would next ask, hoping it might not prove impossible to answer. His hope was misplaced.

"There is a young lady in the case, I believe. Does she know aught of this?"

Francis exchanged a glance with his mother, who closed her lips firmly together. Up to him then. He prevaricated. "You knew of Marmaduke's interest in Richenda Vexford?"

"Vexford? Yes, I believe so. I forget now. Marmaduke received a letter."

"An invitation?"

A faint grimace crossed Gibbon's features. "A summons rather. That is how Marmaduke phrased it. He was amused. I asked him if he had an interest there, if this female would make a worthy helpmeet. Marmaduke was adamant it was not serious, but he had nothing better to do, he said." Anguish ripped through the man's voice. "I could wish he had not gone! He would yet be with us."

What to say? An obvious truth, unless some other accident had befallen. The less said of Richenda, the better. "It is most unfortunate, sir."

Gibbon looked across, plainly distressed. "I wish it was mere misfortune, my lord. Yet I fear Marmaduke was less than plain with me. His friend believes this girl had undue influence over him. Percy had witnessed this in London, he told me. That is why he followed Marmaduke to this place. He sought, he said, to draw him off if he could. Moreover, Percy tells me the father is a man of choleric temper."

"That is certainly true."

"You know him, my lord?"

"Vexford, yes. He is one of our neighbours in these parts. If it comforts you, I should doubt of his ever having been persuaded to approve your nephew for his daughter. Or any other young man, from what I have seen. Marmaduke was in no real danger from Richenda on that score."

This intelligence did not appear to afford Gibbon any satisfaction. His colour rose. "I should like to know what objection he could have to Marmaduke. The boy was my heir. I don't mean to boast, my lord, but I possess a tidy estate. It is not an inheritance to be sneezed at." His face fell. "But all for nothing. It will go to an obscure cousin when I depart this realm. A windfall for him." He rubbed his handkerchief, still held in his fingers, against his nose. "I was blessed with no son of my own, you see. No offspring at all, for my wife could not carry to term. All my hopes have been invested in my poor nephew."

"A sorry loss, sir," came from Sybilla, but in a bracing tone. "We must hope your cousin proves worthy of the unexpected honour."

Gibbon did not look as if this thought afforded comfort, but he nodded in a vague sort of way before turning his attention back to Francis. "I do not know, my lord, if I welcome or dread what your lady wife may be able to tell me."

Small wonder. Francis tried for a neutral note. "It appears there is yet some question on the matter. But we must hope my wife may at the last be able to set your mind at rest."

"Impossible." He shuddered. "I doubt I shall be easy again for a twelvemonth."

"It is understandable you should think so, sir," chimed in Sybilla, "but you will find ease. I have borne enough of such losses at my time of life to be able to reassure you of that."

Gibbon refused to be comforted. "It is kind of your ladyship to say so, but this loss is a hard one to bear."

Francis began to wish Tillie would reappear. If anyone could soothe the fellow, it would be his darling wife. To his inestimable relief, the thought had hardly formed when the door opened and she walked into the room.

CHAPTER NINETEEN

Primed by the butler, Ottilia made directly for the stranger, who had risen at her entrance. "My dear Mr Gibbon, I am so very sorry for your loss. You have come, I believe, to find me. I am Lady Fan. Or, more properly, Lady Francis Fanshawe."

She held out her hand, taking him in the while as he held it lightly and made a small bow. "You are very kind, my lady. I thank you."

Ottilia smiled at him and looked across to her spouse. "I see you have done the honours, Fan."

He was on his feet. "Indeed. Mr Gibbon is much distressed, but I have told him all I can. He is anxious for answers, as you may imagine."

She flicked her eyes heavenwards, knowing the visitor could not see, but turned with an apologetic look to Gibbon. "I will tell you what I may, sir, but first I have a duty to perform." She crossed to the mantel, looking down at her mother-in-law. "Sybilla, I am sorry to be obliged to tell you that Lady Stoke Rochford died this morning."

The dowager tutted. "Another one?"

"Yes, but expected and not in the least suspicious. I did not wish to mention it when I told you I was going out, but the truth is I went to check at her companion's request. I imagine you may guess what she feared. I thought I must inform you immediately as you visited her so recently."

"Yes, but I have not seen her for years. We were never close. I must say she was pretty frail when I met her the other day."

"Just so. It is a pity it should happen at this moment, but I don't believe it has any bearing upon the matter at hand."

Her husband emitted a relieved breath. "Thank the Lord for that!" He then evidently recollected the augmented company, for he turned to Gibbon. "You must forgive us, sir. We have been somewhat exercised by the difficulties attendant upon finding out what happened to your nephew."

"Difficulties?" The visitor almost squeaked the word. "Why so?"

Ottilia intervened at once, moving to join Francis on the sofa where he had taken a seat. "My dear Mr Gibbon, do not take fright, I charge you. It is merely that people's memories of the night in question differ somewhat. It is always so, I fear. The task becomes one of disentangling discrepancies. I regret to say that so far I have not been able fully to clarify matters."

He looked a trifle bemused. All to the good. The less he understood, the better. Ottilia was reluctant to open the subject without first hearing from Francis just what had been said already. How to avoid broaching it? Recalling Mr Pedwardine had directed him to the doctor, she tackled that first. "You have seen Doctor Lister, I understand."

The introduction proved unfortunate. Gibbon uttered a muted cry. "My boy too!" Then he held a handkerchief to his eyes, his shoulders shaking.

Ottilia looked at her spouse beside her, lowering her voice. "What have you told him?"

"Almost nothing," he returned in like manner. "We have learned a little of Marmaduke from him instead."

She listened to his murmured words, her mind working as she learned of the intimacy enjoyed with the deceased by Percy Pedwardine. Not to mention the tale with which that young man had seen fit to regale the uncle. So he came with the intention of putting a spoke in Marmaduke's wheel? He had succeeded with a vengeance. Was it all his intent?

Presently Gibbon's grief subsided and he apologised for the display, what time Francis replenished the man's glass. Ottilia waited until he had drunk a little of the liquid it contained and seemed to regain command over himself. He addressed himself to Ottilia. "My lady, you must forgive me. I have not yet learned to master my emotion."

"It is very understandable, sir. You have sustained a severe blow."

The word brought his chin up. "A blow! Your husband — or no, was it her ladyship there? One of them spoke of a blow."

"A scuffle, I said," came in tetchy tones from Sybilla, her disapproval of the visitor's lack of control clearly visible in both face and voice. "No one is certain there has been any kind of blow, so pray do not fasten upon that detail."

Gibbon ignored this recommendation. "I must, my lady." He looked across and Ottilia met his gaze. "It is of all things the most dangerous for the boy. As I told his lordship, Marmaduke could never engage in fisticuffs. Asthmatic, you see, Lady Fan."

Ottilia seized on this. "I did wonder." She did not say that Pedwardine had dismissed the notion of his friend's condition being serious. "It was reported to me that your nephew did struggle for breath."

"There! You see."

"But he got over it."

Gibbon became agitated. "But his heart! The doctor spoke of cardiac arrest. Was it not so?"

"That was my understanding, sir."

"Well, there it is, my lady. If he received a blow…"

She made haste to soothe. "That was indeed my first thought, sir, but it seems he recovered from whatever difficulty was sustained by the argument. From what I have been able to discover, too much time must have passed between that incident and his unfortunate demise for the two to have been closely related."

It was plain the man was still affected for he appeared to follow this with painstaking concentration. He demurred after a moment. "You may say so, my lady, but the doctor could not be specific as to the time my poor Marmaduke breathed his last."

Francis cut in. "Except that we know it was more than four and twenty hours before he was — er — left at our door. Other than that, my wife has been unable to determine just when the event may have taken place."

Ottilia met the fellow's questioning look with an inward sigh. Small point in prevarication. "I dare say this may distress you, sir, but no one has been able to state precisely when they last saw Marmaduke alive. I do know he was found dead in the morning, but not where one might expect him to be."

The fellow's air became bewildered. "Where then was he? Where should he have been?"

"He should have been at Thorpe Grange, having attended the Twelfth Night party there. In fact, he was found in the summer house at Wyke Hall." She did not add her conviction that his corpse was taken there.

"He went there to meet that girl then!"

"That is what we are supposed to believe, yes."

His brows drew together, the intensity seemingly painful to him. "You don't believe it?"

"Just so, Mr Gibbon."

He hesitated, his glance flitting from Ottilia to Francis and thence to Sybilla before returning. "I don't understand."

Ottilia smiled. "Nor more do I, sir. At least, I have an inkling of the truth but I cannot speak of it without being certain."

Gibbon said nothing for a moment, his gaze fixed upon her as he evidently thought this over. Then he let out a sigh. "I had hoped to travel home within the day, once I have arranged for the transport of Marmaduke's remains." The mention brought a tremor to his voice but he did not break down again.

Ottilia ventured a suggestion. "These uncertainties need not detain you, sir. If you will give me your direction, I will write as soon as I have unravelled the business."

At this, he straightened, visibly stiffening his spine, his head up. "No, indeed, my lady. I owe it to my boy. I will remain. I will see the thing through. Marmaduke could expect no less of me." He rose on the words. "I will leave you now. You have my direction?"

Ottilia rose too, as did her spouse, moving to open the door.

"You may leave it with me, Gibbon. Be sure my wife will inform you as soon as she is able to produce a definite answer."

Gibbon gave thanks and made three punctilious bows before heading for the door Francis was holding open. Ottilia checked him. "Mr Gibbon!"

He paused, turning. "My lady?"

"It may be useful to talk with you again, if you are willing."

"I am at your service, my lady. Believe me grateful. It is the least I can do." He gave another small bow and departed, under Francis's escort.

Ottilia resumed her seat as her mother-in-law let out an exasperated sound.

"Thank heavens that is over. I could not think what one might say to the fellow. He could scarcely keep his countenance."

The indignant note drew a gurgle from Ottilia, which she hastily retracted. "I am not laughing at him. Not everyone has your iron control, Sybilla."

The dowager gave one of her dismissive waves of the hand. "It is a matter of breeding, child. One does not parade one's grief in public. To wear mourning is quite enough of a show."

Ottilia did not waste her breath in arguing the point. "What is of more importance is the role of young Pedwardine. It becomes so contradictory I do not know what to believe."

This aroused Sybilla's interest. "How so? Is he lying, do you think?"

"It would appear so. But then he is not the only one. Richenda is a most unreliable witness, and both the Thorpe men as well as Botolf Claydon are concealing something."

"Do you indeed believe they took the body to Wyke Hall?"

"Yes, I do. But that still does not tell me how and where Marmaduke died. I am half inclined to suspect Pedwardine has fabricated the whole of his tale of what happened at Thorpe Grange between him and Marmaduke. Yet I cannot rid myself of the suspicion that Martin Thorpe knows more about it than he saw fit to tell Francis."

Sybilla rose. "For my part, you are hunting a mare's nest. There is nothing to find. You said yourself there is no question of murder."

Ottilia met the black gaze, speaking the thought in her mind. "I am no longer certain of that."

Having seen off both her mother-in-law and her husband, the one to take her prescribed walk in the grounds, the other to visit Pretty in the nursery, Ottilia retired to her parlour where she found her niece in possession. Lizzy was in the window seat, apparently lost in thought as she gazed out. She did not turn on the opening of the door and Ottilia was moved to wonder if she actually saw the misted hills in the distance. One could not tell from her profile, but the pose gave off an air of dejection.

Ottilia suppressed a sigh. She had put off this discussion too long. She shifted into the room and the movement must have caught Lizzy's attention for she turned her head in a sharp gesture. A little gasp escaped her. "It's you, Aunt. You don't object to my invading your eyrie, do you? I thought I ought not to come in when Marmaduke's uncle was there."

Ottilia went to her daybed and perched upon its seat, leaning on the back and gesturing. "Come and sit with me, Lizzy. It is high time we talked."

Her niece hesitated, biting her lip. She turned back to the window as she rose, peering out. "I may as well. He is out of sight now."

So that was what held her attention. "Vivian?"

Lizzy came around the daybed and plonked down, throwing herself against the back and drumming her fingers on the cushioned seat. Ottilia waited, concern gathering in her breast. With an abrupt transition, Lizzy sat up, turning to face her aunt.

"He does not wish to be married. He sees it as a trap. He wants to be free to go where the mood takes him and — and sketch his wretched drawings!"

Ottilia had to smile. "He told you this?"

"As good as. I don't even recall precisely what he said. Richenda appeared immediately afterwards and I was distracted."

"Understandable." Ottilia probed the anomaly. "The subject of marriage was then discussed? Even though Vivian made no offer."

Colour stained Lizzy's cheeks but she tossed a defiant head. "If you will push me to it, Aunt, I asked him why he would not marry me."

"Ah, did you?"

"Yes, and you need not tell me it was unmaidenly, for I know it already. I have been well served for my boldness." A note of anguish entered. "Except that it wasn't bold. I didn't think of what I should or shouldn't say. It just came out because I wanted to know."

Ottilia took hold of one agitated hand. "I did not reproach you, child."

"Oh, I knew you would not. You are the only person to whom I could confess." A somewhat hectic giggle escaped her. "Uncle Francis warned me not to ask Vivian to marry me, and I didn't, I promise you. But why shouldn't a female bring up the subject?"

"Most unfair, is it not?" Ottilia squeezed the hand she held. "You might consider, however, that it is quite as difficult for gentlemen. They have all the onus of offering and may suffer the ignominy of being rejected. Then, if they are accepted and find they have made a mistake, they may not cry off."

Lizzy did not seem inclined to allow this. "Well, but they have the option not to offer, even when they know full well the female cares about them. They have all the advantage."

"You mean Vivian has all the advantage." Realising the argument was pointless, Ottilia changed tack. "What did you say to Vivian when he intimated that he did not wish to marry."

"I told him he was selfish. That he isn't the man I thought he was, but that is nonsense. He is just the man I knew he was." An edge crept into Lizzy's voice. "Insouciant and uncaring. I ought to have guessed how it would be. I knew it, underneath.

Else he would have offered last year when he came to Dalesford. I told myself he was intimidated because Mama so obviously disapproved. Papa too. But it wasn't so, Aunt Ottilia. He could not bring himself up to scratch because he doesn't want to marry even though he loves me."

"Did he say he loves you?"

Lizzy sniffed, a quiver at her lips. "Not in so many words, but it's what he meant. Besides, I know he does. He would have left by now if he didn't. He has no real reason to remain only to help with your investigation."

Ottilia felt compelled to enter a caveat. "You are forgetting that your uncle insisted he remain."

Lizzy shrugged, releasing her hand from her aunt's hold. "Vivian wouldn't care for that. He goes his own way."

Ottilia did not dispute the point. She was exercised by her own lack. She was so little acquainted with Vivian Maplewood it was hard to make any judgement of her own. It was, however, politic to discourage Lizzy from making any further demands upon the man. "If you value my advice —"

"I always do, Aunt, you know that."

"Thank you. I was about to say that it might serve you best to remain aloof."

Lizzy's nose was in the air. "Oh, you need not think I mean to sue to him. We have scarcely exchanged two words since."

"Excellent. You will abide by that practice, if you are wise."

Lizzy's gaze widened upon hers. "Do you think that will work upon him?"

"It may. It is certainly more likely to do so than if you were to plague him with unwanted attentions."

"Unwanted! They were not unwanted before."

Ottilia groaned aloud. "That is beside the point, child. Keep your distance, Lizzy. Let him come to you. If he is indeed overfond of you, he will find it hard to be left out in the cold."

A deep sigh came in response. "If you want the truth, it is hard for me too."

"I don't doubt it." An idea surfaced and Ottilia regarded her niece with a touch of speculation. It would take the child out of Vivian's orbit for a space and perhaps she might scrape acquaintance with one or other of the young gentlemen, who might well visit Claydon. It could do no harm to let Vivian note the possibility of a rival. "You might visit Etta tomorrow perhaps."

Lizzy's brows drew together. "Visit Etta?"

"I was thinking of your notion of her replacing Teresa Mellis with your grandmother."

The frown did not abate. "I thought you said it is too early to be suggesting it. Besides, I've not yet sounded out Grandmama."

"If Sybilla approves the notion, she will wish to conduct an interview and enquire into Henrietta's family connections. It strikes me that it might be politic to discover the girl's sentiments first."

This drew a hint of Lizzy's mischievous smile at last. "Especially if Grandmama refuses to entertain the notion."

"Just so. That is settled then. You will employ the greatest tact and merely suggest the possibility. There is besides no saying what you may inadvertently find out in that house that may shed light on this Marmaduke business."

Francis took it that his wife had just finished feeding their son when he walked into her parlour, since she was engaged in covering the fabric of her bodice over her breast. She smiled, putting a finger to her lips.

"He is sleeping."

Francis came across and sat down beside her, reaching a finger to stroke the infant's smooth cheek. Luke's minute mouth opened and closed again. Francis kept his voice muted. "He seems contented."

Tillie's expression, as she gazed down at the infant, was tender. A pang smote Francis. He suppressed it.

She spoke softly. "He is just like his papa." A mischievous glance was cast at him. "Once his hunger is satisfied, he is as good-tempered as you please."

"Wretch!"

A muted giggle came. "His appetite is quite as demanding too."

"Any more and I shall walk away this instant."

"No, don't." She slipped her hand into his. "We have not had a chance for privacy this age."

Except in the bedchamber. But Francis refrained from mentioning this since the current exigencies left scant time for discussion as his darling wife was usually too tired to engage much. Nor did he wish to appear curmudgeonly by expressing his oft felt wish everyone would go away and leave them alone. Until the wretched Marmaduke business was settled, there was no hope of that. Moreover, his brother-in-law was likely to arrive at any day.

Tillie released his hand and nudged him. "Pray call Doro for me, Fan, and we can talk."

"In a moment," he said, his gaze catching on his son again. An odd feeling crept into his breast. "He is so very tiny." He measured his finger against the baby hand and, despite that Luke slept, the minute fingers closed about his own. A flood of feeling engulfed him and the words came unbidden. "He has never done that before."

"It comforts him."

Francis had no words. He sat mumchance, mesmerised by the baby grip. It released after a moment and he felt peculiarly bereft. He regarded the perfect little fingers resting against his large one, the tiny nails, the pink hand, all with a sense of wonder.

"It is incredible to think how this small person will grow and become a man at last." His gaze shifted to his wife's as he spoke and found her with tears standing in her eyes. "Sweetheart! Why are you weeping?"

But she was smiling. "I did not dare to hope Luke would capture your heart so soon."

Francis took her hand and kissed it. "Nor did I, to be truthful. I have neither knowledge nor experience of babies." He drew in a breath and sighed it out. "He is a perfect little man. I dare say I will spoil him as much as I spoil Pretty."

He said it to please her, but she made a face. "You won't. You will harry the poor boy and try to turn him into a copy of yourself."

"Of course I won't."

"It is what fathers do."

"With sons? And mothers no less with their daughters no doubt."

She nudged him again. "Fetch Doro, Fan. We will wake him."

Thus adjured, he rose, but with reluctance, and went to the door. Doro was waiting by the balustrade and came at once when Francis beckoned.

"Master Luke is ready, milord?"

"Yes, thank you."

He watched as his wife kissed the child and handed him over. He had seen her do so many times, but this felt different. He saw her at last as his son's mother as well as his wife. More than ever he yearned for the house to be emptied of visitors that they might live as a family in the cosy way they had before the advent of the corpse on the doorstep.

When the door closed behind Doro, he went straight back to the sofa, retook his seat and drew his wife into his embrace. "Do you know how very much I adore you, mother of my son?"

She accepted his caress with fervour, but her eyes quizzed him. "Is this brought on by your discovering Luke's tiny hands?"

"You know well it is. I wish very much we did not have all these persons cluttering up the house. I want my family to myself."

She tucked her hand in his. "Then help me unravel this mess, Fan. I don't mind admitting it has me quite in a puzzle."

Francis was not best pleased to be dragged back to the matter, but if it would hasten the departure of their guests, so be it. "You've not benefited from what Gibbon had to tell us?"

She sat back, her brow creasing. "If anything, it but complicates things further."

"How so?"

He came under the beam of her clear gaze, but her thoughts were obviously elsewhere. "Did someone deliver the *coup de grâce* with a second blow? The boy could not sustain even one, according to his uncle. If so, who was it?"

Francis held her gaze. "Whom do you think it was?"

"I want to say Percy Pedwardine. Everything points to him."

"Does it? Why should he eliminate his friend?"

"That is just it. Why indeed, Fan? The only notion that comes to mind is to sweep Marmaduke from his path in order to have Richenda for himself."

Francis entered an immediate caveat. "But he can't bear that female."

"He might overlook his dislike in order to secure her fortune."

"Over Vexford's dead body."

"Just so."

Francis stared. "You seriously think Pedwardine would dispose of Vexford?"

She shifted her shoulders and squeezed his hand. "There is the difficulty."

"I should just think so. He has only to elope with the chit. Why should he kill off Vexford into the bargain?"

She let out a laugh. "I don't mean that. I can imagine nothing more unlikely."

"Then what did you mean?"

"Merely that Vexford is the bar to such a plan. If he could not stomach Marmaduke for a husband for his daughter, and Percy must know that, how in the world should he accept a fellow with no expectations?"

"How do you know he has no expectations?"

"If he had, he would have said so. He knows well I am looking at him askance. Why not at once remove any possible motive, if he was able?"

Trying, without much success, to unravel all this, Francis arrived at frustration. "Well, if not Pedwardine, then who? Claydon?"

He was treated to one of his darling wife's enigmatic looks. "If I say it, you will laugh me to scorn."

Intrigued, he quirked an eyebrow. "Try me, you witch of a wife."

It was a moment before she capitulated. "Martin Thorpe."

Taken utterly aback, Francis released her hand and turned on the daybed to stare at her. At length, he spoke the thought in his mind. "You're raving, Tillie."

She gave him a mischievous look. "Yes, so I thought at first."

"Well?"

She shrugged. "I do not know. I have not yet pieced it all together."

"Nor will you, for my money."

"You may be right."

He waited for more, but nothing was forthcoming. Irritation burgeoned. "Well, you can't leave it there, woman. What in the world makes you even think of Martin Thorpe?"

She drew a breath. "For one thing, if he was not instrumental in the death, he at least knew Marmaduke was dead and had a hand in moving the body."

"It does not therefore follow that same hand caused the man's death." Francis found his head teeming with argument. "Granted, Thorpe should better have called in a doctor there and then if he discovered the fellow dead. Foolish to remove the body altogether, assuming you have that right. I concede he might have a motive in wishing Jarvis to benefit, but he could not ensure that without ridding himself of the other rivals. Nor could he be certain Vexford would accept his brother's suit. Indeed, it's clear he wouldn't. He thinks the lot of them are unworthy whippersnappers. Moreover," he pursued, warming to his theme, "Thorpe himself told me he has warned Jarvis not to saddle himself with such a father-in-law as Vexford must make. No, Tillie, this won't fadge." He met her gaze as he spoke and found it rueful. "Well, what?"

She gave one of her warm smiles. "You have enumerated every one of my arguments, my dearest dear. And yet…"

"And yet?" Chagrined to have been once again beaten to the post, he waited for her refutation. It did not come.

"My darling lord, I wish I might satisfy you. I cannot even satisfy myself in the matter. Yet it certainly does not satisfy me to think that Jarvis and Botolf alone were responsible for moving the body. And if they did, why? Unless to protect Martin Thorpe?"

"From what? Complicity in the death? You had as well think it of Botolf or Jarvis."

"Just so, but supposing Marmaduke was found, by one or the other, perhaps not yet dead, and in trying to revive or help the man, he succumbed. From the damage of the first blow, if we cannot successfully accept a motive for murder. What then, Fan?"

"Then the obvious thing was to send for a physician."

"Which was not done. Instead, the poor wretch appears on our porch four and twenty hours later."

"Yes, but that does not mean —"

"Figure to yourself, Fan, how it must appear if the boy died on them in such a way. Suspicions, questions, endless difficulty. Bad enough there had been the altercation with Botterell. Now here is a corpse on their hands. What in the world are they to do?"

Impatience claimed Francis. "For pity's sake, explain, Tillie!"

"We know they did not send it to me. They could not do so without arousing suspicion. There would be no point in having concealed the death at all. Therefore they moved it to a far more convenient location."

Francis could not avoid a sceptical note. "Convenient for whom?"

"For the Thorpes, of course. Highly inconvenient, not to mention disconcerting, for its recipient. But a corpse it most definitely was. I only wish I could fathom just how it came to be so."

CHAPTER TWENTY

Lizzy ordered the Fanshawe carriage for her visit to Henrietta Skelmersdale, requesting the attendance of her footman. Charles held the door and she was just about to step up into it when Vivian hailed her.

"Lady Elizabeth!"

Ignoring the instant flurry in her pulse, Lizzy turned to find he had come out of the house behind her. "I did not see you there, sir."

He came alongside, a frown creasing his brow. "Where are you off to?"

Lizzy lifted her chin. "What is it to you?"

His gaze narrowed. "Nothing at all. I was merely interested. Are you on a mission for Lady Fan?"

Lizzy thawed a little. "Not precisely. I mean to visit Etta." Should she mention her true purpose? She opted for simplicity. "She is bereaved, you know."

"Lady Stoke Rochford's companion? Ought I to pay my respects?"

What did this betoken? Was he angling to accompany her? Wary of a too intimate situation, Lizzy probed. "Why should you? You are not acquainted with her."

"I am acquainted with Claydon. I imagine he is also bereaved."

This was said with an ironic inflection so typical that Lizzy was hard put to it not to hit back in the old way. Too flustered to think clearly, she said just what she had meant not to say. "You can come if you wish."

His gaze held hers. "I do wish."

In some disorder, Lizzy climbed up into the carriage and took a seat. Vivian sprang in, crossed her and sat down on the other side. The door closed and the carriage was on the move before Lizzy could think why in the world she had capitulated.

The essence of Ottilia's scheme was to stay aloof so that Vivian might be induced to come to her. Belatedly, it occurred to her that it was exactly what he had done. She turned on the thought to confront him. "You could have asked me at breakfast."

"You could have told me at breakfast."

Irrationally annoyed, Lizzy spat back. "Why should I tell you my proposed movements?"

"Would you prefer to stop the carriage and let me out?"

"Prefer it to what?"

"Conversing with me."

"I am conversing with you, stupid man!"

To her combined chagrin and delight, he burst out laughing. "There's the Eliza I know!"

Lizzy could not decide whether to glare or smile. "You are the most infuriating creature, Mr Maplewood."

"Likewise, Lady Elizabeth."

"Oh, stop it! Did you come with me only to drive me to distraction?"

"Of course. Isn't that the basis of our friendship?"

The burgeoning warmth in Lizzy's bosom was quenched. Was this his desire? To rekindle their former relationship?

"We can still be friends, can we not?"

Had he read her mind? "I don't know, Vivian."

He was silent for a space and the sound of the horse's hooves grew loud in Lizzy's ears. When he spoke again, it was in a tone too soft for her comfort. "Can we try, Eliza?"

She looked round and found an expression in his face that spoke to her heart. Lizzy hardened it. "Half a loaf, Vivian?"

"I don't want to lose you altogether."

Lizzy discovered her muscles were tensed. With deliberation, she sank back against the squabs, looking away from him. "I'm afraid that is inevitable."

There was a pause. Lizzy held her breath. His voice came like a caressing breeze. "Does it have to be?"

Oh, wretch! Wretched, cruel man! Lizzy turned and looked him straight in the face. "There is no help for it. You see, I am not set against matrimony. Did you not say it yourself? My husband, when I come to marry, will not take kindly to my intimacy with a former —" She paused, putting a finger to her chin. "I hesitate over what to call you. Former what, would you say?"

His face, to her secret satisfaction, was frozen, his eyes hard. "You need say no more, Lady Elizabeth. I understand you perfectly."

Next instant, he was rapping on the roof. Lizzy's heart sank as the carriage came to a standstill. Vivian opened the door on his side. He did not look at her as he spoke.

"I will walk back. Good day to you."

Then he jumped out and the door slammed shut. She heard him call to Williams to drive on as a welter of feeling rushed into her bosom. Hateful of him! Why could he not fight for her? What price saying he did not wish to lose her altogether then? Well, it proved he was determined against her, just as he had said on that hateful day.

She was obliged to dash at her welling eyes, berating herself for a fool to be weeping over the worthless creature Vivian had shown himself to be. A mental review of what had been said served to fuel both her fury and her upset and she railed in her mind for some little while. By the time the carriage turned into the rutted lane leading to Lady Stoke Rochford's residence, a creeping notion had taken possession of her mind.

Perhaps this was the best outcome after all. If Vivian truly did not wish to lose her, he might miss her friendship enough to come to his senses. Friendship! How dared he offer merely that when he knew she wanted so much more? Well, Vivian Maplewood might now see what came of his recalcitrance. She hoped he would choke on it.

The carriage halted and Lizzy was obliged to swallow down her distresses. She was here to offer Etta comfort and a glimpse of a better future, not to seek comfort for herself. Though a wish of confiding in someone would not be entirely suppressed.

The former companion was found to be immersed in funeral arrangements. She was seated at a desk in the parlour, a disordered sheaf of paper before her, pen in hand and ink stains on her fingers. She turned as Lizzy was announced, looking across with a frowning countenance for a moment as if she knew not what had been said. Then she uttered a cry and set down the pen all anyhow, leaping to her feet.

"My goodness, how glad I am to see you, Lady Elizabeth!"

"Lizzy will do, if you please." Gratified by the welcome, Lizzy moved forward, meeting her halfway across the room and taking the hand the taller woman held out. "I hope I am not disturbing you, Etta."

The other rolled expressive eyes. "You are and I am delighted. I cannot get on with this list at all. I should have been happy to have been interrupted by anyone." The disappointment Lizzy felt must have shown in her face. Etta set her other hand on the one she was clasping and leaned in. "I don't mean that, Lady Elizabeth — or rather, Lizzy. Pay no heed to me. Of course I prefer you to any other who might come here — saving Ginny perhaps."

Lizzy produced a smile. "I hope I may make a good substitute. I came to see if there is anything I might do or say to relieve you."

"Oh, everything." Etta released her, at once ushering her towards the window embrasure. "For heaven's sake, let us sit down and you may tell me how your aunt is faring in her quest."

A trifle put out, Lizzy allowed herself to be pushed into the window seat and watched Etta plonk down likewise. "I thought you were too troubled to be thinking of that matter now."

A bright smile appeared. "Believe me, I am desperate for the distraction. Botolf has delegated to me the task of preparing the list of who should be invited to partake of refreshments here after the funeral."

"Why could he not do it himself?"

"To tell you the truth, he would have done, but I persuaded him to leave it to me. After all, I know best which of our neighbours had troubled themselves about poor Robina. Yet in the event, I am finding it quite impossible to exclude anyone and I am ready to tear my hair out."

Not finding the problem of particular interest, Lizzy stated the obvious. "Then why try to exclude them?"

Etta shrugged. "Very likely I shan't. Perhaps I am prejudiced. Few cared enough to trouble about Robina in her lifetime. Why should they be honoured? Moreover, if so be it turns out one of them did dispose of that poor young man, I should much dislike to be entertaining him."

It was on the tip of Lizzy's tongue to ask if that applied to Botolf Claydon but she managed to halt the words. Instead she turned the subject closer to the point of her visit. "Are you meaning to remain here, Etta? Has Mr Claydon spoken of your future?"

Her hostess sighed. "Alas, no. I did venture to bring the matter up, but he dismissed it, saying there was time enough to be concerning ourselves over that. Time enough for him. I dare not be dilatory in finding another post." Lizzy's ears pricked up at this, but Etta had not finished. "There is no saying what Botolf intends, after all. He might even sell the place."

"Sell his godmother's residence?" A little shocked, Lizzy eyed her. "And do what with the proceeds?"

"Buy an estate closer to the metropolis, I expect."

"Why, when he has friends and acquaintance here?"

Etta made a face. "Botolf considers this area a backwater, peopled by unfashionable dullards."

Affronted on behalf of her uncle and aunt, Lizzy bridled. "He might count himself lucky to be accepted. Who is he, after all? I take it he had no other expectation than this?"

"Oh, none. Botolf's father was a scholar of note, but virtually penniless except for what he earned by taking in boys as a crammer for the university. He published several volumes much valued in academic circles, I believe. That is how Robina came to be Botolf's godmother."

"Gracious, was she a scholar too?"

"She was extremely well read. She and Mr Claydon senior struck up a correspondence and when Botolf was born, she told me, she wanted to do something for the friend Mr Claydon had become. Botolf was invited for visits as a child, Robina being childless herself."

"But did not Lord Stoke Rochford mind?"

"Robina was widowed when she was a comparatively young woman. Not much older than I am now. She never wished to remarry and as her husband left her the property, she was able to do very much as she chose for the remainder of her life."

Fortunate female. No one was obliging her to marry some titled eligible who would bore her to death within a month. Certain persons who might have been a trifle more acceptable having set their faces against matrimony altogether. Lizzy shook off the painful thoughts. Time to broach her famous notion. "Etta!"

Her hostess looked at her in surprise. "That sounded portentous."

Lizzy dredged up a laugh. "I did not mean it so. It is just that… Oh, I meant to be tactful, but since you have mentioned the matter, I may as well say it without roundaboutation."

A trifle of bewilderment showed in Etta's face. "What matter? Is there some difficulty I should know about?"

"Gracious, nothing like that!" Lizzy cleared her throat. "You met my grandmother, didn't you?"

"When she came to visit Robina, yes indeed. She looks to be quite formidable."

This was not promising. Lizzy hastened to correct an impression she could not but acknowledge to be all too accurate. "She can be, it is true. However, when you get to know her, you will discover she can be perfectly amiable."

Etta laughed. "I am sure I shall not be so fortunate as to get to know her. Is she affectionate towards you?"

"Well, she rarely shows affection but I know she is fond of her family. Or most of them, more especially Uncle Francis and Aunt Ottilia. The thing is —"

"That does not surprise me. Who could fail to like your aunt?"

Lizzy drew a determined breath. "The thing is, Etta, that my grandmother's companion is about to leave her and she must find someone new. I wondered…" She faded out at the expression on the other's face. "Oh! You hate the notion. I was afraid you might."

The features reassembled and Etta shook her head. "It is not that. I ought to be grateful. I am, I suppose. It is just that when you said it, I had a sudden recognition that…"

She faded out and Lizzy, moved, noticed her eyes were watering. "Oh, Etta, you poor thing! I am so sorry. I did not mean to upset you."

Etta waved this away. "You haven't. It catches me now and then, that is all. I grew very fond of Robina. I cannot think how I shall bear to substitute her for another."

Distressed on her behalf, Lizzy tried to backtrack. "I have been precipitate. It is too soon."

Etta dashed at the wetness on her cheeks. "No, no, you were right to mention it. I promise I will think of it. Have you spoken to your grandmother on this subject?"

"Oh, no. My aunt thought it best to speak to you first. And she was quite right. I dare say the idea fills you with horror. Grandmama is nothing if not tetchy, I admit."

"That does not frighten me. I can deal with such crochets. But Lady Polbrook lives in London, does she not? I am used to retirement and quiet."

"She is only in London for part of the Season. For the most part she resides at the Dower House at Polbrook, although she will take off upon occasion. I accompanied her to Tunbridge Wells not long since. And she was with the Fanshawes in Weymouth one summer. I am persuaded you would find it more amusing to live with her than with Lady Stoke Rochford."

She then wished she had held her tongue for Etta's features crumpled again and she dragged a handkerchief from the pocket of her gown. Lizzy watched her blow her nose and tried to make amends.

"Pray don't think of it now, Etta. If Botolf is disposed to let you take your time, you need make no decision until you are ready."

Etta tucked the handkerchief away and produced a smile, though her eyes were a trifle red. "We are getting a little ahead of ourselves, are we not? After all, Lady Polbrook, even if she is disposed to consider my candidature, will wish to assure herself that I am suitable for her purposes." She waved her hands in much her usual fashion. "But let us not dwell upon my troubles. Is Lady Fan any further forward?"

Lizzy disclosed such details as might not prejudice her aunt's investigation, but her mind returned to the little history of Botolf Claydon that Etta had revealed before the unfortunate mention of Sybilla's need of a new companion. What if he was bent upon enriching himself even further? The property he had inherited was modest. Richenda Vexford's portion would no doubt make a welcome addition.

The notion had barely settled in her mind when the man himself walked in, accompanied by two young gentlemen whom Lizzy took to be the cronies of which her aunt had spoken.

Etta took it upon herself to make the introductions and Lizzy was at once flattered and irritated to find that her rank caused an immediate brightening of interest in the two newcomers. The reflection that this might give Vivian cause for jealousy provided a ready excuse for her to be gracious. She smiled upon the chubby features of the shorter fellow.

"Delighted, Mr Botterell. I think it is your aunt who brings you to these parts, is it not, sir? Mrs Honeybourne?"

He nodded, an eager smile appearing. "My maternal aunt. She has ever been kind enough to allow me to run tame in her house."

"How fortunate." Lizzy looked up at his taller, and rather better looking, companion. "And you, Mr Thorpe? Your family is situated in Tangley, I believe."

Jarvis Thorpe's brows drew together. "You are very well informed, Lady Elizabeth."

Before she could answer, Botolf Claydon cut in, an undercurrent of mockery in his tone. "Naturally, Jarvis. She is niece to the incomparable Lady Fan." His lip curled. "No doubt you are here in the furtherance of her cause, ma'am."

Lizzy bridled inside but maintained a cool front. "As a matter of fact, I came to see if I may be of use to Etta."

"Yes, and I am excessively touched by it," chimed in Etta. "If you must know, all of you, Lizzy has just been telling me how that matter is faring. Marmaduke's uncle is here, by the by. I do think you all ought to pay your respects."

Both Botterell and Jarvis Thorpe looked horrified at this, but it was Claydon who raised an objection. "Why in the world, Etta? We hardly knew the fellow."

"No, and only think how embarrassing." This from Botterell, his colour rising. Then he seemed to recollect himself, throwing a conscious glance at Lizzy. "I mean, it would not look well, would it? After what passed."

Jarvis Thorpe set a hand on his friend's shoulder. "Easy now, Aubrey. I don't think it behoves any of us to go badgering the man."

Lizzy could not resist. "No, it is rather he who may come badgering you."

"What?"

She smiled sweetly at Botterell. "Should it enter his head to investigate on his own account."

Thorpe eyed her with misgiving. "Does he so intend?"

"I have no notion. I was not in the room when he spoke with my aunt and uncle."

Etta gave a laugh. "Fie, Lizzy! You have put them all on end for nothing."

Lizzy retained an innocent front. "Oh, dear, I am sorry. I did not mean to startle you."

A flurry of denial came.

"Nothing of the sort."

"I was not precisely startled."

"He may question me all he wants. I have nothing to hide."

This last, from Claydon, drew Lizzy's gaze. "Does anyone have anything to hide, I wonder?"

The question was productive of an uncomfortable silence. Etta broke it. "Did you come in here for a particular reason, Botolf?"

His brows rose. "Do I need one?"

She flushed. "Of course not, I was merely asking in case you needed me."

Lizzy's ire rose against the man. "We were just discussing what Etta means to do. Her situation is difficult."

His face changed. "I have already said to Etta there is no rush. There is much to be done and her help will be invaluable."

Perhaps he was not as bad as he was wont to paint himself. Lizzy produced a smile. "That must be a relief to Etta."

Surprisingly, Jarvis Thorpe moved a little closer to the woman. "We shall miss you, Etta. You have been very much a part of our circle."

"Well, that is kind of you, Jarvis, but I cannot believe any of you will remember me for long."

"Nonsense, of course we will." Thus Botterell, flanking his friend. "You are like the elder sister I never had."

A tinkle of laughter came from Etta. "Ought I to be flattered?"

He reddened. "Well, but what I mean is, always easy to talk to. Never stand on ceremony either. No one else would listen when I wanted to talk of what happened with that fellow." He seemed not to notice his reference, but continued, "Only one willing to hear me out. You made me feel like it was no great matter after all. Or at least, not my fault."

Etta glanced towards Lizzy, a wary look in her eyes, before she answered. "I don't think it was your fault, Aubrey. It was foolish perhaps, but we all know you meant no harm to that young man."

Lizzy looked from one to the other. "You spoke of it together?"

"Gracious, didn't everyone speak of it?"

Botterell became defensive. "If you must know, I came here upon the following day. I wanted to ask Botolf what had become of that fellow, but he was out."

Etta's gaze met Lizzy's. "I had no hesitation in reassuring Aubrey. If blame there is, I dare say we can all point the finger to where it belongs."

Whom did she mean? No one evidently cared to hazard a guess as to where the finger was pointed. Neither Jarvis Thorpe nor Botterell appeared pleased with the notion. Claydon looked merely cynical. Were they all in agreement? She felt obliged to probe.

"Where do you all point the finger, Etta?"

She shook her head. "Least said, soonest mended."

"She means," said Claydon in a tone distinctly patronising, "least said before one who may carry tales to Flitteris."

"I wish you will be quiet, Botolf! I did not mean that at all."

"Then what did you mean?"

Etta fixed him with a stare. "If you insist, I had no wish to offend Aubrey and Jarvis by disparaging Richenda. The whole business may be laid at her door." She turned apologetic eyes on the other two gentlemen. "You have both been her dupes. She never meant to have anyone from around here."

Jarvis Thorpe shifted his shoulders. "You need not feel bad, Etta. I have realised as much any time these past days."

A pout decorated the chubby features of Botterell. "She gave *me* encouragement. Before that fellow came here at least."

Without thinking, Lizzy intervened. "Is that why you took him to task, Mr Botterell?"

"I only wish I'd smashed his pretty face for him. Wouldn't have looked so smug with a bloody nose!"

"Then you did intend to hurt him! It was no accident after all."

Botterell's colour faded, leaving his features white. "Don't say that! A figure of speech. I meant nothing by it. It was not I who dropped him!"

"Dropped him?"

"Be quiet, you fool!"

The hissed admonition came from his taller friend, who dug him in the ribs. Lizzy's gaze flitted from one to the other, and thence to Claydon. He was looking daggers. A little thrill of excitement fluttered in her bosom and she gave it voice. "There is something! You have withheld it from my aunt!"

"Lizzy, hold a minute!"

She swept Etta's objection aside with a wafture of her hand. "No, I have to ask. Mr Botterell, why did you say it in such a way, that it was not you who *dropped* Marmaduke?"

Both Botterell and Jarvis Thorpe shifted back, the latter giving tongue. "He did not mean it literally. We all know Gibbon died that night. Aubrey's attack was not the cause."

Lizzy looked from him to Botterell and back again, seized with a conviction they were concealing something. "Is it possible Marmaduke received a second blow?"

This brought Botterell back into play. "I never gave him a blow! It was no more than a tap. Besides, he was a much larger man than I. I could not have brought him down had I tried."

"But he was brought down? Is that how he died?"

All three kept silent. Etta, surprising Lizzy, intervened. "For heaven's sake! If there is more to tell, then say it. Of what use to hold off? It will be found out in the end. From what I understand, Lady Francis is quite the bloodhound."

"Not only that," Lizzy cut in. "She has a lightning mind. She makes such connections as I can never hope to emulate. And she never fails. You cannot outwit her. It is useless to try."

Botolf Claydon maintained a faintly supercilious look and said not a word. Determined then. Lizzy turned her attention to Jarvis Thorpe and found him with tight jaw and pinched mouth. But Aubrey Botterell was biting his lip and blinking overmuch. The weak link? To her own surprise, Lizzy was hit with a flash of insight. "You have given your word to someone!"

Etta clapped her hands. "Oh, well done, Lizzy! That must be it indeed."

The impact as Lizzy gestured towards Thorpe and Claydon was clear. "You two at least." Lizzy turned on Botterell. "But not you perhaps."

He blenched. "What do you mean?"

Triumph lit in Lizzy. "You did not see it for you weren't there."

"Careful, Aubrey!"

"See what, if you please?"

Lizzy confronted Claydon. "Whatever it was, you and Mr Thorpe were witness to it. Not so Mr Botterell, but he knows. Don't you?"

"You need not answer, Aubrey. Lady Elizabeth has no authority to ask such questions."

Etta threw Claydon a glare. "Perhaps not, but it matters little. It is plain you all know just what happened to poor Marmaduke, and if you gave your word to anyone, it must be to Mr Thorpe. I mean your brother, Jarvis. No one else could command your silence."

Lizzy's breath caught. "Mr Martin Thorpe? Then my aunt must needs sue to him for the truth."

CHAPTER TWENTY-ONE

"What does that mean, Fan, *dropped him?*" Ottilia turned from her niece to her spouse, parked as ever at the mantelpiece and leaning one elbow on its convenient shelf as he listened to Lizzy's account.

"It is boxing cant."

"So I supposed, but what precisely do the words indicate."

Francis quirked an eyebrow. "Just what it says, Tillie. That the victim was felled to the ground by a blow."

Ottilia kept her gaze on him. "Necessarily to the ground?"

"You are thinking of Marmaduke's having died seated?"

"Just so."

"Well, it could equally mean he was knocked into a chair, I suppose."

"Definitely knocked?"

Her spouse lifted an eyebrow. "I think you are making more of it than you need, my love. I dare say Botterell merely meant that Gibbon was found dead thus, assuming your theory about moving the body."

Before Ottilia could question it more, she was forestalled.

"That won't fadge, Uncle Francis. Aubrey Botterell was at pains to point out that it was not his blow — which by the by he insists was merely a tap — that proved fatal. Doesn't that suggest there could have been a second blow? Isn't that what you suspect, Aunt?"

Ottilia hesitated. She had so suspected, but in relation to Percy Pedwardine. She could make out a case for his having dealt his friend a death blow, knowing as he did how vulnerable was Marmaduke to the danger in fisticuffs. Yet withal, the business was problematical.

"I have cogitated much on this, I admit," she said at length. "It does seem to me a far-fetched notion that one of these young men would go to such lengths to sweep a rival from his path. On the other hand, we have known jealousies to prompt otherwise seemingly innocent individuals to resort to murder." She glanced at her spouse. "Have we not, Fan?"

"You are thinking of that business at Witherley? But that was premeditated, Tillie."

"As this was not? I cannot but feel it was more likely to be accidental, were any of these fellows involved. One can scarcely accuse Martin Thorpe of deliberately assaulting a young man who was a guest in his house."

"But the others, Aunt? Not Aubrey, for I am sure he had no hand in it. For my part, I can believe Botolf Claydon capable of anything."

Francis expressed the thought in Ottilia's mind. "But not Jarvis Thorpe?"

Lizzy's brows drew together. "Well, he is certainly in on it, but he did not strike me as a man of violence."

"How can you possibly tell?"

Ottilia intervened. "I dare say Lizzy is thinking of his being quite controlled, Fan. I noticed it myself."

"Which Aubrey Botterell is not. I believe they confided in him and he is really not very good at keeping mum."

"If they did, it was after I spoke to those three. Botterell certainly had no knowledge of it then. I dare say he pumped his friends after our interview."

"I am certain he knew, Aunt. Moreover, he would have told me if we had been alone, I am convinced of it."

"Well, it is a pity none of them broke, Lizzy, but you have gained more than we could have hoped for." Ottilia threw her husband a quizzical glance. "Did I not insist upon Martin Thorpe's involvement?"

He snorted. "You recited me a rigmarole of whys and wherefores until my head was whirling."

"It was not, Fan, you fiend!"

"I could scarce think straight for hours afterwards."

"You were perfectly well able to think and you know it, horrid creature. You argued your case with aplomb." He grinned as he blew her a kiss and she gave an exaggerated sigh, turning to Lizzy. "You see what I am obliged to endure?"

She found an odd expression in her niece's face, akin to sadness. Or was it envy? Had matters worsened with Vivian Maplewood? He had not been seen since breakfast and Ottilia assumed he had gone off sketching. Best not to enter into the subject at this moment. Especially in her husband's presence. Francis had no patience with this pair of star-crossed lovers.

In the event, it was he who continued the discussion at hand. "Are you then intending to beard Martin Thorpe, Tillie?"

The thought elicited another sigh, of resignation. "I suppose I have no choice."

"Do you wish me to do it for you?"

She smiled across at him. "That is a generous offer, Fan, but I think I had best tackle him direct."

Ottilia took opportunity upon the following morning. The day being fine and Ottilia well wrapped up in her warm cloak, she commandeered Hemp's services to drive her to Tangley in the phaeton. Mrs Thorpe being out, she was not obliged to do the pretty and was shown directly into an upstairs drawing room where Martin Thorpe joined her in short order.

His aspect was wary as he entered the room and fixed Ottilia with a frowning gaze. "Lady Francis, how do you do?"

Ottilia had taken a stance by a window overlooking the lawns to the back of the house where a terrace below looked to be the family's preferred station for the outside. Benches were strategically placed within a central parterre from where a path led down a flight of stone steps to the lower wide lawns, adjacent to a wooded area which must provide a pleasant walk in summer. She turned to survey Mr Thorpe's lean features. "I am well, sir, I thank you."

The wariness increased. "The infant too, I hope?"

Deflection? "Our little Luke is thriving, I am happy to say."

"I am glad." He gestured to a long sofa set against the wall closest to the fire. "Will you not be seated?"

Ottilia shifted back into the room, casting a glance about the drawing room. Sofas and chairs were ranged around the walls, interspersed with pier tables and massive Chinese vases with several mirrors that served to make the space look bigger. Had this been the scene of that little contretemps at the Twelfth Night party? She paused by the sofa he had indicated but did not sit. "Was it in here that young Mr Botterell took issue with the unfortunate Marmaduke Gibbon?"

Thorpe's mouth became pinched. "I told your husband everything I knew, Lady Francis."

Ottilia produced a smile. "Ah, but I don't think you did, sir."

His eyes grew cautious. "Indeed? What do you suppose was omitted?"

She had to laugh. "Come, come, Mr Thorpe. You cannot have truly imagined I would not discover there had been more to the business than you saw fit to disclose. Far too many persons knew."

"Knew what, ma'am?"

She ignored the question, holding his eyes. "Your young gentlemen have been admirably close-mouthed. Unfortunately, they none of them have yet learned the art of schooling their countenances. In this, they are not in your league."

A faint quiver attacked his nostrils but he gave no other sign. "I fail to understand you."

"I think you understand me very well, Mr Thorpe." She waited, but nothing was forthcoming. With a sigh, she took a seat at last, inviting him with a gesture to do likewise.

Thorpe hesitated a moment before moving to the mantel where a small fire blazed and settling there in a position to warm his coat-tails, his hands behind his back.

Ottilia watched these manoeuvres with rising amusement. If he hoped to intimidate her, he was doomed to disappointment. The stance was too formally masculine for words, too obviously the master of his house confronting an unwelcome intruder.

She adopted a soft tone. "Will you tell me, sir, why you despatched Marmaduke's corpse to Lord Vexford's summer house?"

Shock leapt in his eyes. Excellent. She had disconcerted him. He recovered with speed. "Of what are you talking, madam?"

Ottilia uttered a dismissive sound. "Pray don't waste my time, sir. Richenda found Marmaduke dead in the summer house upon the morning following your party. She it was who sent the body to me in the evening."

The pinched look returned to his face. "What has that to do with me?"

Ottilia sighed. "I seem to have gone over this time and again. Marmaduke had sent his carriage back to the inn. He rejected his friend's offer to drive him. He was, at the least, incapacitated. How did he get from here to Wyke Hall in the night hours without assistance?"

"I have no notion."

"I find that very strange, you see. You claim not to have seen Marmaduke leave the house. So does everyone else. Therefore he did not leave."

"That does not follow. He could have begged a ride from anyone."

"Certainly. Only no one admits to having supplied him with such. Had he begged assistance in your stables, I imagine you would know of it."

"Not necessarily."

Ottilia lost patience. "Oh, don't be so ridiculous! It is time and past we ended this farce. You, together with your brother and Botolf Claydon, connived at removing Marmaduke's dead body from this house and taking it to a place where Lord Vexford must be thought complicit in the death." She waited for denial, but it did not come. Martin Thorpe maintained a stony silence. Ottilia resumed. "Vexford happens to be the one person who did not have a hand in this business. Or he and Miss Grindlow's guardian, Seth Newton. Virtually every other man involved most certainly did."

Her quarry shrugged lightly. "If you know so much, ma'am, why come to me?"

A sliver of triumph lit Ottilia's bosom. It was not precisely a confession, but at least he was no longer protesting its truth. "I come to you for the facts I don't know, Mr Thorpe."

His eyes held on hers, narrow and suspicious. "Facts such as what?"

She drew a breath. "Marmaduke died here, but when and precisely how? Did you or one of the young gentlemen find him thus? Or did you see him expire?"

He threw back his head and let out a long groaning sigh. Then his shoulders drooped and he reached a hand to the mantel, gripping its edge.

Ottilia was conscious of pity. "You have been holding this secret for a full week, Mr Thorpe. Too long, I fear. Unburden yourself, I conjure you."

At that, he dropped his gaze. Then he backed a step and sank into the chair conveniently set to one side of the fireplace. Ottilia waited, watching as he put a hand to his forehead, rubbing at it as if he had the headache. At length, he dropped both hands and clasped them between his knees, looking up at last towards her.

"I had to make a rapid choice. Botolf came to me in my library. I thought everyone had gone. I went in to take a nightcap before retiring."

"Your wife had already gone to bed?"

He nodded. "I was not particularly surprised to see Botolf. He is Jarvis's close friend, comes and goes pretty much as he pleases. But on this occasion he brought dread tidings." A little shudder shook him. "Botolf had found Marmaduke still sitting in the breakfast parlour. Sleeping, as he supposed. He went to rouse him." A hoarse little cry escaped him. "You cannot imagine the horror."

Ottilia did not speak, her mind working. Did Claydon find him? Or was he responsible for his condition?

"A guest in my house, dead! I went directly to ascertain the truth of it. I found him just as Botolf described. I knew not what to do."

Send for a doctor? It would seem the logical choice, but Ottilia refrained from saying as much, unwilling to stop the man's loosened tongue.

"By the time I was certain life was extinct, Botolf had fetched Jarvis. Botterell, my brother said, had already left. Thankfully."

Then the story of a meeting between Jarvis Thorpe and Botolf Claydon at the Plough was another fabrication. Thorpe had fallen silent and Ottilia was obliged to apply a prompt. "When did you decide to remove the body from your house?"

"Not immediately." He got up and paced as he spoke, evidently restless at the memories evoked. "We waited, discussing our options. I wanted to be sure the servants had gone to bed. Quite when the notion came to me I no longer recall. I know only that I wanted to be rid of the business. The complications were too dreadful to be borne. And all the time, while we talked, knowing that boy was sitting there, for all the world as if he slept. I tell you, it has given me nightmares."

Ottilia was not surprised. She refrained from pointing out that he could have avoided all such distresses by reporting the death at the outset. "How did you manage the transfer?"

He halted, looking a trifle less oppressed now the story was told. "The boys took care of it. Jarvis saddled the horses and I helped them load the dead man onto Botolf's mount. A cool customer that boy. He rode while holding the body." Another shudder. "I could not have done so."

Ottilia made no comment on that point. She already knew enough of Botolf Claydon to believe him capable of such insensitivity. "I had supposed you used a carriage for the purpose."

Martin Thorpe made a gesture of dismissal. "We dared not risk it. On horseback, the boys might hope to enter Vexford's grounds unperceived. Jarvis told me they rode around the back, walking the horses on grass. It was accomplished without incident, much to my relief."

"I imagine so." She regarded him as he stood in the middle of the room, his face grey and defeated. "What made you choose Vexford?"

He emitted a harsh laugh. "Who else? Besides, it was the likeliest scenario, knowing the fellow's attachment to Richenda."

"Why the summer house?"

"Jarvis knew Richenda was wont to use it for assignations. He had met her there once or twice."

Scarcely a surprise. The inimical nature of Richenda's father towards her suitors made it certain she would conduct her flirtations in a clandestine fashion.

"You did not then choose Vexford in hopes he would take the blame?"

"Good God, no! In my mind there was no questions of— of —"

"Foul play?"

"He looked too peaceful to have been slain. Why a young fellow should die suddenly is a mystery, but —"

"You were not seeking to protect Aubrey Botterell?"

He shifted away. "Not specifically. Though that foolish argument was in my mind. If questions were to be raised…"

"Better they should be raised on Vexford's account."

"No! Not that." He made a motion at his head as if he might tear his hair, had he not been wearing a wig. "I wanted the body off my premises. The most convenient place was the one I chose. That is all."

Ottilia had no comfort for him. "Sadly, it was not all, since Richenda saw fit to pass the problem on to me."

He sighed. "Had I foreseen that, I think I should have acted differently."

Ottilia got up. "I am glad you decided to tell me the truth at last."

A grimace came. "You gave me little choice, Lady Francis."

Ottilia was moved to a spurt of laughter. "It is a little habit of mine, I fear. You may thank your stars you were not the one who found Marmaduke."

Martin Thorpe's face changed. "You mean you suspect Botolf had a hand in it?"

"It is possible. He, or one other."

"Who?"

Ottilia smiled at him. "You kept your secret, Mr Thorpe. You must allow me to keep one of mine."

Sounds of a commotion from the hall brought Francis out of his study. A female voice he could not at once place was raised in quivering alarm.

"Either her ladyship or Lord Francis I must see at once! I cannot waste a moment!"

"I will ascertain whether his lordship is available, ma'am." Rodmell, attempting to inject calm.

"He must be available, if he is here. For heaven's sake, send to him to come to me at once!"

Francis made for the main stairs and ran down to the hall where he could see the duenna from the Vexford household who was just inside the front door, subjecting the butler to an agitated waving of her arms as she spoke.

"Why have you not gone? Speed is of the essence, man!"

"If you will allow me to conduct you to the morning room, ma'am —"

"Don't conduct me anywhere, but go, I charge you! Fetch your master to me this instant!"

Francis intervened, calling out as he marched across the chequered floor. "I am here, Miss Poynton. What is amiss?"

Both she and the butler turned their heads, the latter visibly relieved. Miss Poynton threw up her hands, staggering towards Francis. "Aid, my lord! Aid, I beg you!"

He caught the hands as she reached him, holding her off. "Calm yourself, Miss Poynton! Of course I will help you, if I can."

"If! Yes, I must hope you can. Mercy me, where will it all end?"

He realised she was shaking and signed to Rodmell. "A little brandy, I think. In the morning room."

About to escort the afflicted woman across the hall, he was arrested by his mother's voice from above. "Francis, what in the world is afoot? What is all this shouting?"

"I don't yet know, ma'am."

"Who is that?"

To his annoyance, Sybilla began to descend the stairs. He did not trouble to answer but again tried to shift Miss Poynton in the direction of the morning room. "Can you walk, ma'am?"

She threw a startled glance up at him. "Walk? Yes, why?"

"I think you will be more comfortable if you can sit down."

She uttered a cry. "What does my comfort signify in this calamity?"

His patience was sapping fast. "Come, if you please. We cannot discuss —"

"What calamity?"

His mother had arrived on the scene. Miss Poynton wrenched away from Francis, turning towards her. "I hoped for Lady Fan in this extremity."

"Well, you will have to make do with me and my son. What calamity?"

A groan escaped Miss Poynton. "I can hardly speak of it."

"For heaven's sake, woman! If you want help, you had better open your lips."

"Don't fluster her, ma'am." Francis abandoned the attempt to retire to a more private accommodation. "I take it something has happened to Richenda?"

"If that were all!"

Here a new voice entered the fray, much to Francis's irritation. "Gracious, what is happening?"

"That, Lizzy, is precisely what we are trying to find out." He spoke with asperity, noting that the company was augmented not only by his niece running down the stairs, but also by Vivian, who came in by the open front door. Ignoring the lot of them, Francis addressed the duenna again. "Miss Poynton, pay no heed to all these people, but attend to me." He put up a hand as his niece opened her mouth. "No, Lizzy, be quiet. Let the woman speak."

"Quite right, Francis." His mother, just as if she had not been the worst of all, waved an imperious hand. "Be quiet, all of you!"

Curbing a wish to retort, Francis concentrated on Miss Poynton, taking up the likeliest scenario. "Has Richenda eloped?"

Miss Poynton shuddered. "It is worse than that, I fear. She would not have left her father lying injured, no matter how much they quarrel. Lord Francis, I am very much afraid she has been abducted."

A raft of unnecessary sounds of astonishment broke out around him, but Francis fastened on the salient point. "How is Vexford injured?"

"We think he was hit. His head is bleeding. He was no longer unconscious when I came away, but he is groggy."

"You've sent for a doctor?"

"Yes, and our fellows have taken him to his room. Our housekeeper is detailed to bathe his wound." She seized Francis's arm. "But I dared not delay. Richenda is gone. Someone has taken her!"

At this, Lizzy cut in. "Are you sure she has not ridden out like the last time?"

Miss Poynton waved frantic hands. "I thought of that at once, but her horse is in the stables and the grooms have not seen her today."

A number of possibilities were racing through Francis's mind. "Did you check her chamber to see if she has packed anything?"

"I did think of it. I went there directly, as soon as I had seen to Lord Vexford's needs. I knew she was not there for I had sent her maid to fetch her when her papa was found, but I hoped she might have come back."

"Where was he found?"

"On the drive, out near the stable block. Which is most odd, because I am sure I saw him earlier, making for the summer house."

Sybilla exclaimed. "This pestilential summer house again!"

Francis gave a silent curse. "Is it possible Richenda had an assignation and Vexford caught her at it?"

"But she would not attack her own father," Lizzy objected.

"That is not what I am supposing."

"What then, sir?"

He looked at Miss Poynton. "If there had been some sort of meeting and Lord Vexford found a man with his daughter, what do you suppose he might do?"

Miss Poynton did not hesitate. "Cosmo would set about him."

"Then I dare say we may assume that is what happened. The fellow defended himself and Vexford was hurt. He must have still been able to walk if he was found elsewhere."

His mother was nodding along. "Until his wound overcame him? Well reasoned, Francis. But what of the girl?"

Dragged away, it would seem. But Francis did not voice the thought. "Whether or not she went willingly, it behoves us to find her in short order."

For the first time, Vivian spoke. "Which of those of her admirers did it, do you think, sir?"

"A very good question, my friend, and I think you may be able to find out."

"Vivian? How?"

"Quiet, Lizzy. Now, listen to me, all of you." He had spoken in his soldier voice of command and the result was gratifying. Even his mother looked all attention. He tackled her at once. "Ma'am, I must beg you will go back to Wyke Hall with Miss Poynton here and render whatever assistance you can."

"Very well, but I had best take Elizabeth. She may run any errands for me."

Lizzy did not look best pleased, but Francis encouraged her. "Just what I was going to suggest. Lizzy, you may take opportunity to go to the summer house and see if you can find signs of any altercation, a weapon perhaps, or any little item that may have fallen or been left."

His niece brightened. "Look for clues? Yes, indeed. I shall come with you, Grandmama."

"Well, if you want to be useful, you may go and fetch me a cloak and get yourself a pelisse, girl." As Lizzy hurried away towards the stairs, Sybilla turned to Francis. "What will you be doing?"

"I am going after the runaways."

Miss Poynton seized his hand again. "Thank you, my lord, thank you a thousand times."

He released himself. "You may thank me when I return your charge to you. Mama, I leave Miss Poynton in your care." He found the butler hovering with a tray and became aware that several other servants had gathered. "Give Miss Poynton the brandy, Rodmell. Tyler!"

The footman, who was among those present, stepped forward. "My lord?"

"My curricle, if you please. Tell Ryde to be ready to accompany me. As quick as he can."

Tyler shot off to the nether regions and Francis, seeing that his mother was supervising the administering of brandy to the afflicted duenna, turned his attention to Vivian, who came smartly to attention.

"Your orders, my lord?"

Francis gave a laugh. "I'm glad you are ready to assist."

"It's the least I can do, sir. What do you need?"

"You'd best take a vehicle, I think. Riding will be too slow."

"I have my own carriage, never fear."

"Excellent. I want you to track down as many of those young men as you can find."

Vivian frowned. "You want them to help too?"

"I want to know which of them has taken Richenda. If you fail to locate one, we will have our man."

CHAPTER TWENTY-TWO

Stepping down from the phaeton, Ottilia passed a glance across the façade of Flitteris Manor. Hemp had helped her down and she released his hand.

"It is oddly quiet, Hemp."

He threw a look one way and then the other. "It does not seem any different to me, milady."

"Well, for one thing, no one has come out to greet me, or even opened the door as they usually do. For another, there are a great many hoofprints and carriage tracks decorating the drive." She indicated the wheel marks carved into the gravel and the distinct, if partial, prints in the shape of horse shoes.

Hemp's brows drew together as his gaze took in the impressions. "I had not noticed, but you are right, milady."

"You had your attention on the horses, Hemp, but it struck me as we turned in at the gates. I was expecting to find several vehicles."

"One at least has passed around to the back, milady." Hemp pointed to a definite track leading away from where the phaeton stood.

Ottilia became brisk. "We had best find out what has been happening here."

Even as she spoke, the front door opened and a figure with which she was not greatly familiar moved into the aperture. A voice she recognised called out in jovial tones which yet had a touch of exasperation. "Ottilia, thank the Lord! I thought I had come to a mausoleum. Where the deuce is everyone?"

"Dalesford!" Ottilia started forward and her husband's brother-in-law came out of the house, meeting her in the porch. She gave him her hand, smiling a greeting. "My dear Gil, how unfortunate you should arrive just at this moment."

He grinned. "Or at any moment, perhaps. I gathered the place was full to bursting already."

"Nonsense, I am delighted to see you. As to where everyone is, I am as much in the dark as are you."

He wagged a finger, laughing. "Ah, but I am before you there. Rodmell tells me they are all gone off on some wild goose chase to do with this investigation of yours."

Ottilia broke into laughter. "I hope it may not prove to be wild." She turned to give thanks and dismissal to Hemp and found he was already leading the equipage and pair off, no doubt heading for the stables. She turned back to the newcomer. "Let us go in, Gil, and we will enquire of Rodmell just what has occurred."

Gilbert Fiske, Earl of Dalesford, was a slight man closely resembling his daughter, Elizabeth, though with a nose more prominent and a firmer chin, and characterised by a pair of humorous grey eyes and an insouciant manner. He followed Ottilia in as he resumed the conversation. "I suppose I need not be surprised at my daughter's charging off somewhere."

"No, indeed. Lizzy has been eager to participate."

"I make no doubt of it, the little minx."

He did not, to Ottilia's relief, refer to the matter that had brought him. How she was to explain to Lizzy's papa the turmoil in which her niece found herself in relation to Vivian Maplewood was a question she did not care to contemplate at this present. Thankfully, the butler, who had evidently opened the door, now coughed to draw attention to himself.

"Rodmell, just the man we need. I hope you mean to tell me what has set the household by the ears. But first, have you and Mrs Bertram seen to Lord Dalesford's accommodation?"

"Mrs Bertram is attending to the matter now, my lady. I was about to offer his lordship refreshment."

"Not before time," chimed in Gil, his tone cheerful. "I breakfasted in Winchester but I am peckish. Anything you can rustle up, Rodmell, will be welcome."

Ottilia moved towards the stairs. "Give order for it, will you, and then pray come to the withdrawing room directly."

"As you wish, my lady."

"I hesitate to give orders in your house, Ottilia, but —"

"But you would be glad of a glass of something?"

Gil laughed out. "Fan always says you are one jump ahead."

Ottilia had to smile. "It wasn't difficult. But you need have no fear. Rodmell is also expert at reading the signs." Ottilia turned to the butler. "You are able to give me the needed account, I trust, Rodmell?"

The butler looked unhappy. "As near as I can, my lady, but I must at once confess that I did not fully follow his lordship's reasoning."

"I just wish to know what happened. But let that wait. Lord Dalesford's needs are paramount."

"You are the perfect hostess," said this worthy as they began to mount the stairs together. "How fares the Fanshawe son and heir?"

"Thriving, I thank you. He promises to take after his papa, at least in his eating habits."

Gil shouted with laughter and Ottilia was relieved to find that his daughter's vagaries had not impaired his habitual good humour. She enquired after his son in her turn. "And Gregory? Does his limb mend?"

"That imp? You would not suppose from his antics that he had broke his arm so recently. He has suborned his young brothers and his little sister into running around after him while he sits there like the Sultan of Arabia."

Ottilia's maid met her at the top of the stairs and took the cloak she shrugged off. Then she led the way to the front withdrawing room as Gil continued to talk of his offspring, the pride in his voice unmistakeable. Lizzy was the eldest of five, outstripping her nearest brother by some years. It had been a solace to Ottilia when she discovered that her sister-in-law Harriet had been obliged to wait for the heir after giving birth to Lizzy.

"I lost two in between, Ottilia," she had confided by way of consolation for Ottilia's loss, "but in the end, we had Gregory and the other three followed in short order."

At the time, it had not served to ease the deep-seated ache, but the advent of little Luke had given Ottilia hope of birthing another child. If not, she had Pretty, and there was yet time for her to accept her for a mother.

Gil's anecdotes were brought to an end as the butler entered, Tyler in his wake with the promised tray. The visitor pounced on the decanter the moment the footman set it down on the pier table.

"Ah, this is just what a man needs!"

Rodmell signed to Tyler to retire and himself stood back, allowing the visitor to serve himself. "Cook is preparing a tray, my lord."

"Capital. Ottilia, may I pour you a glass?"

Before she could respond, the butler coughed behind his hand. "Her ladyship will take coffee, my lord. It is in hand and will be here directly."

She had moved to the fire and was engaged in warming her hands, but she turned at this. "Oh, Rodmell, I am so fortunate in you all, to know my tastes so precisely."

Gil twinkled as he came across to join her at the fireplace, glass in hand. "I should have remembered your addiction. Fan has spoken of it countless times."

"He may call me an addict, but I maintain it is merely a preference. I reserve wine for dining." Growing impatient of delay, she called across to the butler. "Rodmell, pray come and enlighten us, if you please. Where have they all gone?"

He moved to a position closer but still at a respectful distance. As she took her customary seat, she reflected he was the only person in the household who attempted to maintain formality.

"As far as I could ascertain, my lady, all were despatched in different directions."

"But what caused it all?"

He gave that butlerian cough, a sign he must break discretion. "The lady from Wyke Hall came, my lady. She is, I believe, Miss Vexford's companion or erstwhile governess."

"Miss Poynton?" Ottilia's mind flew. "Richenda again? What is it this time?"

Rodmell coughed again. "I understand Lord Vexford suffered some sort of attack."

"What, a seizure?"

"No, my lady. Miss Poynton spoke of his receiving an injury to the head."

"You mean someone attacked him?"

"So I understand."

This became interesting, though she was sorry for the man despite his abominable manners. "But that would not require the assistance of so many."

"No, my lady." Another cough. "Miss Vexford, so it was said, was not upon the premises."

"Good heavens, has she eloped? Or was she taken?"

At this point, Gil, who had been listening in frowning silence, seemed to wake up. "Eh? Who is this girl?"

Ottilia made a silencing gesture. "I will explain it all to you presently, Gil." She turned her attention back to the butler. "I take it his lordship took charge of matters?"

"Yes, my lady. I am not fully informed. I know my lady Polbrook went with this Miss Poynton, accompanied by Lady Elizabeth."

Gil sat back. "Well, that's a relief. If she is with her grandmother, she can't come to much harm."

Ottilia refrained from demolishing this fond belief. In her view, Lizzy was quite capable of haring off on some perceived fancy of her own in the belief she was helping matters. "His lordship, Rodmell? Where did he go?"

"He ordered his curricle, my lady. I think he intended to go north."

"What, Gretna?" Gil had been raising his glass to his lips, but he brought it down again. "Good grief!"

"I cannot imagine Fan has any intention of driving so far, Gil. He probably hopes to catch them up, assuming there is a *they* in the case."

Another cough emanated from the butler, bringing Ottilia's head round. "Yes, Rodmell?"

"His lordship despatched — er, requested, I should say — Mr Maplewood to go in search of certain young gentlemen. I do not know precisely whom, but your ladyship will guess, I surmise."

"With ease, thank you." Had Francis sent Vivian to discover which of Richenda's suitors might be missing from the area? Was it an abduction then? Her mind leapt to the one person who could benefit from forcing Richenda to the altar, if that was his intention. But had there been an altercation with

Vexford? It must take a callous individual to deliver a blow and remove without ascertaining whether the man lived. Which indicated that such callousness might have operated in the case of Marmaduke Gibbon.

She was recalled from her thoughts by Gil. "Do you mean to chase after them all, Ottilia?"

"Heavens, no! Fan is more than capable of handling whatever he may find. Besides, I scarce know which path I might choose to follow. No, I will remain here and await events." She smiled. "Oh, and service your needs."

He did not reply and Ottilia thanked the butler, dismissing him. When he had left the room, Gil opened fire.

"While we wait, Ottilia, I will be glad of a round tale. You will oblige me, I am sure. Fan says you are nothing if not direct. Am I to resign myself to accepting this Maplewood fellow for my son-in-law?"

There was solace in having a part to play in the crisis, providing Vivian with respite from brooding upon his mishandling of the wretched female who now seemed set against him. Eliza's manner towards him since the little incident in her carriage had been altogether distant. By contrast, her caressing ways with her relatives were meant, he was convinced, to taunt him. An ambition in which, to his chagrin, she was succeeding. Try as he would to ignore it, or dismiss it for sulks, he could not quite banish the pricks. Conscience? In some part. Yet they found their mark. He knew he had hurt her. The reciprocation was perhaps deserved, but that made it no less painful.

He drove with a trifle more speed than was strictly necessary in country lanes, excusing himself by way of necessity. Lord Francis needed his information as soon as he could get it.

It did not take many minutes to reach the Plough where Vivian had first encountered the three young gentlemen involved in this fiasco. Taking this for his first port of call, he might hope to obviate any further search.

Leaving the vehicle in the charge of his groom, he jumped down and strode into the inn. He was in luck. Jarvis Thorpe was in the act of picking up a tankard from the counter as Vivian entered the taproom.

"The very man I want!"

Thorpe paused with the tankard in his hand, his brows drawing together as he turned. "Maplewood!"

Vivian wasted no time. "Are you here alone?" He swept a glance across the taproom. "Ah, no, I see Botterell is with you." Aubrey Botterell was seated by their customary table near the window. He was staring at Vivian in lively dismay. Vivian paid him no heed. "Where is Claydon?"

Thorpe set down his tankard and gave a shrug. "At home, I presume. We've seen less of him since he inherited. Seems to have a great deal of business on hand." The frown deepened. "Why do you want him?"

"I don't want him. I just want to know where he is."

"I've just told you."

Vivian sighed. "But you don't know it for certain. I perceive I must go on to Penton Mewsey." He looked Thorpe in the eye. "I've not been there before. You'd best show me the way, Thorpe."

A haughty look came his way. "Why the devil should I?"

"Because I'm in a hurry. There's no time to waste."

At this point, Botterell came up, looking anxious. "What is it? What is amiss?"

"Just what I was going to ask, Aubrey. What has happened, Maplewood?"

Vivian looked about to check they were not overheard and lowered his voice, leaning in a little. "It seems Richenda has gone off, whether willingly or not we don't know."

"Gone off?"

"Gone off where? What do you mean, gone off?"

"That is the question. But Vexford has been injured, attacked as it is thought."

Thorpe exclaimed and Botterell stared. "Old Vexford attacked? How? Why?"

"Again, unknown. But the inference is that he interfered when some fellow was taking Richenda and —"

"And you thought it was one of us?" Jarvis Thorpe's outrage was patent. "That's why you came looking here? Good God, I ought to call you out!"

Vivian held up placatory hands. "For heaven's sake, don't take an affront into your head! I am acting for Lord Francis. He asked me to find you."

"For the purpose of accusing us? How dare you, sir?" Thus Botterell, his chubby features becoming suffused.

Impatience overcame Vivian. "Take a damper, both of you! You are suitors to Richenda, are you not?"

"Yes, but —"

"That doesn't mean —"

"Therefore," Vivian continued, riding over the protests, "it was necessary to eliminate you as potential suspects."

"Suspects?"

Vivian retreated a pace before Botterell's thrusting glare. "Unfortunate choice of word. Witnesses?"

"It makes it no better, sir."

Vivian let out an exasperated sound. "Look, time is of the essence. Lord Francis has set off northwards. It would be a deal more helpful if you two will lend a hand to help unravel this mess, instead of taking umbrage for nothing."

His words appeared to have gone home, with Jarvis Thorpe at least. Botterell was still gobbling. His friend dug him in the ribs. "Cease, Aubrey! He has a point." His gaze returned to Vivian. "Why does Lord Francis think they have gone north? Not Gretna, surely?"

"He had to pick one direction and that seemed most likely. If we can ascertain whether there is any sign of them in another direction, that might help."

Thorpe picked up his tankard and took a pull, his face thoughtful. What time Botterell gave Vivian another of his glares for good measure and then turned to his friend. "We might try towards Winchester."

Thorpe nodded. "Yes, but you go. One of us needs to show Maplewood how to get to Penton Mewsey."

Vivian almost spoke his relief, but instead merely thanked him. "Have you carriages?"

"No, we both rode. I'll ride alongside you. Best if Aubrey takes the other route."

Vivian turned to the shorter man, whose indignation was turning to excitement. "I'll ride like the wind."

"I should take it easy, if I were you. Don't neglect to ask at any hostelry at a suitable distance if any carriage was seen."

"That's easy. They will know Richenda along that route. I can ask if they've seen her."

"With a gentleman, don't forget, Aubrey."

"I know that, Jarvis. There's no need to instruct me." But he turned a questioning gaze on Vivian. "Should I go all the way to Winchester?"

"How far is it?"

"Twenty odd miles."

"I should imagine it will become clear sooner than that if they have gone that way. They cannot be very far ahead. The duenna raced over to Flitteris as soon as she had seen Lord Vexford suitably bestowed."

With Botterell on his way, Jarvis Thorpe downed the rest of his tankard and accompanied Vivian out of the inn. It did not take many minutes for the other man to retrieve his mount and Vivian was soon tooling his curricle as he followed where Thorpe led on horseback.

The way was smooth until they turned into the drive of the establishment that now belonged to Botolf Claydon, when Vivian was obliged to slow down to negotiate the considerably rutted way. By the time he had reached the entrance, Thorpe had already dismounted and left his horse standing while he jangled the bell hanging outside the front door, of carved wood grown dark with age.

Vivian did not trouble to get down, instead waiting to learn whether the quarry was in the house. The door opened and Jarvis Thorpe conferred with the footman before taking several loping steps to the curricle.

"Botolf is not at home."

A flitter of excitement mingled with disbelief went through Vivian. He opted for caution. "Does that mean he wants no visitors or is he absent?"

"I'll find out, though I think he wouldn't hesitate to see me." Saying which, he went back to the footman who had come out onto the porch. The conversation was too low to be made out, but it was plain Thorpe had become insistent. Did he too fear his friend might prove to be the aggressor in this case?

In a moment, he left the man, who went back into the house and returned to the vehicle. "He's definitely not there. I tried to get out of the servant where he might be, but he insists he doesn't know. I could go in and ask Etta, but I doubt Botolf would confide his movements to her. They don't get on."

Vivian hesitated. "Well, if he's not here, there's small point in hanging about."

"Where to then?"

"Wyke. There's one other I must discover."

Thorpe dropped back a pace. "I ought to have thought of him at the outset. That fellow Pedwardine."

"By all accounts, however, he is no suitor to Richenda Vexford. The reverse, if anything."

Thorpe's gaze became fiery. "He means her harm, the blackguard!"

"Or he means to profit by her dowry."

"If that isn't doing her harm, I should like to know what is?"

Vivian did not argue. It was plain Jarvis Thorpe was ready enough to have Pedwardine for the villain. Would he be as eager if it proved to be Claydon?

CHAPTER TWENTY-THREE

Francis made good time without springing his horses. The team were fresh and it took all his skill to hold them in from racing away along the familiar roads. He took a route through Andover, travelling east. At Basingstoke he turned north for Reading without checking the coaching inn there. Assuming Gretna was the goal, it was safe to assume the runaways would take a northerly direction and, considering the clandestine nature of the journey, avoid being seen where Richenda might be known.

"It's to be hoped we find word sooner rather than later," he remarked to his henchman seated beside him.

Ryde grunted. "If so be as this is the right way, m'lord."

"Or even if the girl is with one or other of these young fellows." Francis had not hesitated to confide his mission to his groom, who had been with him since his soldiering days and was wholly to be trusted.

"Seems as someone were anxious to fetch the lady away, m'lord, seeing as they saw fit to batter the old gentleman."

"That is precisely what induced me to come out on this fetch. I only hope I am not wasting my energy."

A dour laugh escaped the groom. "Leastways, it'll give this lot some exercise. Been too long lazing in the paddock."

Francis ran an eye over the glossy brown backs of the bays. "They don't look to be gaining flesh."

"Wouldn't let 'em, m'lord. I take them out now and now if you don't."

Aware he had been less inclined to journey any great distance since Tillie's confinement, Francis made a mental resolve to try and get out more. If he could persuade his darling wife into an outing when she was up to it, they might jaunter down to Winchester. Tillie would enjoy replenishing her wardrobe with these newfangled gowns. She had more than once expressed a wish she might have been able to wear such during her pregnancy.

"Can you imagine how comfortable, Fan, with these high waists and soft materials?"

But before any such pleasurable excursion could be anticipated, this afflictive mystery must be solved. Not to mention ridding the house of extraneous persons with whose company he could well dispense.

"There's a hostelry coming up, m'lord."

Ryde's comment took his attention back to the matter at hand. He glanced at the swinging sign up ahead and slowed his team. "We'd best find out if anything has been seen of our runaways. They might have rested the horses here."

"Unless they are travelling post, m'lord."

"Unlikely, I think. I suspect Miss Vexford is too fly to show herself in a posting house too near to home. The fellow must be using his own vehicle."

"Which fellow, m'lord?"

Francis cursed as he directed his horses into the open space in front of the Bear. "Now you ask, I don't suppose any one of them owns a coach. Yet who in their right mind would drag a female off in an open carriage and hope to undertake a journey of several hundred miles?"

"They might do for the start of the journey, m'lord."

"And hire a coach at Reading? Yes, that's a possibility, Ryde."

No ostler came running, which confirmed, had such been needed, that the place was not a coaching inn. Reflecting that this was likely a waste of time, Francis nevertheless brought the vehicle to a standstill and waited for Ryde to jump down and go to the horses' heads. Once they were under the groom's control, he descended and walked into the inn.

A bustling female came into the square hall from a door to one side, presumably leading to the tap, and dropped a curtsey. "Is it refreshment your honour was wanting? We've ale a-plenty and I can do food if you want, though the full meal's not yet ready. There's —"

Francis held up a hand. "Neither, thank you. I stopped only to enquire if a young lady and gentleman might have alighted here for a space. Within the last couple of hours?"

The woman's eyes opened wide under the mob cap she wore. "There now, and I suspicioned all weren't as it should be!"

Surprise and elation leapt in Francis. "You've seen them?"

"Well, if so be them is one and the same as your honour asked for. You wouldn't be the father as the young lady were worrying over?" Her gaze devoured Francis's features as she spoke. "No, you couldn't be, sir. You don't look old enough, if you don't mind me saying."

"Quite right, I'm not her father."

Before he could check he had the right female, the woman was off again.

"Well, and if you ask me, your honour, she weren't best pleased as that feller wouldn't nowise turn back again. If she begged him once, she must have done a dozen times to my ears, only he wouldn't budge, that one."

Francis cut in as she paused for breath. "Can you describe the lady, if you please?"

"That I can. Dark-haired she were, and lots of it under the hat. Looked to have a comely figure too the way her coat were

319

fitting. I can't abide them skinny females what eat too dainty to have no more flesh on them than a chicken." Then Richenda was dressed for travel? "Pretty face too, I'd say, if she weren't scowling like she was."

Quarrelling? Because of the injury to her father perhaps, rather than having been forcibly dragged upon the journey. Or that was what it looked like.

"What of the gentleman?"

"Oh, he were powerful cross too. No matter how many times she asked, like I told you, he wouldn't budge, he wouldn't. Said as he'd not go back for nothing, not to face her pa."

"What did he look like?"

"He were a slim fellow, darkish hair. Hadn't got no patience it seemed to me. Cross as crabs he was, though why he would be if he were wishful to wed her I don't know."

Francis's senses prickled. "How do you know he was wishful to wed her?"

The woman pursed her lips. "Well, I don't, your honour, not for sure. But he were mighty anxious to be off and why would he be escorting her otherwise? Without no maid nor chaperon. And he weren't nowise her brother, that I'd swear to, for as he'd have been as anxious for his pa, now wouldn't he? Only he didn't care nothing for that. Told the lady off to do her business quick so they could get on."

Using the facilities of the house? An excuse to try to effect an escape? Yet Richenda had apparently been in agreement with this journey. What was the wretched wench playing at now?

"One more thing, if you will. Were they travelling in a coach? Or an open carriage?"

"Well, the roof were up, but it was one of them like your honour come in. I saw you from the window in the tap, which is why I come out."

"A pair of horses or a team?"

"Only two as I saw."

Then he stood a good chance of catching them. Francis thanked her and left the place before the garrulous dame could break into speech again. He was grateful for her information, but time was pressing.

He relayed what he had heard to Ryde as he set the equipage in motion again, urging the team out onto the dirt road. "Although nothing to indicate which of those fellows it was," he finished on a note of dissatisfaction.

"You'll find out soon enough, m'lord, if so be he's only driving a pair."

"Yes, it's my hope we'll catch up with them before my team are blown."

"They'll make it to Reading, m'lord. Nor it wouldn't surprise me, from what you've said, if Miss Vexford don't insist on stopping for a bite."

"So she can make another attempt to persuade her escort to turn back?"

"Or if they meant to hire a post chaise, m'lord, it would make sense to bait before they go on."

"Yes, I dare say, but to my mind, it begins to look as if Gretna was never the goal."

Recalling what his wife had said of Richenda's trickery, Francis mulled over what possible game she had on hand this time. The suspicion could not but obtrude that she might have over-reached herself if her accomplice, assuming that was the role of her escort, had other ideas.

He was growing irritable by the time he drove the curricle into Reading and he was relieved to roll down King Street and see the George come into view.

"We'd best bait the horses here, m'lord."

"Yes, if we are in luck. Otherwise I must try the Crown."

"We can mebbe hire a team if you need to go on. This lot must rest now."

"Let's hope I don't need to go on. If the gods are with us, we may find them either here or at the other coaching inn."

He turned off the road and drove through the arch leading to the yard of the George. It was not busy. A couple of ostlers were lounging at the entrance to the stables, but seemed in no hurry to service the one chaise, its shafts empty, presumably awaiting a fresh team. A second vehicle drew Francis's interest.

"A curricle, Ryde. This looks promising."

Without more ado, he gave the reins into his groom's hands and jumped down. There was no need to give order to Ryde to see to the comfort of the horses, but he bethought him of the fellow's earlier words. "Check if there is a spare team we can hire, Ryde, just in case."

He found the back entrance and went into the inn. A wide hall gave access to two doors either side and a passage beyond. Francis had no need to shout for a servant came hurrying in from the back.

"How may we serve your honour?"

Francis lost no time in repeating the query he'd made at the previous hostelry. He was gratified to learn that a young lady and gentleman had taken refreshment and were ensconced in a parlour to the left of the hall. The servant gestured and took a step or two towards the indicated door.

Francis passed him as he spoke. "Capital. I will announce myself."

He flung open the door and marched into a parlour typical of these places, furnished for utility with the basic necessities of a swift visit. There was no sign of Richenda Vexford, but standing at the mantel, his startled countenance turned towards the newcomer, was Botolf Claydon.

"Lord Francis!"

Francis eyed him with a rise of contempt as he shut the door behind him. "The late Lady Stoke Rochford's estate not enough for you, Claydon? Where is your inamorata, if I may be so bold?"

The young man's mouth had not its habitual curl and he reddened, but his eyes sparked fire. "You are mistaken, my lord. I have no interest in Richenda's fortune, if that is what you imply."

"Indeed?" Francis strolled further into the room. "Then if this is not an elopement, what is it?"

"You may well ask!"

"I am asking. Cut line!"

Claydon drew himself up. "I am not obliged to give an account of myself to you, Lord Francis."

Francis sighed. "Pray don't imagine I desired to come on this chase. I am acting on behalf of Miss Poynton who came to Flitteris for aid. I take it you are aware of Vexford's condition?"

"I don't doubt he'll recover soon enough, the old rusty guts."

"Rusty guts he may be," Francis said with asperity, "but Richenda is under age and Vexford has the law on his side. Now, since you deny eloping, if you don't wish to be had up for abduction, you'd best explain your conduct."

With visible effort, Claydon curbed his unamiable tongue. "I am here in support of Miss Vexford, sir. She demanded my aid."

"One of her schemes, I must suppose?"

Claydon let out a frustrated breath and shifted away from the fire. "I should have guessed what she would be at. I've known her from a child and she was forever play-acting then."

Francis lost patience. "Give me a round tale, Claydon. What did she want of you?"

He shrugged. "I suppose to give her father a fright. She sent to me to come urgently to Wyke Hall." A little of the sneering look returned to his mouth. "Not that I was her first choice, as she was quick to tell me when things went awry."

Francis strove for patience. "You went as requested then."

"Yes, and I wish very much I had pleaded stress of work. It's not as if I haven't got a mountain of business to deal with."

"What precisely did Richenda ask of you, Claydon?"

He let out a groan. "To pretend to elope. She is bent upon inducing her father to take her to the metropolis again but at present he is too incensed with her over all this furore to consent. Richenda thinks if he fears she will marry one of us, he will decide to take her only to find a more worthy suitor."

Francis could not withstand a guttural curse. "What a devious wench she is! I hope to heaven my Pretty won't lead me this kind of dance in years to come."

To his surprise, Claydon gave a laugh that sounded quite genuine. "You are not in Vexford's mould, sir. I feel sure you are safe."

"Let us hope so." He bethought him of how Pretty, now she had settled into her new life, was inclined to be demanding and a rueful affection swept his breast. But he was not now concerned with his adoptive daughter. He brought his attention to bear on the matter at hand. "Where is Richenda now?"

"She went off to use the facilities after we had consumed a light repast." Claydon gestured to the remains of their meal on the table near the window, and then frowned. "She ought to have been back by now."

"Were you intending to proceed, or had she managed to persuade you to turn back?"

Claydon stared. "How did you know she wanted that?"

Francis could not suppress a grin. "The landlady at the Bear betrayed you. She was, fortunately for me, most interested in your conversation."

"Well, I did agree, though as I told her, I won't attempt to persuade Lord Vexford that my intentions were serious."

Spying a bell on the table, Francis made for it. "As far as I can make out, Vexford is in no condition to ask you anything." He picked up the bell and rang it.

Claydon's face had changed when he glanced back at the man. "Is he that bad?"

"I don't know. My mother and my niece went with Miss Poynton to discover the situation and help if they could. What happened to Vexford?"

A shrug came. "I have no notion. I met Richenda in the summer house and then we repaired to the stables where I had left my curricle. As we drove off, Vexford came running, or rather stumbling, down the drive, yelling after us."

"From which direction did he come? The stables?"

"More like the summer house. He must have gone there seeking Richenda. She urged me to whip up the horses at first, but then she cried out that we must stop."

"Why?"

"She thought her father had fallen."

"Then why didn't you stop?"

Claydon shuddered. "If you had heard him roaring, you wouldn't ask. I confess I didn't believe he could be incapacitated, even if he fell."

"But Richenda thought otherwise?"

Annoyance surfaced in the young man's face. "You would think, after the way he treats her, she wouldn't care. She has said often enough she wished him underground. She claimed she hated him."

Francis gave a somewhat grim smile. "Blood, my friend, will out for the worst of us. He is virtually the only parent she has known her lifelong. Besides," he added, recalling Tillie's remarks about the girl, "this enmity is likely something of a game for her. I have no doubt she would mourn her father's loss as much as any daughter."

A horrified look came over Claydon's features. "It's not as bad as that?"

"For all I know, it may be. Which is why we must make haste to return Richenda to her home."

A knock at the door produced a buxom woman, who came in and dropped a curtsey.

"Ah, in good time. I suspect you are the very person I need. Have you seen the young lady who was dining in this room?"

The dame's gaze relaxed. "Why, yes, sir. She went out for a breath of air."

"Thank you." Francis made for the door and the woman shifted. He threw a command over his shoulder. "With me, Claydon!"

He did not look to see whether the young man obeyed him but strode out into the hall and thrust through the back door. The inn yard appeared to have become a good deal busier in the few minutes in which he had been inside. The chaise had acquired a team and was turned facing the other way, ready to leave. His own curricle stood empty by the entrance to a wide stable, and a second curricle had just drawn up, its driver staring back towards the chaise.

It was a moment before Francis recognised the fellow holding the reins as Vivian Maplewood. Astonishing he had caught up so fast. Had he done what was asked of him? Not that it mattered now.

Francis hailed him. "Hoy there, Maplewood!"

Vivian looked round. "Lord Francis, I'm glad I caught you!" He leaned down as Francis came up to the curricle. "I've just seen the oddest sight, sir."

"Well, what?"

"See that chaise? A moment since some fellow bundled a female into it. I'd swear it was Richenda Vexford."

Francis wasted no words, taking off on the instant just as the postboys set the chaise in motion. "Hi, there! Hi, you there! Wait!"

The rumble of wheels over the cobbled yard must have drowned his shout, for the chaise took the turn and disappeared under the arch.

Little point in trying to give chase on foot. Francis turned back and yelled at Vivian. "Get after them, for pity's sake!"

"But my team needs rest!"

"Never mind it. They may break presently. I will follow as soon as I may and take over. Go!"

Thus adjured, Vivian went into action and Francis was gratified to see how well he handled his horses as he turned the curricle in the confined space and set off in pursuit.

Francis called to his henchman who was just coming out of the stables. "Ryde! Get a team harnessed with speed! We've a chase on."

The groom replied with a grunt and vanished back into the stables. An instant later, Francis heard his voice at a pitch of command and an ostler came running out, heading for the waiting curricle. The sound of shod hooves followed and Francis caught sight of a glossy maned head before he turned away.

He beheld an open-mouthed Botolf Claydon standing just outside the door of the inn. "Why are you dawdling there? Bustle, man!"

"You want me to come too?"

"Of course I want you to come, you halfwit! This is your doing."

"But it might not be Richenda."

"Where then is she?"

Claydon's temper flared. "I don't know and I don't care! The wench is a dashed nuisance and I'm hanged if I waste more time on her."

Contempt rose in Francis. "If you've no spunk for it, go back to Flitteris and await me there. Don't fail, because I'm by no means done with you, my friend!"

Claydon groaned. "All right, I'll come. But don't blame me if it proves to be a wild goose chase."

Francis merely nodded. There was no saying it would not be, but with two curricles on his tail, the quarry would not get far. With Tillie's suppositions in mind, he had a fair notion which of the young men had captured Richenda, assuming she had not entered the chaise willingly. Anything was possible with Richenda Vexford. But Vivian's words had resonated in his head and a lightning notion of just what had occurred had entered there. Were there two schemers involved? Neither of whom, it would appear, had anticipated the other. Vexford's injury might now be explained.

Claydon had headed off towards the stables, shouting for his groom, but Francis had not long to wait before his henchman called for him.

"All set, m'lord."

"Capital." Francis crossed to the curricle and swung into the seat, taking the reins from his groom. "We're not far behind. Let them go!" This to the ostler holding the heads of the lead horses.

The man released the bridles and sprang out of the way as the team moved forward. The leaders were strong chestnuts, the second pair blacks. They responded well enough, but Francis at once missed his own horses.

"It's to be hoped we won't be too long on the road with these beasts."

"Best I could get, m'lord. Them postboys took the cream."

"Who shall blame them? Though it's to our disadvantage if they are too good. Do you suppose I may spring this team at a pinch?"

Ryde gave his dour laugh. "Not unless you have to, m'lord."

"We'll take the Oxford road. I can't doubt now that Gretna is intended."

In the event, the curricle had covered only a matter of a couple of miles past Caversham when Francis caught sight of Vivian's vehicle up ahead. "Aha! There's our quarry, if I am not mistaken."

"I see it, m'lord."

Some way beyond Vivian's curricle, the chaise could also be seen, travelling at a sedate pace. Vivian had sensibly waited for Francis without attempting to intervene. Francis followed for several hundred yards as the road twisted and turned, waiting for a straight stretch.

"We'll see what these beasts are made of, shall we?"

Francis whipped his team up to a faster pace, gaining swiftly on Vivian, who looked over his shoulder and waved his whip in acknowledgement. Francis signalled to him to give room and the young man slowed his horses and guided them closer to the side of the road.

"It's tight, m'lord."

"I can see that, but I can get by, I think."

Francis slowed a trifle as he came up with Vivian, swinging out for the pass. His curricle made it with half a foot to spare as his groom pithily informed him.

"Spare your scold for the next pass, Ryde. The chaise is even wider."

He was obliged to stay back as a cart coming in the opposite direction made its ponderous way past both chaise and curricle. Another series of bends held him up again, but the moment he saw the road clear ahead, he gave Ryde the office. The groom lifted the yard of tin to his lips and blasted a warning. The chaise at once slowed, shifting to one side and Francis dropped his hands.

The curricle rattled past and Francis kept going for a couple of hundred yards at the same pace.

"We've outstripped 'em, m'lord."

"Good." Francis slowed the horses and brought them to a speedy halt. "Take the reins. Pull the curricle across the road if they look like they won't stop."

Throwing the reins to his groom, he jumped down and began walking back towards the oncoming chaise, putting up one hand in a holding gesture as he took the centre of the road.

The postboys evidently had no notion of ignoring the request, for the chaise, which was already moving at a slower pace, slowed still more and came to a stop a few yards in front of Francis, who was still moving.

He did not stop, but carried on past the staring postboys, thrusting a hand into his pocket and throwing them a brief explanation. "Hold, will you? I need a word with your passenger."

The one addressed looked nonplussed but made no attempt to stop Francis as he passed on and walked up to the chaise, pistol now in hand. He seized the handle and wrenched open the door. A shaft of satisfaction ran through him as he recognised the features of the man within, chagrin written all over them. A little shriek emanated from the woman beside him, but Francis paid no heed, his eyes on the perpetrator.

"I thought so." Francis levelled the pistol. "Get down, Pedwardine. Your game is done."

CHAPTER TWENTY-FOUR

Before the demands of hospitality could once again claim her, while Lord Dalesford was refreshing his person in his allotted chamber, Ottilia had time to make a foray to the nursery where she found the infant Luke fast asleep. Upon spying her, Pretty put a finger to her lips in an imperious gesture. The child was ensconced on the rug before the fire, engaged in a game with various toys which looked to be taking tea from the circle Pretty had placed them in, tiny cups set before each one.

Amused, Ottilia nodded her understanding and crossed to the cot, taking a few moments to enjoy the sight of her son at rest. The wet nurse, Susannah, seated in the nursing chair, was suckling her own babe. A dame of middle years, she nodded and smiled at Ottilia, making signs indicative of Luke's sleeping state. Ottilia mouthed a thank you, leaned to tuck the blanket more securely about her son's little person and moved to greet Pretty, dropping to her haunches and keeping to a whisper.

"Is this a tea party?"

"I am At Home, Auntilla. They are visiting."

"Ah, I see. I had best not disturb them then."

Pretty rolled her eyes. "They don't talk. I have to do it all."

No difficulty there then. With her acceptance of her new familial connections, Pretty had lost all her initial shyness and chattered without cease. She looked upon Luke as a brother, although she had not yet recognised how Ottilia fitted into the picture. Luke's mama she might be, but Pretty persisted with Auntilla.

"Where is Papa?"

The inevitable pang could not be avoided. Ottilia swept it away. "He had to go out. He will be home soon, I hope."

Pretty turned back to her toy visitors and Ottilia was obliged to own the child had lost interest in her. With an inward sigh, she rose and left the nursery, heading back downstairs.

She would welcome a respite in her parlour, but Gil would be down shortly and as everyone else was abroad, Ottilia must perform her duties as hostess. She was making therefore for the withdrawing room and as she passed along the gallery, the front door bell pealed. Pausing, Ottilia looked over the balustrade. Was it Francis at last?

Tyler appeared from the nether regions and crossed the chequered hall. He opened the door and the well-known tones of Ottilia's niece wafted in.

"Oh, thank you, Tyler."

Lizzy stepped into the hall and Ottilia did not know whether to be glad or sorry. With Lizzy's father in the house and about to make an appearance, she foresaw a trying time ahead. But her attention caught on the fact her niece was escorted only by Jarvis Thorpe as Tyler closed the door behind them both. She leaned over the banister rail and called down.

"Lizzy!"

Her niece looked up. "Aunt Ottilia, thank goodness you are here!"

"Where is your grandmother? Did she not go with you?"

Lizzy was moving across the hall. "She stayed with Miss Poynton. Mr Botterell will escort her back presently."

Ottilia felt considerably behind the fair. Vivian had gone in search of the young men, so how it came about that Jarvis Thorpe brought back Lizzy needed explanation. It seemed safe to suppose he at least was not involved in Richenda's escape. Nor, it would appear, was Aubrey Botterell.

She waited for Lizzy to arrive at the top of the stairs and addressed Jarvis Thorpe who was a few steps behind. "Thank you, Mr Thorpe. I hope you mean to remain for a space. You may well be able to throw light on obscure places, if you will be so good."

He gave a slight bow as he reached her. "I must return Lord Vexford's phaeton, but I am at your service meanwhile, ma'am."

She smiled her gratitude, took Lizzy's arm and drew her towards the withdrawing room, lowering her voice. "Your papa has arrived, Lizzy."

"*What?*" A pinch on the arm made her drop from a shriek to a hissing protest. "Why must he come today of all days?"

"We have been expecting him for an age, don't forget. He will be down at any moment, so you had best prepare yourself."

Lizzy grimaced. "Is he furious with me?"

Ottilia drew her through the door into the front room. "Not noticeably. You may look upon the happenings of the day as an advantage. At least it diverts attention from your matrimonial tangles."

"They are scarcely matrimonial, Aunt."

There was a brittle edge to the words and Ottilia patted her hand before releasing her. "Take courage, child. All is not yet lost."

Lizzy's gaze fixed upon hers. "Why, what do you mean, Aunt? What do you know?"

Ottilia brushed a finger across her mouth and raised her voice, turning to the gentleman standing by the door. "Do come in, Mr Thorpe. Take a seat."

He waited politely until she had seated herself on the sofa. Ottilia glanced at Lizzy, who sank into a chair by the fire, visibly disturbed. Jarvis Thorpe took one of the stray chairs opposite the sofa and looked expectantly at Ottilia.

"I understand Mr Maplewood was sent to find you and your cronies."

"He found me and Aubrey. Botolf was not with us."

"Ah. You've had no word of him then?"

"None at all. Maplewood requested me to show him the way to Lady Stoke Rochford's house — or rather Botolf's as it is now, but he was not there."

Ottilia's mind buzzed. "Was he not indeed?"

"Gracious, was it he who took Richenda then, Mr Thorpe?" Lizzy, rousing herself from her inner thoughts.

Thorpe shifted in obvious discomfort. "I cannot say, Lady Elizabeth. I hope not. I would not have thought it of him."

Ottilia leapt in. "Thought what of him? That he might elope with her?"

"It's not in his style, ma'am. I know he's apt to take on with those affectations of his, but we've been acquainted for years and he's a good man at bottom. He wouldn't behave scaly, go underhand like that. I'd stake our friendship on it."

An accolade worth knowing. Yet Ottilia's instinct could not ignore Richenda's persuasive powers. Lizzy forestalled anything she might have said in response.

"Well, someone behaved scaly. Lord Vexford did not hit himself on the head!"

"Ah, now I was hoping you might have news of that matter, Lizzy. Did you find anything of note?"

Triumph lit in Lizzy's face. "I did and that is why I asked Mr Thorpe to bring me back. I guessed you must be here by now and you will wish to hear of it at once."

"Well, what, Lizzy? Don't keep me in suspense."

"Lord Vexford was attacked in the summer house."

"How do you know?"

"I found traces of blood. Quite fresh too for it had not altogether dried. And his wig was on the floor!"

Amused at the ringing note, Ottilia could not resist. "Conclusive then. Assuming it belonged to Lord Vexford."

"Who else would leave one in his summer house, Aunt? Moreover, none of the younger men wear wigs, do they, Mr Thorpe?"

"Not to my knowledge, ma'am."

"You see? Whoever hit him did so there. But he must have managed to get up for he wasn't found there. He was near the stable block, lying in the drive."

"Then it is safe to assume his injury did not overcome him at once." Ottilia looked back to Jarvis Thorpe. "After you failed to find Claydon, sir, what did you and Mr Maplewood do?"

"Maplewood went to look for that fellow Pedwardine. He had asked Aubrey to try for Richenda along the Winchester road so I rode east and west, just in case. We knew Lord Francis had gone north, so when I failed to find any sign, I went back to the Plough to await Aubrey's return."

Ottilia revised her ideas. Was Francis on the right track? Could Richenda have been heading for Gretna after all? "What took you to Wyke Hall?"

Thorpe shifted his shoulders. "We know Richenda well, Lady Francis. It seemed probable we would find her there."

"You suspected a trick?"

"She's mischievous like that. Drove us near demented as a girl. You never knew what she would be at."

Ottilia had to smile. "I have to say I wonder then at your courting the adult." Thorpe compressed his lips and she relented. "Well, perhaps the reason is not far to seek after all."

His features grew taut. "I've more conduct than to take this kind of measure, ma'am." The tone of arrogance dropped to a sulk. "Besides, I'd not face old Vexford for twice the fortune, if I had thought of eloping."

"How did you find him? Has he recovered from his injury?"

Lizzy took this. "He may not recover, so the doctor says."

Alarm swept Ottilia's bosom. "Don't say so, Lizzy!"

"No, no, ma'am," said Thorpe, his brows drawing together. "He took quite a knock, but he won't die of it, if that's what you fear. Only the doctor thinks he may be much changed if his brain is affected."

Ottilia was not entirely relieved. If, as she suspected, the injury had been deliberately inflicted, she might yet be obliged to call in a justice of the peace. She had hoped to conclude this whole business without that.

Before any further discussion could take place, the door opened to admit her husband's brother-in-law. Gil swept one glance around the room and fixed his gaze upon his erring daughter.

"There you are, you abominable minx! What the devil do you mean by it, eh?"

Lizzy had risen, but Ottilia, conscious of the presence of the strange young man whom Gil had clearly not noticed, intervened before her niece could speak. "Gil, you will allow me to present Mr Thorpe, if you please. He is one of our neighbours and kindly escorted Lizzy back from Wyke Hall. This, Mr Thorpe, is Lady Elizabeth's father, Lord Dalesford."

Gil turned upon the young man the sort of appraising look to be expected from a man with a marriageable daughter. "How d'you do? My thanks."

Ottilia read his expression without difficulty, frustrated as he clearly was in tackling Lizzy there and then. She looked relieved and seized the chance to proffer her own thanks.

"Yes, indeed, it was most kind of you, Mr Thorpe. I ought not to detain you further."

Jarvis Thorpe stood with alacrity, clearly only too happy to take his leave. But his proposed departure was prevented by the unmistakeable sound of horses and carriages approaching down the drive. Several, by the sound of it.

"Wait! Do you hear it?" Ottilia, eager at the thought of who must be arriving, rose and moved to kneel on the window seat. "Yes, it is Fan!"

She found Gil at her elbow, also staring out. "What in the devil's name is he doing with all those people?"

"One, two — no, three carriages." Ottilia recognised the occupants as the two extra carriages pulled up behind her husband's curricle, which was no longer fully visible from this window. "Lizzy, it is Vivian, and he has Richenda with him." She flicked a look over her shoulder and found both Lizzy and Jarvis Thorpe hovering close to the window embrasure. "Your friend Mr Claydon is here too, Mr Thorpe."

"Then it was he who —"

"That is not certain. My husband has Mr Pedwardine with him."

Lizzy broke out at this. "Do you mean it is Percy Pedwardine who abducted Richenda?"

Ottilia turned away from the window, gesturing them both back as the doorbell pealed. "We will soon find out. Lizzy, do you go down and take charge of Richenda."

"Shall I bring her here?"

"Of course. We need to find out just what mischief she has been brewing."

Francis having sensibly separated the various parties involved in the debacle, Ottilia found she had only to tackle Richenda at the outset.

"I've left Maplewood with Claydon in the dining parlour and Hemp has Pedwardine under guard in the morning room. Lizzy has taken Richenda to her chamber, but will be back directly." He turned to Jarvis Thorpe. "As for you, sir, you can make yourself useful and go to Wyke Hall."

"I've just come from there."

"Well, go back again. Someone needs to inform Miss Poynton that we have her charge safe and you're the only one available at this moment."

Thorpe looked altogether discontented. "I'd like to see Botolf first."

Francis had given him an appraising look in which Ottilia read a trifle of doubt. Or was it suspicion? He glanced at her. "I've had his story so I suppose it can do no harm. Off you go then."

Thorpe slipped out of the room in some haste and Francis was able to greet his brother-in-law. "Trust you to arrive just when all hell has broken loose, Gil!"

Dalesford laughed as he shook hands with his usual vigour. "I shouldn't think I'd find anything else where you two are involved."

"On the contrary. We'd been quiet for months until that pestilential girl chose to drop a corpse on our doorstep."

"If I'd known I wouldn't have allowed that child of mine anywhere near the place."

Ottilia judged it time to cut in. "For shame, Gil. Lizzy has been most useful."

He threw up his eyes. "Yes, well, I dare say we may discuss that minx's vagaries at a later time. I can see Fan is big with news and you are eager to hear it. Shall I withdraw?"

"Perhaps when Lizzy produces Richenda, if you don't object."

"Good God, no, Ottilia. I've no wish to be dragged into these deep waters." He then took a seat, looking expectantly up at Francis.

Ottilia gave an inward sigh. She would much have preferred to hear her spouse's account without an audience, but it could not be helped. "What happened, Fan?"

The tale of his doings and those of the individuals involved served to settle Ottilia's ideas. It was much as she had suspected for some days. Whether one could prove it remained a question. The first hurdle was to get a factual rendering from the instigator of the whole business.

When Lizzy brought Richenda in, Gil left them, much to Ottilia's relief, and Francis took his usual stance at the mantel. Ottilia patted the sofa beside her.

"Sit by me, Richenda."

Richenda was for once somewhat subdued, her face blotched, her eyes red-rimmed. She came across and sat down, dropping her gaze and clasping her hands together in her lap.

Lizzy hovered until Ottilia signed to her to take the chair opposite. "I've told her the news about her father, Aunt."

Startled, Ottilia threw her a questioning look. "All of it?"

Richenda's gaze came up and the dark eyes caught hers. "What do you mean? Lady Elizabeth says he is going to recover. That is what the doctor said, you told me." The accusing note was directed at Lizzy.

"Yes, yes, that's right, he did say so."

"Then what else?"

She was nothing if not quick. Ottilia gave it as good a turn as she could. "Your papa may not be just as he was. His mind may be affected."

"His mind? How affected?"

"I doubt anyone can tell at this stage, my dear. If I must hazard a guess, from a like situation my brother dealt with some years ago, the patient became quieter."

Richenda's head tossed. "Well, that will be no bad thing."

"And sometimes a little confused," Ottilia pursued. "Or forgetful."

Richenda drew in a sobbing breath. "At least he can't punish me this time."

Ottilia exchanged a glance with her spouse, who rolled his eyes. Self-centred to the last was this young woman. She abandoned the subject. "Be that as it may, I wish you will tell me what you were trying to achieve with this ill-considered flight, my dear."

"It wasn't a flight! I never meant to go far. I just wanted him to think I was going."

"Your father?"

"Who else? No one cares what I may do except him. And now not even he, if he is going to be changed."

Ottilia ignored this, going directly for what she needed. "You began by asking Mr Pedwardine, I gather?"

Richenda tossed her head. "He ought to have helped me. He owed me that much."

"Pardon me, but I fail to understand what you feel he owed you."

Richenda's tone became sulky. "It was all his fault. Had he not come harrying poor Marmaduke, none of this would have happened."

Undoubtedly, but Ottilia refrained from agreement. "What exactly did you ask him? And how did you make contact? You did not again go to the inn to accost him, I take it?"

Came a toss of the head. "After the way he behaved the last time? I sent him a note to meet me in the summer house."

With difficulty, Ottilia suppressed an exasperated sigh. "Could you not for once have behaved with circumspection, child? Had you not taken Percy Pedwardine's measure?"

The pansy eyes showed puzzlement. "I thought he might be trusted because he disliked me. How could I guess he would come after me?"

"Dislike you he may, but he is far from misliking your fortune."

Richenda gave a gasp. "He did not mean to carry me to Gretna, did he?"

"Where did you think he was taking you?"

"I supposed he had thought better of his decision. He grabbed my hand and said I had best come with him rather than Botolf Claydon. He said he was ready to serve me as I wished."

A scornful laugh came from Francis. "Yes, serve you up before a parson." He dug a hand into his pocket and brought forth a folded paper, holding it up. "He had a common licence in his possession."

"Then Gretna was not his goal," said Ottilia.

"Any willing priest would have served his purpose, provided both he and Richenda were unknown to the fellow. I dare say he had someone in mind."

"Indeed, Fan. He is nothing if not thorough."

Richenda was looking more and more bewildered. Her gaze travelled from Ottilia to Francis and back again. Anything she might have said was forestalled by Lizzy, however.

"Are you saying Mr Pedwardine intended this from the first, Aunt? Is he the one who —?"

She broke off as Ottilia waved her to silence. But it was too late. Richenda rounded on her.

"The one who what? What are you saying, Lady Elizabeth?"

Lizzy looked guilty, but Ottilia intervened before she could be provoked into response. "Never mind that for the moment, Richenda. Pray tell me just what you said to Mr Pedwardine."

Richenda's frowning gaze came back to Ottilia. "I told him I needed his help to fool Papa. I wanted Papa to think I had eloped. Papa has behaved so cruelly to me over this business, refusing to take me to town for the Season. I w-wanted to m-make him think I would m-marry Botolf, or any of them, only so that he would take me out of their orbit." Her voice became husky. "I never m-meant for him to be hurt. And when I saw Papa fall, Botolf wouldn't even stop the carriage!"

Ottilia nipped the burgeoning hysteria in the bud, her tone tart. "Let us stick to the point, if you please, child. What was Pedwardine's reply when you asked him this?"

That brought the habitual indignation to the fore. "He was excessively rude. He swore he would have nothing to do with such a stupid scheme. And it was stupid, I see that now. Only he had no right to say so. If he truly thought it why should he change his mind and come after me?"

"As has already been said, he did not change his mind, Richenda. He seized the opportunity. He may have guessed you would ask another perhaps, or —"

"He knew, for I told him." This said in a shamefaced way. "I said if he was determined to disoblige me, I would ask one of my suitors." Her gaze altered all at once and she put a hand to her mouth. "He even asked me which one and I told him."

"You said you would ask Botolf?"

"Yes, for I knew neither Jarvis nor Aubrey would do it. Botolf doesn't care about convention the way they do. I was persuaded he could be induced to oblige me."

"As we see," put in Francis on a dry note and Ottilia received one of his ironical looks. "Ill-judged, but I don't doubt she is capable of any amount of cajolery."

Ottilia could not but agree. "What means did you use to persuade Botolf to do your bidding, Richenda?"

Defiance showed in her face and she did not answer for a moment. Fearing the worst, Ottilia waited. An overwrought giggle escaped Richenda. "Well, if you must know, I said if he didn't oblige me, I would tell Papa that Botolf had kissed me."

"Good grief! And she doesn't even have the grace to blush!"

"There, Uncle Francis! You thought *my* conduct reprehensible."

"I've never known you to be unscrupulous, Lizzy."

Ottilia had to laugh. "No, that is left to me, is it not, Fan?" But she was watching Richenda, who had cast down her eyes but still had the ghost of a smile upon her lips. "My child, your methods are disgraceful. Had Miss Poynton not come to us, you might well have found yourself riveted to a man far more ruthless than you will ever be."

It did not take Ottilia long to garner corroboration of Richenda's story from Botolf Claydon. Upon being urged thereto, he had confessed to having succumbed to Richenda's trickery.

"The thing is, ma'am, if she had told her father such a thing of me, he would come after me with a horsewhip."

"That is why you wouldn't stop when he came running out?"

"Yes, for how could I know Richenda had not already made some such representation about me? Old Vexford has the devil of a temper on him and I was damned — saving your presence, ma'am — if I would face him. Especially when he had actually seen me driving off with his daughter."

Ottilia could appreciate this and said so. "But you would have had to face him at some point."

Claydon grimaced. "I didn't think of that at the time. When I agreed to bring Richenda back, I was planning to drop her at the gates and make off right speedily."

"To lock yourself in your house, no doubt. Well, you may count yourself fortunate. The chances are he will remember nothing of today's happenings when he recovers his senses. Before you go home, however, I desire you will detour to return Richenda to her home." His look of horror amused her. "Be content. You need not fear to meet Vexford. He is far too indisposed."

Released, the young man exited the room, what time Ottilia took the chance to inform Vivian that his fate was at a crossroads.

Vivian's jaw tightened. "I am aware, ma'am. Eliza's father is here, is he not?"

"Ah, you've heard then." She touched his arm. "What do you intend, my dear boy?"

He straightened his shoulders. "Unlike Claydon, Lady Francis, I am prepared to face the music."

"Bravo! You may thank your stars that Gilbert Fiske is a far better tempered and sensible man than Vexford."

She left the room and he followed her into the hall where Ottilia found a coterie of persons engaged in argument.

"But I don't wish to go with Botolf," Richenda was protesting.

"Nor do I wish to take you, if you want to know."

To Ottilia's relief, her spouse intervened. "Enough! Jarvis Thorpe has already left so there is no one else available to take you home at the moment, Richenda."

"Yes," added Lizzy, who was escorting Richenda with a hand at her elbow, "and only think how worried poor Miss Poynton will be."

"Precisely. High time you were restored to your duenna. Go, Claydon!"

He waved the pair away and Richenda, grumbling, allowed herself to be led to the door where Lizzy pushed her out and closed it behind the pair. Turning, she froze, staring at Vivian Maplewood.

Ottilia signed to him to proceed in search of Gil and swept across. "Lizzy, have you yet spoken to your papa?"

Her eyes were on the young man as he mounted the stairs. "I've not had a chance. Where is Vivian going?"

Aware of the foreboding note, Ottilia slipped an arm about her. "He is off to find Gil. I think it will be best if you stay out of the way for a space."

Lizzy's eyes were moist. "I don't think I can bear to, Aunt."

"Let them have it out, my child."

"But it is my fate they are deciding!"

"Nonsense, Lizzy. You are the arbiter of your own fate and if there is a decision to be made, you will make it yourself."

Lizzy hesitated. "Will you wait with me?"

"I cannot. I must speak to Mr Pedwardine."

Lizzy was, predictably, at once diverted. "May I come?"

Ottilia squashed this without hesitation. "You may not. Go up to the withdrawing room, or you may make use of my parlour if you prefer, and possess your soul in patience."

A derisive snort sounded and Ottilia turned to find her spouse looking particularly sceptical. She hid a smile and urged

Lizzy in the direction of the stairway. "Up you go. Upon no account disturb the gentlemen!"

Lizzy blew out a breath and at last moved towards the stairs. Ottilia crossed the hall to the little morning room where Francis was awaiting her.

"You don't for a moment believe she will obey that injunction, do you?"

Ottilia grimaced. "For a little while, I hope. But be that as it may, we can no longer delay with this interview."

He set his fingers on the handle of the door, but he did not immediately open it. "Have you thought what you will say to him?"

Ottilia touched a hand to his chest. "My dearest dear, I have thought of little else these many days. I suppose it must depend upon his attitude."

"You'll accuse him?"

"Certainly, but perhaps not immediately."

He nodded and turned the handle. Ottilia preceded him into the room and found her steward in the way.

"Guarding the door, Hemp? Thank you."

Hemp glanced behind him to where Percy Pedwardine was to be glimpsed, seated on the sofa. "He has made no attempt to escape, milady. Do you wish me to remain?"

"Yes, if you please. I don't want a scuffle, but if you need to lay hands on him, do so."

The low-voiced conversation must have reached Pedwardine's ears, for his head was turned towards Ottilia as she stepped past Hemp to confront him. He did not rise and Ottilia was not surprised when Francis strode up to the sofa, his tone menacing.

"Get up, man! Where are your manners?"

Pedwardine looked up, a sardonic expression in his face. Then he got to his feet in a leisurely way and turned to Ottilia with an ironic little bow. "Lady Francis."

Ottilia crossed to a chair near the fire that faced the sofa and took a seat there. She gestured. "Do sit down again, Mr Pedwardine."

A glance at her spouse was enough to induce him to take a step back, but he remained near enough to intervene, his stance altogether a threat.

Pedwardine's lip curled and he threw himself down into the sofa again, his body splayed in a fashion as negligent as it was insolent. "I must say I had expected at least an offer of bread and water in my dungeon."

"Wine?"

"I dare say that would meet the case."

Ottilia signed to Hemp, who went across to the bell-pull and tugged upon it. Then he returned to stand before the door. Francis, looking distinctly irate, nevertheless retired to a less immediately threatening distance. It was plain the man's impudence had infuriated her spouse. Pedwardine little knew with whom he had to deal. Ottilia tried for a light note.

"I suggest, sir, that you mend this intransigence. I cannot answer for my husband's temper if you continue to treat me to this display."

A growl from Francis bore this out, but it had little effect upon his intended victim. Pedwardine's lip curled the more.

"I have no expectation of receiving aught but insults and abuse in this house, ma'am. I must beg you to hold me excused."

Ottilia shrugged. "As you wish. We will finish this bare-fisted then."

"Boxing cant? You are an original, Lady Fan."

"So I have frequently been told. You, on the other hand, are a murderer, sir."

He had not been expecting it, that was clear. Pedwardine sat up in a bang, his brows snapping together, his eyes narrowing. His voice came harshly. "I trust you can substantiate that supposition, madam?"

"Substantiate, yes. Prove, no. But you already know that."

His eyes glittered and the smile reappeared. Ottilia all but shuddered. Pity Richenda if she had put herself into this man's power.

"Well, ma'am?"

"It is far from well, sir. I perceive you have abandoned your pose of inconsolable friend. You played it well, that I must concede." He made no answer, instead regarding her steadily and without expression. His nerve was admirable, if one could admire such in the villain he undoubtedly was.

A knock at the door induced Hemp to open it. He had some low-voiced colloquy with whoever was outside and shut it again. Ottilia met Pedwardine's gaze. "Your wine will be here directly."

"I thank you."

Ottilia braced. "Meanwhile, let me try if I have gauged matters with any accuracy." Her adversary inclined his head in a manner as confident as it was patronising. He would not break readily. "You gave me, I surmise, a mouthful of falsities when you told me what happened that night."

His brows flickered. "Which night, Lady Francis?"

Her husband cut in before she could answer. "You know well which night, man. Don't make this harder on yourself than you need."

Pedwardine's head turned. His tone was silk. "I am at a loss, sir. Harder on myself? Has your lady wife then sent for the constables? Am I to be led forth with gyves upon my wrists?"

Francis made a hasty motion and Ottilia quickly put out a hand. "Pray don't allow him to goad you, Fan." And to the culprit, "You would do better to hold your tongue. This discussion may not end in the way it ought, but I have promised Mr Edmund Gibbon a faithful account."

This had an effect for Pedwardine's cheeks darkened and his regard wavered, flicking away to the mantel, the window, the door and returning at last to Ottilia. Seeking a way of escape?

Satisfied, she pursued her course. "You did not quite account for everything, did you? So far from Marmaduke having an assignation, I think you had in fact promised him a lift back to the inn. You had every intention of keeping your appointment with Richenda and would have abducted her then. Indeed, I suspect you did keep it, but Richenda was prevented from doing so by her papa. I acquit you of planning Marmaduke's death but the quarrel with young Botterell played neatly into your hands."

He was silent, again regarding her with that enigmatic look. But this time Ottilia noted the tautness in his cheek and the tighter look to his mouth. He was not as composed as he would have her believe.

"Go on, Tillie."

She acknowledged the impatient note in Francis's voice with a nod and pressed on. "Together with Claydon, you helped Marmaduke into the breakfast parlour, perhaps as suggested by Mr Thorpe. Your friend had not quite succumbed, which would have been far more convenient, I dare say, but I imagine the idea was burgeoning already. You got rid of Claydon on the pretext of his arranging for water to be brought and took your chance."

Pedwardine raised his brows. "This is a fairy tale. What chance?"

"You knew only too well how dangerous it was for Marmaduke to engage in fisticuffs. You were quite aware of his weak heart. All it took was a more directed and more powerful blow."

He did not speak, but a muscle shifted in his jaw and the steady gaze became almost glassy. Ottilia could not even triumph, the enormity of his crime against this, his closest friend, coming home to her with a vengeance. Her voice, to her chagrin, was unsteady.

"The only thing you had to do, so far from helping him to the door as you told me, was to pretend to help him, at least to stand. You could not administer the *coup de grâce* when he was sitting. It might not have been strong enough. He dropped where he stood, poor Marmaduke, did he not? The only mercy is he may never have known what happened to him. Cardiac arrest was likely instantaneous."

There was silence for a space. A glance at her husband found his features writ large with a mixture of distress and disgust. She felt it no less herself.

The door opened, producing Tyler with a tray upon which reposed a glass of ruby liquid. Hemp took it from him and the footman retired. Ottilia nodded and the steward brought the tray across, proffering the glass to Pedwardine.

He stared at it for a moment, almost as if he knew not what it was. Then he seized the glass, put it to his lips and tipping back his head, drained it in a few quick swallows. He set it back down on the tray, wiped a hand across his mouth and thereafter ignored Hemp as he retreated and disposed of the tray on a convenient surface. Pedwardine met Ottilia's gaze. "What then, ma'am? Did I walk calmly out of the place and take my leave?"

Ottilia eyed him. "I doubt you were entirely calm, but you had a part still to play. Marmaduke's body must needs be left in a convenient spot. You did not want him discovered too soon. You moved his chair to face the fireplace so that he was not immediately visible from the doorway. You did not want light shed upon the corpse, so you doused the candles all but one and left that close to the door. Only then did you stage your exit."

"Stage?" The question came from Francis, his brow furrowed by a frown. Had this business particularly troubled him?

"Our friend here had to ensure he was known to have left the house. You took the trouble to take leave of your hostess, took advantage of the general flurry of departure and made good your escape, leaving Thorpe with the problem of the corpse. I dare say if he had not panicked and taken pains to remove Marmaduke from the premises, your perfidious betrayal would never have been remarked, let alone discovered. But the disposal of the body first to the summer house and then to our doorstep undid you, I fear. Only you did not know it, for you went off just as planned on the excuse of a boxing match, believing, I have no doubt, that the body would not be found until the morning."

Her victim said nothing, but Francis wore a look of disgust. "I have never heard of anything so callous!"

"Quite so, Fan." She was watching Pedwardine. He had himself well in hand, she guessed, for the supercilious smile was back. The wine had been a mistake perhaps.

"This is pure fantasy, Lady Francis. Marmaduke died a natural death. My part was exactly as I told you at the outset."

"Including your activities today?" This from her spouse in a hard tone. "It won't fadge, Pedwardine. You will scarcely deny your intentions towards Richenda. I caught you in the act."

A low laugh came. "That was very much spur of the moment. Why should I not benefit if the silly wench was bent upon ruining herself in any event?"

"This is beyond words! I suppose you will claim it was not your hand that gave Vexford a blow either. What did you do, hide near the summer house, lying in wait for the poor fellow? I dare say you never left the place at all after refusing Richenda, is that it? Once you were sure she had gone with Claydon, you had nothing to do but to hire that chaise and go after them. Does that hit the mark?"

Ottilia intervened. "He will admit nothing, Fan. It is useless to expect it of him."

"You are correct, Lady Francis. A farrago of nonsensical proportions you have concocted. I venture to suggest that none would believe it if you were to spread the tale abroad."

Francis strode up to him, fist raised. "Is that a threat?"

Pedwardine threw his hands palm up. "By no means, my lord. I am merely pointing out to her ladyship the folly of attempting to indict me with these fustian accusations."

"I have no intention of indicting you, Mr Pedwardine. As you have pointed out, there is no possible way I could prove it. It is even on the cards that Mr Gibbon will refuse to believe you capable of such villainy."

The man's smile grew and his voice purred. "He has known me for a very long time. He regards me with almost as much affection as he did my poor departed friend."

Ottilia longed to wipe the smile off his face. He had not even the grace to make denial, so sure was he that he would get away with his crime. She held back from speaking her mind. This was not a man one should make privy to one's true intent.

"Well, we shall see, Mr Pedwardine. Conscience may do the work on my behalf." A little devil prompted her. "You may like to know, for instance, that you are sitting on the very spot where Marmaduke's body lay while I examined him."

Pedwardine swung up from the sofa in a hurry, turning to look down at its long seat. Revulsion? He recovered faster than Ottilia expected, turning his once more bland features upon her. "I take it I am free to go?"

In her turn, Ottilia remained silent, merely regarding him in a manner she hoped was as enigmatic as his own had been. He laughed and turned for the door, coming up short before the bulk of Hemp, still positioned as guardian.

Francis flicked a gesture, redolent of feeling. "Let him go, Hemp."

The steward stood aside and Pedwardine left the room. At a sign from Francis, Hemp followed, hopefully to ensure he left the premises. A moment later, the sound of the front door shutting behind him roused Ottilia to the latent fury she had been holding in.

"Despicable man! I shall ruin him, see if I don't."

Francis came up to her chair and dropped down beside her, taking her unquiet hands. "My dear one, you were splendid. He almost broke at one point and I thought you had him."

Ottilia gave a little shiver. "He knew he was unassailable. Fan, I feel quite sick."

"I'm not surprised. It's enough to turn anyone's stomach. Come, don't let him win, Tillie."

She allowed him to draw her to her feet and took comfort in his arms as he held her close. Presently she shifted in his embrace, leaning back to look up into his face. "I don't believe any have struck me as so vile as this one, Fan. His closest friend."

"I know. It hardly bears thinking of. But it is over. You will have to repeat this story several times, I don't doubt. That will numb you to it a little, I hope."

She sighed. "Perhaps. I ought not to feel glad that I must, for it goes against the grain to start what I fear will prove to be a whispering campaign."

"Well, you said you wanted to ruin him."

"In the heat of the moment."

"It's inevitable, my darling. You can't stop it. There are too many people involved."

She found a smile from somewhere. "You are wise, my dearest dear. I wish I might refresh myself with Luke, but I fear we have still to settle this business between Lizzy and Maplewood."

"Oh, good grief, I had forgot that. Heaven help us all!"

CHAPTER TWENTY-FIVE

Vivian ran his quarry to earth at last in Lord Francis's study where he found Lord Dalesford making use of the implements at the desk to pen a letter. He turned on the opening of the door and Vivian was conscious of a sliver of anxiety as Dalesford's gaze registered recognition.

"Ah, it's you, is it?" He rose from the chair and turned to confront Vivian. "I was going to discuss this business with my daughter first, but perhaps it is as well."

Vivian moved into the room, struggling a little to keep his eyes from wandering away from Eliza's father's face. He did not look to be infuriated, but his aspect was far from genial.

"I believe I owe you first an explanation, sir."

"Several, I imagine."

The dry note rankled. Vivian balked. "I don't intend to sue to you for mercy, my lord. I am aware how the situation must appear."

Dalesford's brows rose. "Are you indeed?"

"I am, sir. You suppose I concocted this scheme to make a clandestine assignation with Eli— with Lady Elizabeth."

A snort greeted these words. "Good God, man, do you think I don't know my own daughter? I'm perfectly aware it was Lizzy's doing to arrive here when she knew you would be present."

Vivian jumped to her defence. "She would not have done so had I not informed her of the circumstance. It is quite my fault."

A look of surprise overspread Dalesford's features. Did he suppose Vivian had no sense of responsibility?

"Well, that's something, I suppose."

He said no more and Vivian likewise waited, puzzlement brewing. The other man regarded him with what looked suspiciously like lurking amusement. Goaded, Vivian broke. "Are you not going to ring a peal over me?"

The brows flew up again. "To what purpose?"

Vivian frowned. "I thought you came here for that."

"I came to discover just what mischief my wayward child had got herself into. And, if possible, to extract her out of it."

Unaccountably annoyed, Vivian found himself arguing the point. "She isn't wayward, sir. She is merely forthright in pursuing her aims. I find it an admirable trait."

"Oh, do you? You've not spent the better part of nineteen years worrying over what trouble the chit might get into next. Believe me, my boy, she is a handful."

A bubble of mirth rose up and Vivian could not suppress the laughter. "I know it." To his own surprise, he added, "I like it. So much so that I fear I will be obliged to overcome my own scruples and..."

He faded out, of a sudden realising where his words were tending. Words? His thoughts! What possessed him? Had he not specifically weighed the thing in his mind and come to the only possible decision? Only half realising what he did, he shifted away to the window, staring out across the terraces, though he hardly noticed what he saw. In his mind's eye he was recalling Eliza's image, her face when she had made that plea. *Why won't you marry me, Vivian?* He could no longer remember his reasons. What had he said? Some words that made no sense, words that sprang from some foolish notion of retaining the freedom of his bachelorhood. An empty freedom, as it appeared to him now. How had he ever thought it could better serve him than to share his travels with Eliza? He turned on the thought, words tumbling out of him as he stared at Lord Dalesford, feeling as if he understood for the first time.

"I didn't see it, sir. I thought I needed my freedom. I wanted to travel, so to sketch and live untrammelled. I didn't think I wanted the burden of a wife, of Eliza tagging along. But that was blind of me. As if she would simply tag along! A companion she would be, but of course she would go her own way, make her own adventures for that is what she is. The perfect helpmeet for me, sir, only I had not the wit to realise it."

His focus altered and the face confronting his became clearer. Lord Dalesford was regarding him with a twisted smile, a twinkle in his eye.

"I had no slightest intention of handing her over, but I rather think I am changing my mind. You will do very well with my Lizzy, Maplewood. If, that is, you are asking for my permission to address her?"

Vivian straightened, his voice free and clear. "I am, sir. I know I am not the suitor you wanted. She ought to marry some titled fellow. But I will inherit my father's estate, a modest one but adequate."

Dalesford held up a staying hand. "We can go into all that later." He leaned a little towards Vivian. "Confidentially, my young friend, I have had my doubts these many years that any of the fellows I had in mind would be capable of managing my minx." He straightened again and there was challenge in his face. "Are you, Maplewood?"

Vivian laughed out. "I will learn. She cares for me, I know that. I think that makes a difference."

"Don't you believe it! She adores her father but I confess she has too many times baffled my attempts to control her. You are welcome to make the attempt."

Even as he spoke, the door was pushed open a trifle and Eliza's face poked around it.

The waiting had proved unbearable. After pacing back and forth in her aunt's parlour, speculating upon what might be said between Papa and Vivian, Lizzy's patience gave out. It did not take many minutes to run the two to earth in her uncle's study. She put her ear to the woodwork to no avail. She could recognise the mumble of male voices, but not the words spoken. It would not do. She must know. The doorknob turned in her hand almost before she made the decision to open the door. Her father was the first to remark upon her arrival.

"Ha! You're there, are you? You'd best come in, wretch of a female."

His genial tone belied the words and Lizzy's gaze shifted to Vivian. His colour was high and he looked decidedly ill at ease. She shot the burning question. "Have you decided my future then between you?"

Vivian's gaze dropped and her father took the bait. "Come in, shut the door and hold your tongue! Or I'll decide something you won't care for, my child."

Lizzy obeyed the first two commands, but put up her chin. "Threaten me all you wish, Papa, but I cannot be silent."

He threw up his eyes and turned to Vivian. "Give us five minutes, Maplewood."

Vivian hesitated, causing Lizzy surprise. "I hope you don't mean to inflict punishment on her, sir. I've said the blame was mine."

"If I haven't laid a hand on her in all these years, my boy, I'm not likely to start now." Lizzy met her papa's gaze as it veered. "But she still has a trifle of explaining to do."

Torn between gratification that Vivian had taken the blame and a burning desire to know what had passed between the two, Lizzy watched his retreat from the corner of her eye. The moment the door closed behind him, she broke out.

"Papa, it is of no use to scold me and a waste of breath besides. You need not fret either because he does not want me, so you and Mama win in any event."

Her father's brows rose and an odd sort of gleam appeared in his eye. "He does not want you, you say? How can you know that, Lizzy?"

She thrust her chin in the air. "Because I asked him."

"The devil you did!"

Defiance rode her. "I did, Papa. I asked him why he would not marry me."

"Lizzy, you wretched child! Have you no conduct? Anyone would suppose you had not been properly raised — not that such is news. What Harriet would say I dread to think."

An irrepressible giggle escaped Lizzy. "Mama would have a fit, of course." She moved a step closer. "I had to, Papa."

"Yes, that's what you always say." He sounded rather resigned than angry. "Why did you have to? Not that I need ask. I may guess the poor fellow showed no inclination to address you and you, shocking female that you are, felt obliged to turn the tables."

"Well, I did and I was well served for my boldness. Vivian was perfectly frank. He prefers his freedom to me and that is all about it." Her overburdened heart crumpled. "Oh, Papa, I am so very unhappy!"

She threw herself at him as she spoke and he received her in a comprehensive embrace, drawing her to him in the tender manner he had always used towards her. It was comfort to a degree, but failed to quiet the agitation of her spirits.

Her papa's soothing tones came in her ear. "There now, my sweet, there is no occasion for all this despair."

Lizzy lifted her head in a bang. "There is, there is! Oh, I know it is good news to you and Mama, but —"

She was silenced as he put a finger to her mouth. "Quiet! You misunderstand me, child. I cannot speak for Harriet, but I dare say she will come round when she realises how your heart is touched."

"There is little point in her realising it, is there? She will be glad rather that I am willing to compound for some unfortunate of her choosing."

Much to Lizzy's annoyance, her papa fell into laughter. "Unfortunate to be saddled with you? Yes, I have myself been puzzling over who of the eligibles might have gumption enough to contend with the vagaries of Lady Elizabeth Fiske."

"It is no laughing matter, Papa. I shall be a pattern card of correct behaviour."

"I wish I may see it."

"I will, because I won't care. It doesn't matter who I marry if Vivian won't have me."

Her father's lips twitched. "Then it's a good thing I've given him permission to address you."

About to retort in kind, Lizzy abruptly realised what he had said. "What?"

His grin emerged. "I thought that might knock you acock."

"Papa! Is this a jest?"

"I hope not. It didn't sound like it."

Lizzy's veins were behaving in a manner that threatened to undo her. "But he doesn't want me. He said so."

"Apparently he has changed his mind."

"Why? How?"

"Ah, that I will leave to the fellow himself to explain. In fact, I think he had best do precisely that right now." He crossed her, heading for the door.

"No, wait, Papa!"

He halted, turning, brows snapping together. "Don't tell me you have changed your mind. Are you no longer desirous of marrying him?"

Lizzy hesitated. Not, she wanted to say, if he had been coerced somehow. "You did not force him, did you?"

"I? Why in the world would I, child? It's not the match I planned for you."

"Then why have you given him permission?"

Her father rolled his eyes. "Saints preserve us! Let the man speak for himself and you'll soon see why." With that he continued to the door and opened it. "Maplewood!"

Lizzy heard Vivian respond and had to seize the back of a chair for fear she might faint. Her father went out and she heard his voice in the corridor.

"In you go, my young friend. I don't know whether to wish you good fortune or offer you a brandy for courage."

"I'll take a celebratory glass of something, sir. Later. I hope."

Then Vivian was in the room, the door was closed and Lizzy straightened, shifting away from the chair the better to confront him direct. She wasted no time.

"Why does Papa say he has given you permission to address me?"

Vivian's gaze met hers and she thought she read anxiety in his eyes. "Because I told him I am in love with you."

A jolt hit Lizzy's chest. "Why would you say that? It's not true!"

His gaze narrowed. "How would you know? Are you privy to my heart?"

"I wish I might be, Vivian, but the only thing I'm privy to is how you broke mine."

His face changed. "I know. I hurt you."

Lizzy tossed her head, that same hurt riding her. "Was it to make amends you lied to Papa?"

"It was no lie!" He came up to her, seizing her by the shoulders. "For heaven's sake, Eliza, let me speak for once!"

She did not throw him off, a sliver of hope sneaking into her breast. But she was not yet ready to succumb. "Well?"

He released her, slumping a little. "If you want the truth, I have been in love with you for an age."

"Not noticeably."

"Oh, be quiet! You know — you've known all along that I care for you. If I didn't say it, it's because I was fighting it, Eliza. I didn't want the complication."

Lizzy's demon rose. "Now you do? For what reason when you made your preferences clear enough."

He sighed. "I knew you would not make this easy for me. Why should you indeed?"

"At least in that we are of one mind."

His mouth shifted and a faint smile appeared. "I must have taken leave of my senses. You will drive me demented. Your father was right to warn me."

Lizzy's chin shot up. "Warn you? Of what, pray?"

"Of the difficulty of controlling you. You would try the patience of a saint, Eliza, and I'm no saint. Yet I am willing to compound for a lifetime of reining you in, if only to have your enlivening company."

Lizzy eyed him, uncertainty warring with burgeoning elation. "You think you can rein me in, do you, Mr Maplewood?"

363

"I do, Lady Elizabeth. You will answer to my hand on the reins because you love me." All at once, Lizzy found herself trapped in a close embrace. "You do, don't you?"

Mesmerised by the latent power she could feel, in his arms, in his gaze, Lizzy melted. "So much, Vivian."

His kiss, waited for, imagined for an eon, did not disappoint. Presently, a convenient window seat provided an opportunity for Lizzy to thrash out the matter of his changed mind.

"Truthfully, it hit me when I was talking to your father, but I've been miserable for days." He lifted the hand he was holding to his lips and kissed it. "Ever since that abortive carriage ride. Losing you was more than I could endure."

"But you said nothing even then, Vivian."

"I thought I had wholly alienated you. You seemed not to be troubled, or not nearly as much as I."

Lizzy was not prepared to let him off altogether. "Then you didn't intend to ask Papa for my hand even today."

"I confess it, no. Until it struck me that I had cut my own throat with what I said to you that day."

"Truly?"

He turned to her, an echo of pain in his eyes that went straight to her heart. "If I hurt you, I hurt myself the more. What price my so-called art if I had not you by my side?" He smiled. "Will you come adventuring with me, Eliza?"

Lizzy's voice became a trifle constricted. "Try if you can to stop me, Vivian."

CHAPTER TWENTY-SIX

Not much to Ottilia's surprise, Marmaduke's uncle appeared stunned by her revelations. Rather than risk running into Mr Pedwardine at the Fox, she had sent a note requesting Mr Gibbon to visit her at Flitteris. She had only hinted at her business with him but it had brought him hotfoot, almost before she was prepared.

Ottilia received him, along with her spouse, in Francis's study, the withdrawing room being overly inhabited. Lizzy's engagement had injected a euphoric atmosphere into the house which was not shared by Sybilla. Ottilia left her reeling with the news as conveyed to her by Gil and hurried away to undertake the unpleasant duty of informing Mr Gibbon of her findings.

He had not taken a seat and stood staring, the colour coming and going in his cheeks. Ottilia exchange a glance with her husband, who took a hand.

"You had best sit down, Gibbon, before you fall down."

The visitor allowed himself to be pushed into a chair by the window, what time Ottilia took the one from before the desk and set it down close by. She sat and reached across to place her hand on Gibbon's.

"I am very sorry to be the bearer of such fell tidings."

Gibbon's brows drew together and he withdrew his hand from under hers. "I don't believe it!"

An exasperated sound from her spouse threw Ottilia into speech. "I do not blame you, sir. It must be hard indeed to hear such a thing of one who has been, as I understand it, a welcome guest in your home for many years."

Gibbon shook his head with some violence. "Such a blow? For such a purpose? He could not have done it, not Percy. He cared for Marmaduke. What possible reason could he have?"

Ottilia took this, speaking with a calm she did not feel. "It was not premeditated, that I will swear to. I fear it was a decision made on the spur of the moment, the temptation too strong to be resisted."

"Temptation? Why should he be tempted to dispose of poor Marmaduke? That is what you are saying, is it not? You say that Percy killed my boy?"

"I do say so. Indeed, I believe there can be no doubt."

"But why? *Why?* They were friends. Impossible. He could not have done it."

Ottilia looked to Francis who raised an eyebrow. "This was to be expected, my love. There is nothing for it but to give him your reasons."

"You mean Percy's reasons, Fan." She returned her gaze to the suffering uncle, whose eyes darted between them, a hint of suspicion therein. Ottilia repressed a sigh. "You will like this no better than the fact itself, Mr Gibbon, but what you must understand is that Mr Pedwardine coveted Richenda's fortune. He claimed to believe that Marmaduke was not serious about a possible match, just as you said yourself."

"Because Marmaduke told me so."

"So you said," Francis cut in. "It seems he may not have been quite open with you." He held up a hand as Gibbon showed signs of growing red in the face. "Before you snap my nose off, sir, pray consider for a moment. Marmaduke took pains to be sure of Richenda's attention, even going so far as to flirt with another female to make her jealous. Whether Richenda had any real interest in marriage with Marmaduke is another matter altogether, as my wife will agree."

"But that has naught to do with Percy. He came here to dissuade Marmaduke from becoming entangled with the girl, for he told me so."

Ottilia gave him a sympathetic smile. "Just so. He did his utmost to keep your nephew from her and traduced her character into the bargain."

"Well, then!"

"My dear sir, this was all in vain. We cannot know whether Marmaduke indeed had serious intentions towards Richenda, but we may deduce from Percy's conduct that he thought it was so. He could not hope to rival Marmaduke, either in looks or eligibility. Indeed, he knew his only chance was to entrap Richenda into an elopement, which was just what he intended on the night of the tragedy."

Gibbon was looking more distressed now than angry. "Would he behave so dishonourably? Cut his own friend out?"

"He would have if he could have. This would be bad enough, you might think. It may have been in Percy's mind that Marmaduke's reaction was not to be contemplated. That thought may well have contributed to the temptation to sweep your poor nephew from his path. Dead, Marmaduke could neither object nor stand in Percy's way. He would have a free hand to prosecute his design to carry Richenda away to be married."

For several moments, Gibbon did not speak. His countenance demonstrated the teeming thoughts going on behind haunted eyes. Compassion stirred in Ottilia and she knew not how to relieve the poor man. A glance at Francis found him similarly perplexed, a frown creasing his brow.

At last the sufferer spoke, a challenge in his tone. "Can you prove all you have said?"

"I cannot."

"Then why should I believe you?"

Ottilia drew a breath. "At the least, there can be no doubt of Mr Pedwardine's intentions towards Richenda for he had a marriage licence on his person when my husband caught up with him. As I explained at the outset, the facts support my suppositions. Do you wish me again to relate those anomalies?"

Gibbon waved this away in haste. "I don't desire to hear that recital." His gaze fixed upon her. "To whom else have you mentioned these matters?"

Francis took this. "As to Pedwardine's escapade with Richenda yesterday, they are known to several who were with me. That news is bound to travel, sir. Moreover, since a number of persons have been under suspicion, it behoves my wife to reassure them."

"At the expense of Marmaduke's best friend, no doubt?"

"That is inevitable."

There was another silence. All at once, Gibbon drew a heavy breath and let it out in a bang. "I cannot endure this!" He rose. "I must go. I will take my boy home and bury him with due ceremony."

Ottilia received a look with eyebrows raised from her spouse. She got up as the visitor made for the door. "Mr Gibbon!"

He turned, casting an unloving look upon her. "Madam?"

"I am sorry to have burdened you. It cannot be but that suspicion will gnaw at you. I can only regret the disappointment you must feel at the last when you come to realise the truth of what I have told you."

A bleak look answered her. "I had hoped Percy would be of some comfort to me. You have doubled my loss, ma'am."

At this, Francis took a stride towards him. "My wife, Gibbon, had naught to do with either of your losses! Look to the true culprit and don't accuse one whose only care has been to discover the truth. If you can't accept that truth, that is on your head alone. Don't blame my wife!"

"Fan, pray leave it!" Ottilia hurried to the visitor's side, putting out a hand. "I feel for you, sir, and I fully understand your dilemma. If I could have turned it otherwise, I should have done so with a whole heart."

Gibbon visibly wrought with himself before he took the proffered hand. "I wish I might find it in me to be grateful. I thank you at least for your honesty. Good day to you." He nodded towards Francis and walked out of the room in some haste.

Ottilia stared at the door as it closed behind him, sagging a little. In a moment, she felt her husband at her back and his arms came about her, holding her close against him. His murmured words brought balm, of a sort.

"Never mind it, sweetheart. He will learn in due time. Never mind it."

"I am astonished Dalesford agreed to it. Both he and Harriet have ever averred that nothing less than a peer would do for Elizabeth. And where, pray, have they all gone off to in such a hurry?"

It was a relief to Ottilia that Sybilla had waited until the departure of the betrothed couple and Lizzy's father before speaking her mind. Admittedly, she had been a trifle grudging in her congratulations, giving poor Vivian Maplewood a somewhat austere look as she condescended to shake his hand. Nor had she participated with any show of enthusiasm in the celebratory dinner last night. Her remarks therefore came as no surprise to Ottilia.

"I suspect, Sybilla, that Gil was won over by Lizzy's quite evident affection for that young man. He only wants her happiness."

Francis let out a snort worthy of his mother. "Nothing of the sort, Tillie. Gil told me he thinks Maplewood may prove to have a far more capable hand on Lizzy's rein than he has ever managed to hold."

Her spouse was occupying his favourite stance at the mantel in the withdrawing room, whither the depleted party had repaired after bidding the cavalcade farewell, Lizzy, her maid and Gil occupying the family coach in which he had travelled to Flitteris with Vivian following in his curricle. The footman Charles, sent with Lizzy for protection, had been despatched back to the family home in Buckinghamshire by stagecoach.

"Well, it is to be hoped he may be capable of controlling the wench," said Sybilla on a sceptical note.

"As to where they have gone," pursued Francis, "it seems Maplewood wished his prospective father-in-law to see for himself the estate he will eventually inherit, and in addition to meet with his parents."

"Pish! If you ask me, Dalesford is bent upon putting off the evil day when he must break the fell tidings to Harriet."

"Oh, Sybilla, no. Harriet will come round."

"Not without a deal of protest and rodomontade, Ottilia. I am glad I will not be there to hear it."

Francis rapped upon the wood of the mantelpiece. "As I was saying… Maplewood wished more particularly to present Lizzy to Maplewood senior. She has met the mother, of course. In Tunbridge Wells."

This drew Ottilia's attention. "I did like Annis Maplewood. I dare say she will prove an influential mother-in-law for Lizzy."

"If Elizabeth does not drive her to distraction. That child wants conduct."

Ottilia, seated in the window seat to catch the warmth of the sun, had to smile. "That I cannot deny. I expect marriage and babies will sober her a trifle."

"They haven't sobered you, my dear one. I see no reason to suppose Lizzy will change in the slightest degree."

"Fiend! I would be perfectly sober if impulsive young women would refrain from sending corpses to my doorstep."

"On which matter, Ottilia, how do you propose to proceed against that abominable villain?"

Ottilia sighed. "There is little I can do, Sybilla. I have seen Mr Gibbon and that was distressing enough."

Francis straightened. "You told him the truth, Tillie. It is not your fault if he refuses to accept it."

"I wish I might have spared him, but I could not reconcile it with my conscience to allow Percy Pedwardine to walk away without some form of retribution."

The dowager gave one of her explosive snorts. "The villain ought to be incarcerated."

"Have no fear, Mama. Whatever Gibbon may believe, the inevitable whisperings will blacken Pedwardine's name. I can't imagine his credit will survive. He will be ruined. With luck, he will leave the country and so rid Society of one of its vilest members."

Finding the prospect of rumour set abroad by her agency exceedingly distasteful, Ottilia turned the subject. "Have you thought whether you will consider that girl Etta for your companion, Sybilla?"

Her mother-in-law stared. "What in the world are you talking of, Ottilia? Who is Etta?"

Ottilia felt blank of mind for a moment. "Henrietta Skelmersdale. Lady Stoke Rochford's companion, do you not recall?"

"I hardly spoke to that female. Why should I think of her?"

Light dawned. "Lizzy did not speak to you of it, did she? I suppose she forgot in all the excitement." Ottilia rose and shifted into the room. "It struck Lizzy that Lady Stoke Rochford's demise left Etta without employment. Fortuitously, perhaps, you are in need of a new companion."

"Gracious heaven, can that child never refrain from poking her nose into other people's affairs?"

"She meant well, Sybilla. She may have mentioned it to Etta. As it chances, I told her to sound the girl out, but matters came to a head before I heard whether she did or no and I forgot to ask."

Sybilla pursed her lips, delicate brows drawn together, but she said nothing. Ottilia exchanged a glance with her spouse who quirked a comical eyebrow. To her everlasting gratitude, he took a hand.

"It could do no harm to talk to the girl, Mama. It might solve your difficulty at a stroke."

Eager to encourage this theme, Ottilia crossed to her mother-in-law's chair and dropped down beside her, reaching to cover one of her hands. "I do think it may be a very simple solution, Sybilla. Only think. She is young, intelligent and forthright. I believe you will like her."

The dowager patted her hand, producing a wry smile. "You are nothing if not persuasive. Such a matter cannot be decided all in a moment, however."

"Indeed not. Besides, I dare say she is much occupied at this present with the aftermath of the death. But would it not be politic to secure her, if you can? Assuming you find her congenial."

"She won't find me congenial," declared Sybilla in a rare spurt of self-knowledge.

Ottilia had to laugh. "I expect Lady Stoke Rochford had her moments too. Etta is a resilient girl. I doubt even you could crush her spirit."

Sybilla snorted. "I thank you." She withdrew her hand from under Ottilia's and made to rise. "I may as well essay the thing at once. Ring the bell, Francis. At least we shall know one way or the other."

With Sybilla safe on her way to Lady Stoke Rochford's house, accompanied by her maid, Ottilia seized the chance to escape to her eyrie where her spouse very soon followed.

"I thought I should find you here, my dear one. Have you to feed Luke?"

From the daybed where she was seated, Ottilia held out a hand to him. "Presently, when Doro brings him." Her spouse took the welcoming hand and sat down beside her. Ottilia found herself the recipient of a searching look. "Well, what, my dearest dear?"

"You look jaded."

"It has been a difficult week, Fan."

"That is not all, is it?" Francis gave a grimace. "You are not happy. Is it Gibbon's reaction?"

She drew his hand to her lips and kissed it. "You read me so well, my darling lord, but it is more than Mr Gibbon. There is the rest of the world."

He squeezed the hand. "Tell me."

Ottilia could not repress a painful breath. "I do so hate to be the instrument of damning gossip."

"You won't need to be, Tillie. You have only to give the facts to those involved, did I not say so at once? They will do the rest."

"That does not exonerate me, Fan."

He gave a wry grin and kissed her. "You have the busiest conscience of anyone I know, my loved one."

Ottilia accepted the kiss but was yet troubled. "My heart misgives me."

"How so?"

She looked him full in the face. "What if I am wrong? As I was obliged to confess to Mr Gibbon, I have no proof."

His brows snapped together. "You are not wrong, Tillie. That villain all but confessed by his very attitude. He deserves his fate."

"Condemnation by mere gossip? Ought anyone to be subjected to that?"

Francis let out an exasperated noise. "You can't stop it, Tillie. Unless you leave it at Gibbon and lie to the rest."

"I cannot do that."

"There you are then."

"Yes, I know where I am, Fan. Between the devil and the deep blue sea." Ottilia tried to accept the truth of this but a vague apprehension persisted in her bosom. "I feel as if I am unleashing something monstrous."

"Tillie, I won't let you do this. You did not deal young Marmaduke that killing blow. By rights, Pedwardine should be in the hands of the authorities at this moment. That he is not is due only to the lack of evidence. You know he did it. He won't be the first to escape the consequences of his crime."

"Yes, but he is not going to escape them, is he? Not if I —"

"You have no choice. If you keep mum, your conscience will plague you."

"And if I speak, it will do so in any event."

There was a silence. Ottilia met his gaze as he eyed her, reading both concern and frustration in the brown depths. She essayed a smile which went hopelessly awry. Francis emitted a heavy sigh and took her in his arms, drawing her close. Ottilia wept a little, but the solace of his embrace had its usual soothing effect.

As she pulled away, she found her spouse was holding out a handkerchief. A gurgle escaped and she took it, making use of its snowy folds. "What in the world would I do without you, my dearest dear?"

"Founder, of course." He grinned. "Now tell me I am the prince of husbands."

Her laugh was genuine. "You are and I love you with all my heart."

"Except that part of it which now belongs to Luke."

"Oh, that goes without saying." But she accepted his kiss with fervour.

Francis straightened, looking across to the door from behind which a childish treble sounded along with the recognisable footsteps of Doro. "And here come our demanding progeny, if I mistake not."

A knock produced Doro, carrying the infant Luke and accompanied by Pretty, who no sooner saw Francis than she rushed across to him with a shriek of "Papa". He lifted her onto his lap and Ottilia's formless unease melted as she watched him slip into his fatherly role.

She accepted her baby son into her arms and began to adjust her bodice. The reflection could not but obtrude that there was far more importance in the felicity of her domestic life than in the possible fate of a murderer.

A NOTE TO THE READER

Dear Reader

Setting this story in and around Flitteris Manor where the Fanshawes live meant I had to research the area better and choose places and families to become neighbours. It had to be a careful exercise because once done it cannot be undone. Flitteris is bound to reappear in future books and no doubt neighbouring individuals may rear their heads again.

It was also necessary to work out the layout of the house. As I am not a planner, I had to go back and find everything I had described in earlier stories to make sure I didn't suddenly invent a completely different home. Fortunately, I have a lot of illustrations from the period and Pinterest is a great source for blueprints of houses. That is in addition to various helpful books in my research library.

While I was poring over a general map of the country looking for names — it's how I find surnames for characters — I ran plump into Botolph Claydon and Stoke Rochford. Far too good to miss. Both found their way into the story, though I did adjust Botolph to Botolf as that is how it was spelt in my Oxford Dictionary of English Christian Names. One of my research bibles.

Medically, when I was researching cardiac arrest, I discovered this rare condition whereby an individual (young males apparently) has dropped dead without apparent cause. Theories abound, but at that time it seemed to be generally accepted that a defective heart was to blame. In the eighteenth century, lacking sophisticated technology and equipment, medicos did not know nearly as much about the heart as they do now. I seized on this rare phenomenon immediately. Luckily, Ottilia had heard of it!

Research aside, I truly had nothing in the bank when I began writing the story beyond the body being dropped at Ottilia's door. To say I didn't know what I was doing would be a gross understatement. I hadn't a clue. Somehow the story evolved, clues and suspects appeared and eventually, along with my heroine, I found out the how, who and why of the murder. I confess that at one point I became so confused I had to write a timeline of exactly who said what and when.

One of the joys in writing this series is developing the family background and pursuing the ups and downs of Francis and Ottilia's marriage. Their growing family, together with the changes occurring in the extended family, are interesting for me as the writer because I never know what's going to come up. For example, it was a revelation to me when Pretty stole Francis's heart. Then again, while writing the first draft of the next story which I have been doing these last months, all at once I discovered a future event for the Fanshawes and was able to sow that seed. It's quite exciting but my lips are sealed.

It is serendipitous moments like this that make writing resemble some kind of magic. The Inner Writer, as it's known, seems to be capable of flights of fancy that never occur to the analytical part of one's mind. I think that is why I changed (many years ago now) from planner to "pantser" — writing by the seat of one's pants or into the wind. Too much analysis interferes with my creative process. I have to trust the Inner Writer to come up with the goods. Once there's a first draft, I can draw on my analytical side to fix any flunks and add whatever is missing.

The end result is what you get to read, and I am crossing everything in hopes it has proved enjoyable for you once again.

If you would consider leaving a review, it would be much appreciated and very helpful. Do feel free to contact me on **elizabeth@elizabethbailey.co.uk** or find me on **Facebook**, **Twitter**, **Goodreads** or my website **elizabethbailey.co.uk**.

Elizabeth Bailey

Sapere Books is an exciting new publisher of brilliant fiction and popular history.

To find out more about our latest releases and our monthly bargain books visit our website:
saperebooks.com

Made in United States
Orlando, FL
20 April 2022